The Art Guardian

VEGA

Maribel Vega
2406 E State Road 60
PO Box 2022
Valrico, FL 33594
IFP2911@gmail.com
https://www.facebook.com/WhyIHateMyJob
https://www.instagram.com/maribelvegaofficial

Prologue

After being orphaned at the age of eight, Lizbeth learns about her family lineage of Art Guardians. Who posses the power to travel into paintings. Without having fully mastered her powers yet, Lizbeth falls in love and finds herself in a love triangle that can cost the lives of everyone she holds dear to her heart. Forced to submit to the obsession of her first lover. Lizbeth finds a way to master her powers, save the ones she loves, and entrap the obsessor. Using the power to enter through the gate of any painting,

When I was a young girl, I would sit for hours in the day with my grandmother in her yard. As she would paint her masterpieces on canvas. Her favorite works of art to paint were those of the ocean. She loved painting fierce waves and calm waters. Sometimes she would add a small fishing boat or beautiful colored fish. I always wondered if they were from her imagination or if she had really seen these majestic fish. Every time I asked she would respond the same way, "There is only one way to find out, and that is by traveling into the unknown". I never really knew what she meant by that at my young age.

My grandmother and I were very close. So you can imagine my sadness when a few months after my eighth birthday she passed away. Her friends were at the funeral. There was also many people I had never seen before. Some were strange looking and very much to themselves. Except for one who did not seem strange at all. She smiled and waved at me from across the room. I waved back. She was about my same age. We looked so similar. Almost like sisters. Except, here hair though long like mine. Mine was black and her was light brown. With her hand she invited me to follow her. I looked around to be sure she was inviting me. When I looked back at her, again she invited me to follow. I carefully passed through the crowds, being sure to not get too much attention. When I got to where she had been standing, I looked around for her, but couldn't see her anywhere. Then past the kitchen and down the hall I spotted her near the staircase. I again made sure no one was looking at me and followed after the mysterious girl. When I got to the steps, I looked around for her again. Then I looked up and she popped her head out from the second floor. I ran up the steps after her. I had to know where she was going. When I reached the top of the steps, once again she had disappeared. I took a few steps in the direction I assumed she had gone and there she was, standing in front of the attic door. She invited me to follow her, but I was sure the door was locked. I would have known, because grandma never let me up to the attic. She always told me it was too dusty up there and that it was full of spiders. I was about to tell this mysterious girl that the door was locked, when she suddenly turned the knob and opened the door. She invited me to follow her again and went up the attic stairs. There was no way she could do that, so I ran over to check the doorknob to the now opened attic door. I tried turning the knob, but it was locked. I thought to myself, how could she open a locked door. I had to know who she was. I ran up the attic stairs, but then came to a sudden halt with what I saw. There was no dust or spiders. The attic was beautiful. Slowly I continued going up the steps. There was this feeling of awe and wonder that came over me. The attic was so well lit with the sunlight that came through the many windows. I hadn't remember seeing so many windows from outside the house before. The sun also hit brightly onto the many solar powered lights that hung over the many many paintings on the walls. There was almost no open wall space. Paintings were inches apart hung from the ceiling to the floor. The ones hung on the ceiling had wooden ladders beside them. The frames on each painting were elegant and gold colored. I almost thought it was real gold until I touched one. Somehow the wood was painted in such a way it looked and shined like gold. The attic was even better than any museum my grandmother ever took me to. The floors of the attic were covered in padding. Almost like a giant sized quilt with light colored patterns stuck to each other. The padding on the floor was sturdy enough to walk on without fumbling, but soft enough to break a fall. After I was able to get past the shock of the beauty of the attic, I looked over at the girl who was standing in the middle of the room. I slowly approached her. We looked at each other and she smiled at me.

"My name is Tiara".

"My name is..."

"I know your name. You are Lizbeth. Your grandmother told me".

"You knew my grandmother?"

"I did. Many of us know your grandmother. She has helped us all, so very much".

"Helped you? With what? Did you know about this attic? Why did my grandmother not allow me up here? How do you know my grandmother?"

"Your grandmother was right".

"Right about what?"

"She said you would have many questions and that you were very curious. Which is why she knew you would be the best person to inherit her title"

"Her title?"

"Yes, the title of 'The Art Guardian'".

"Art Guardian?"

"Yes, come with me I will explain it all. We will have plenty of time for me to teach you before you become an adult".

"An adult, but I am only eight"

"And I am ten. We have much time and you will learn all the secrets of your grandmother. She was not supposed to die so soon. She wanted more time and she was going to wait until your sixteenth birthday to share the secrets".

"What secrets?"

"Come, I will show you".

At that moment Tiara took me by the hand and walked over to a painting of a forest. She then reach out her other hand towards the painting and it began to glow with a golden light. The light became brighter and brighter. Then suddenly I felt a pull on my body, so out of fear I shut my eyes. Then I heard birds chirping around me and when I opened my eyes, I was staring in a forest. Startled I looked at Tiara and she giggled.

"It's okay, there is nothing to fear".

"Where are we?"

"We are inside of the painting".

"The...painting...that's not possible".

"Ah but it is. If an only if you posses the power of travel".

"The power of travel?"

"Yes, The Art Guardian...I mean your grandmother felt it were best to use common words and titles, like 'Art Guardian' and 'Power of Travel'. This way whenever we spoke of things in the real world, it would not raise questions".

"The real world?"

"Yes, outside of this painting. The days spent in the painting are the same as in the real world. One day there is one day here. Yet here there is no time. Like, there is no day or night. It is this way all the time and it does not change".

"You mean this forest does not get dark and there is no night?"

"That is correct. You see, you do catch on quickly. Each time you enter a painting, you must wear a watch so you know how long you have been here. If you do not, you can lose track of time and what you may feel are hours can actually be days. Then it will seem like you are missing in the real world".

"How can that be so? Would not you feel tired and hungry? Should that not let you know it is time to come home for dinner and to go to bed?"

"No, Lizbeth. Have you ever taken a nap in the day and felt like you only slept a few moments, but when you see the time, hours have passed? And when you are hungry the painting feeds you. So it is easy to let time slip away. Worse yet, it is easy to get lost for hours, days, or even years within a painting. So you must be very careful."

"How do you not get lost? This forest is so big".

"Look here. This marker shows you where the gate is. The gate we used to enter. Is the same gate to return. The Art Guardian, your grandmother, placed them in all paintings after...she just placed them for us to know".

"After what? Tell me".

"After your parents were lost in a painting".

"My parents? Lost in a painting? Why did my grandmother not tell me this? We can go and find them?"

"After your parents were lost, your grandmother was so sad that she promised to not share this secret with you at a young age, so you would not get lost as well trying to find them. Lizbeth, they're gone".

"What do you mean gone?"

"Your grandmother entered every painting searching for them. Her search turned into months, then years. She brought you along with her on every search, because you were just a baby and there was no one to care for you. She carried a watch to know when she had to return. Finally she entered...this painting...and found...let me show you".

Tiara took me by the hand and led me deeper into the forest. We climbed upward onto a flower pathed hill. At the top of that hill were two tombstones. I released Tiara's hand and approached the tombstones. One had my mothers name and the other my fathers name. Sad, I turned to look back at Tiara. She walked over to me and put her arm around my shoulders.

"This is why your grandmother did not want you to know about these powers yet. She was afraid to lose you too. Your parents were lost here for many years. Your grandmother searched and search through every painting. Then one day she found two bodies that were only bones, but one of the bodies had your mothers scarf. A scarf your grandmother had given her as a gift. Your grandmother had them buried here. This way no one in the real world could question how this happened. No one would believe your grandmother, that your parents were lost in a painting. After that, your grandmother was sure to create a mark, to allow us all to find our way back. And she made the rule of never entering a painting without a watch. Lizbeth, The Art Guardians are passed on from one generation to the next. If there is no Art Guardian then the paintings die and all those within them."

"I don't want anyone else to die".

"I do not want anyone else to die either. Which is why I will teach you how to be the Art Guardian. This way you can protect everyone. But first there is the matter of this worlds guardian for you. As we speak there is a woman who is very close to your family, whom will act as a long lost aunt to you. She really is not, but your grandmother knew how to work around that, just in case anyone was ever needed. She has a son your age, but he cannot travel just like you cannot. I will teach you both".

Tiara took me gently by the hand and led me away from where my mother and father were buried. We reached the marker my grandmother had placed, also known as the gate. Within seconds of the golden bright light we were back in the attic. Just then a man in a black suit was climbing down the wooden ladder. He was tall and strange looking. He had a mark on his cheek that looked like a paint brush stroke. He recognized me and Tiara. When he leaned in to speak, his voice was very deep and he spoke slowly.

"Hello, Lizbeth. Granddaughter of the Art Guardian. Tiara, am I late for the funeral?"

"You are not, you have made it in time".

"Good, I had hoped to return in time to bid my farewells to our great Art Guardian. Young Lizbeth, I truly hope you will take on this task of Art Guardian. I love very much visiting this world. Yet, I also love very much my homes. Your grandmother has been very kind to us all. In turn, we provided her with all that she needed to....well care for us. You my child shall never lack either. I have brought this for you".

The strange man reach out his hand in a fist and slowly opened it to real a chunk of gold. I stared at it in awe. I have never seen such a large piece of gold before. I looked at it and back to the strange man. Tiara reached out and gently took the gold from his hand.

"This is still all very new to Lizbeth".

"I can see that. Take good care of her, Tiara".

"I shall".

With that the strange man turned and went down the attic steps. I did not know what to say. All I could do was look at Tiara with shock. She giggled and placed the chunk of gold in my hand. Then she led me to the painting he had climbed out of.

"He's just come from the caves of gold. Do not let the word cave fool you, it is a beautiful place. Come, look, here is

the land of pearls. And there is the mountain of diamonds.
For years they all have provided riches to your family. This
way they had no need to work and could remain here
guarding the paintings".

"So she was not allowed to leave?"

"Oh no, she lived a normal life. She went on vacations and
enjoyed life as anyone else would. Yet whenever she was
away, she would leave someone in charge of guarding the
paintings. This way they would not be stolen, destroyed,
or worse".

"There is worse?"

"They are protected from falling into the wrong hands.
Any evil one that can get a hold of any of the paintings
could use the painting riches for their own greed and
entrap the painting and all the people in them. Come, we
must return to the funeral, before anyone from this world
realizes you are missing".

Tiara grabbed my hand and we ran down the stairs from
the attic, across the hall and down the stairs from the
second floor to the first. Once in the living room the priest
from the church saw me and reached out his hand.

"There you are blessed child. Please come, we are to
begin".

The funeral began and the priest read from the Bible. As he
did so I looked around at everyone. Now I understood why

some people looked so strange. They were from the paintings. There were so many. Too many to leave abandoned. My grandmother protected them all. I could not leave them alone. And I certainly could not allow an evil one to entrap any of them. I stood there thinking for so long, when I suddenly heard the priest ask if there was anyone who would like to speak. I slowly stood up from my seat.

"Blessed child. Did you want to say something?"

"I do".

"Come, stand by me here on this chair so you can be seen by everyone. Speak child. Tell us what your hearts yearns to share".

"I...know my grandmother loved you all very much. I also know now why she loved art so much. I will not allow anyone to be abandoned. I will continue in her work. I will be.... The Art Guardian!"

There was a sudden sound of gasps and whispers that covered the room.

"What does she mean about becoming the art guardian?"

"Her grandmother was very into the arts and cherished every piece".

"I see, I'm assuming all these strange people are the artist her grandmother worked with".

"Oh, I am sure they are".

A strange man stepped forward. He looked almost like royalty with all the jewels he wore on his very fancy garments. He stood before me with his hand on his heart.

"Young one. Young Lizbeth. We of the art are all in your debt. Thank you, for choosing to carry this task".

He bowed his head at me and all the people from the artworks did the same. I looked around at them and though I was only eight, I felt the enormous responsibility in ensuring to keep them all safe. For I now was the Art Guardian.

After that faithful day, I was allowed to live in my grandmothers home with my new guardian and her son Philip. He was like the brother I never had. We did everything together. Tiara was with us all the time as well. Mainly during the summers when we were out of school. She would grow immensely bored whenever Philip and I had to go to school and had to work on things like homework, essays, projects. We both would have been "A" students had we not missed so many homework assignments. Due to Tiara pulling us into another painting for fun and games. We had adventures that no story book could begin to describe. We rode on flying dragons and swam with mermaids. We ate the sweetest of fruits and wore the most extravagant clothing. Tiara and I noticed early on that Philip did not like the plain mens attire selected for him. So his clothing was made to his liking, with more jewels and glow just as ours. We were all three the best of friends. The childhood I had was almost like a fairytale.

We were sure to wear our watches and return back home in time. Well, not always on time. As we grew older, we really did enjoy our teen years as we partied a little more than we should have. We went from medieval bars to open sky parties, or what they called within those paintings "Gatherings". We tasted the best wines and cheapest beers. The real world could never compare to the late night parties we enjoyed. And the boys, oh my. Such gentlemen, so strong, such warriors, such...hunks!!!! Yes, they were so cute. Compared to a real world football player, these were the hottest of the hottest guys. They were muscular, handsome, strong, they rode horses and swung swords, they were brave, and did I say handsome. We all loved being around these amazing handsome men.

"Tiara, Lizbeth, I think I am in love".

"Again. Weren't you in love with the last guy you met in the other painting?"

"Ugh, you are so judgmental, Tiara".

"Or jealous".

14

"That is it, Lizbeth. Tiara is jealous because she liked the other guy from the other painting and she did not know he liked me".

"Ah, so I am jealous now I see. Fine then this jealous girl will not be taking you both to the next party I heard about".

"Party? Where? Do tell, Tiara. Lizbeth and I are truly sorry. You are not jealous. You are the bestest friend ever and you take us to the best parties".

"No! No more parties tonight. Guys, it's three am. We have to get back."

"Oh Lizbeth, why do you always have to ruin the fun. You're seventeen, but one would think your seventy".

"I am the only one who thinks responsibly here. And Philip, your mother would kill us if we got back too late. Remember she said not more returning after midnight. It is way past that time".

"Ugh, Lizbeth. Tiara is right, you are such a party pooper. It is not like we are out of the house. I mean, technically we are at home. And I'm super drunk, but I'm not driving. I just need to flop out of this painting, drag myself across the floor and down the attic stairs to my room. Mother won't even know".

"Maybe she will not know, but I will not be a liar to her. I promised to obey her rules, and we are way past curfew".

"Tiara, help me out here".

"Oh my dearest Phillip you are on your own. Tonight I stay with the hunter".

"The hunter! No, he's here?"

"He is indeed, my dearest Phillip. No! Don't turn so quickly. You don't want to make it so obvious. Look back slowly".

"Oh my my my, Tiara. That is one of the best paintings every painted of all the paintings covering the walls".

"Indeed he is. Farewell you curfew teens. I am not a teen nor do I have a curfew".

"I do hate you".

"My, my, who is jealous now, dearest Philip?"

"I am not ashamed to admit that I am boiling with jealousy right now. The hottest painting in the painting world is looking right at you. Tiara, please please tell me you don't want him so I could have him".

"I may be half painting, but I am not real world dumb. He is mine and you better get back home, before mommy grounds you until your twenty-first birthday".

"I hate you Tiara, you know that right?"

"I love you too, Philip. Good night to the both of you".

"Philip, we are leaving now".

"Oh Lizbeth, Tiara is the luckiest creature in existence".

"And will will not be unless we get back. Come one!"

I had hoped we had returned in time before Philip's mother noticed we were way past our curfew. But sadly that was not the case. As we climbed out of the painting, I threw Philips arm over my shoulder and helped lift him up. We hadn't taken three steps when I heard Philip's mother.

"Do either of you know what time it is?"

Philip immediately straightened up on his own.

"Mother! I though you would be..."

"Fast asleep? No, I was not. I have been waiting all night for the both of you. I never sleep until I hear you both come down these attic stairs. That way I know you are both back and safe. This is another reason why I gave you both a midnight curfew. Is it midnight now?"

"Well..."

"Don't answer that Philip. Get your drunk bottom down these steps and do not defy me again or you will be grounded from paint hopping for an entire month."

"Mother! A month. That hardly seems fair...."

"Neither does defying me. Downstairs now!"

Phillip quickly went down the stairs. I followed behind when suddenly Philip's mother pulled out her arm to stop me. Philip fumbled down the stairs on his own and into his bedroom. The slamming of his bedroom door being could be heard in the attic.

"Lizbeth. I know you are aware of the responsibility that is on your shoulders as the Art Guardian. I expect these actions from Phillip and Tiara, but you? You do not have this luxury of doing as you please".

"I am aware, it will not happen again".

"It will not. It cannot. For this reason I have spoken with the painting elders and we have all decided that it is best you train with another. Tiara is young and impulsive. She has not lead you down the right path, or shall I say paths. You still do not even know how to travel. You always need either Tiara or a passer buy from the painting to open the gate for you and Phillip. As the Art Guardian you should be able to travel. This way you can warn others, send messages, or whatever needs to be done. Now, I have done all of these duties for you to allow you time to have a normal life. Next week is your eighteenth birthday and within a few more months you will graduate from high school. What is it that you plan to do?"

"I...I do not know".

"Child, you are not expected to have all the answers. But at least a plan. I will not be here forever and I am growing old. I will help you for as long as I am able to do so. But the burden you carry is not a light one. These paintings you love so much, need protection. Your protection. Now, off to your room. You will have plenty of time to think of a plan. A month to be exact".

"A month..."

"The same time you and Philip will have grounded from traveling. Now, I expect you to use that time wisely".

"I shall".

"Good, that is what I want to hear. Now go and get some rest".

The following week my eighteen birthday came. Phillip and I celebrated in the real world with a very sweet party his mother did for me. Friends and neighbors were invited. Philip and I sat in a corner by the living room window. I smiled and nodded at everyone. Philip complained.

"Can this party be any more boring. I mean really, you have turned eighteen not eighty".

"It's not so bad".

"Not so bad? Look around you Lizbeth. It looks like a retirement home in here. Is there anyone under fifty besides you and I?"

"There are no younger people, because we did not make friends in school. There was no one we could invite. Your mother did what she could to give me a party with guest".

"Well, did she have to raid the retirement home to find guest for your eighteen birthday party? Besides, we did not have the privilege of making friends at school. I mean honestly, how do you tell someone 'I go paint hopping want to come?' Yes, laugh, Lizbeth, ha ha so funny".

As I laughed, Phillip received a text message that read;

T: I'm upstairs, are we celebrating or what? ~Tiara

"Philip, don't you..."

"What, kidnap you so you could have some fun on your birth-day! This party is almost over anyway. Bid your farewells to everyone and lets go upstairs".

"We are grounded from traveling..."

"Up but but. What mother does not know won't hurt her. We will just act like we are going to my bedroom to watch a movie or something."

"And when she comes upstairs to your bedroom and does not find us there?"

"I will take ALL the blame. It is your birthday today, she will understand".

"Uh, Philip".

"Oh Lizbeth, get up, get up".

Philip pushed me up from my chair and accompanied me to every guest to thank them for coming to my party and bidding them farewell. He was sure to push and pull me every so slightly to ensure I did not linger too long with each guest. I did look over to Philip's mother and I could tell she had a suspicious look on her face. After saying my last farewell Philip pulled me up the stairs. We ran across the second floor foyer and right before opening the attic door we heard Philip's mother.

"Where do you think you're both going? If my memory serves me correctly you were both grounded from traveling. There are still three weeks left in this grounding".

"Mother, please. It is Lizbeth's birthday. Must she celebrate her eighteenth birthday with the Sunshine retirement home entourage. Just one day and you can add an extra day onto our punishment".

Philip's mother hesitated for a moment. Then she raised up her index finger and pointed it at us.

"Midnight! I want you both back by midnight!"

"Oh yes mother, yes. Midnight it is! You are the best mother on the whole planet earth of the real world and the painting world, muah".

Philip's mother nodded in disagreement and sighed with a slight smile on her face. Then headed down the steps and back to the party. Philip opened the door and pushed me up the stairs with a rush. When we reached the stop of the steps, there was Tiara waiting for us.

"I thought the two of you would never come. What took so long?"

"We were serving our community by taking care of the elderly. I managed to save Lizbeth, so let's go".

"Guys, where are we going?"

"Oh you will see. Tiara has a great celebration ready and waiting for you".

Tiara stretched out her arm towards a painting we had not traveled to before. She shut her eyes, took a deep breath in and out, and the gate began to open.

"Ready!"

"You know we are! Let's go Lizbeth!"

We wrapped our arms around each others shoulders and jumped into the painting together. When we made it to the other side I heard a loud in sync yell of "Surprise!". Every single one of our friends were there. When I looked around I realized we were in a huge cabana that fit hundreds of us. There was music, drinks, food as far as the eye could see. And just a few feet away was the clearest bluest ocean waters I had ever seen. Almost like flexible glass waves were hitting the shore.

"This is so amazing".

"I knew you'd like it, Lizbeth".

"I had never seen anything like it".

"Well, Tiara had a painter paint it with all the specific details, foods, ocean waters, and all. Then she brought it here and we mounted it on the wall. Isn't it great?"

"Greater than words can even describe".

"I knew you'd like it. Sure beats the very fun party Philip tells me you were having downstairs, does it not?"

"It does...IT DOES! WHOOO LET'S PARTY!"

"YEEEES!!!"

"THIS WAY GUYS!!!!"

Tiara led us right to the beach where we ran into the waters. There were no rocks or shells to prick our feet. Just smooth, soft, warm sand on the beach and in the water. The water was perfectly warm. There was no shallow or deep level. It remained a little above the waist no matter how much further we walked into the ocean. We were careful to not wonder too far into it of course. In the real world or in paintings, the ocean can always be unpredictable. After hours of swimming, eating until our bellies couldn't fit anymore food and all the piña coladas we could drink. We laid on the loungers to soak up the sun. Sun that did not burn or scorch us. It was almost as if someone set the temperature of the sun to seventy-eight degrees and no hotter. After lounging around I lifted my arm to reach for my drink when I noticed the time on my watch.

"Oh no!"

"Oh no, what?"

"Tiara, it's almost midnight. We have to go back. We promised Philips mother we would be back on time. Philip wake up, we have to get back".

"Leave me alone, I'm taking an afternoon nap".

"Not at afternoon nap, an almost midnight nap. We have to get back!"

"Midnight! Not afternoon?"

"No, we have to go now. Tiara lead the way to the gate marker".

"This way follow me".

We made it to the marker just in time and Tiara opened the gate. We went through and ran down the attic stairs. On the second floor foyer, was Phillips mom waiting with her arms crossed. She lifted her right wrist and looked at her watch.

"Just in time. Good night both of you".

She walked into her bedroom and closed the door behind her. Philip and I gave off a sigh of relief and began laughing quietly. Philip hugged me.

"Good night buttercup. Happy eighteenth birthday. I need some serious sleep now".

"So do I. Goodnight".

We parted ways and I went into my bedroom. I pulled the covers back and threw myself onto my bed. I don't remember what happened next, except that I was fast asleep. Before long I was having a dream. At least I thought it was a dream, but it felt so real. It began where I was walking down a dark hallway with no doors. I had never seen this hallway before. Whispering could be heard, but I could not make out what they were saying. I yelled out "hello" and my voice echoed. Again I yelled out "hello". This time it did not echo. Then I suddenly heard a cry for help. It sounded like a woman.

"Help me! Can you hear me? I'm on the island. The painting of the island. I have been trapped here for many years. Please help me!"

"Which island? I have seen them all and no one is trapped in them. Which island is this? Where is this painting?"

"In my husbands home. It the hall of artwork. Please help me. I have been here so long. Can you hear me?"

"I can hear you!"

"Can you hear me? Please don't go, please help me!"

"I want to help you, where is your husbands home?"

"Please! Can you hear me? Please help me!"

I woke with a startle and sat up on my bed. That was so strange. What painting of which island? I pulled the blanket back and rushed out of my bedroom and pass Philip's mother leaving her with a "Good morning" in her mouth. I flung open the attic door and ran upstairs. I desperately looked for any island paintings I had never seen before. I had been in all of them though. After several moments Philip's mom came upstairs.

"Darling Lizbeth? Are you okay? "

"I must find the painting of the island, to save her".

"Save who? Lizbeth, please calm down and look at me. Save who?"

"The woman who called out to me for help in my dream. She said she was in the painting of an island".

"Did she say anything else?"

"Yes, she said it was in her husbands home. In the hall of artwork".

"She could be anywhere Lizbeth. Did she say anything else. Did she tell where her husband's home was? Anything at all to help find her".

"No, no, she did not give me any further clues....why is what I am telling you not surprising to you? Has this happened before?"

"Come with me young Lizbeth, it is time we have a serious talk".

Philips mother gently lifted me up from in front of the island painting I was kneeling at. She walked me down the attic stairs and abruptly opened Philip's bedroom door.

She then walked in to wake Philip up. He was spread across his bed asleep on his stomach with his mouth open. She yanked his leg.

"Not now mother, I'm sleeping".

"Philip this is important, wake up".

"Please, a few more hours and I promise I will do my chores".

"Philip! This is important, wake up!"

"Mother, you're scaring me. What's wrong?"

"Come. Lizbeth will need all the help she can get and where else can she get that help except through a true friend. I will gather what we need and go downstairs to make you both a cup of coffee. A very strong cup for you. You will need to be sobered up to pay close attention to what I have to share".

Philips mother quickly left the room and went to her bedroom. I ran toward Philip's head and kneeled by his beside. With his head still lifted up he looked at me with confusion.

"What is going on? I have never seen my mother like that".

"I had a dream about a woman calling out for help. She said she was in an island painting in her husband's home. In the hall of artwork".

"Okay, that sounds creepy. Do you think it had anything to do with Tiara's new painting?"

"No, Tiara's painting was of a beach. This woman said she was trapped on an island".

"Beach, island, aren't they the same thing?"

"No, she mentioned she had been there a long time. If it were here wouldn't we have noticed someone trapped by now".

"Okay, this just became a very scary situation".

"I think your mother knows something. None of this surprised her".

"Okay, now I have to know what's going on. Let's go".

We tidied up and changed our clothes and ran downstairs at the same time. When we got to the kitchen the counters and table were full of some old and new looking books. Philip's mother walked up to us and handed each of us a cup of coffee. Philip's eyes were wide open as he slowly went for the first sip of his coffee.

"Uh mom, are you okay?"

"No time for questions yet. Listen closely, do not interrupt and pay close attention".

Philip and I looked at each other with fearful concern wondering what was going on. Then Philip took another sip of his coffee. I followed with a big gulp from my cup of coffee.

"Here on the kitchen counters you will see newer journals. Some of these here were written by me. Lizbeth, these were written by your grandmother, and your great grandparents. On the kitchen table you will find older journals. These were written way before our time by your ancestors, before your great grandmother and further back. Your generation has been Art Guardians since the first painting was created. In these journals it will share how it all began and what has gone on through the years".

"What does that have to do with my dream about the woman needing help?"

"I remember your grandmother sharing a story with me about a rescue. This was of a young boy who desperately wanted to learn how to open the gates. But he was no kin to you. In his nosey ways, as any young child would be, he accidentally saw a pair of your twin cousins traveling into and out of a painting from a museum they were visiting. He befriended your cousins and became close to them. As you are with Phillip. However, unlike Philip, this young boy became very greedy and wanted terribly to travel on his own. He tried to learn everything that he could. Then one day he gathered enough strength to open the gate. The problem was, he did not know how to return. Of course after your twin cousins learned he was missing, they searched for him within all the paintings. That took so much time, because no one knew which painting he was stuck in. After several weeks of searching within the paintings and the real world thinking he was kidnapped or a runaway, your cousins found him. They opened the gate and brought him home. Sadly, grateful he was not. He was furious. Furious that he could not travel how he wanted to. Your cousins forbid him to return and sent him away. He threatened to tell everyone the truth, but he knew no one would believe him. So instead, when everyone was asleep, he snuck into the house and stole as many paintings as he could carry. Right around that time you were born, Lizbeth. Sadly around the same time your parents went missing. Your grandmother was distraught and your cousins feared the boy would return. So your grandmother was entrusted with all the paintings protection. Which she brought to this house and placed in the attic. Now the paintings were protected, but your parents were still missing. So she searched and searched until she found them".

"Right. I remember. Burying them in that painting, to not raise questions about their disappearance and death".

"Mom, what happened to the young boy?"

"He moved away with his family and we never heard of him again. Sadly we do not know where he moved. We heard it was out of the country, but we never learned where. Had we known, your twin cousins would have gone to retrieve the stolen paintings".

Philips mother turned the page and there was an old black and white photo of twin boys and another young boy with them.

"Who are those kids in the picture?"

"Don't know, but we can clearly see two of them are twins. These must be your cousins. Let me turn it around. Ah, it reads the names of your twin cousins and 'Neptune'. I guess they called the boy Neptune".

"Well, we now know there was a rescue. Did they dream of the boy nicknamed Neptune, like I dreamt with the woman?"

"No. Your dream is unique. This is what we want to figure out. You Lizbeth will start with your grandmothers writing. Do not worry about my writings, there is nothing in there about something like this. Philip and I will go through the older journals. If there was a rescue similar to your dream it should be written in these journals".

Philip downed his last sip of coffee and grabbed Lizbeth's cup and gulped the rest of her cup. They nodded in agreement and began their search. The morning hours soon turned into late night. The stacked books were made into a mess opened and laid out almost everywhere in the kitchen and into the living room. Where they all three ended up on the couch, in front of the fireplace and on a recliner. Philip was in front of the fireplace laying on his stomach when he perked up.

"I think I've found something!"

"What does it say, Philip?"

"Okay, so Lizbeth's great, great, great grandfather named Eric wrote about a rescue of a woman in a painting. He shared that he dreamt with a dark hall with stone walls and no doors or windows".

"Just like my dream, but in mine the walls were not stone, they were just like our walls today".

"It says he heard her cry for help. He asked her where she was and she told him she was in the kings hall of art. Inside of the....here it is. Inside of the battle painting. Oh that is a terrible painting to be stuck in. Who would want to be stuck in a painting where there is a battle all day and night".

"Philip, forget that and tell us how he found and saved her".

"Well, your great, great, great grandfather Eric did not work in the castle. He was a steel worker and he made weapons. So he decided to make two great swords. One for himself and one to give as a gift to the king. This gave him an excuse to get inside the castle. It took some time to do, but his plan worked. He then was granted an audience with the king and was able to give him the sword. The king was pleased with the gift. Then he asked Eric what he could give him in return. Eric asked to see his hall of art. The king thought it was an odd request, but he granted it. He sent a soldier with Eric who led him to where the hall was.

Afterward, Eric walked down the hall alone. It looked just like the stone walls in his dream, except these walls had paintings on them. There were many paintings of battles".

"How did he find her then?"

"It says here he searched each painting for something odd. Then he saw only one painting with a woman in the back of the battlefield sad and hugging herself".

"That had to be the one".

"Indeed it was mother. He opened the gate and the second sword he made for himself, he used to fight through the battle to reach the woman. When he did, he found her weeping under a tree. He asked if she was the woman from his dream who called out for help. She looked up at him with surprise, then stood up and ran into his arms. Oh, he wrote she was the most beautiful woman he had ever seen."

"How romantic".

"Romantic indeed, Lizbeth. He was like her knight in shining armor"

"Romance shmomance, what happened next?"

"Okay okay mother. Well, he goes on to share how he snuck her out of the castle and brought her to his home. There he sat with her and she told her story about how she wanted to run away from a betrothed marriage with the king. She remembered seeing a golden light in the hall and she walked over to it. Next thing she knew a man ran out of the painting. She quickly moved out of the way, but tumbled and fell into the painting".

"Who left the painting?"

"Doesn't say. Whoever it was they left in a rush. What I can see here is that Eric wrote, that he fell in love with the woman and they married. So this rescued woman ended up being your great great great grandmother, Lizbeth".

"Does it say her name? The name of the woman Eric married".

"Yes, here it is. Her name was Sophia".

"Okay, so I just need to look for my great great great grandmother Sophia's journal".

"Good idea Lizbeth. Philip look through your pile to see if you find it and I will look through mine".

"Got it! Got it! Sophia!".

Phillip, his mother and I hovered over my great great great grandmother Sophia's journal and began searching for clues. Sadly there was nothing that could help me with learning how to find the woman from my dream.

"Dearest Lizbeth, I am truly sorry. I had hoped this could help."

"Do not be sorry. This helped immensely. At least I know I am not going crazy. Hopefully, I can someday find this woman and help her".

"Oooh you guys are going to call me a genius. Lizbeth, why don't we open up a museum where we recycle paintings. All kinds of older paintings. If she had been stuck in the painting for quite some time, and we know it's not a newer work of art. People can donate their old artwork or sell them to us. You've got more than enough money to do so. Let's face it your rich, so money would not be an issue".

"Oh my goodness Philip, you are a genius. If I cannot find her, maybe just maybe she will come directly to me".

"I know of an old abandoned building, that they have wanted to tear down for years to build condos. Advocates will not allow it, because it is a historical building. It is a very big building and perfect to store artwork".

"Now I know where I get my genius from, mother".

After a few months we were able to officially move into the building. There were so many legalities and paperwork. Philip was sure to turn over every rock and cover every corner so to speak, when it came to protecting everything that was brought into the building. This way no one, from advocates to the city officials could take our paintings away. The building was theirs, but whatever was brought into the building was legally ours. This assured us that all artwork would stay in our possession as it should. We named the new museum "The Guardian". I also played the artist part so well, with my slick back ponytail done on my hair, black turtleneck tops and black famed blue light glasses. I was an art gallery protégée. During my spare time I read a lot of books and watched tons of videos on artwork. Just so I could understand the lingo when speaking with artist.

No painting had a permanent home. With every new painting being donated or sold to us we had to adjust the wall space time and time again. Even Tiara found herself with less paint hopping and more working. As we unpacked new paintings Tiara as usual shared her thoughts.

"With all this artwork, specifically all these island ones, shouldn't we have found this woman already? You haven't dreamt with her again, maybe this is a lost cause".

"I'm not giving up Tiara. I need to find this woman".

"Lizbeth, your obsession with finding this woman has made you even more tight wound. Your less fun than before and you barely go paint hopping with Philip and I. Where is that fun Lizbeth I knew as a kid who loved flying on the dragon and swimming with the mermaids?"

"That girl is long gone, Tiara. Miss Lizbeth now is a business woman. For fun, she now reads books on art. Give up your dispute, I have already tried over and over".

"Why do you both make me out to be some up in age woman who has retired from having fun in life".

"Lizbeth, your obsession with finding this woman can takes its toll on you if you are not careful. I just don't want you to get to crazy about this and lose yourself. We don't know how she got into the painting to begin with. What if it wasn't an accident and she is like the young boy who was evil and determined to travel?"

"Then in that case she got what she deserved and should stay on the island".

"Philip! Tiara, I understand your concerns. Yes, I am still trying to find the woman to save. However, in the process I have had the ability to do something that I have grown to love. Look at all of this amazing artwork we have collected."

"Yes, artwork you have not allowed me to take you into so you could enjoy".

"Not every painting needs to be traveled into. Sometimes it is enough to just protect it. Which is what I am responsible in doing".

"Yes, yes, I know. As the Art Guardian. But how do you expect them to know who you are if you do not meet the painting and the people who live in them".

"I guess you are right".

"Oh she is right indeed, Lizbeth. Tiara, confirm my doubt, is this an original or a copy?"

Tiara reaches out her arm to the painting Philip puts before her. She takes a deep breath in and out and nothing happens. No light, no open gate, nothing.

"Yup, it's a fake. Surely not the original work. Only originals allow the portal to open".

"I thought so, I will store this one in the basement with the others. If the original reaches our hands we can give this one away and check the original...for this so called lost woman".

"Will you now tease me as well, Philip?"

"I said nothing. To the basement I go".

"That's it, tonight we are going...uh...there. That one looks fun. And I don't want to hear any excuses, Lizbeth".

"Did I just hear we are going paint hopping?"

"I thought you were headed to the basement, Philip".

"Well, I overheard paint hopping so if you guys are going then so am I. What time will this be?"

"Tonight. 8pm. The museum is closed so no excuses, Lizbeth".

"Yay! Now I am going to the basement. Toodles".

"Toodles?"

"He heard it in one of the paintings we hopped into".

I agreed to travel that night and we entered the painting Tiara chose. I do admit we did have lots of fun that night. Yet, I could not help but look around from time to time searching for the woman who needed help.

"She is not here, Lizbeth. I can assure you if she was, we would have found her already".

"I guess you are right, Tiara. But it is late anyway and we are not in the attic at home".

"Fine, I agree. Yet, do you really want to interrupt Philip's fun right this second".

I glanced over to where Philip was and could not help but burst out laughing. Tiara laughed with me. He was indeed having way too much fun dancing by the beach fire and yelling out "Whoop, Whoop" over and over. We stood a tad bit longer and when Philip was all out of "Whoops", we traveled back to the museum. All three of us climbed into the car and I drove us home. Before I could fully stop the car Philip jumped out and started to "whoop, whoop" into the house. Tiara and I laughed as I parked the car. After doing so, we stepped out and that's when we heard Philip yell. We ran into the house and found Philip beside his mother who was on the kitchen floor. I ran over to them.

"What happened Philip?"

"I don't know I walked in and found her like this".

"Tiara, call an ambulance".

She did so and they quickly arrived to take Philip's mother. We then all three jumped into my car and followed the ambulance to the hospital. The minutes that passed felt more like hours. Suddenly the doctor walked into the waiting room and Philip wasted to time in asking about his mother. The doctor agreed to allow all three of us to go and see her, especially since we said we were all her children. Philip was distraught when he looked through the window and saw his mother so weak. She looked over at him and gave him a weakly smile. Tiara pulled open the door and Philip rushed in. We followed behind him. Philip sat by his mothers side and took her gently by the hand.

"Mother, what's wrong? Why did I find you on the kitchen floor? The doctor said you asked him not to tell me anything and that you wanted to tell me yourself".

"My sweet boy. I love you so much. You know that right?"

"I do know that, but what's wrong mother? Please tell me".

"I'm dying. I have cancer".

"What? Mother, no no no. You are healthy and strong, I don't understand. Why wouldn't you tell me, I could have taken care of you?"

"I kept it from you, because I wanted you to enjoy your life, not worry about me all the time. Which is what you will continue to do even after I am gone".

"No, I can't lose you mother. This is wrong. This is all wrong".

Philip laid his head on his mothers chest and cried like a little boy. She cried with him. I felt helpless. Once again, another woman in need that I could not help. Then I felt Tiara nudge me. I looked at her and she signaled to follow her out to the hall. We both stood up from the chair and stepped out of the room. Tiara closed the door behind me. Then she stood there looking at me for a moment, hesitating to speak.

"What is is Tiara? Speak".

"I think, I might have a plan. I am not sure it will work, but it is worth a try".

"What plan is that?"

"What if we brought Philip's mother into a painting? Any painting of her choice. And allowed her to live there, without cancer."

"Your saying there is a chance she could live without her illness inside of the painting? Has this been done before?"

"I have heard rumors, but I have never witnessed it. It is a whole lot better than doing nothing. We have to try".

"I agree. What if it doesn't work?

"Then she will at least die peacefully on a beautiful sunny beach, as opposed to this dreary hospital room".

"Good idea. Should I tell him or should you".

"You tell him. You are the Art Guardian. Besides, I would hate to break his heart further if it doesn't work. After all it was my crazy idea".

"But it is better than no idea at all".

Tiara gently pushed open the door and she and I both popped our heads in. Philips mother stopped crying and look at us. Philip lifted his head and looked at his mother. Then he turned to look at Tiara and I. I looked at Tiara and she looked at me, when then looked back at Philip, without planning it we said the words, "We need to talk" at the same time. Philip wondering what was going on slowly stood up and joined us in the hall. We told him the possible plans and he became hopeful. He immediately began the process of requesting that the hospital release his mother and allow her to die peacefully in her home. It was not until morning that she was released to us. We gently helped her into the car and drove home. Once we got there we rushed up the stairs carrying her and laid her on the soft floor pillows.

"Choose mother. Any which one you want. Tiara will take you through".

"That one right there has always been my favorite to travel too. The sun is so bright, the breeze so cool, the coconut and mangos are to die for in there. Literally".

"Mother, not time for jokes you are way to weak and we must travel now. Tiara open the gate".

Tiara stretched out her arm, took a deep breath in and out, and the gate began to shine golden bright as it opened. We then all three gently lifted Philips mom up and entered through the gate. Once in the painting the gate closed and we laid Philip's mother on the sand. She closed her eyes and took deep breaths. Those seconds felt like forever. Then suddenly she spoke.

"Philip, help me up. The pain stopped".

We were astonished and then we broke out with rejoicing. We helped her stand to her feet and she was like brand new.

"Oh my this is unbelievable. All the pain is gone. I feel like my old self again. How?"

"I do not know, mother. But I am so glad we tried. Thank you Tiara, thank you so much".

Philip grabbed Tiara in a tight hug and cried in her arms. After that we remained within the beach painting for days with Philip and his mother. I only left the painting to put a sign on the museum door. That read it would closed until further notice and to update our website to when we were going to reopen.

We stayed and wondered to ourselves if Philips mother could ever return to the real world.

"Look, if a day here is a day in the real world. Then days go by as normal, physical clock time does not count, but its days do and age does".

"Do you guys think if my mother went back now, the cancer would be a week old and still growing?"

"I think it would, Philip". I am half paint and half human, first made. My father was paint and my mother was human. So I have been traveling all my life. When humans stay in a painting they grow old and die as they would in the real world, yet the paint people are immortal unless they leave the painting. Your mother still has regular changes in the real world. Yet here, it seems that she would only age."

"Well, there is only one way to find out for sure. Let me go back. If the cancer is still there I will feel the pains, I am sure".

"No mother, you cannot. What if within a week you are dead in the real world. If you walk through the gate, you could collapse and be dead. Then there would be no time to pull you back through, because you would be gone".

"I think Philip has a point. But to know for sure. What if one of us waits in the real world, while the gate is open and you reach your hand through. If you feel any pain we will know that the cancer still has your body in the real world, but in this painting you can live the rest of your days, cancer free".

"That's a good idea, Lizbeth. Can we do that, Tiara?"

"It is worth a try. I will open the gate. Lizbeth and I will step into the real world and wait for Philip to reach through, holding his mothers hand. If she feels any pain, he can pull her back or we push her back into the painting".

"I like this plan. Philip, no matter what happens. I will be just fine here, if I cannot return. Promise you will be okay with that".

"I can't promise anything just yet mother. Let's give it a try first".

We all rushed over to the marker and Tiara opened the gate. She and I went through and waited on the other side.

When suddenly Philip's hand holding his mothers began to slowly come through. Then their arms. Once her shoulder and side were coming through the gate, she and Phillip immediately returned. Tiara and I looked at each other and stepped into the painting again. Philip's mother was kneeling on the beach breathing heavy and Philip was in front of her trying to ease her scare.

"What happened?"

"It did not work, Lizbeth. Once her shoulder and side were passing through she felt the pains of the cancer. And stronger than a week ago when we entered the painting".

"Then that answers that question. Philip, your mother may never return to the real world or she will surely die from that disease. Lizbeth and I will give you both some time alone".

Tiara nudged me and we walked away to give Philip and his mother some alone time. We went to the tiki bar and sat down. I couldn't help looking over my should back at them as they spoke. Tiara ordered a strong long island ice tea. The bartender then looked at me.

"And for you madam. What would you like to drink?"

"Anything with your delicious coconut and mango mix".

"Coming right up, madam".

"Tiara, I still can't get over the fact that you never have to pay for anything in a painting and you get such great service. Nothing like the real world".

"Now that is truth".

The waiter handed me my drink and right after my first sip, I heard the best sound ever. From behind us Phillip and his mother broke out in laughter. I abruptly asked the waiter for two more coconut and mango drinks. When they were ready, Tiara and I each carried one and rushed over to Philip and his mother. When we reached them, Tiara sat by Philip and handed him his drink. I sat by his mother and handed her the drink.

"All is well?"

"It is, Tiara. My mother made a point. She won't be dead right now and instead she will be on a forever vacation".

"That is what I said. Think about it, what person can live the rest of their days this way, on a forever vacation."

"That wasn't the only thing you said mother".

"Oh what, are you judging me now".

"Judging? Now I need to know what was said".

"Tiara, what I said was that the bartender who never closes the tiki bar, will now have to do so from time to time to fill me with his....coconuts and mango whenever I want him too".

"Ugh mother!"

"What? I mean the drink, this drink. You all have such dirty minds".

There was a very much needed burst of laughter between us four.

We stood for hours and hours on that beach. Which then turned into more days, then weeks. Philip was not ready to go back home. Nor was Tiara. I returned to have arrangements made on a fake funeral for Philips mother. We planned to have it done with a closed casket so no one would notice there was no body in it. We also used one of our fake funeral homes that were run by people from the painting, to be used for times like this. I had remembered reading about them in my grandmothers journals. They lived out of state, but were glad to travel and prepare everything to make it looks just right. Phillip returned to the real world for the funeral. He still cried immensely. Though his mother was still alive, he cried because she could not come back to the real world. He also cried because he did not know how to open the gate himself yet. He promised his mother he would learn, so that he could visit her anytime he wanted to. Tiara promised to stay by his side until he did.

After the funeral I filled my days with working at the museum. The majority of the time Philip and Tiara were in the painting with Philip's mother. No matter how many times she begged him to return and live his life like normal, he refused to leave her side. Philip would not allow me to linger as long as he did either. He knew I had to protect the paintings both in the attic and in the museum. It began to feel pretty lonely in the real world without Philip, his mother, and Tiara. I had missed them dearly. I longed for Tiara to drop by the museum insisting that we go paint hopping and have fun. Yet, I knew Philip needed time, and he needed Tiara to learn how to open the gate. Patience was the key. So he patiently took each lesson. And I patiently awaited to see my friends again.

Across the oceans in the country of Portugal, lived a man in his late forties who had a fascination with artwork. He was a very rich and powerful man. So powerful he was even asked to advise the president on matters of state from time to time. His name was Leonardo Ferreira, but many called him Leo. He lived in a lavish mansion with very expensive furnishings that added to his homes elegance. But where he could always be found during the morning hours, was at the head of the very long dinner table in his dining room that could sit twenty people.

On this breezy sunny morning, Leo sat at the head of the table as he always did, to eat his breakfast and read his newspaper. One of his men walked into the dining area, then stood waiting. Leo knew he was there, yet kept reading his newspaper. He then closed, folded, and placed it off to the side. Then he leaned in to start eating his breakfast.

"Speak".

"Mr. Ferreira, you asked me to let you know when the museum named Guardian would reopen. I have received notice that it has now reopen".

"Good. I must take a visit to this museum then".

"Yes sir, but I have also learned that the artwork collected is not for sale".

"Not for sale? What do you mean, not for sale? Everything has a price".

"The artwork in this museum was either donated or purchased by the owner named Lizbeth and her colleagues".

"I see, and does this Lizbeth own the building as well?"

"She does not sir. It is a historical building owned by the city".

"In that case, have my people call their people. If she does not give me what I want. I want to know what I can use to persuade, this, Lizbeth. Have the maid pack my things. I would like to leave tonight".

"Yes sir".

"Ah, one more thing. Do you know anything of my sons' whereabouts?"

"No, sir. Nothing yet".

Leo reached the U.S. and settled into his hotel, with about an hour before Lizbeth's museum scheduled closing time. He had his driver take him there. The driver reached the front of Lizbeth's museum and Leo stepped out of his car. He looked up at the building and paused for a moment. Almost as if he was familiar with its design or it reminded him of something. He then continued to approach the building and walk inside. Two of his bodyguards followed behind him. After he was inside his bodyguards opened the double doors that were painted in navy blue with gold trimming. Leo was pleased with the design. He slowly stepped into the hall of paintings and was impressed. The decoration was beautiful and paintings reached as high as the ceiling. Neatly and perfectly organized. He took some time viewing the paintings. Then he saw one he very much liked. He stopped to admire it.

"This one. Yes, this is the one I want. Get me the owner, this Lizbeth".

As the bodyguard walked off to find Lizbeth, Leo spoke to himself.

"This old woman named Lizbeth has done well with her collection. I will be pleased to take this one off of her hands".

Just then the bodyguard walked back into the hall of paintings with Lizbeth following behind him. Leo turned to see her as his bodyguard walked off. When he did so, Leo was able to get a good look at Lizbeth. He was amazed at how young and beautiful she was. Lizbeth boldly approached him and reached out her hand to shake his.

"Allow me to introduce myself. My name is Lizbeth and I do not take kindly to threats. So let me be clear, none of my paintings are for sale".

"Threats?"

"The city officials called and said that if I did not sell you what you wanted, that I could lose the building. I would rather sacrifice the building, before I let go of any of my paintings".

"I see. Please, allow me to introduce myself now. My name is Leonardo Ferreira, but everyone calls me Leo".

"Well, Mr. Ferreira..."

"Please, call me Leo".

"Mr. Leo, as I have said. None of my paintings are for sale".

"No need to worry. I will not try to buy any of your paintings. After all, I thought I was looking at the most beautiful creation ever made, but I was wrong".

"Oh, how so? I believe all the artwork in this museum is the most beautiful works ever created".

"This is not true. In order for you to see the most beautiful creation, Mrs?"

"Miss".

"Ah, Miss Lizbeth. As I was saying, in order for you to see the most beautiful creation...you must first look into a mirror. Then and only then will you understand why my eyes have now seen, such true beauty".

"Sir.."

"Again, please call me Leo".

"Uh, Leo. I do thank you for such kind words. Yet, I do not understand. If you are not here to force me to sell you one of my paintings, then why have you come?"

"I would like to ask for your forgiveness on any misunderstanding you city officials may have caused you. I am a collector of art and I love to see what is out in the world, besides my own beautiful collection in my home. My request to visit your beautiful museum must have had them assume I wanted to purchase one of your beautiful pieces. I merely wanted to see what you displayed, nothing more. Yet, I was surprised to have my breath taken away, in meeting you. There are not many young woman as beautiful as you, that show interest in artwork as exquisite as this. Again, forgive my intrusion and any discomfort I may have brought to you this evening. I will take my leave and leave you to your work".

"No! Wait. I am sorry. I was so rude towards you. It's just that I am very protective of my work. It is not for profit that I do what I do. It is because I feel responsible in caring for it, and because I love it".

"Miss Lizbeth, you have truly inspired me this evening. I hope I am not being too forward in asking you to have a cup of coffee with me, so you can tell me more on how you have come to acquire such a beautiful collection".

"Oh, coffee at this hour for me would not be the best..."

"Tea then. Any which one that could allow you to feel at ease before you go home to rest. For example chamomile tea, perhaps? There is also green tea, or peppermint tea, or...."

"Tea is fine. I will join you for tea".

"Wonderful. We can go in my car. My driver will take us to one of my favorite places where they serve the best cup of coffee...and tea".

"That is very kind of you. I will actually go in my car and meet you there".

"This is fair. You barely know me. For now I am just a stranger to you. Here let me give you the address. I will wait for you there".

Leo snapped his finger and one of his men rushed over with his phone, where he pulled up the name and address of the restaurant Leo was inviting me to. I searched it on my phone. After doing so Leo smiled and left my museum. I felt so nervous inside. I was not sure exactly why though. Was it because I was riled up and ready to dispute the non-sale of my paintings with this man, or because he asked me out on a date. No, not a date. It was just a cup of tea. Wouldn't that be considered a date though? I believed I was thinking things over way too much. It was just a cup a tea and that was it. Yet, I couldn't help finding myself in front of the mirror making sure I looked okay. Then I thought, no blue light glasses. I look too studious. Nope, blue light glasses are a go. I am not trying to impress anyone. Glasses it is. I locked up the museum and got into my car. Right before turning on my car I pulled down the visor and looked into that mirror.

"What are you doing, Lizbeth? What I am doing is having a cup of tea with a very nice older gentleman, who happens to be very handsome for his age. Oh Tiara, Philip, what would you guys do? You would both go. No, wait, I am neither Tiara nor Philip, I don't just go. I follow the rules and I keep it together. But if I don't go, he will come back to the museum wondering why I stood him up. What excuse would I give them? Ugh, I have no excuse and no reason why not to go. Fine, I'm going. After-all it is just tea."

I closed the visor and turned on my car. After my cellphone GPS led me to the restaurant I parked my car and looked over at the entrance. Then I grabbed my phone to message Tiara and Philip.

L: *"You guys we need to talk. I think I am going on a date with a person from the real world. Message me back as soon as you get this message (crazy emoji/heart emoji)".*

There, done. If any of them returned to the real world they would surely get my message. Before getting out the car, again I opened the visor and checked how I looked. Then I took a deep breath and stepped out of the car. As soon as I slammed closed my car door I was startled by one of Leo's men.

"Miss Lizbeth, this way please".

What kind of a man summons for me by sending his henchmen every time he wants to speak to me. This was new, really new. Actually, when I thought about it, it was all new. I had never gone on a date with anyone in the real world. I was always afraid they would see me as odd or crazy because of my paintings. So painting men were the only kind I dated and kissed. Well, it was one kiss. Just a tap kiss on the lip. Tiara and Philip had more experience with these things. Oh how I had hoped to speak with them. But unless Tiara was outside of a painting, she could not receive any of my messages. And with Philip in the painting for so long, forget getting my message unless he returned. I walked into the restaurant and it was very lavish. It looked very expensive. As rich as I was myself, I had never entered any establishments like this. Leo's man led me right to his table. Leo immediately stood up and pulled out a chair for me. I guess that meant for me to sit in it, so I did and he gently pushed my seat in. He sat in the chair beside me. Very close to me might I add. I thought he would sit across the table, but oh no, he sat right beside me. The waiter then walked over to our table and quietly waited. Leo smiled and turned to me.

"So, Miss Lizbeth. Have you decided on which tea you would like. All you need to do is ask and you shall receive".

"Thank you. Chamomile should be fine".

"The lady will have a chamomile tea".

"Very good choice my lady, would you like anything in your tea? Sugar or milk perhaps?"

"Actually, I prefer honey. Floral honey if you have any".

"Excellent choice Miss Lizbeth".

"And for you sir?"

"I will have the same as the beautiful lady. Please, add sweet milk to mine".

The waiter nodded in agreement and walked away.

"Tell me Lizbeth, have you ever tried your chamomile tea with sweet milk?"

"I don't think I have every tried any tea with milk in it".

"Ah, then you do not know what you are missing. Please, you must try some of mine".

The teas were quickly brought to us and Leo lifted his cup and gently placed it close to my lips. I know it was just a cup a tea, but for some reason it felt like such a sensual experience. I closed my eyes and took a sip of the tea.

"That is delicious".

"Ah, I knew you would like it. Would you like sweet milk added to your tea?"

"I would".

Leo called the waiter over and asked to have sweet milk added to my tea. The waiter nod in agreement and rushed to get the milk. He returned with an adorable mini pitcher and every so eloquently poured sweet milk into my tea. I picked up my spoon and stirred the tea with milk. Leo and I picked up our cups of tea and began to drink and talk. We talked about so many things. We started with teas, then paintings, about life and then we ventured into more personal conversations about relationships.

"With so much desire to talk art and tea, I failed to ask you Miss Lizbeth. Is there a boyfriend I should be concerned about. I do not want to cause anyone any jealousy".

"No, there is not boyfriend".

"No boyfriend? Forgive my shock. A woman as beautiful as you should have men fighting for a chance to at least speak with you. I consider myself the luckiest man then, to have had the chance to sit with you and enjoy your company and your beauty. What ever fool you let go of in the past, I am sure feels the regret of losing you".

"Actually, there is no boyfriend now...nor any from the past".

"No. It cannot be. I do not believe you. What fool would allow a beauty like you to slip past him. If it were me, I would follow you around like a helpless puppy. Do not laugh Miss Lizbeth, I mean this. You are beautiful, well educated, you have great taste in art, and you are now well learned on tea with sweet milk".

"You do have a way with words. But your flattery will get you nowhere. Especially if this is to trick me into selling you one of my paintings".

"Aha, she is funny as well. Yet, there is no trickery here. I do not want to buy any of your paintings. However, I believe you will find me often in your museum, hoping to get another quick glimpse of the most beautiful work of art I have ever seen".

Leo reached for and took me by the hand. I freaked out. I did not know what to do, so I gently pulled my hand back and stood up from my chair. Leo stood up from his chair as well and stepped closer to me.

"Oh my it is late. I need to head home now".

"Is there any one waiting for you at home. Mother, father, children, perhaps".

"No, there is no one. I have roommates that live with me, but they are out of town right now. I have work in the morning so I need my rest".

"Then I bid you good night. Under one condition".

"What would that be?"

"That you join me for dinner tomorrow after work".

"I don't know..."

"Or lunch. You work all day, you have to eat don't you. Lunch or dinner you choose. We can eat here. You know now where it is. I can have my driver pick you up or you can meet me here as you have done this night".

"Dinner is fine. And I will meet you here".

"Thank you for accepting my invite. I look forward to our dinner tomorrow night".

"Good night".

"Good night, Miss Lizbeth".

I walked towards the exit of the restaurant as calmly as I could. I knew Leo would be looking at me. I couldn't help it though, so I looked over my shoulder and sure enough he was looking right at me. Once the door attendant opened the door I walked out of the restaurant and rushed to my car. I sat inside, slammed the door closed and began to hyperventilate, then I started laughing like a crazy person. I had to get home. I needed to shake off this craziness. I turned my car on and drove home.

As soon as I parked my car in the driveway I heard my cell phone alert. I picked it up and it was a message from Tiara that read;

T: *"Get up here now".*

I quickly jumped out of the car, unlocked the front door, slammed it behind me and ran upstairs to the attic. Tiara was standing there looking at the painting Philip and his mother were in.

"What is going on? Is everything okay?"

"Wait for it".

"For what, what are we waiting for?"

"Shh, just wait".

We stood there silent for a moment when suddenly the painting Philip was in sparked a small gold light. Almost like the gate was opening, but not quit fully open. The best way to describe it was like almost a circular plastic flap sliced in four places. I could see Philips hand coming through pulling on the plastic. Then it widened some to fit his arm. Then his head. It was grotesque to say the least. Almost as if the painting were giving birth to Philip. Little by little he pushed his body through. Finally when he was through, Philip was covered in sand as he dropped to the ground and sand poured out of the painting and fell to the ground as well.

"What is the world did I just see?"

"That was Philip learning how to open the gate, just enough to force himself through. Philip, you need more practice to fully open the gate or you will be pushing yourself through these tiny port holes, every time".

"Ugh, don't you think I know that now. That was terrible. And I am covered in sand. I have never come out so messy from a painting before".

"Well, actually there was this one time where..."

"Shut it, Lizbeth!"

"I also remember a time where…"

"You too, Tiara!"

"Gross, I need a shower".

"Okay, go shower and when you are done. I need to talk to both of you".

"This sounds serious, maybe a shower can wait till later".

"No, you go shower and then I will tell".

"Lizbeth went on a date!"

"A what? Lizbeth doesn't date real world people".

"I've got the text right here".

"Oh my gosh! Tiara, you go back and tell my mother I will be staying here tonight. I am going to take a cat bath shower. We will meet downstairs in 30 minutes. Then I want to the know the details. HURRY!"

Before I could say a word Tiara disappeared into the painting and Philip was already downstairs on the second floor yelling "Lizbeth went on a date!"

We all met in the kitchen and Philip kept looking at me funny as he went into the fridge to pull out the glass pitcher filled with juice. Tiara keep grinning at me. Philip poured his juice without hardly taking his eyes off of me. Then he took a sip of his juice.

"Start talking".

"Okay, so I got a call this morning from a city representative..."

"Your dating someone from the city!"

"No, Philip".

"I was going to say, they are usually only old guys".

"That's not necessarily true, Philip. Let Lizbeth talk, don't interrupt".

"Thank you, Tiara. As I was saying, someone for the city called to tell me that a very important man was flying in from Portugal. He was an art collector. They also mentioned he was very rich and had powerful connections, so I should not refuse the purchase of any of my paintings. If I did not comply then they would remove me from the building".

"The paintings are not for sale".

"Exactly what I told him, Tiara. When I confronted him earlier this evening. I was very strong towards him and willing to lose the building, but not one of my paintings".

"What does that have to do with a date....wait did you go on a date with the Portugal guy?"

"Well Philip, see, maybe not a date. It was more like we had a cup of tea. With sweet milk might I add, and it tasted really good".

"Oh my goodness Tiara, Lizbeth is in love".

"I am not!"

"That's it. You are in love. Virginity gone to the Portugal guy".

"You are exaggerating now, Philip. It was just tea. And I do not plan to give up my virginity to just any guy. I'm waiting for marriage".

"Oh Philip, the virgin Lizbeth and her holy ways will not submit until marriage. Bets are open to see if she will wait or give it up now".

"I take you up on that bet, Tiara. Wait, how old is this guy? Was he married? Kids? How powerful is he? And what kind of art does he collect?"

"Questions I do not know the answer to yet. I know that he is older than me. I'm sure he has been married before".

"If not still married, make sure he is not trying to make you the 'other' woman".

"Oh my goodness, I didn't even think of that. I will ask him at dinner tomorrow night. If he is married, then forget it".

"Wait, your going to dinner with him tomorrow night? Hold on, why wait to ask those questions. What do you think the internet is for?"

We all three looked at each other then ran to the living room. Philip was the first one to beat us to the laptop, we hovered behind him.

"Okay, what is his name".

"It's Leonardo Ferreira".

"Searching, searching. Oh there he is. Well, not bad. He is older, a lot older, but he's a very good looking man for his age".

"Says here he is very rich and powerful in Portugal. He has influences on the political world. Keep scrolling Philip. Lizbeth, did he talk any politics with you".

"Oh, here it is, here it is. It says he was married, but his wife mysteriously disappeared almost 10 years ago. Okay, now that sounds creepy".

I stood up not liking the whole wife disappearing bit. Especially after that dream I had about year ago. I walked over to the fire place and let Philip and Tiara keep searching on the web for more information on Leo.

"Philip, check to see if he has any children".

"Here. He has one son. He looks like he can't be any older than twelve or thirteen though".

"Yeah, I agree. Well, Lizbeth this just means that you have to stay alert. Ask questions and don't believe everything you hear. Make sure to figure out if he is one of the good guys".

"Yes, you both are right. You know what, I won't go to that dinner. This is crazy. I am the Art Guardian and my sole purpose is to protect the paintings and that is what I shall do".

Philip and Tiara looked at each other in concern and Philip closed the laptop. Tiara walked over to Lizbeth and sat beside her on the couch.

"Lizbeth, honey listen to me. Being the Art Guardian does not mean that you abandon your personal life. You are allowed to date, fall in love, have children. You are not meant to spend the rest of your life dusting paintings and dying alone. Besides having children to continue the generation of Art Guardians is a must. Who will protect the paintings after you are gone?"

"Tiara is right Lizbeth. I thought about that too. In this world my mother is gone. That leaves us three to protect the paintings, but after us who will do so?"

"Either of you can fall in love. Tiara you could have children. I can be their aunt and teach them everything I know".

"But they would not be the lineage from your bloodline, Lizbeth. Someone from your bloodline needs to be in the real world or the gates will close forever".

"What are you saying, Tiara?"

"Didn't anyone every tell you that? Your bloodline must continue in order to have the ability to open the gates. Philip, hand me the oldest journal. Look, here is the first journal written by your ancestor Rose. In it she tells how she fell in love with a man in a painting. Knowing that he was not real and that she could never love him in the real world, in anger she took the painting to the river and threw it in. Rose regret her actions and jumped in after the painting. After saving the painting and putting it on dry ground. Nothing was ruined. Not a drop of paint smeared or bled. Yet, when she looked down, there were two brightly shining golden seeds. She picked them up and took them both with her. When Rose got home she placed the painting back on the wall and placed the seeds in front of the painting. Day after day she wondered what the seeds did and why they were on the ground. She tried planting one of them, but after a year passed, nothing grew. She tried cracking open the seed, but it was indestructible. Finally, she decided to swallow one. When she did, she felt this rush from within her body and the gate opened by itself for the first time on the painting of the man she fell in love with".

"Whoa, what a story. So that is how the first gate opened. The man must have pushed the seeds out of the painting after being dropped into the water".

"That is what we believe Philip, because it says here that the man who was in the painting was madly in love with Rose and told her he waited a long time to meet her. Maybe the water softened the painting enough to allow the seeds to pass".

"This painting. Where is it now?"

"This painting was called the seed sower and it burned many years ago in a fire that took many other paintings with it. The man in the painting of course already lived here in the real world with Rose".

"That's terrible".

"Terrible indeed. In the journals that followed Rose's daughter and granddaughter possessed the power of travel. But Rose's granddaughter named Sarah did not have children. Instead she remained alone. After she died the ability to travel died with her. Everyone who was able to open the gate like myself, and Philip who is learning, could not longer do so. Those who were from the real world, that had traveled into paintings were trapped inside. And others who traveled outside of the paintings were trapped in the real world. One of Sarah's cousins tried to find a solution to save her brother who was trapped in one of the paintings. So she desperately searched until she found Rose's journal. With it, in the same chest she found the seed in a gold and jewel covered box. After reading the journal she knew what to do. So she swallowed the last seed and was able to open the gates again. That is when they knew that the power of the seed past on from mother to child in the womb. Which is why a Guardian is needed. To be a Guardian does not mean you only protect the paintings. It also means you protect the power within you and share it forward. Though the power to open the gates can be shared, there can be only main carrier per generation. With the carrier gone, we all lose our power as well".

"Why would my grandmother never share this with me. Why did she leave me with so many unknown secrets!"

"Calm down, Lizbeth. I am sure she did not expect anything of what happened with your parents and raising you alone. Let along dying before she could teach you".

"Tiara is right, Lizbeth. My mother was just starting to learn things when your grandmother suddenly passed away. Many of us were left with unanswered questions and unknown secrets. Which is why your grandmother was sure to make my mother aware of the journals. So we had something to learn from".

"I am sorry for sharing this with you so late, Lizbeth. I thought that by now you had already read all of the journals and knew this".

"Well, I did not. So if you both will excuse me, I will gather each of these now".

"Careful, that is a lot of books".

"I don't care. I am taking them all to my bedroom and I will spend the night reading them all, this way there are no more hidden secrets that I know nothing about. Philip, could you please place a sign on the door and on the web that the museum will be closed tomorrow".

"Sure thing, Lizbeth".

I angrily marched up to my bedroom, trying not to trip or tip over the huge stacks of journals in my hands. I slammed the door behind me then threw the journals on my bed. I spent the entire night reading through the journals. I learned so much. I became angry, I cried, I smiled. My ancestors had their struggles, their losses, and their loves. I do not know how long I was reading or what time it was, but I do remember the sun starting to come up and laying one of the opened journals on my chest. I slept until midday I guess, when Tiara and Philip came into my bedroom with a warm cup of coffee.

"Good morn...no, good afternoon sleepy head. Here, drink and fully wake yourself up. We know you have been reading all night, and we will not allow you to be swallowed up into these journals. Once you are done with that coffee you, me and Tiara are going shopping, to find you the sexiest dress in town for your dinner date tonight".

"What? Sexy? I don't know about that".

"Oh Philip and the hair".

"Yes, I agree Tiara. Let me run and make her an appointment with my hair stylist".

"No wait, guys".

They picked up all the journals, placed them on the chair beside my bedroom window and left the room, closing the door behind them. This was Tiara and Philip, there was not disputing with them. So I sat up on my bed and sipped away at my coffee.

First stop was the hair dresser. Total makeover. Tiara and Philip were more excited then I was with finally changing my hair style. I liked my long shiny straight black hair. Apparently that wasn't enough. I needed some bangs and some wave in this limp hair. Dress shopping was next. Seven stores later, Philip found the dress "he" liked on me and Tiara had to agree. After making them happy with the dress selection, which was supposed to show enough cleavage. Not too much to say I'm slutty, but enough to say I'm available and in Philip's words, I'm hungry. The shoes were easy, we all three have always had the same taste in shoes.

It wasn't long before the evening rolled in and they were helping me finish up my make-up.

"Okay, that should be good. How much more do I need?"

"Hush now Lizbeth, this is your first official dinner date and you have to look great. And done. Oh, I am a genius. Tiara, what do you think about my masterpiece".

"Whoa, Lizbeth. You look amazing. Philip, you did a great job".

"Yeah, well I hope Lizbeth learned something along the way. I won't be here forever to do your make-up so you gotta be sure to put it on".

"I got it, I got it. Oh my gosh, I have to leave now or I will be late. Where is my dress?".

"Right here".

I quickly threw on my dress and slipped my feet into my shoes. I rushed towards the door, with Philip and Tiara behind him. I did not even remember my keys or wristlet, which Phillip had. Or my phone which Tiara had.

"Oh my goodness, where are my keys!"

"Here".

"My phone?"

"Right here".

"My wristlet".

"Dearest Lizbeth, that is right here. Now stop and take a few deep breaths before you get behind the wheel of that car. Better? Okay, now go have fun. And maybe even get laid for once".

"Saving myself for marriage! Bye!"

I carefully rushed down the stairs and to my car. It was not long before I reached the restaurant. Once again I took a deep breath, stepped out of my car, and expected one of Leo's men to lead me, so I wouldn't be startled. There he was right on time leading me in to see Leo. As I walked into the restaurant I remembered Philip's words, "I am a diva and I better walk like one". So I did. I pushed nerves aside and confidently walked into that restaurant. I smiled at Leo as he stood up from his chair. When I reached him he just stared.

"Is, everything okay?"

"Oh, yes. Forgive me. I am without words tonight. You look extravagant. Wow, I surely am the luckiest man in this entire restaurant to have such a beauty dining with me tonight".

"You are so very sweet, thank you, but flat..."

"Yes, yes I know. Flattery will get me nowhere. However, I feel that all I can do is shower you with compliments. I held many of them back the first day we met, but tonight my compliments will be poured out like sweet milk. There is that beautiful smile. I am glad I can make you laugh. Please, sit".

"Thank you".

"You have changed much since our last meeting, last night".

"Ah yes, my friends returned from out of town and heard I had my first date. They wanted to help, and so they did".

"Your friends have great taste. This must have been why the museum was closed today. I am now flattered you closed the museum to ready yourself for this date".

"How did you know the museum was closed?"

"I stopped by with a gift this afternoon. This gift. Two dozen long stemmed red roses".

"They are beautiful".

"Yes, well I had them put into this vase filled with water so they would not wither.....as I do whenever I see you".

"In truth, I did not close the museum to only go shop with friends today. I was up until late last night reading books on art and how it all works".

"Ah, I see".

"But I was up within hours, to shop and get myself ready for tonight".

"Then you sacrificed your beauty rest to prepare yourself for me. Now, I feel special again. Let us celebrate this night with some red wine. I chose this one specifically for you on this night".

"Thank you. Wow, that is delicious".

"It is indeed. It takes years to cure, which is why it cost $1,000 a bottle. Are you okay, Lizbeth!

"Sorry, I choked a little there".

"Do you not like the wine?"

"No, the wine is delicious. It just, $1,000 a bottle?"

"Yes, I drink this wine only on very special occasions. There have not been many in my life lately. Until tonight that is".

"Please, go on. I would like to learn more about you. I have told me all I can tell about myself. I grew up with parents who were both artist that loved painting. They passed away in an accident when I was very young. My grandmother raised me until she too passed. I have been an orphan ever since, with my two bestest friends to keep me company. They are more like siblings to me. I shared my parents love for art. However, not having any artistic abilities myself I decided to open the museum. So I could home the orphaned paintings".

"Yes, and named it The Guardian. Peculiar name for a museum".

"The same way I feel my parents guard over me, I guard over the paintings. Now, tell me about you".

"There is much to tell and I am glad you are interested in knowing more about be. So, where would you like me to start?"

Leo seemed very sincere as he shared about his life. From his youth and into his present. With some stories he made me burst out laughing. With others, I found myself reaching out for his hand. He was so kind and gentle with me. I felt like I could have spoken to him all night.

"Leo, though I am having a very nice night with you, I must now take my leave. I did not realize it was so late".

"Fair enough. I do remember you sharing that you were up late and awoken before getting a full rest. I would not want you to drive home feeling tired. Allow me to walk you to your car".

Leo requested the check, and after paying it he walked me to my car. I unlocked it and opened the car door. As I turned to thank him again, I almost bumped into him because of how close he was standing to me.

"Good night my beautiful Lizbeth".

He gently lifted my face by the chin and softly kissed my lips.

I nervously smiled at him and sat in my car. He shut the car door for me and I drove off. I began to take deep breaths and couldn't' wait to get home to tell Philip and Tiara about the amazing date I had with Leo.

Leo sat in his car and waited until Lizbeth drove off.

"Follow her".

Leo's driver drove off following Lizbeth. After she made it to her house she jumped out of the car. Leo's driver pulled up at a distance and Leo watched Lizbeth walk up to the porch where Philip and Tiara were excitedly waiting for Lizbeth. They all three embraced each other and quickly went inside the house. After the front door closed. Leo told the driver to go and they left.

"Okay, I need to know everything. Every detail every every".

"Well Philip, we spoke a lot and he told me a lot about himself".

"Let's focus mainly on the important stuff. What happened to his wife and did he remarry?"

"He was married. He shared how much he loved her and how they were your typical love birds, but things changed as he became richer and was much busier at work. She wanted him home more often, but work demanded a lot from him. He said she was unhappy and threatened to leave him often. He of course thought she would not. Yet. she would leave from time to time and spend weeks to months away. Then she would return home. He thought these breaks would clear her mind, but when she returned home she would be angrier than before. They argued often. Then one day he returned from work and her clothing and luggage were gone. Not like the first times, where she would only take a few things. This time she took everything. Clothes, jewelry, even some decor in the home. He was sure she wanted a divorce, and waited for the letter. But months turned into a year and he began to send for her to be found. But no one knew where she was. The only thing they found was a registered a flight out of the country before her disappearance, but after she landed she was no where to be found. Even her son has not heard from her. Yet, this was something she did often when she disappeared for weeks or months at a time. She would not even contact her son".

"Oh my and ten years later, nothing".

"Leo said his son blames him that his mother ran off and hasn't spoken to him in years".

"Why would the son blame him?"

"Leo said his son heard their arguments, where the mother threatened often to leave if he did not change his ways and excessive work habits. She complained often that she was bored with him and their marriage. In their last argument Leo yelled out he wanted a divorce. The argument ended there and his wife walked out of the room".

"Sounds like a fair story. I say, just watch yourself Lizbeth. Either way you have a huge responsibility on your shoulders now. So just be careful with the Leo guy".

"I agree with Tiara. With what you carry, Lizbeth. Just any guy cannot do. Yet, it may be just a thought, but if he works so often, this would leave room for you to take care of your work of the paintings. And with his influences, maybe just maybe you can get your hands on much more artwork. Maybe even come closer to..."

"The lady trapped on the island painting. Yes, I thought of that as well".

"Still, be careful and feel him out. One date is not enough to decide on what kind of a person he will be in taking part of guardianship of the paintings. Especially if you guys have children together. How would he take that on? His kids opening gates into paintings"

"Tiara, that is a typical day in Lizbeths world. Painting hopping is the new thing".

"You guys are funny. Yet, though he is very sweet and handsome, I do also want to be careful. Not anyone can be trusted with this kind of secret. Especially a political man who knows so many people and has no private life".

"You are right, Lizbeth. People in politics find it hard to have privacy".

"For now I think it is best to keep him as a friend. Eventually he will have to return home to Portugal. I can then go on with my life and who knows, meet someone that has a more private life, like I do".

Though this is what I wanted to do. I found myself far from it. Especially after Philip and Tiara returned to the beach painting, so Philip could be with his mother. I found myself alone again and going on more and more dinner dates with Leo. That then turned into lunch dates as well. He knew I could not leave the museum often, so he would bring lunch and flowers to me almost every day. I began to enjoy his company. We talked a lot about life and things we would love to do, given the time. He made me laugh often, which is always a good thing. We even had one of the most romantic evening dinner dates ever, where he set up the middle of the museum floor with a picnic. There was fruits and appetizers, drinks, and candles. It was the most romantic thing I had ever seen. His men closed the museum for me and waited outside. We stood inside eating, drinking and talking about the paintings. He looked over at one specific painting.

"If I could travel into any painting in here, it would be that one right there".

"Oh, why that one".

"Just look at it. It has a little hut on a farm full of fruit and vegetables. It is both humbling and peaceful. That would be where I would want to stay for the rest of my life. With the right person of course".

Leo then looked right at me and smiled slightly. I looked back at him. He leaned in closer and closer to me. A part of me wanted to move back, but another part wanted what was coming next. Leo gently touched my lips with thumb and I closed my eyes. Then he leaned in and softly kissed me. Again and again he gently kissed my lips. After the fourth kiss, I leaned in closer to him and kissed him back. Next thing I knew our lips were locked together and we were passionately kissing. I did not want him to stop. I wanted more. He then wrapped his arm around my waist and by then I knew I could not resist. He went down kissing my neck as I gently gripped onto his. I felt like I was about to fall over. But I did not fall. He slowly laid me down and gently placed my head onto one of the decorative pillows. He kept kissing my neck, then back to my lips, then back to my neck again. I could think of nothing else, except for how much I wanted him right at the moment. He then placed his other hand on my knee and slowly moved up my thigh, lifting my skirt as he did.

Then just what I needed to happen, did happen. He accidentally hit the open wine bottle that tipped over spilling and leaking onto me. The cold wine was exactly what I needed to cool off my highly heated hormones. I slowly pushed him off and stood up.

"I'm sorry. I...am so sorry. I can't. We shouldn't. I will be right back".

I ran off to the restroom and locked myself in. I was breathing hard and trying to get myself together again. I fixed my blouse and my skirt. I look right into the mirror.

"You better not Lizbeth. Keep it together and keep your hormones under control".

After I gathered myself I went back out to the museum floor room and sat beside Leo. He looked somewhat disappointed. Then he stood up and paced the floor.

"Lizbeth, I am sorry. Truly I am. I don't want you to see me as the kind of man who only wants to...".

"No. Leo, I understand. We are adults here and we have feelings for each other. I mean, I hope you have the same feelings I do....that I have for you".

Leo rushed over and sat close to me.

"Lizbeth, what I feel for you, I cannot even describe into words. I think about you everyday all day. The moment I awake in the morning, I smile thinking of you. I get out of bed saying your name out loud. Sometimes I think I am in my teens again, because you make me feel so young and vibrant. I don't know maybe I am going crazy...or...maybe I am falling in love. It has been a long time since I have felt this way for anyone else after my wife left. I can't return home, because it means I will not see you each day. It is a sacrifice I am not willing to make. I stay here, so I can see you again. Here you laugh at my ridiculous jokes. Watch you bat your eyes every time I make you feel nervous. Yes, just like that. Everything about you has me lovesick. I do not know what to do, because I cannot think straight."

Leo pulled out from underneath one of the small decorative pillows, a small silver box.

"You will think I am crazy, but I am not getting any younger and time is not my friend. I would rather try then spend my time wondering. I brought this for you".

Leo opened the small silver box and in it was a beautiful diamond ring.

"Lizbeth, would you marry me? You don't have to answer now. I can give you time to think about it, but I had to ask. I want you to know that I want something more for the both of us. I want to spend the rest of the life I have left....with you".

I was momentarily speechless. Leo was everything I wanted. He was attentive, gentle, kind, and he loved paintings. I was sure given the right time, I could share with him the truth about me. He lowered his head with a sad look thinking I would not answer. I placed my hands onto his cheeks and gently lifted his face.

"Yes Leo. I will marry you".

His face lit up and he stood up and leapt for joy. I laughed at his boyish reaction. He then threw himself to the ground in front of me and pressed his lips against mine. He then poured wine into my cup and his.

"Let us drink what is left in this bottle, to our engagement!"

Within two months time Leo had met Philip and Tiara and wedding plans were being made. My bachelorette party was of course done in the painting where Philip's mother was. We could not let her miss the party. Tiara brought some special invites from other paintings. The best ones of all were the samoan male dancers. I liked their dancing a whole lot more than I would have liked a male stripper, that is for sure. We danced and drank all night and day. I honestly lost track of the time. My bachelorette could have easily lasted two days, maybe three. When we were finally ready to return, I bid my farewell to Philip's mother. She could not be there at the wedding, but I promised to come visit as soon as I returned from my honeymoon. Leo said it would be no longer than two weeks in Portugal. Then he promised to allow me to come back home as he made arrangements to move his life out here. This way I could be close to the museum and my home, which I left to Phillip and Tiara. Once I was settled into my new life, I could move the paintings to the home Leo and I would be buying, leaving Phillip the one with his mother and any others he and Tiara wanted to keep and protect. We all three promised to spilt the work, while still remaining together. I had hoped that maybe after about a years time of I and Leo's marriage, I could share the truth of who I was. I also protected myself from having children. I wanted to be sure Leo would understand and accept who I was before I bore children. Yet, my heart told me that he would as long as we had our love. Philip and Tiara did not like the idea of waiting so long, but they also understood how important it was to keep our secret. In the journals we had read, there were many of my ancestors who never told their husbands out of fear they would not understand. I did not want to live all of my life not telling Leo, but I knew I had to wait for the right time.

After we returned from the painting I jumped right into the shower. Then I walked over to my bedside table to check my phone. Thirty-five alerts in total between text and missed calls. All from Leo. I quickly looked through the text and they were all in asking how I was enjoying my bachelorette. Then they read like demands in wanting to know where I was. I immediately called Leo.

"My love, you sound worried in your messages. Forgive me for not responding sooner. My signal was bad".

"Lizbeth, where are you?"

"I am home".

"Then where have you been? I have been worried sick".

"Please forgive me. Philip, Tiara and I were celebrating my bachelorette".

"For three days!"

"Was it that long?"

"Yes, it was that long. Three days you disappeared. I heard nothing from you".

"Leo, I am not going anywhere. I will not disappear again. Please do not be afraid. All is well".

"Okay, forgive my concerns. I just did not know where you were. I hate not knowing where you are".

"Forgive me Leo, it will not happen again".

I understood his pain. Especially since his wife disappeared on him in this way before. I did my best to comfort his fears, but he would not let me hang up the line. He said he wanted to keep hearing my voice after not being able to do so for three days. We spoke for a few hours and I was able to disconnect the call. Then I went downstairs with Philip and Tiara.

"About time, I thought you fell asleep after all that partying. Here I made heart shaped pancakes, bacon and eggs. Oh, and toast".

"Yes, yummy. Thank you Philip. It was Leo, he was so distraught. He said he thought I disappeared on him".

"Oh like his wife did?"

"Exactly, Tiara. I assured him that all was well. He was so worried that he had not heard from me in three days".

"Wait, three days? We were partying for three days?"

"Looks like, Philip. And of course I left my phone beside my bed. Thirty-five alerts I had from him".

"Oh my, poor thing, he must have been so worried. But who can beat a three day bachelorette. It was the best ever".

"I am sorry to have caused him all that worry, but I do admit it was the best bachelorette a bride-to-be could ever ask for".

Leo was standing in front of the wall sized window in the hotel he was staying in. One of his men walked in.

"Sir?".

"I sent for you to ask you one more time. Did you see my bride-to-be leave her house? Did she go anywhere?"

"No sir. We had men surrounding her house at all hours of the day. Some watching the back of the house and others watching the front of the house".

"No one came to visit? Any men?"

"No sir. No one came in or out of the house for three days. There was one thing that was strange. At night there was only one single lamp lit in the living room. And there seemed to be no movement in the house during the day or at night".

"And her phone. When it was tracked?"

"It showed it was in the home sir and never moved from there".

Leo waved for the man to leave as he stood looking out the window deep in thought. Then he became very angry.

"Where did you go Lizbeth? Why would you lie to me? Did you allow another man to touch you? I will kill him, Lizbeth. No one touches you. No one but me. You are mine!"

He then lifted a vase from off of the living room table and threw it across the room. It hit the wall and chattered into pieces. Leo tried to regain his composure and walked off to his bedroom.

It wasn't long before my wedding day came and I was awoken the best way possible. With my two bestest friends in the world jumping on me.

"Wake up, wake up! You are getting married today!"

"Philip you are going to crush the bride before she can get married".

"I don't care. This is the last time we could wake her up this way, because after today she will be waking up in her matrimonial bed.

"Philip, you have a point. In that case...SCOOCH OVER!"

Both Philip and Tiara flopped on me as we laugh and yelled out. Then it got pretty sentimental, starting with Philip.

"I'm going to miss you, Lizbeth".

"Awe please don't cry, Philip. You are going to make me start crying. Besides I won't be gone long. Just a few weeks max and I will be back"

"Well, don't rush back on our account. Enjoy your lives together. Your both in love".

"I guess I agree with Tiara. Go enjoy yourself, have fun, then get your butt back home".

We laughed together and they got me up and going. They helped me do my hair, put on my make-up, and get my dress on. When I was ready to go, they helped me down the stairs. Within seconds there was a knock on the door. It was one of Leo's men who came to pick us up in a limo. We sat inside the limo. Then served and toasted with the champagne Leo left for us as the driver drove off.

The wedding felt like a dream. Philip walked me down the aisle and Tiara was my maid of honor. Leo had no one, since everyone he knew was in Portugal. The wedding reception was very sweet and intimate. Very few guest. Leo was in such a good mood even allowed some of his men to have a drink or two and eat.

Right after the sunset, Leo had his driver put all of my belongings into his car. I changed into a more comfortable dress and then went and bid my last farewells to Philip and Tiara before driving off with Leo. Philip and Tiara then jumped back into the limo and were driven home.

After they got home, they changed their outfits and went up to the attic. On the wall we had installed a shelf with a wireless battery charger to place cell phones on. This was so the batteries would not drain out and the phone shut off, if they were in the painting too long. Then they could immediately see when I called or text. I told them I would not leave any voice messages unless it was important, but that I would check in by calling. Philip and Tiara placed their cellphone on it.

"Okay Philip, are you ready?"

"I am".

"Remember. Concentrate. Don't push it, just be at ease and once you find that peaceful place, the gate will begin to open. I've told you guys this hundreds of times. Now find that place".

Philip reached out his arm aimed it at the painting and took a deep breath in then out. A bright golden light began to shine, little by little the gate opened for Philip.

"I did it! I can't believe I did it! Oh why did Lizbeth have to leave now she had to see this!"

With excitement Phillip and Tiara walked in through the gate and into the painting, to tell Philips mom all about the wedding and how he opened the gate.

Leo and Lizbeth were several hours into their flight to Portugal on his private jet. With all the excitement and nerves Lizbeth had fallen asleep in her seat. Leo had men with him on the private jet. One in specific couldn't help but look at Lizbeth often. Leo took notice. After the man stood up to use the restroom and came out, Leo walked over towards him, but before passing the man Leo stopped within ear shot to the man.

"Beautiful, isn't she".

"Yes sir, she is very beautiful".

"If you look at her again with your lustful eyes, I will have my men open this airplane door and throw you out of it... without any parachute on your back. Do I make myself clear".

"Very clear, sir".

Leo then walked back to his seat. The man that had been looking at Lizbeth became afraid. He sat down and turned to look out the window instead.

After a very much needed nap, I had awoken feeling Leo's gentle hand strokes on my cheek.

"It is time to wake up my love. We will be landing soon".

"Already?"

"Already? You have been asleep for quite some time. Sleep you very much needed to help with the time zone difference. Also, well rested enough for us to have our special wedding night. I want to make it the best night ever for the both of us".

Leo gently kissed me, then the co-pilot approached to let us know we would be landing. Leo helped me with my seatbelt then held my hand.

After landing in the private jet, there was a car waiting. My luggage was quickly placed into the trunk of the car and the driver drove off. We reached Leo's beautiful home around 11pm Portugal time. When we stepped inside I was amazed at how big and luxurious it was. Bigger than I could have ever imagined it to be.

"Your home is beautiful, Leo".

"Indeed 'our' home is beautiful, but there is no time for a tour tonight. I will take you to the only room we need to be in at this moment".

Leo took me by the hand and led me upstairs in the direction of these two big decorated double doors. He grabbed onto both knobs and pushed open the doors. Inside the bedroom was lit with many candles. There was champagne in a sterling silver bucket of ice and two flute glasses. On the bed was a very sexy white lingerie.

"This is for you on our wedding night".

"Leo, I do not know what to say".

"Say nothing at all, this night is not for words. The language of love will be spoken through our bodies".

"I will go freshen up then".

I went into the large elegant marbled bathroom. And when I say marbled, I mean marbled. Everything from the counter to the floors and the walls were covered in gold trimming marble. I wasted no time admiring the bathroom anymore and opened my luggage. I pulled out everything I needed. Steps included in washing my face from the wedding make-up and putting on new light make-up. I brushed my hair and put on the lingerie. The hardest part was the garter belt buttons and stockings. After struggling to do so, especially since I had never wore any before, I fanned myself off. Then I lightly sprayed some perfume and was ready to go. I slowly opened the door and Leo was waiting for me with two glasses of champagne, wearing nothing but a pair of silver silk sleep pants. I was amazed that at his age he was so fit and strong looking. I very shyly walked over to him. He handed me a glass of champagne.

"Drink this. It should ease your nerves. After-all you have nothing to be nervous about. You look so beautiful. I am the luckiest man alive. And I promise to be gentle".

Leo then gently took me by the hand and led me to the edge of the bed. He placed my half drunken glass of champagne on the bedside and gently placed one of his arms around my waist as he pulled me closer to him. Then with his other hand he caressed my hair and my face. I closed my eyes as he softly passed his thumb over my lips. I felt his lips touch mine. Again, another soft kiss of the lips. Then once more a soft kiss. Leo slowly laid me on the bed and began to kiss my neck. At that point I was already his to do what he wanted. I was weakened my the touch of his lips on my skin and his hands that caressed my body. There was no part of my body he left untouched. He was so gentle with me that every part he touched he left me wanting more. I remember being afraid of my wedding night, but with how Leo was with me, I was no longer afraid. Instead I wanted more and more as I tightly gripped the bedsheets in my hands. I wanted to open up my mouth and beg him not to stop, yet there was no need to. He was just getting started. The night seemed to go on and on. He had me three times. Each time felt like a first time and I just kept thinking to myself...more...more...don't stop. He did not rush a thing and took his time with me. We kissed so much and for so long I almost felt like my lips were no longer there. They were not my lips anymore, they were his, he owned my lips and my body. They were his to do what he wanted.

I do not know how much time passed. Our love making seemed endless. At least I wanted it to be. So I cannot remember when or what time I drifted off, but I was awoken by a soft warm breeze. When I opened my eyes I was facing the left side of the bed where there was a balcony. With all my nerves the night before, I did not take notice that the long thick elegant curtains that reached as high as nine or ten feet tall were opened to reveal the double glass doors to a balcony. The sun was shining and a breeze keep blowing inside the bedroom, lifting the sheer curtains right above the double doors. The scene was something out of a storybook, or even a painting. I stood up from the bed, wrapped the blanket around me and walked towards the double doors. The sheer curtains lifted again with the breeze and so did my hair. I walked out to the balcony and the view was mesmerizing. There were gardens and what looked like vineyards, but of flowers. I felt like I was in a dream. I stepped back into the bedroom and grabbed my phone. One text is what I sent in a group message to Philip and Tiara. It read;

This girl right here is no longer a virgin. Leo was amazing. I am glad I waited. I'm so in love. TTYL (muah emoji, champagne bottle emoji).

With excitement I put the phone down and ran off to shower and get dressed.

After my shower I put on some makeup to look beautiful, yet natural. A little foundation, a little setting powder, no eyebrow drawing, just eyebrow filling, light natural looking eyeshadow with a hint of shimmer, and mascara. Oh and some lipstick. No! Lipgloss, yes. I brushed my hair and left it loose. Then I put on the white long sleeveless sundress, with the sexy split up the middle. Philip helped me pick this one out. He said it would be so appropriate for a new bride to wear. Oh and of course the gold braided tie belt. The one Philip said would make me look like a goddess. After I looked in the mirror I actually felt like one. I couldn't have been more happy. I sat on the edge of the bed to put on my white lace up wedge sandals. All done, I was ready to explore. I walked over to the bedroom door and turned the elegant brass doorknob. It was hard and the door was heavy. The door was made of wood, but very thick and strong. I had to give it a little pull to open it. After doing so I walked out of the room, but did not know which way to go. The halls seemed to be never-ending both to the left and to the right. I decided to go straight towards the stairs. I looked over the railing to see if I could get a glimpse of Leo, or at least hear his voice. It was so quiet. So I slowly went down the stairs. The home was beautiful and so elegant, yet it had a very eerie feel to it. In my opinion even though the house was beautiful, it did not feel like a home. Either way I continued my search for Leo. I walked through great large sized rooms and down halls. At one point I was sure I was lost. Finally, down one hall I could see Leo at a distance sitting at the head of a table with a newspaper. I hurried my steps and when I reached the entrance of what I believed to be the dining room I slowed my steps down before walking in.

"Good morning".

"Lizbeth, I was not expecting you to be up so soon, my love".

Leo stood up from his chair and walked over to me. He wrapped his arms around my waist and kissed my lips.

"After last night I had expected you to sleep until the afternoon at least".

"What time is it now?"

"Early, very early".

Leo then kissed me. We kissed until the maid walked into the dinning room.

"Ah, there you are. Breakfast for my new bride."

The maid seemed very odd. She was older in age and very serious. She nodded at Leo and walked off.

"Come wife, sit by me. I had a special breakfast made for you with the sweetest and ripest of Portugals fruits. They will melt in your mouth like butter".

"Sounds delicious".

"It is very delicious, but nothing compared to how delicious you taste".

He suddenly scooped me up. Startled by his action I let out a yelp, followed by laughter.

After breakfast he toured me around the house. Especially after I told him I believed to have gotten lost earlier that morning. The tour took quite some time. There was so much house, anyone could get lost in it. Leo shared the history behind the home to help me get a better understanding to its appearance. Yet, it still did not take away from its eeriness. The last stop was the hall of artwork. He had all kinds of artwork, from paintings to sculptures. It was smaller than my museum, but still a very large hall for a house. Much larger than my attic. There were also many paintings to explore. Especially those of the islands. I noticed a painting that had a woman sitting by the shore reaching for the sun. She was wearing a red dress. I thought that was odd for a painting of an island. Who would paint it with a woman in a red dress. Usually artist paint with more neutral colors. There was also a rhinestone broach that I had to a closer look at to see what it was. After a closer look I could tell it was an initial of the letter "A". Leo took noticed that I lingered on that painting.

"Does that piece intrigue you?"

"It does. It is very different. Artist do not usually paint this way".

"You know your art well. I also found it to be somewhat different. Which is why I purchased it and placed it there. Come now my love, I will tour you around the gardens".

Leo walked over to me and turned my face from the painting and kissed me, then he took me by the hand and led me away from the painting.

After touring the gardens it felt like hours had passed. And surely they did. We finished our tour on the outdoor deck patio where lunch was waiting. But there was only a place setting for one person.

"Here we are. I was sure to have lunch ready for you".

"What will we be sharing this afternoon".

"You are too kind and caring my love. You think we would be sharing? I wish it were so. Sadly I cannot join you for lunch. I must work today, but only for a few hours. I will return before dinner".

"But we are on honeymoon. Could you not take time off of work?"

"This is true. Yet I took too much time off of work already. Waiting for that special beauty to take notice of me, date, me and accept my marriage proposal. How long was it that I was out of work following, my queen? Ah, yes, almost two months. I am more than sure she would allow me to work a few hours each day to make up for time lost".

I could not dispute with that. Leo was right. He did stay a long time in my hometown. And he did do it for me. I sadly accepted his leave for work.

"I will be back before you know it. Besides, I cannot stay apart from you too long. You will not be alone in the house. The maid is here and I have men roaming the house to keep you safe. You will not see them, nor will they see you, but they are around. If you need anything at all just ask the maid, her name is Clara".

Leo kissed me and walked off. I sat at the table alone looking out into the gardens. I did happen to get a quick glimpse of a few men roaming the gardens. But they appeared and disappeared quickly.

The hours passed and the night sky began to creep in. Still, no Leo. I missed him and wondered when he would be back. I checked my phone several times. No messages, no missed calls, nothing. I went back downstairs to the foyer and paced a little, when I suddenly heard a car drive up. I stood still and waited. After a few seconds two of Leo's men opened the doors and Leo walked into the house. I smiled a great big smile and as soon as he stepped in I ran to him. The doors closed behind him right before I reached him and embraced his neck.

"My word, what a welcome".

"I missed you. You said it would only be a few hours. Yet, it has been many hours".

"Forgive me my love. You are right. It has been too long. I have missed you as well".

"Leo, your hands. They are stained with red ink".

"Art, my love. Art. My men and I had to help with painting the night red. I must have gotten caught up in my work".

"Painting?"

"Well, I was not doing the painting. Just witnessing the work of art. I got to close and stained my hands. When the masterpiece is finished you will be the first to see it. Let me tidy myself up and wash off this paint".

We went upstairs to our bedroom where Leo washed his hands and changed his shirt.

"Are you hungry? Dinner should have been ready hours ago. Did you not eat?"

"Clara did make dinner and asked if wanted to eat, but I did not. Not without you again. Yet, I am not hungry. For food that is".

"I wonder then dear Lizbeth, what are you hungry for?"

Leo kissed me, but he did not do so gently this time. He kissed my lips and neck as if he hadn't seen me in weeks. He did so zealously and aggressively. I admit...I liked it. I grabbed onto his hair and shirt and he kissed my neck this way and I couldn't help but let out moaning sounds, which only made Leo grow wilder. He gently nipped my chin, licked my neck, sucked on my lip. Again, I did not want him to stop. I wanted more. I wanted him to do whatever he wanted to me. I suddenly fell on top of the bed with Leo on top of me. We then forcefully took each others clothes off. I wanted him. I wanted him badly. Before long he was making fiery love to me and I found myself gripping onto the headboard rails and yelling out his name.

Leo was sitting in the bed with his upper back against the headboard. As Lizbeth slept in his arms he caressed her hair while looking down at her.

"Lizbeth, you are mine. All mine. I will never let you go, ever. You may not know it yet, but you have already come to your castle, where you will remain with me. Here. This is your home".

Leo looked over at Lizbeth's phone, then went deep into thought.

"I can't allow you to have any distractions. You cannot disappear on me ever again. I will not allow it. And your friends. They are a distraction. In time you will forget them and we will be happy together....here, in this house".

Leo gently laid Lizbeth onto the pillow. He then carefully climbed out of the bed to not wake Lizbeth, put on some silky sleep pants and walked around to Lizbeth's nightstand. He picked up her phone and walked out of the bedroom.

The next morning I awoke, again with a breeze and the light of the sun. I turned in the bed thinking that I was alone again. Instead, I saw Leo walking towards the bedroom door. He opened it and Clara rolled in a silver cart with breakfast on it. Then she left the room and shut the door behind her. Leo then began to uncover what was on the silver cart and bring a plate to me.

"Good morning my love. I thought it would be best that I did not leave you today or the rest of this week. You were right, this is our honeymoon week. So I have had breakfast brought to us and I want you to have it in bed with me.

Leo handed me a plate of breakfast, he then went back for his and sat beside me.

"How very romantic of you".

We kissed and ate together. The rest of the day we spent it roaming the gardens where he would hide from me within the bushes and pop out to frighten me. We were like young teens. We laughed and kissed and make love on a bed of soft grass surrounded by flowers. It was like living in a dream. Every moment of that week and the next, we spent it together. It was like being inside of the paintings, because I lost track of time and days. If it were not for the night sky and the day sun, I wouldn't even know another day had passed.

Half way through the third week I wanted to check-in with Philip and Tiara. I had them in mind often, but Leo kept me so busy I did not check-in with them yet. So after I stepped out of steamy shower with Leo, where we again made love together, I placed my white towel robe on and went to get my phone. It was not on the nightstand, in the draw, or on the floor. It was nowhere. Leo had finished in the shower and noticed me searching.

"Are you looking for something my love".

"I am, my phone. Have you seen it?"

"Clara, must have moved it. You do not need it either way. I do not have my phone. Not for all the time we have been together".

"Actually, I do need it. I would like to check-in with my friends. To let them know I am well and so very happy".

" I will speak with Clara in the morning and ask her if she has seen it".

"Thank you".

Leo then walked over to me and took me by the waist.

"You belong to me. But this robe you are wearing does not. Since you belong to me, this robe is interfering with what is mine. So you know what that means?"

"It must come off?"

"It, must, come, off".

After a chase of robe stripping between the both of us we laid in bed together, made love, and from exhaustion, we fell fast asleep in each others arms.

The next morning when I came down for breakfast, I noticed Clara leaned over towards Leo who was sitting at the head of the table. They were whispering something to each other. As I came closer Clara nodded in agreement, stood up, and walked away to the kitchen.

"Good morning. Did you ask if she had she seen my phone?"

"Good morning my love. And yes, I asked. Sadly she thought it was of no use and got rid of it. Being that nowadays so many people walk with their phones in hand everywhere they go and she had not see you with one at all. She thought it was meant to get rid of, especially since it was in the same place, never being used or moved".

"I did use it. Just to check-in why my friends. And I do not walk with my phone everywhere, because there is a life out there that can be enjoyed without a phone".

Just then Clara walked back into the dinning room with my breakfast plate and placed it in front of me.

"I couldn't agree with you more, my love".

"Lady Lizbeth, I ask for your forgiveness. Over a week ago I removed the phone and held it in the kitchen to ensure it was indeed trash. No one inquired about it and after a week had passed I threw it away. I am truly sorry".

"No, Clara, it's okay. Maybe I can get myself a new one".

"Well, with what Clara shared, I already took the liberty of having one delivered to the house early this morning".

Leo handed me a white box with a red bow on it. I opened it and it was a brand new phone.

"Leo, thank you. I will call my friends now to share the new number".

After hearing what Lizbeth said, Clara looked at Leo and he gave a quick smile. Clara then left to the kitchen as she normally did. Once she was in the kitchen and not seen by Lizbeth, she rushed over to a corner of the wall where there was a tiny curtain. Clara pulled open the curtain to reveal a signal distorter plugged into the wall. She turned the switch on and closed the mini curtain. Then she went near the dinning area to listen in. Just then she heard Lizbeth.

"The call dropped. It did not complete. I don't know if it rang on their end or not. If so they will not know it's me".

"Let me check my phone as well. Ah, no signal either. This happens often in this house, Lizbeth. Possibly because of the size of the house or it's artifacts that block the signal. Give it time, it will pick up signal again and once it does you can make your call".

Clara smiled and walked away back into the kitchen.

It had been almost a month now. Leo began to return to work and would be out practically all day and evening on some days. He would leave on specific days right after breakfast and not return until late evening. Other days he would leave midmorning and not return until late into the night. Some nights I would be asleep by the time he got home. I began to understand why his prior wife argued so much with him about his job. I did not want to be like her and leave him. I loved Leo too much to do so. I knew if I were patient things would change. After-all he was moving away with me. He promised to do so. I was supposed to only stay in his home for two weeks and then return to the states. This way he would take care of things here and begin the move with me out there, so I could be close to home and my museum. Yet, I did not see any movement at all. No boxes, movers, nothing. Maybe, if I left first this would get Leo going. It could have been that he was waiting on me. I never asked, so he said nothing. Our two-week honeymoon had turned into a month long. I had to connect with Philip and Tiara. I picked up the phone Leo gave me and still no signal. I wandered outside into the gardens. Nothing. I wandered farther than I had before and there was some sign of movement for signal. So I thought if I wandered further away from the house, whatever was affecting the signal would be too far away. I kept going and then....I got it! Finally, some signal. As soon as I began to dial Philip's phone number I heard one of Leo's men shouting at me.

"Mrs. Ferreira! Mrs. Ferreira! Forgive me but you must return to the house".

He slowly coaxed me several steps back toward the house.

"Sir, I understand your job is to protect me, but I am only trying to make a call".

I tried moving forward again and he pulled his hand out not allowing me to do so.

"I have strict rules from Mr. Ferreira. You cannot go past this line".

"Line? What line?"

I looked to the ground and there it was. Painted on the grass was a white line that extended out to both sides of the house. I did not understand. Why not past the line. I was able to get signal there. I decided to follow the line going towards the right. Leo's men followed me diligently. The line kept going and going all around the house. Something was not right. I then reached my arm with the phone and quickly one of Leo's men ran to me and demanded I stay behind the line.

"I am behind the line. I am just reaching my arm to get signal".

"Again, Mrs. Ferreira you must stay behind the line".

Now I was sure something was wrong. Pass that white line was cell phone signal. Why could I not get any? I was furious and I marched back into the house. When I looked back to Leo's men, I saw one of them making a call. There was phone signal pass the line, but why was I not allowed pass it.

Angrily, I waited for Leo to get home. The hours passed and still he did not return home. I tried to stay awake as long as I could, but somehow feel asleep on the chaise in front of the fireplace in my bedroom. I do not remember it, but he must have lifted me up and placed me on the bed, because that is where I found myself in the morning. As soon as I did wake up, I climbed out of bed and went in search for him. I found him where I usually do every morning. Sitting at the dining table. I slammed the phone he gifted me on the table.

"There is no signal in this house. Yet there is signal passed the white line. A line I am not allowed to cross over. Why is that?"

"Good morning my love".

"Leo, please answer me. Why can I not pass the white line?"

"It is not safe".

"Not safe? There are dozens of men out there. How is it not safe to stand a few feet passed the line to make a call".

"It is in range of snipers. All the men I have out there could not stop a bullet from a sniper".

"A sniper? That is your excuse? Snipers can shoot from an area or distance. Even if I am behind the white line".

Leo sat there and said nothing. Then he looked up at me and was deep in thought. I tried to calm myself. Maybe he was trying to protect me, though I did not buy that spew about snipers. I sat in the chair beside him.

"Forgive me Leo. None of this seems to make sense to me. Yet, I believe I am to blame that we have not moved back to the states. I'm assuming you've been waiting on me. I won't linger our stay any longer. I will pack my things tonight. Send me back home on the earliest flight possible. This way I don't have to worry about signal. I will wait for you there, so we can go house hunting as you had promised before our wedding".

"As you wish my love. Now, I must be off to work. And no need to worry, I will not be coming home late tonight".

Leo stood up, lifted my chin to face him, kissed me and walked off. I sat there so upset. Then I stood up and went to my bedroom to pack. After everything was packed I placed my luggage by the bedroom door.

That evening I waited for Leo in the balcony. Clara knocked on the door then opened it to let me know dinner was ready.

"Is Leo back?"

"He is not".

"Then I will not eat dinner until he returns".

It was not until pass midnight when I heard the bedroom door latch open, then close. I knew it was Leo. He went into the bathroom and closed the door. After a bit, he stepped out of the bathroom and slowly climbed under the bed covers next to me. I had my back turned to him and though I was awake, I was still angry. He embraced me.

"My love? Are you awake? I brought you a gift".

He laid in front of me a new phone.

"Maybe this one will work".

I was happy to see he tried to remedy the issue so I turned around.

"Ah, you are awake".

"I am. I was angry with you".

"No, my love. You cannot grow angry with me. You can love me, lust me, maybe even fear me a little. But I never want you angry with me".

"Fear you? I do not fear you. You are too kind and caring to be feared. Maybe a little overprotective, actually a lot overprotective, but not fearful".

Leo smiled and kissed me. Then he began to slowly undress me, I closed my eyes and allowed him to. We then made love. I awoke in the morning to find that Leo was not in the bed with me. When I looked over at the bedroom doors, my luggage was gone. I was sure he took it downstairs. Maybe my flight was available today. I jumped out of bed and into the bathroom. Then I froze and had chills run up my spine. All my stuff was laid back out onto the bathroom counter. I opened the draws and everything was in them again. I ran to the closet. All my clothes were back on hangers. Everything, I mean everything was back in place. But my suitcases were gone. I ran downstairs to speak to Leo, but he was not sitting at the table. Just then Clara came out of the kitchen.

"Ah, Mrs. Ferreira, your husband left you a note. And this".

She handed me a large box. I placed the box on the table and opened the note. It read:

My love,
*   I know it must have surprised you to see all your belongings unpacked. Clara was ordered to unpack your things last night as you slept so soundly and peacefully. I have a good*

explanation for this. But first I want you to join me tonight for a party. It is a business party and I did not want to bring you along to matters of business, but the wives or mistresses of all the men were requested to attend. You being my wife of course, and me not needing a mistress, I ask that you accept the gift of this beautiful dress to wear and attend the party tonight. I have hired a group of ladies to come by this afternoon to pamper you as the queen you are and get you ready for this party. Forgive my absence. We will speak soon. I cannot wait to see you tonight.

Love Leo

I had no idea what to think at this point. I threw the note on top of the box, picked up the box and walked back to my room. When I got up there I laid the box on top of the bed and opened it. It was a beautiful and sexy red dress. Definitely something Philip would have picked out and I would have made him put back. Also in the box were shoes, hair accessories, jewelry, even a gorgeous clutch. I sat at the edge of the bed confused. Just then I remember the new phone Leo brought me. I ran around the bed and picked up the phone, turned it on and desperately waited for it to start up. After what felt like forever, the phone did nothing. No signal or any kind. Not even internet. Nothing. I thought, fine. I will attend this party. But when we get home, I need answers. I especially want to know why my things were unpacked.

Before the afternoon rolled in, I was pacing the entrance foyer. At 12pm exactly the doorbell rang. I rushed to the door and opened it. Three very happy ladies greeted me.

"You must be the beautiful Mrs. Ferreira. It is a pleasure to meet you".

"I am she. Please come in".

The first two woman stepped in, but before the third one did she noticed something lying on the ground. It was a white padded envelope with a label stuck on that had an address I was not familiar with. I slowly peeled off the stuck on label to reveal it was a package sent from Philip and Tiara. But it was sent to the address I had given them before I left. The same address Leo gave me. Yet, the address Philip and Tiara sent the package too was not the same as the sticker that I peeled off. Was the home I was staying in a different address than what Leo had me give them. I quickly replaced the sticker and hid the package underneath my arm. Just then Clara stepped into the foyer.

"Ah, I see the ladies are here. I will let Mr. Ferreira know".

I sent the ladies upstairs to my room so they could get things prepared. Clara saw I had a package under my arms. She stared at it and me.

"What is it that you have in your arm, Mrs. Ferreira?"

"Just something one of the ladies said she recommends I wear under my gown. A lingerie that will drive Leo crazy when he undresses me. Did you say you were going to let Mr. Ferreira know the ladies were here? Do you have a phone with signal? Or any internet of some sort?"

"Oh, no, of course not. What I meant was I would let one of the men know so whenever they get phone signal they could let Mr. Ferreira know".

Clara nervously and quickly walked away. I knew she was lying and I was not going to let this go. I would find out what was going on.

I went upstairs to meet with the woman. I do admit. These woman did liven up the dreary home. They played music, joked and laughed as they did my nails and pedicure. They made me miss Philip and Tiara all the more.

"So, Mrs. Ferreira my friend here is afraid to ask, but I am bold enough to do so. What is it like being the wife of the handsome Mr. Ferreira?"

"Leo? He is an amazing man. He is so kind and gentle towards me".

The girls looked at each other.

"What is it?"

"Well, with his line of work, we expected him to be more... you know.."

"What my friend here means to say is, we thought he would be more like a ferocious lion".

"Oh, that. Yes. He can be when he wants to. Did you say, in his line of work?"

"Well, sure. In his line of work you have to be pretty tough to do what he does day in and day out".

"I'm sorry, I thought he worked in an office".

The girls looked at each other afraid and would not respond to my assumption of Leo working in an office.

"So Mrs. Ferreira I hear you are wearing red. Blood red. In that case I have the perfect matching blood red nail color to match your dress. Ah, here it is. I will even add some rhinestones onto your nails to match the diamonds on your jewelry and accessories".

"Diamonds? These are not rhinestones?"

"Oh Mrs. Ferreira, you are truly as sweet as everyone says you are. Mr. Ferreira would never dress you in rhinestones. Diamonds are what you will be wearing tonight. Even your bag is covered in them".

Hours later after the girls helped me prepare they left. My hair was done up with a diamond headpiece and curls going down the both side of my neck with a string of diamonds following the shape of each curl. Every piece of jewelry had diamonds on them. I didn't even want to think of the cost of it all. I was not a stranger to diamonds. I traveled into paintings that had more diamonds in them then the eyes could see in one day.

There were still a few more hours before Leo was to come get me for this party. So before putting on my red dress, I locked myself in the bathroom while in my lingerie. This way if Clara came in she would believe I was still changing. I then opened the package that Philip and Tiara sent me and to my relief I found three more packs of birth control and a letter. I literally swallowed my last birth control pill last evening. The timing couldn't have been anymore perfect. I immediately opened the new birth control wrapping, placed the new pack into the plastic hard case and took the first pill. Then I took the hard case and packets and put them away in the back of the draw and covered them wit my undergarments. Then I sat down on the velvet stool to read their letter that read:

Dearest Lizbeth,

What is up with you? It has been two and a half weeks now. We got one call and that was it. I'm sure you must be busy helping Leo with packing. I knew you wouldn't be able to come back home without him. You also might want to turn your phone on. We keep trying to call and it is going directly to voicemail. That is when we just KNEW you did not have enough birth control for all the love making you and Leo are doing. I know we sent way too many packs. Well, let's be clear here. While I was taking care of the museum, Tiara picked up your refills and she didn't put just one as I had instructed, she put all three into the package. I'm surprised she remembered my letter. I did not know when you would be receiving this so we shipped it as soon as possible. Lizbeth, how primitive is this where I am writing you a letter instead of texting you. Then again my mother lives in a painting, so we can't necessarily call our lives normal. Anyway, we love you. We miss you and can't wait to see you back.

The one, the only, Philip the great!

I admit I had the biggest smile after reading that letter. I missed them all so, much. If only....then it hit me. I ran out of the bathroom and to my nightstand. I left the new phone Leo bought me on the nightstand so he wouldn't notice it missing, but I took the old one from my nightstand draw and quickly placed it inside the diamond clutch bag. Then covered it with tissues. Once I had a chance to be alone, I could call Philip and Tiara. I was doubtful of Leo's intentions, so I felt it best not to tell him of my plans.

As the evening rolled in I was ready for the party. A little anxious as well. Hoping my plan to call Philip and Tiara would work. I waited in the balcony until I was able to see at a distance a car drive up to the front of the house. I knew it was Leo. After a few moments I heard the door and stepped in from the balcony. Leo looked surprised.

"Is there something wrong?"

"Wrong? Nothing is wrong. Once again you have taken my breath away. You look just like the queen you are".

I smiled and Leo slowly walked over to me admiring me the entire time. He truly did know how to make me feel special. Then he kissed me and laid his forehead against mine.

"You are mine, Lizbeth. You will always be mine. I am the most luckiest man to ever live. Stay close to me tonight. I know every man in that room will be admiring you. I want them to be clear that you are all mine".

Leo kissed me again, then took me by the hand and led me out.

The party was very extravagant. There were gorgeous chandeliers, artwork, and sculptures. The furniture was antique and very expensive. It was like being in a ballroom to a renaissance party. I would know, I have traveled into plenty of them.

As Leo and I walked in, there were many people who turned to look and stare at us. Of course I now knew why. After having the girls over earlier that day, I did learn that many people were curious to know who I was and what I looked like. No one had seen Leo with a wife or a mistress in quite some time. He had a few lovers. But never did he walk in with another woman under his arm after his wife disappeared so many years ago. One of the hired servers passed up by with a silver platter holding champagne glasses. Leo reached for two and handed me on. We continued walking until we stopped at a group of couples. About four couples to be exact.

"Leo, it is great to see you have joined us tonight. This must be your beautiful new wife, Lizbeth".

"You would be correct. Lizbeth, this is Eduardo, he is a long time colleague and friend. And this is his wife Anna".

"It is a pleasure to finally met the wife of Leo. Eduardo and I wondered to ourselves when we would meet the woman who kept Leo away from his work here in Portugal so long. I can see now why he was detained for quite some time".

"You flatter me. I hope I have not caused any harm in delaying Leo's return".

Just then a younger man walked up to Eduardo.

"Father, a word please".

"Ah, Lizbeth. This is our son Paolo.

"Yes, and now he wants to pull his father away for work. He is very dedicated to our work. Paolo, please meet my friend Leo's wife Lizbeth".

"A pleasure to meet you, Lizbeth".

Paolo's eyes were fixated on Lizbeth. He was amazed by her beauty. He leaned forward to shake her hand. Lizbeth reached toward Paolo and smiled as she shook his hand. He could not get his eyes off her so his father Eduardo interrupted.

"So, what was it that you wanted to speak with me about, Paolo?"

"Ah, yes. May we speak alone father".

"Business before pleasure, is it not what they say".

Eduardo and Paolo walked away together. Paolo looked back at Lizbeth who was talking to Anna. Leo took notice that Paolo was looking at Lizbeth and grew jealous. He tried to hide his jealousy and smile.

As Leo stood there making small talk with his group, the music suddenly stopped and the room filled with a sudden wave a whispers. Some men were rolling a dolly carrying something that was covered to hide what it was. When they reached the other side of the room, beside the piano they picked up this covered item and placed it on the floor. The rolled the cart away. I looked at Leo and he was smiling.

"Come, Lizbeth. There is something I want to show you".

We approached the covered item and Leo left me standing there alone as he walked over to it and stood by it.

"Ladies and gentlemen. With permission of my dearest friend Eduardo, I wanted to share the latest addition to my collection. This one is like no other artwork ever seen. Its beauty is unmatchable. The rarest of its kind. And it is all mine. Ladies and gentlemen, allow me to present to 'The Keep-her'."

Leo pulled back the cover to reveal a portrait of me, dressed the exact same way I was. Every detail was displayed in the painting. Even the diamonds that were wrapped around each one of my curls. I was in total shock. I did not even know what to say. Leo stepped forward and took me by the hand. Then gently spinned me around so all could see the amazing likeness. The people were amazed and astonished. They then began to clap. Leo then led me away as the people gathered around the portrait.

"Do you like it my love?"

"I am without words, Leo. I have never...I would have never...I don't even know what to say".

"Say nothing. Your loss of words is enough to ensure me that it is to your liking".

Eduardo and Anna along with their son Paolo and the other couples joined Leo and I.

"Magnificent work, Leo. What made you think of such a great idea as to dress your wife the exact same manner as the portrait you revealed tonight".

"Anyone can take a picture, but to paint a beautiful woman like my wife, takes true talent. My Lizbeth is not a mere picture, but a true work of art".

"Oh, Eduardo, why can't you say beautiful things like that to me".

"I am not as romantic and adoring as Leo is. Brave Leo, you will have people talking for years to come".

"Will there be copies made. For others to add to their collection? It is such an exquisite work of art".

"No, Paolo, there will be no copies made. I will be the only and true owner of this masterpiece".

There seemed to be some tension between Paolo and Leo. Yet I had no time to concern myself with them. I had to find a way to slip away from everyone in order to make that call to Philip and Tiara.

"Leo, where is the restroom?"

"I will show you Lizbeth. I am need of some freshening up myself".

Anna joining me to the restroom was not part of the plan. She freshened herself us and I acted like I was doing the same, with a little extra lipstick and powder on the cheeks. We then exited together. As we walked back, I noticed a balcony with the double doors wide open. Surely Anna would not follow me outside to the balcony as well.

"Just what I need. Some fresh air. I think with all the excitement tonight this would do me well. Could you let

Leo know I will be outside enjoying the night breeze for a moment".

"Surely I can Lizbeth. Go ahead, I will let Leo know".

"Thank you".

Anna picked up a fresh glass of champagne and returned by Eduardos side. Leo looked back for Lizbeth.

"Did my wife return with you, Anna?"

"She did, but she went outside to the balcony to get some fresh air. She said with all the excitement tonight she needed some of the night breeze. I can only imagine how overwhelming this can all be. Meeting new people, of portrait of herself, a new environment altogether".

Anna went on and on. As she spoke Paolo looked for Lizbeth and saw her walking towards the balcony. Leo noticed Paolo looking for Lizbeth. When he noticed Paolo eyes fixated in on direction he looked that way and saw Lizbeth go out to the balcony. Paolo smiled and excused himself. Then walked off toward the balcony. Leo did his best to control his jealousy. So he quickly drunk up his glass of champagne and requested another.

I walked across the room as discretely as possible. When I reached the balcony I quickly walked to the edge of it and slightly leaned over the railing so no one could see me as I pulled out the phone. My hands were shaking. I was so nervous. I could not believe I had to do this in hiding. I did not care to ask questions, I had to make this call so I began to dial the number, when suddenly I was startled by Paolo and the phone slipped right out of my hands. I stood frozen and in shock as I saw it dropping and fall right into the bushes below.

"Did I startle you, Mrs. Lizbeth".

"Uh, yes, no, I mean. I wasn't expecting anyone to be out here".

"Neither was I. Yet I understand your need to get away for a moment. I myself need time away sometimes".

Paolo kept talking, but it all sounded muffled to me. I didn't really hear a word he was saying. I just kept thinking that my opportunity to make the call slipped from my hands and was down in the pushes. My heart was racing, I felt like I was going to pass out. Then I had an idea.

"Paolo, do you have a phone?"

"Of course I do. Who doesn't".

"Can I borrow you phone? I seem to have left mine at home".

Paolo seemed surprised at my request and paused for a moment. Then he began to reach into his jacket pocket to pull out his phone. He handed it to me and it was locked.

"Oh, uh you have to unlock it".

"Yes, of course. Silly me".

He unlocked the phone and as soon as I began to dial Philips number Leo walked out to the balcony.

"Lizbeth?"

Again I froze and slowly turned to look at Leo. He walked over to me, looking at Paolo and me suspiciously.

"Yes, Leo?"

"I was wondering where you were. Let us bid everyone a good night. We are going home now".

"But the night is still so young, Leo. Besides Lizbeth does not look the least bit tired".

"My wife may not look tired, but I know her well. What she wants right now is her bed and me, by her side, so we could fall fast asleep together".

Paolo leaned over towards Leo's ear and spoke low, but I still heard what he said into Leo's ear.

"With a beautiful wife like yours, who could think of sleeping, when there are much more pleasurable things to do together".

Paolo then proudly walked back into the house. Leo grabbed me by the arm and I could tell he was angry. We said our goodbyes to his friends and Leo walked me out of the party and out of the house. The driver drove up with the car and Leo almost pushed me inside of it. He sat inside the car and angrily told the driver to go. Leo did not say a word to me the whole drive home. After the driver pulled up in front of the house, Leo climbed out of the car and walked over to my side. I did not wait for him to open my door and I opened it myself. Before I could step out of the car he grabbed me by arm and pulled me up the steps. The men opened the front doors and we walked into the house.

"Leo, you are hurting me".

He still did not speak. Instead he pulled me up the steps. I had to balance myself to not fall over.

"Leo, let me go. You are hurting me. What is wrong with you?"

When we got to our bedroom he opened the door, pulled me inside and closed the door behind him. As I turned to face him, with the back of his hand he struck me so hard I fell to the floor. My cheek was throbbing in pain. Shock and fear is what I felt as I stood on the bedroom floor.

"How dare you make me look like a fool in front of all those people. I unveil of portrait of the woman I love and later you are found alone in a balcony at night, with another man! You were flirting with him weren't you? How dare you abuse of my trust in this way".

Leo pulled off his tie and his jacket. Then he went to serve himself a drink. I stood up from the grand and unzipped my dress. It was hard to move my legs in it because of it tight design. The dress dropped to the ground.

"You are at fault for my anger. You made me do this to you".

"No, this is not true. I made you do nothing. You took it upon yourself to lift your hand up and strike me. Do not blame you cowardly decisions on my actions. Your are responsible for your own actions. If you cannot control them, you should not be married then".

Leo angrily slammed his drink down and when he turned to look at me, my shoe hit his face. I swung by second shoe, which he blocked from hitting his face.

"Lizbeth! Never, hit me again or I swear I will....".

"What! What will you do?"

Leo came chasing after me and I began to grab whatever I could reach to throw at him. He dodged everything I threw and right when he was about to get close enough to me I jumped onto the bed. He grabbed my arm and pulled me

131

off the bed and onto the floor. I lost my balance and fell back first back onto the bed. He then held me down. Just when he was about to strike me again I lifted my left leg and kicked his hand away. Then I rolled over to my side of the bed, jumped off of it and continued to pick up whatever I could find to throw at him.

"Okay, enough! Enough! I will not hit you again".

I slowly put down the lamp I was about to throw at him. We stared at each other for a moment. Both of us furious and filled with anger. Then he suddenly jumped onto the bed to chase after me. I ran, but did not get far. He caught me by the arm and as I tried to hit him with my other arm he grabbed my face and pushed me up against the wall.

"Stop it! Stop! Calm yourself!"

"Let me go then!"

"I will not let you go. I will never let you go".

"Stop talking to me like this. You struck me. Your words are void to me now. They are nothing. Let me go!"

I fought as best as I could swinging my arms and trying to kick him. He somehow he got a hold of both my wrist and held them together behind my back, with one of his hands. Then he grabbed my face again with the other hand.

"Enough! Stop fighting me!"

"I hate you! I hate you, let me go!"

"If you hated me you would not be crying right now. Calm yourself, please".

"I am crying because you broke my heart. You struck me for no reason....".

"I struck you out of jealousy! Just the thought of Paolo being as close to you as he was, made me lose control over myself. I could not contain my anger".

"So you saw me as Paolo and struck me instead of him, is that it?" I am to blame that he followed me outside? I hate you Leo. Let me go. You are a coward. You won't strike a man you are jealous of, but you will strike an innocent woman. LET ME GO!"

"Lizbeth, please. Fine I will let you go. Please calm yourself. You are right, I did wrong in striking you. It will never happen again, forgive me. I was not thinking straight. I am so in love you with, I lost control. Please Lizbeth. I do not want you to hate me. I would rather choose death than to lose your love."

Leo began to cry and laid his head on my shoulder and released my face. I began to calm down and he slowly began to release my wrist.

"I have never loved anyone as much as I love you. This is too much for me to comprehend. This love, this jealousy, this hunger to be my your side. When I am away at work I miss you so much. I think I am going crazy. I don't even know who I am".

He put both his hands on my cheeks and looked at me.

"Please do not hate me. I beg of you Lizbeth. I never wanted to take you to that party. I knew this would happen. Men would lust after my wife. I know these men. They will try to seduce you and take you away from me".

"I do not want any of those men Leo. I fell in love with you. I do not care for any of them".

"Prove to me that I am the only one".

"How do you want me to prove this to you?"

"By showing me how much you love me, kiss me. Kiss me, Lizbeth".

Leo kissed my lips and I tried to turn my face, because I was till angry with him. He released my cheeks and grabbed my waist then began kissing my neck.

"Leo, please. Just stop".

"Never, I will never stop. I love you, Lizbeth. You are mine. Only mine. Give yourself to me and prove to me that you are mine. Love me again".

With these words he slowly took me down to the floor, where he continued kissing me until I no longer wanted to fight back. Instead, I let him make love to me.

The next day when I awoke Leo had already left for work. He did not return until late at night after I was asleep. The second day I awoke and again he had left early for work and did not return until I was asleep. I began to rethink this marriage and realized that I could not share my secret with Leo. All I wanted at this point was to return home. I missed Philip and Tiara immensely. I decided to write them a letter.

When Clara left for her midday shopping I snuck into the kitchen and checked every draw and cabinet in search for some stamps or anything I could use to send a letter to Philip and Tiara. I needed to tell them things were not well and that I would be returning home as soon as I could. But there was nothing. No stamps anywhere. Then I thought, what would be better than a letter, was me telling them myself. So I looked everywhere to find either my luggage or any piece of luggage. In one of the first floor bedrooms I found my luggage hidden deep inside a closet. So I rushed back to my room and packed my things. This time I took them downstairs myself and left them by the front door.

That night, once again I had fallen asleep before Leo returned home. The next day I got out of bed and saw that all of my belonging had been unpacked again. I could not contain the frightful feeling I had in the pit of my stomach, which was telling me that I would not be leaving this house. I covered my mouth and did my best to not be heard as I yelled and cried.

After I gathered myself, I marched downstairs. Leo was not in the dining room. I barged into the kitchen and found Clara working.

"Go and tell Leo's men to contact him now. I want to speak with him!"

"Ah, Mrs. Ferreira. Mr. Ferreira is in his office. He asked me to tell you that he wanted to talk to you when you had awoken".

I walked out of the kitchen and barged into Leo's office. He was talking to one of his men. They stopped whatever conversation they were having and with Leo's approval the man walked out of Leo's office. He shut the door behind him.

"Good morning my beautiful wife".

"Don't my beautiful wife me. Why do you keep having my stuff unpacked. I want to go home. Leo, I don't need my stuff in order to leave this house. I can leave with just the clothes on my body. Have one of your men drive me to the airport. I will get my own flight home. You cannot keep me here".

"Lizbeth, please sit down".

"I'd rather stand".

"Lizbeth, my darling wife. You are already home. Your stuff as you say, continues to be unpacked, because there is no need for you to leave your home.

"Leo, this is not my home. We had an agreement before we married. Two weeks max and I returned home. You would then follow behind. Two weeks! It has been a month now".

"Lizbeth, you understand that my work is here. My life is here, I cannot leave everything behind".

"That is not what you promised me! You lied to me and my friends. You deceived me so I would I trust you".

"I told you what you wanted to hear".

"Even if it was all lies? I cannot, I will not, trust you now or ever. Stay back! Do not come near me. I want to go home. Let me go, Leo. I want to go home. Either you take me to the airport, or I promise you...."

Leo pinned me against the wall and grabbed my face again with his hand. I tried pushing him back and struggled to get his hand off of my face.

"Promise me what? Lizbeth, you will not be leaving this house. This is your home now. Our home. Here we will build our lives together. We are husband and wife. No one can break that bond. We will make it stronger, by having children. How many Lizbeth? Do you want two, three. We can have all the children you want. This will keep you happy and you won't feel alone in your home. This is where you belong. This is where you will remain".

"Get your hands off of me! I will not give you children. You are a liar and a deceitful man. My life is not here. I have a life, I have friends, a home, I have...."

"No! Your life is here, with me, by my side. In time you will forget your friends and the life you had. This is your new life now".

"It's not! It's not! Let me go!"

I managed to push Leo off of me and move as far away from him as I could. Then I moved to the other side of the leather couch in his office to have something between us.

"Leo you are truly insane. There is something really wrong with you. You don't deceive, lie, and try to manipulate people".

"Why is that? I do it everyday".

"I think I am going to be sick".

"My love..."

"No! Stay back. I don't want you to touch me. Don't touch me ever again".

"That is not what you said the other night. Or the nights before. Or even on our honeymoon week, where your body practically begged for my touch".

"That was before I knew who you were. You have changed, or actually you have now shown who you really are. Now, I have changed and I do not accept your terms. I will be leaving this house. I care nothing for your stupid white line. Your men will have to shoot me, because I will not stop".

I quickly made my way to the door so I could leave his office and as soon as I had opened the door, Leo grabbed me from behind. Wrapping his arms around mine making it difficult for me to push or grab him.

"Let me go!"

"Never! I can keep you here and I will keep you here. The only choice you have is how you will remain in these walls. In your bedroom with lock and key or willingly to walk these halls as the queen you are. This is your home now! You belong to me!"

My arms were pinned with the way he wrapped his arms around me, but I managed to kick his leg as hard as I could. He loosened his grip and I broke free. Then I opened the office door and ran out as fast as I could. I didn't know which way to go, so I thought of the phone I had. I ran upstairs to my room and jumped onto the bed, opened the nightstand draw and grabbed the phone. Then I ran back out of the bedroom, just then Leo was reaching the top of the steps. I hid behind the door so he would not see me. As soon as he went into the bedroom I ran down the stairs, through the foyer and out the front door. I looked around for Leo's men and could not see any. I looked at the phone and saw no signal so I ran and ran through the bushes, looking everywhere for Leo's men as I did. Finally, I was almost to the white line, but there were no more bushes to hid behind. So I first entered Philip's phone number then stood up and ran as fast as I could past the white line, at the same time I hit the send button to dial the number. Just then Leo's men saw me from a distance and came running towards me. I ran to buy some time for the call to connect. I did not know which way to run, Leo's men were coming from everywhere. Suddenly I heard voicemail. Philip's voicemail, then the beep and I began to yell.

"Philip, I'm trapped! Leo is not who he says he is. He's kidnapped me and won't let me return home. The address he gave us is a fake. I...."

One of Leo's men grabbed my arm and snatched the phone away from me. But before he could delete the message I hit to end the call. He checked the phone.

"It's too late. She ended the call".

That man handed the phone to another man. Then he handed it to Leo who walked up right behind me.

"She sent the call Mr. Ferreira".

Leo looked furious. It happened so fast, but within seconds Leo struck me again and I was on the ground. This made me furious. I refused to be a trapped battered woman. I yelled and stood up from the ground and charged Leo, but his men grabbed me.

"I told you to never strike me again! I will rip your eyes out! Let me go!"

"Take her to her room and tell Clara we will need the key".

"Yes, Mr. Ferreira".

"No! Let me go! What key! Don't you dare lock me up Leo! Don't you dare!"

It took three men to take me to the bedroom. One on each of my arms and another holding me through my ankles. I went screaming and fighting the whole way up. They then threw me onto the bed and rushed out of the room. I climbed out of the bed and rushed towards the bedroom door, when it suddenly began to close and I could see Clara handing one of the men a key, which they used to lock me in my bedroom. I banged on the door and yelled.

"Let me out! Leo, let me out! I hate you Leo! I hate you!"

Leo reached the top of the steps just in time to hear Lizbeth yelling how much she hated him.

"You all may go".

The men all left as Leo ordered. Only Clara stood with Leo.

"You know the drill, Clara. Let her calm herself and we stick to the plan. Come with me".

Leo walked back down the stairs and to his office, where one of his men were waiting. Clara followed behind. Leo handed the man the phone Lizbeth had.

"Disconnect this line and destroy it. We do not want them to trying to call or track this line".

"Yes, Mr. Ferreira".

The man rushed out of Leo's office and Clara shut the door behind him.

"What will we do Mr. Ferreira. She is very strong willed. When we spoke by phone you made her seem..."

"I know! I know what I said. She was not this strong willed before. I guess she and I are now both showing our truest colors, are we not?"

"She would be hard to tame, sir. She is much stronger willed then your previous wife. She defies you, threatens you, easily disobeys..."

"Clara! We stick to the plan. She is wild, but there is no stallion I cannot tame".

"Would you like my advice sir. Maybe a child. This one seems like she would be more submissive if she had a child. She loves strongly, as we can see with her friends. Being that they are all she has. If she bore you a child, I am sure she would love it strongly and..."

"Yes, she would know that if she tried to leave, she would not be able to do so with our child".

"This would make her afraid to leave you sir."

"And she would have not other choice than to remain with me. There is only one problem, Clara. She hates me now. How will I get her to give herself to me. I cannot wrestle and fight to take it from her each time. This will not work".

"You are right. The struggle might also cause her to not conceive. Her submission would not be a problem, I assure you Mr. Ferreira. Leave it to me. You will have your wife completely submissive and she will think it is all a dream".

"And how will you do that?"

"With an old recipe I can add to her drink, or food. It is tasteless, so she won't even know. Within the hour she would be hungry for your touch and craving you. This way she is calm and you can have her as many times as you want until she conceives".

"This is great, Clara. But would this drug or 'recipe' have a negative effect if she is pregnant?"

"I know her menstrual cycle now. I can tell you when she will be ready to conceive. The drug would have no affect on her conceiving. Now, once she is pregnant, it cannot be given again, as it can have a negative effect on the child. Possibly even cause her to lose the child".

"I see. Once we have a child together, I will show her how much I love her and our child. She will forget her friends and her old home and return to me. I like this plan".

"Very well then. I will begin to work on the recipe today. It will take about a week to prepare. Its ingredients have to be collected and carefully mixed. They will heighten her sexual desires to where she will have no control over herself and want only one thing....you Mr. Ferreira".

Leo smiled proudly.

"Go Clara, prepare this mix. We will give her two days to calm herself and then maybe she and I can at least speak. For now only bring to the bedroom her meals. Have two men accompany you so they can enter first to guard her, and you. Then just roll the cart in and out each day".

"It shall be done sir".

"Ah and Clara, the signal machine will not longer be needed. It had no affect on my phone or yours with the technology I had installed in them. Yet, let us ensure there

144

are no electronics anywhere in the house that Lizbeth can use to communicate with anyone. If we need it on again I will let you know when to turn it on".

Clara nods in agreement and leave Leo's office. Just then Leo gets a voicemail alert on his phone. He puts the message on speaker.

"Hello, father. Its is your son Alex. I wanted you to know I was back in Portugal. Just landed now. I will be spending three days here in the city, then I will take a drive home. I did not come to argue with you, so please let us be at peace".

Leo frustratedly ended the call.

"The timing could not have been worse, Alex. I needed more time to tame Lizbeth. No matter. I have three days. She will be obedient or she will lose her friends with a bullet to each of their heads from one of my mens guns. She will have to choose. Be obedient to me or suffer the loss of her friends".

I sat in the bed curled up and crying. I couldn't believe this was happening to me. I don't know how many hours had passed. This was like being in a painting. But no kind of painting I have been in before. This was a nightmare.

Trapped in eerie renaissance painting with a mad man. No Philip, and no Tiara to open the gate so I could escape.

Honestly though, I believe the reason why I cried so much, was because my heart was broken. I love him. I had fallen in love with Leo, but now my heart was broken. The man I fell in love with, did not exist. Some art guardian I was. I couldn't even get away from an obsessive lying.....I suddenly heard the door was unlocked and it began to open. I quickly sat up on the bed and in walked in Leo. As calm as he could be. He did not look at me. He just walked in and shut the door behind him.

"We need to talk, Lizbeth".

"I have nothing but hateful and resentful words to say to you".

"Those will have to wait. After what I tell you, they might be even worse, but you will have to keep them all to yourself and be the calm obedient wife I want you to be".

"I'd rather die".

"Funny you should say that. What if it wasn't your life at risk, but the lives of your friends?"

"You would't dare, Leo".

"I would. To get what I want, I would. As long as you remain here and obedient to me, your friends will be able to live a long healthy life. Without you. If you defy me and try to run again. Well, let's say before you make it home your friends will be gone".

I began to cry obsessively. Leo ran over to me and caressed my hair and cheek. I stared at him angrily.

"My love. I did not want it to come to this. You forced my hand by wanting to disobey me. Is it my fault that I fell in love with you. You stole my heart and now I cannot let you go. I would rather die...or kill. Then lose you. You are all that matters to me. And when we have a child, you will be more at peace here. A child will make you happy and we will be a family and you will turn that anger back into love again for me".

"A child?"

"Yes, my love. That is what we need, you need. It will make you happy and connect us always. You know you cannot leave me if we have a child together. I would never let you take my child from me. I would never let you go either. We will be happy here and raise our children and grow old together, as any married couple should".

Tears kept running down my cheeks and Leo would wipe them away as he spoke these words. I tried to speak through the tears.

"We are not any married couple. This marriage was founded on deceit and lies. You are not who you made yourself out to be. And now I am a prisoner".

"You are not my prisoner.."

"I am. You are ensuring that I am. If I try to escape you, there are consequences. How am I not a prisoner?"

"Lizbeth, please".

"The man I thought I married was a sham. He does not exist. Behind this mask was a monster, who would kill innocent people to control one person".

"Come now. This is not a new thing. It may be new to you, but you never asked me what kind of work I do. Lizbeth, I am a hired hitman agency. I send men to kill for me and sometimes I kill them myself. You would not believe what people pay to have someone taken out to obtain what they want. I understand their desires and I appease them in taking these lives".

"Taking lives? You consider yourself powerful enough to choose who lives or dies? You are truly a monster. And I will not allow my body to have a child from someone like you. Not with the responsibility this baby would have...."

"Responsibility? What responsibility? My love, the only responsibility they would have is to grow strong and make us proud. I will teach them all I know. My children will be strong and..."

"No! I will not bare you children. I would rather die!"

I pushed Leo away and stood up from the bed, he then grabbed me and I tried to back away, but he pressed me against the wall and kept trying to get me to look at him as I turned away.

"Look at me! You will not die. Not even death will take you from me, do you understand. My plan is a good plan and you will submit to it. Your death will cause the death of your friends either way, because in the rage of losing you I will kill them myself. Would you be selfish enough to take your own like and cost them theirs?"

"Selfish? How dare you talk to me about being selfish when you are the epitome of greed".

Leo kissed me as I tried to turn my face away and push him back. He still reached my lips as he spoke.

"I admit I was a selfish man, but when I met you it was like you ignited those flames even more. I have never felt this way for anyone, Lizbeth. You think me to be a man of greed? Then so be it, but I have no self control over the greed I feel with you. You are mine. I will kill for you if I have to, but I will never let you go. Never".

Leo tried to contain his lust and anger by hitting the wall beside my head. He then backed away and rubbed his face and head with his open hands.

"You do not understand what you have done to me, Lizbeth! Do not fight me! Just submit and no one will be hurt!"

Leo rushed out of the room like a crazy man, locking the door behind him. I couldn't help but cry as I slide down the wall to the floor.

I wiped my tears away and wanted to know what time it was. I crawled my way towards the bed and lifted myself up. Inside the beside table was my watch. It was 4pm. I rushed to the bathroom and opened the draw, then reached back and pulled out the birth control. I popped out the pill and swallowed it, then drank water from the faucet to take the pill down. Then I hid the birth control. Leo could never know that I had birth control. I had three packets. That was three months I had to try and escape, but how. Philip and Tiara's life were at risk now. Leo was crazy. All this time I had been dating and then married a killer. I sat back on the bed then laid into a fetal position where I cried and cried until I feel asleep.

The next morning I awoke with the sound of the door being unlocked. Then it opened. Two men walked in and stood guard. Behind them was Clara pushing the silver cart. She left it at the foot of my bed and left the room. The men followed behind her as they closed and locked the door. I laid my head back onto the pillow.

This happened again and again for two days. I was brought breakfast, midday lunch and dinner. Each time was the same. The men opened the door, Clara rolled a new cart in, took the old one out and they closed and locked the door. How was I not a prisoner. After dinner I went to soak myself in the Jacuzzi. I filled it with anything and everything I could find to ease my stress. Lavender, lots and lots of lavender.

Leo was in his office. He was walking towards to the door to leave his office, when he overheard the men who would unlock and lock Lizbeth's bedroom door as she was brought her meals. They were walking by and having a conversation.

"I think I could get used to guarding the maid".

"Agreed, with every entry to that bedroom we get a glimpse of that beautiful woman".

"She is just wow. Would we be lucky enough to come in when she is changing one day".

"Who knows. I would love to get a glimpse of that. Remember, we were told if she is not in the bedroom, we are to search for her, wherever she is".

Both men laughed amongst each other and Leo grew furiously jealous. He stepped out of the office and looked in the direction of the men. Then he turned around and went to Lizbeth's bedroom. He unlocked the door and walked in. She was not in the bedroom. Leo searched for her and slowly pushed open the slightly closed bathroom door. There was Lizbeth soaking in the jacuzzi. Leo slowly stepped in unnoticed and leaned against the wall staring at Lizbeth. She remained in the jacuzzi with her eyes closed and did not take notice that Leo had been standing there. He smiled.

"You are truly so beautiful".

Lizbeth was startled and look over to see Leo standing there.

"How long have you been there?"

"Long enough to admire how lucky I am to have you in my life".

"What do you want, Leo. Why are you here?"

Leo walked over to the Jacuzzi and sat on the edge. Then he dipped his fingers into the wanter and gently swayed it back and forth.

"You said I treat you like a prisoner. No queen should be locked in her tower. We have come to an agreement and..."

"There was no agreement. You threatened me. Nothing else".

"Well, either way you understood the request. So, I feel that you have earned the privilege to walk amongst your castle again. You know what the consequences are if you disobey my orders".

Leo stood up and was about to walk away. Then he stopped.

"And another thing. I don't want my men to see you anymore. Their job is to protect me and you. Not gaze upon and lust what belongs to me. If you see any of my men, turn your face. I would hate to start killing good men for looking at you and whispering about how beautiful MY wife is".

Leo walked out of the bathroom and left Lizbeth's room. He closed it behind him, but he did not lock the door.

After Leo left, I got out of the jacuzzi and put on a bathrobe. Then I marched downstairs and into the kitchen where Clara was.

"Mrs. Ferreira? Is there anything...."

"Sine I am a prisoner in this house and you are my husbands warden, then I guess you must be the person I speak to when I need something. I want sheer fabrics. In all colors. Some silk sample pieces as well, to match the sheer fabric. And I want it no later than tomorrow".

I walked out of the kitchen and back upstairs to my room. I slammed the door behind me and paced back and forth full of rage. Then I sat in the chair and thought for a moment.

"How? How do I find a way to escape this madness?"

Then I had a thought. I put clothes on and went back downstairs. I slowly walked the halls until I reach the hall of artwork. I stepped into the hall and stopped. I looked up and around. Then I began to cry.

"I failed. I failed them all. If I do not have a child the power dies with me and everyone is trapped. Even Philip and Tiara. We are all trapped".

I walked down the hall of artwork and saw a painting to my right. It was a sad painting of an old wooden boat in the middle of the ocean waters. All alone, just like me. I walked over to the painting and placed my forehead onto it.

After I lifted my face from the painting I gently touched it, to feel every lifted ripple of the painted wave. I suddenly felt like I was already in the painting. I closed my eyes and thought I felt water. I pulled my hand back and smiled. When I opened my eyes, my had was wet. There were drips of water on the painting itself.

"How?"

I tried again by touching the painting and nothing. I stood back and reached out my arm. Closed my eyes and breathed in and out, just as Tiara always taught us. Nothing. I must have done something to have been able to touch the waters. I spent the rest of my night trying to figure the paintings out. Did I open the gate for just a moment? If I did, how do I reopen it? The hours passed and nothing. Suddenly I was startled when I heard Leo.

"Lizbeth? What are you doing there?"

"Since I was freed from my bedroom prison, I wanted to visit a room where I felt more like myself. A room where works of art are framed and put on a wall to be displayed for the collectors satisfaction only. Am I not another display to be added to your collection?"

Leo walked over to me and caressed my face with the back of his fingers.

"You are much more than that to me Lizbeth. Come, let me show you what was delivered today".

Leo led me out of the hall of artwork and into his office. On the wall above his fireplace was the portrait painting of me that he displayed at the party. He leaned in and caressed my face and had me look at him.

"You stand alone. You are its own masterpiece. A masterpiece that can have only one owner. I am that owner. I do not want to imprison you Lizbeth. I want you to smile and laugh as you did when we first met. Do you remember that night. The chamomile tea with sweet milk. I knew that day, I had to have you. You worked with art. Have you never felt the need to protect what is yours. You had no owner. No man who left his mark on you. I am that man. Your first and only. I may have not been fully honest with you. Yet, had I been honest would you have given me a chance. You would have judged the artwork for its appearance and not it message. That painting of the boat in the middle of the oceans. You would have judged it as sad and maybe even depressing. Yet the artist named it 'Strength'. Because through the crashes of the waves, the boat still endured. It does not break or sink. That is why I had to have it. As dreary as it looked, I had to have it".

I closed my eyes because I did not want to look at Leo anymore. He had a way with words that made me feel weak. I refused to fall into his trap again. But instead of leaving me alone, he came in closer. He pulled me in closer to him through my waist and laid his forehead against mine. Then he wrapped one arm around my waist and place the other on the back of my head, to not allow me to back away. He came close to my lips and as he spoke his lips would touch mine with the words he kept speaking.

"When I saw you Lizbeth, a feeling came over me that was different to what I felt for any work of art. You were in a room full of art, reproaching me about buying any of your art pieces. You did not give me a chance to explain. Instead you stood out from all the beautiful artwork and took my breath away. I wanted to ask you to marry me there and then. I had to contain myself".

Leo began to steal a tap kiss as he spoke, making me weaker and weaker.

"Remember the picnic on the floor of the museum. Remember how you felt. Remember what you wanted. Don't fight it, Lizbeth. Allow me to return that feeling again. That's it. Don't fight it. What do you want Lizbeth? You are allowed to be loved and feel love. Your body craves it, give it what it wants".

"I can't. I can't".

"You can. Lizbeth. Lizbeth".

I tried to push Leo back, but then he passionately kissed me and slowly went down my cheek and onto my neck. I opened my eyes and when I did I saw the painting of me, smiling. Then I remembered the times Leo hit me and threats he made. I gathered all me strength and pushed one time as hard as I could. Leo lost his grip and I was free from his arm.

"Lizbeth, please".

"No. The man I knew in the states is not the same man I have come to know here. The man I see before me feels pleasure in hitting me and threatening to kill the people I love. I will not give myself to you willingly, ever again. I would rather die".

"Lizbeth, I do not find pleasure in these things you have said. You leave me no choice".

"That is not true! You had plenty of choices. You could have started with keeping your word and allowing me to return home. Happy and in love with you, to wait for you as you promised. You could have chosen to leave the kind of work you do...."

"It pays well!"

"I do not need your money! I never cared for your money. I have plenty of my own. I wanted your love and to be loved".

"I can love you, I do love you..."

"No! If you loved me you would not threaten to kill my friends. You would not lock me in a room. You would not seek to hurt me, but to protect me. You are not a man I can love and you are not a man that can love".

I turned around and barged out of the room, slamming the door behind me.

After Lizbeth walked out of the room Leo began to pace in anger. He served himself a drink and took the first cup down. Then another. He served a third cup and instead of drinking it he threw it against the wall. Then in a rage he began to throw things to the floor. Heavily breathing and still angry he opened his office door and began to yell out Clara's name. She came running from the kitchen down the hall and entered Leo's office.

"Mr. Ferreira?"

"How long Clara? How much longer will I have to wait for your mix to be ready?"

"I am glad you asked sir. Lucky I was able to find all the ingredients needed. I am finishing the mixture now. We can give her the first drops in her drink tomorrow night".

"Good. I want my wife. I want her now. When we have children together she will no longer see me as a monster, but as a father to her children and her husband".

"Yes, sir. Please remember after she has taken the recipe and she desires to make love. Do as you please to her. When you are done, you must leave everything as it was. She will think it was all a dream and we can continue to give her the drink. If she learns of what we are doing she will not eat or drink and you will not have her become submissive".

"I understand. Now go and finish this mix".

"Yes sir".

Clara rushes out of Leo's office and he walks over to the liquor and takes a new cup. He pours himself a new drink and sits in his chair.

"Submissive and obedient. That is what you shall be with me, Lizbeth. Submissive and obedient".

Alexander was woken by the hit from a pillow on his bed.

"Alex! Get up!"

"What? What?"

"You asked me to wake you up before I left".

"I did? Benjamin, remind me why would I do something dumb like that".

"For the hundredth time, it's Ben. I will have have enough with hearing my parents call me Benjamin for the next few months. And you asked me to do something as dumb as wake you up, so you can get up and go home to see your father. Here, coffee".

"Where's the rest of the guys".

"They went home to see their parents. All of them as miserable as you and I in having to do so. Hmm, let's see. To choose between being stuck in the middle of the ocean with sharks swimming around us, or face our parents".

Both Alexander and Benjamin replied at the same time, "Sharks".

"Well, I am off. My bus gets here in, oh thirty minutes and it will take twenty to get to the bus station. I so look forward to my four hour bus ride home".

"Why did you not have your parents driver pick you up?"

"And risk my mother or father coming with the driver, then talking to me about my life decisions on the four hour drive back home? Not a chance. I would rather a nice bus seat, the company of the cat lady beside me and the breeze through my open window. See you next term".

"See you next term".

Ben left the room and ran towards the bus stop. When he got there he was just in time. He boarded the bus, placed his backpack underneath the set a began to pop his earbuds in, when a really pretty girl came down the aisle looking for her seat number. Which happened to be right beside Ben. When he looked up, he was surprised to see a pretty girl. She sat down and placed her backpack underneath the seat.

"You don't look like a cat lady at all".

"Are you disappointment?"

"No, not at all".

Ben looked out towards the window and opened it. The breeze blew right in. Then he whispered to himself, "I am so glad I took the bus".

"Are you speaking to me?"

"Oh no, just thinking out loud".

"About the cats or the lady?"

"Well, now I am curios. Do you like cats?"

"Funny that you would ask. I do like cats".

"Oh no, I am dog person myself. They are wild and playful".

"Well, so are cats".

"Not the same see, let me explain why".

"Please, do so, we have plenty of time. This is a long bus ride. We will see if you can convince me of which is better".

And the bus drove off.

Alex got out of the shower and wrapped the towel around his waist. He then pick up his backpack and pull-out a pair of jeans and a t-shirt.

Once he was dressed and ready, he checked out of the hotel and outside waiting for him was one of Leo's other drivers.

"Alex, glad to have you back!"

They both embraced each other. Then the driver opened the car door.

"Where is my father?"

"In matters of business as always. Did you expect him this time?"

"I did. It is the 10 year anniversary of my mothers disappearance. I would have thought he would be here. He always comes to pick me up during this time".

"Well, with the new wife, I am sure this date has already slipped his mind".

"Did you say wife?"

"Your father did not tell you he remarried?"

"My father and I rarely speak, but he could have a least sent you to tell me this news".

"Well, have a seat. There is much to tell".

Alex sat in the car and the driver closed the door. He then he ran over to the driver side and got into the car and drove off.

I was standing in the balcony sipping on my coffee when Leo walked into the bedroom. He stepped out onto the balcony.

"Good morning".

"It is an okay morning".

"Just okay? With a sun so bright and breeze so warm?"

"When the heart is happy, a mind can take notice of such beauty. When a heart is sad, it takes no notice of anything, but sorrow".

"I did not know you were such a poet, Lizbeth".

"I am not a poet, I speak truth".

"How I wish this were not your truth. If you gave me the chance you could be as happy. As you once were when you first came here".

"Had I known the truth, I would have never come here to begin with and I would not have known such sadness".

Leo took steps closer to me and gently glided the back of his fingers on my arm.

"Lizbeth, I will come to you tonight. I want to speak more in depth with you. But that is not why I have come now".

"Why have you come?"

"I would like to make a request. You are no longer to be locked in your room and you are free to roam the house and the gardens. However, I ask that you do it as least as possible in the coming weeks".

"What do mean? Your asking me to willing stay locked away in my room? What for?"

"My son is coming to visit. He might be as long as a week or two the most. He never stays long. You will grow accustomed to his quick visits. He likes to bring his driver into the house from time to time and they move about the house. I do want you speaking to them. I would prefer they not even see you, but the less they do the better for them...and you".

"Why? Will you strike again if any one of them says a word to me. Let us hope neither one says good morning or good afternoon, because I am sure I will be struck and locked in my room".

Leo stood there staring at Lizbeth as she angrily nodded in disagreement and anger. Leo slightly turned to leave. Before doing so he looked at Lizbeth one more time.

"We will be together tonight. I am sure you will be in better spirits and yearning to have me close".

"I do not see how that would ever be possible".

"We shall see, Lizbeth".

Leo left Lizbeth's room and went down the stairs. Then towards his office. Just then Clara came up the stairs and into Lizbeth's room. She saw Lizbeth standing outside on the balcony.

"Mrs. Ferreira? Here are the fabrics you requested".

Lizbeth slightly looked back then turned her face. Clara shrugged her shoulders, place them on the bed, and left the room.

"Wait, so you are saying in two months time my father left to the states and returned with a bride. No one knows anything about her?"

"Nothing except that she is young and very beautiful. She is much younger than your father".

"Then she married him for his money. I thought my father would have been smarter than that".

"When you get a good look at her, you might see why your father fell so quickly. I have heard he is very jealous with her as well. He has since his marriage doubled the men outside the house and they are not allowed to pass a white line painted on the ground".

"A white line?"

"The men cannot pass it to come near the house and there were rules that your father made in regard to her passing the line. No one can cross each others side".

"That sounds ridiculous".

"The house maid has also mentioned to me that they fight often. She is very demanding with your father. Clara fells your father gives into her every whim and is spoiling her even more. Her demands keep growing and she spends her time yelling and throwing things around the house, if she does not get her way".

"This woman sounds terrible. Why would my father marry such a woman?"

"Beauty, my young friend. For beauty".

"I don't care how beautiful a woman is, if she has a rotten soul, the beauty is not enough to build a relationship with them. I think my time at home will be short. The last thing I want is to hear a spoiled woman making demands all day".

As I stood standing in the balcony I grew angrier and angrier. I slammed my cup of coffee down and marched over to the bed where I picked up all the fabrics in both my hands. Then I left my bedroom and marched downstairs and toward Leo's office. When I got there I barged in. He turned around and laid the paper he had in his hands onto the table.

"Lizbeth?"

In my rage I began to throw fabrics at him. Of course with their light weight they did not reach him and instead floated in the air landing on his desk.

"Pick! Which color do you want? If I am to live my life hiding myself from people to help you find some way on controlling your jealous rages, then pick a color! That way I can cover my face and live hiding from the world. Look! Purple, I can take this and make the perfect hijab and veil to hid myself from everyone. Maybe even the birds in the air won't be able to get a glimpse of me. Wouldn't that make you happy?

Just then Alex walked into the house with his driver beside him. They could hear Lizbeth yelling from a distance. Alex and the driver looked at each other.

"I guess the rumors are true my friend. I think it best to take my leave and to not be under the same roof with a woman like that".

"No, don't leave....."

The driver quickly left the house and shut the door behind him. Alex took a deep breath and started his way to his fathers office. When he walked in Lizbeth was still yelling.

"What's wrong? Now you have nothing to say. I'm surprised. Did you not want me to be obedient? Here then, choose a color so I may be an obedient wife. I will have all of the veils made immediately. I want the seamstress working all night to make them for me in all colors. No one will get rest until they are all made and delivered to my room...".

"Hello?"

Lizbeth froze and took deep breaths to try and calm herself.

"Ah, Alexander my son!"

Leo immediately rushed over to his son to embrace him.

"Did I come at a bad time father?"

"No, no, of course not. Just silly little matrimonial disputes. Come meet my wife".

Lizbeth did not want to meet Alex and instead she turned around and paused for a moment. Alex looked at Lizbeth and was surprised to see how beautiful she was.

"You must be my fathers new bride".

Lizbeth walked passed Alex and left the office. She rushed up to her room and threw herself across her bed and wept.

During the evening Clara was preparing Lizbeth dinner. She added exactly three drops to her cup of juice. Then placed it onto the silver tray. Clara then picked up the tray and exited the kitchen passing the dinning area where Leo and Alex were eating.

"Is that for my wife, Clara?"

"It is, Mr. Ferreira".

"Were you sure to make it the way she likes?"

"Oh yes indeed, sir".

"Good".

Clara continued walking up the stairs where she laid the silver tray on a cart and began pushing it towards Lizbeth's room.

"Father, why does your wife not sit with you at the dinner table. And did I hear you tell Clara to ensure that she made her food the way she likes? How demanding is this woman? Clothing, meals, not to mention very impolite".

"Lizbeth is a very high maintenance and demanding woman, but she can be very kind when she wants to be. She has been hurt in the past, so she does not trust easily. Her rages and rants are just a way for her to seem strong. Yet, with me she is different".

"It did not seem that way to me in your office earlier today".

"Ah, that. She is demanding new dresses be made. She feels I have neglected her and she is made to look poor with the clothing she has. No worries, I have got her handled well. I will order her some dresses and once she has what she wants, she will stop raging with anger. You know how woman are with their clothing and accessories. It is never enough".

"Mother was never so needy. Did you remember that today is the 10th year anniversary of her disappearance?"

"I remember it well. But as I have told you in the past, why remember the date that your mother decided to leave us. I hope wherever she is, that she is well. Not a call or even a letter to let us know that she is alive and well. This is not a time I wish to remember".

"I have not stopped believing that I will someday see her again".

"Enough about her. Tell me about you. Are you taking a quick break from classes?"

"Father, the term has ended. We are in summer now. I have the whole next two months to myself, before the next term begins".

Leo became nervous to hear this. He did not want Alex around Lizbeth too long.

"Ah, yes, that's right. I have to remember to submit the payment for the next terms tuition. Well, since you will be around the house for the summer, then I will warn you now. Keep your distance from Lizbeth. I don't want her to grow jealous with you, thinking I favor you more. Which, I actually do. We are trying to have a child. Nothing yet, which is why I think she has been so angry lately".

"You are trying to have a child?"

"Yes, and she has not become pregnant yet. After having so many negative test results, you can now see why she is so angry".

"Don't you think it is too soon to have children with this woman? You barely know her, father".

"It is never too soon with Lizbeth. I know her well and she knows her place. This is her home, she will never leave this house. Why not allow her to have the children she wants to fill this home with laughter. Just as you did when you were just a boy".

Alex was doubtful of his fathers decision, but didn't want to say anymore about the matter.

Clara entered Lizbeth's room and rolled in the cart with her dinner. She then left the room slightly closing the door behind her. Clara waited in the hall watching through the door as Lizbeth walked up to the cart and picked up the cup of juice. She then sipped the juice and walked back out to the balcony. Clara smiled and evil smile and snuck away. After about an hour Clara came back for the tray and noticed the Lizbeth drank all of the juice. She rolled the cart out of her room, placed it where it goes and lifted the tray. When she reached the bottom of the steps she walked into the dinning room and from a distance saw Leo in the patio chatting with Alex. Leo looked back and saw Clara, who nodded to confirm that Lizbeth had drunk the mixture.

"Alex, it is getting late. I have an early day at work tomorrow. I will be off to bed now. Stay and enjoy the night breeze. Welcome home again my son. Good night".

"Good night, father".

Leo rushed off and up the stairs. He went to his bedroom where he began to run a hot shower. Lizbeth had just finished her shower and was standing in front of the mirror wearing a white towel robe and a towel over her wet hair.

After a few moment she began to gently touch her lips. As she did so, she closed her eyes and let out a breath. Then she slowly touched down her neck and chest. With the backs of her fingers she stroked her breast underneath the robe. Letting out deep breathes as she did. As she caught herself doing so, she came to an immediate stop and continued trying to put creme on her face. Again Lizbeth felt the need to sensually rub the creme on her face and followed with rubbing down her neck with both her hands.

The towel on her head fell off and she began to untie the white towel robe. At this point Lizbeth felt lightheaded and tried to hold on to the bathroom counter. Carefully she tried to take steps out of the bathroom letting the bath robe drop to the ground. She did her best to rush over to the bed, letting out small moaning sounds. When she got to the bed she crawled on it and laid on her stomach, then turned around moaning and groaning touching neck, face, thighs. The feeling grew stronger and she moaned even more, gripping the bed sheets as she did, almost as if she was begging to be made love to. Just then Leo walked through the bedroom door and saw Lizbeth's state. He immediately shut the bedroom door behind him and locked it. Then rushed over to Lizbeth.

"I am here my love. I see you are ready for me. I will not disappoint you".

Lizbeth moaned and reached out to Leo, who was untying his robe as fast as he could. He then climbed onto Lizbeth. He kissed her as he spoke and caressed her. As he did so she moaned even louder.

"My love. I told you I would come see you tonight so we could be together. I have missed you. I have longed to see you desire me in this way again. You are mine, Lizbeth. Mine!"

I awoke the next morning naked under the covers. I looked around the room and saw the robe where I dropped it.

What came over me last night, or was it a dream. It must have been a dream. I would have known better than to let Leo touch me again. Each time I closed my eyes I saw him on me and I remember feeling his kisses. But it seemed like a blur. I was sure it was just a dream. Could it have been the new birth control pills I was taking?

I could't lose too much time thinking on on that. I spent most of my days trying to figure out how to escape, and that morning was no different than the rest. I needed to figure out a plan. I dressed myself and thought I needed to think thing from a different angle. So I decided to have breakfast in the dinning room patio. Leo had already left for the day, so this gave me time to look out and see what I could do or where I go. I wanted to know how many men there were watching the house. Where they stood and for how long. If they changed shift, what time did they do so. Anything that could help me gain some knowledge and possibly a way of escape. I stood there watching for hours. That is when I noticed a midday shift change. I tried to watch how it was done, but just then all the men disappeared behind the bush.

Alex had just come downstairs and was passing through the dinning room. He reached out for a pear on the table when he noticed Lizbeth out in the patio. He felt annoyed with her and walked over to the patio. When he got there he leaned against the door way and watched Lizbeth as she slowly paced back and forth. He couldn't help himself from admiring her. At one point he tried to turn away, but then looked at her again. Her legs, her neck, her hair that blew in the breeze. He tried to fight what he was feeling.

"Whatever you are planning, just know it will not work".

Lizbeth was startled and she abruptly turned to face Alex.

"Excuse me?"

"My father is a very smart man. He will know how to figure you out".

Alex began to approach Lizbeth until he was standing in front of her. She took a few steps back.

"I haven't figured you out yet, but I will. And I will be sure to let my father know of all you plans".

"How dare you. You and your father are so much alike. Watch all you want and try to figure me out all you want. I will find a way".

Lizbeth tried to walk away and Alex grabbed her by the arm and brought his face close to her.

"You will not toy with us. In the end you will be the one losing".

Lizbeth snatched her arm away from Alex and walked away. Clara had been spying on them and later that evening she reported this to Leo.

"This is good news. The rumors we started about Lizbeth have taken root in my Alex's mind. He will detest her, which will keep him away from her so he will not know the truth".

"Or fall in love with her, sir".

"Yes, or fall in love. The more he hates her the less I need to worry about him falling in love and trying to help her escape. For now, he is my only son. I do not want to have him killed for trying to take what belongs to me".

Days passed and I wandered the house often. Whenever no one was watching, I would sneak into one of the rooms and search in them to see if I could find something. Anything to help. A laptop, a tablet, an extra phone, a landline, anything. If I did find something, there was never any signal. It made me furious.

Some days were difficult for me to do my searching, because though I acted like I did not notice him, Alex would be watching me. I was sure his father sent him to do so. On those days I was careful with the movements I made. Instead I would go to the hall of artwork, where I studied the painting of the boat. Trying to once again get at least my hand in the painting, just like I did before. Somedays, I would spend hours in that hall. I would see Alex pass by a few times. Even Leo would pass by since it was on the way to his office.

"Again, my love? I see how much you truly appreciate the arts. If you'd like I could build you an entire room of art. Or right on these grounds I could have an enormous building built to fit all your artwork from your museum..."

"No! Do not touch my artwork. It is all my friends have left of me. I am sure Philip and Tiara are caring for all of it. It belongs to them now"."
Leo nodded in agreement and walked off.

"What do you mean there is nothing you can do. Our friend is in trouble. You heard the voicemail she left us".

"I truly am sorry, Philip. As I have said. There is nothing we can do. Your friend, uh what was her name?"

"Lizbeth!"

"Yes, Lizbeth. Willingly married this man and left the country. It is out of our hands. The happens often where men come to marry woman from the states and take them back to their country. The only thing she can do is call the police where she is now. Hopefully they can help her get into contact with us and they can protect her until she flies back to the states".

"This is unbelieved, our friend is being held against her will and no one can help her? I have no other choice, but to go down there myself and rescue her".

"I would not recommend that. As I have said, if you leave the state you are no longer under our protection either, which means, if this man is as powerful as you say he is, there could be men waiting for you to either kill you or trap you away with her".

"So what? We do nothing?"

"We wait. Maybe she can get a hold of the police and tell them her situation. Once she does then maybe she can be helped. For all we know she could already be under their protection and we just have to wait to hear from her. Especially if she has to be put into hiding. It could be months before you hear from her again".

Philip grabbed his phone from on top of the officers desk and barged out of the room. Tiara sighed.

"Thank you officer. You can tell we are under a lot of distress. We are really worried for our friend".

"Please believe me when I say that I feel for you both, I really do. I don't mean to offend, but two months to marry and leave the states was a little too soon. It would have been best to wait longer, at least before leaving the states with someone she met two months prior. This happens more often than you can imagine. I wish I could do more".

Tiara nods and gets up from the chair and walks off. She meets up with Philip outside, who is frustratedly waiting by the car with his arms crossed.

"Philip....."

"No, no, no. That is not okay. No one can do anything to help our friend. She is all alone trapped with that evil man. We should have seen this coming. We should have been smarter. She is the Art Guardian for goodness sake. We should have protected her. All this talk about having babies, we pushed her into this, so we would not lose our ability to open the gate, and now look".

Tiara grabbed Philip in a tight hug as he cried on her shoulder.

"We have to find a way Philip. We just need to put our heads together to figure this out".

After a few moments, Philip jumps back.

"I think I might have a plan. Let's go home, I will tell you all about it on the drive home".

He runs over to the passenger side and Tiara opens the car door and climbs into the drivers seat and they drive off.

Leo was seated at the dinning table when Clara walked in with his breakfast and laid it in front of him. He folded his newspaper and placed it off to the the side.

"Well?"

"Nothing sir. Lizbeth passed her menstruation as she normally does. It ended a few days ago".

"I do not understand. Shouldn't she have been with child by now. I knew she had birth control when we I first brought her here. But this was two month ago. Shouldn't she be ready by now? I do not understand how that works".

"It is too soon to tell, Mr. Ferreira. We could try again tonight if you'd like. Now is when she would be ready and ripe".

"Yes, my wife needs something to bring her joy. She walks this house with so much sadness. I wish to no longer see her this way. Give her the mixture tonight. I will be with my wife. Maybe it will take this time and she will be filled with joy after having our child".

"Yes, sir".

Before leaving to work that morning, Leo came to my room. I was in the balcony as always. If I was a bird I would have already flown away to escape my fate.

"Good morning my love".

"What is it that you want?"

"Lizbeth, it has been a month now. Will you still not forgive me?"

"In total it has been two months since I was deceived, kidnapped, and imprisoned. The only way to forgive is to be freed. But you know this already".

"What if I moved your museum, your friends, and all that you had in the states and brought them all here. Would that make you happy?"

"Leo, how could you even ask me this. People are not couches or lamps that you can throw into a moving truck and place in your home for display. I would never ask you to entrap my friends as you have done to me. I only stay to keep them safe and happy where they are".

"Then tell me, how else can I make you happy..."

"By setting me free! Let me go home".

"Anything, but that. To let you go would be like putting myself to death".

"Oh we would not want to cause you any pain now would we? As long as Leo has what he wants than all is well".

"Do not mock me, Lizbeth".

"How else then should I respond? Tell me".

Leo rushed up to me and grabbed me in a tight embrace. I tried to push him off and instead he pushed me up against the wall.

"Stop! Just stop fighting me for one moment. Have you thought for maybe one second, that if you obeyed my request and did what I asked, you could have eventually seen your friends again".

"How long Leo, how long would that take? Years? To deceive me and strip me away from all I love is a way of torture. Why should I submit to someone who takes pleasure in harming me this way".

"Lizbeth, I do not want to harm you. My actions may not seem right, I understand this. But I cannot think straight with you".

Leo let me go, turned away from me and stood close to the balcony railing.

"I am not the same man. I was stronger, but now I have been weakened, because of you. I know no other way of obtaining what I want, except in taking It by force".

"You could have had me freely, without using force, but you chose deceit instead. What did I do so wrong to you to be treated in this way?"

He turned abruptly and grabbed me again. This time with both arms around my back, pinning my arms between our chest.

"You did nothing wrong my love".

"Leo, let me go".

"That is the problem. I cannot. I do not know how, nor do I want to. I want to hold you in my arms tightly and never let go".

"Stop saying these things. Please, you say them to me all of the time and I do not feel loved, I feel owned like a piece of property.

"Let me show you that I love you. Let me prove it to you".

"Love is doing anything to avoid causing another harm. Even if it means making sacrifices. You sacrifice nothing and only take. And you take by force. That is not love".

Leo suddenly let me go and stared at me for a moment. Then he turned and walked away. I heard my bedroom door slam as he left.

That evening I took my birth control like I normally did. I had only two packs left. Two months to keep myself safe in case Leo tried to take me by force. If he did, he would not be able to get me pregnant. I think my fears got the better of me, because I believe I had another dream where Leo and I were making love.

Clara knocked then entered Leo's office.

"Mr. Ferreira, I wanted to inform you that the flower is ripe, should not be long now".

"Thank you, Clara".

Leo leaned back in his chair and smiled. Then he slowly stood up and began walking out of his office. He took his time going up the steps.

Lizbeth had almost finished showering as she washed off the soap from her body. Suddenly she smiled and sensually rubbed her arm. Stroking softly up her arm and onto her neck. She began to moan and laid her back up against the shower wall to avoid losing her balance. She moaned louder and Leo heard her when he entered her room. He shut the door behind him and locked it. He could still hear Lizbeth moaning in the shower. After he walked into the bathroom he looked at Lizbeth moaning and trying to hold onto the shower wall. He began to take his clothes off. When he was naked he opened the shower door and stepped in. Lizbeth took some steps forward and landed in his arms.

"This is how I want you, Lizbeth. Just like this".

He roughly kissed her and she kissed back. Within moments Leo was making love to Lizbeth with her back against the shower wall.

Afterward he wrapped her in a towel and carried her to the bed where he laid her down. He removed her towel and his. Then lied beside her.

"Let me hold you tonight. I have not held you this way in many nights".

Lizbeth was still under the affect of the mixture so she caressed Leo's hair and face. Leo lifted his head and kissed Lizbeth. It was not long before he was making love to her again. After the second time he made love to her, the mixture had Lizbeth sound asleep. Leo also was asleep with his arms wrapped around Lizbeth.

A little before the sun came up, Leo had woken up. He realized he had overslept. He slowly tried to slip his arm out from underneath Lizbeth. Then he climbed out of the bed and quickly walked to the bathroom where he put his pants on and picked up the rest of his clothes and shoes. Then he rushed out of Lizbeth's bedroom.

When Lizbeth awoke, she thought she had another crazy dream of making love with Leo. Yet this time she found herself naked and two towels were on the ground. She stood up form the bed and walked into the bathroom. When she looked toward the shower, the flashbacks were so vivid. Lizbeth took a step back and stepped on something. When she looked down she saw a tie. She picked it up and knew it was Leo's tie. Lizbeth rolled up the tie and placed it in her draw.

I said nothing about the tie. But I was sure something was wrong. I was beginning to think that these dreams I've had where I am making love with Leo, are not dreams at all. It must be happening, but how? Was I being drugged? And if so, how? Was it in something I ate or drank. Was it in my bath salts or shower wash. What could it be and why was he doing this? All I did know was, it was during the night. When I came to think of it, it was not long after dinner. Within the hour of eating dinner, I would feel relaxed and sensual. Then everything would become a blur, like a dream. I had to find out what was going on and I had to be aware of when. If I was being drugged, then whatever was being used had to be in the kitchen. Clara must be serving it to me.

I waited until the day I Knew Clara would leave the house to do her shopping. That day I carefully roamed the house. Leo's driver was gone, which meant Leo had left as well. The only one I had to watch for was Alex. When I saw him pass, I hid. Then I rushed off to the kitchen. Desperately I began searching and searching. Anything that could prove I was being drugged. A vial, a small bottle, a pill, anything.

I did not find what I was looking for, but behind a small curtain I found something worse. I was a signal jammer. This was why I could never use my phone, why the tablet I found had no signal. This was what Leo used all along to avoid me for speaking to Philip and Tiara. That is why I could not get any signal within the white line he had painted outside the house.

After my shock I stepped back for a moment and realized that now I could make a call, I turned the jammer off. After the jammer had no power I ran upstairs to my bedroom. I looked everywhere. All the draws, under the bed, the closet, everywhere. I could not find the second phone Leo gave me. I then ran towards the bedroom where I had once found a tablet. Once I got there I rummaged through everything, the tablet was gone. I began to panic. I knew now why there was no signal, but all the electronic were gone. There was nothing, nowhere to be found. I was infuriated. No matter what I did, I was trapped. I could not control my anger and I went to the kitchen to search for the biggest knife I could find. When I looked around I saw on the wall was a shiny new chef's knife. I pulled it off of the magnetic strip, then I pulled the jammer out of the outlet and placed it on the counter. While holding the knife handle with both my hands I lunged the knife into the jammer.

I knew Leo had the means to purchase another, but I wanted to send him a message. I then lifted the knife with the jammer on its end and walked to Leo's office, where I placed it on his desk and walked out of his office.

Lizbeth exited Leo's office and ran into Alex. He stood back and looked at her suspiciously.

"This is my father's study".

"I am aware of that".

"What were you doing in there. He is not here. He stepped out for a moment and will be returning shortly".

"I do not care about your father's whereabouts".

"Then why enter his study if...."

"Why so many questions?"

Lizbeth tried to walk away towards her bedroom and Alex blocked her. She then walked into the living room. Alex followed behind her and reached for some cherries in a bowl on the table. Lizbeth turned to face Alex and in anger she slapped the cherries right out of his hands.

"What is it with you? Did your father send you to spy on me? Is that it, he sent you to spy?"

"I do not know what you are talking about and I do not spy on you".

"Oh no, then why every time I am walking the halls and I look over my shoulder, there you are watching my every move".

"Fine, you want to know why I watch you? I want to know what your game is. What are you plotting and planning against my father. He has given you everything and still you seek for more. You are an ungrateful woman".

"How dare you! Ungrateful? You believe me to be ungrateful? You barely know me".

"I know woman like you Mrs. Lizbeth. Self-seeking and ungrateful".

Lizbeth already angry became even more enraged with Alex's word and she slapped him. He responded with more words and so did she. To the point they were both yelling over each other. Just then Leo walked into the house and heard the yelling. He ran over to the living room. After a few moments Clara also stepped into the kitchen with two grocery bags and she could also hear the yelling and went towards the living room.

"What is going on here with you two?"

"What is going on here father is that your wife is an ungrateful woman, who feels she can strike a man when it pleases her".

Lizbeth was about to jump on Alex to hit him when Leo jumped in front of her to calm her down.

"Lizbeth, enough!"

"No! Enough with the both of you! You are both so much alike. Father and son. You both speak and nothing but wickedness comes out of your mouths. The father is the deceitful one and the son is the spoiled imp".

"Imp? No one speaks to me like this..."

"That is quite enough. Lizbeth please. I will escort you to your room".

"I do not need escorting, I already know the way".

Lizbeth turned around and walked off. When she got to her room she slammed the door closed.

Clara walked over to Alex.

"Come, I will make you a tea to calm your nerves. She can be a difficult woman sometimes".

"Father, I...."

"Alex, please. Go with Clara, drink a tea to calm your nerves. Then we can speak".

Alex walked away with Clara and Leo stood there and grinned.

"Perfect. The two hate each other. This worked out better than I thought".

Leo then turned and walked towards his office, when he walked in he saw something on his desk. He got closer to find the jammer with a chef's knife through it. This made him angry so he turned and went to Lizbeth's room. When he got there he barged into her bedroom.

"What is the meaning of your ridiculous display of rebellion! Are you trying to provoke me, Lizbeth?"

"You are both cut from the same evil cloth. Alex and you..."

"I am not talking about Alex! I am talking about the message you left me on my desk".

"Ah, that. So you want explanations now do you? Well, so do I!"

Lizbeth walked over to her bathroom and roughly opened the draw shaking everything inside. She then pulled out Leo's tie that she found. He followed her to the bathroom and stood in the entryway. Lizbeth held up the tie, then threw it at Leo.

"You place jammers in the home so I could never call for help, you drug me to seduce me and make me think it was just a dream. But in your foolishness you left evidence behind. Did you think I was stupid enough to never question what was happening to me? You are truly a monster. There is no other word for you than that".

"Lizbeth, please. I can explain the tie. I want us to have a child together, but you will not give yourself to me. I had to find a way. It was a harmless mix added to your drink at night. I have done no wrong, you are my wife. I did not want to take you by force, this was the only way...."

Just then Leo bumped into the draw that Lizbeth had the tie in. She had not closed it after removing the tie. When Leo looked down he noticed something. Lizbeth's anger turned to panic.

"Leo, no!"

"What is this? Is this birth control? Where did you get this? This is why you are still not pregnant from me".

Leo held up the packet staring at Lizbeth. She looked back at him in fear and gently nodded.

"Please. Leo. I cannot have a child from you. I cannot. You do not understand what that would do.....LEO NO!

Leo began to press the pills through the packaging allowing them to fall down the sink drain. Lizbeth yelled and pleaded, trying to grab the packet from his hand.

Alex heard the yells and quickly stood up.

"Ignore them, Alex. They fight like this all the time".

"That does not sound like a fight, it sounds like Lizbeth is in trouble, what is my father doing to her?"

"Ignore them...."

Alex ran out of the kitchen and up the stairs towards Lizbeth's room. Clara followed behind. When Alex reached the top of the steps he ran into Lizbeth's bedroom and saw her struggling with Leo.

"Leo I beg of you, please don't".

Leo had already emptied the pack of pills down the drain and turned the faucet on. He then grabbed Lizbeth by the shoulders and threw her to the bathroom floor. She was crying uncontrollably.

"All I asked is that you obey me! You deceived me!"

"That is all you have done since the day I met you. You DECEIVED ME! Now I am your prisoner!"

"You are my wife!"

"I AM YOUR PRISONER!"

Leo rushed over to Lizbeth and grabbed her by the hair. She did her best to fight back.

"FATHER!"

Leo abruptly turned around to see his son standing there.

"Alex, this is no concern of yours. Leave and shut the door behind you."

"Father I will do no such thing, you are hurting her".

"No more than she has hurt me. Now leave!"

Alex did not agree with his fathers actions and looked towards Lizbeth and back at his father. Clara coaxed Alex out and he slowly turned and walked out of the room. Clara then shut the door.

"Come Alex. In time you will grow accustomed to their rants".

Alex acted like he was going down the stairs, then paused.

"Clara, I am going for a swim. All of this has been too much for me today and I need to do something to avoid hearing the sound of yelling echoing through these halls".

"Good idea, Alex".

Alex continued acting like he was going down the stairs and Clara turned to go down the service steps that led to the kitchen. Alex waited, then came back up the steps and ensured that Clara was gone. Then he came back towards Lizbeth's bedroom door to listen in. He could not hear anything yet, because Leo and Lizbeth were still in the bathroom.

"Tell me. Where did you get those pills. Who gave them to you? Was it any of my men? Who was he, I will kill him with my bare hands".

Lizbeth would not talk. Then Leo began to pull out her draws and flip them. As he did, he did not take notice on the birth control pills inside the hard cover, because they rolled up between some of Lizbeth's intimates. However, after making a huge mess he did find the padded envelope Philip and Tiara sent.

"I see. Your old faithful friends, again interfering with our business".

"I hate you. I hate you Leo, I wish I had never met you".

Leo turned to Lizbeth and pulled her up from the bathroom floor and pushed her up against the wall.

"You must make the decision to turn that hate back into love".

"No, that will never happen".

"You will have no more of anything to stop you from having a child with me. What will you do then? Hate our child? Would you be as cruel as to hate an innocent child?"

Lizbeth covered her face and cried. Then she gathered herself and looked at Leo.

"I could never hate a child that is of my blood. I would love my child and protect it with my own life, but you. You I will always hate".

"Not true, Lizbeth. You will learn to love me again. You will".

Leo began to forcefully kiss Lizbeth on her neck. She tried fighting him away, but couldn't push him back. As he continued to kiss her neck he began to confess.

"I did order to have all signal blocked. This way you could reach no one, but me. I am the only one you need. I ordered you to be drugged so you would not fight me. Lizbeth, each time was like our honeymoon night. You desired me, you wanted me, and I gave you what you wanted. I made love to you as you held me, yearning for more".

"Stop! Please stop!"

"Never!"

Leo grabbed Lizbeth by the shoulder and shook her once.

"I will never stop! You have to make a choice. You either give yourself to me willingly as my wife. Or I will drug you every night and have my way with you. Do not make me take it by force, or I will Lizbeth. I will!"

Lizbeth could not take it anymore and went into ranting rage.

"STOP IT! STOP IT!

Leo let her go and she ran into her bedroom collapsing onto the floor. This was when Alex could hear their conversation more clearly.

"I am losing my mind. Is that what you want? To drive me crazy and send me to an early grave. Then continue. Maybe that will free me from this prison".

"Lizbeth, not even the grave will get you away from me".

"Shut-up, stop talking. All you do is spew poison and threats if I do not do what you say".

"I give you choices…"

"Choices? It is not a choice when you tell me that I am to remain here with you to save the lives of my friends. And if I dare try to leave you, then they will be killed with one bullet to each of their heads. That is not a choice, Leo. You are not giving me a choice in having a child with you. The proof was just washed down the drain. That birth control was the only thing that protected me from birthing a child from a monster. You took everything from me and imprisoned me here. Clara and Alex are your spies whom you have watch me so I do not escape. And now you tell me that not even the grave will save me from you. I beg to differ. I don't know when or how, but I will get away from you. Even if we have ten children. I will find a way to run away with all of them, even if it means risking my life in the process. I WILL BE THEIR GUARDIAN, not you!"

Leo grew angrier with Lizbeth last words and rushed over to her and picked her up off the floor. He then took her over to the bed and threw her on it. He climbed on top of her as she struggled.

"Let us find out if you will be able to fight me, Lizbeth. You believe yourself to be so strong. I will show you who has the power here. You won't give yourself to me I will take you by force and we will have children that you will never take from me. And you will never escape me".

With Lizbeth's struggle she managed to scratch Leo's face, and it began to bleed. This made him stop. She pushed him off and rushed out of the bed.

He calmed himself and stood up from the bed.

"You leave me no other option. I will bring the drug to you myself and make you drink it. Then once you cannot contain yourself, I will take what is mine. Or shall I say, you will beg and willingly give me what is mine".

Leo began to go towards the bedroom door. When Alex heard this he hid in the hall. Leo came out of Lizbeth's room and closed the door behind him. Then turned around, pulled out a key, and locked her door. Then he went downstairs.

Several days passed and Lizbeth had been locked in her room. The door was unlocked only to bring her meals. Every meal tray that came out of Lizbeth's room had the juice untouched. Lizbeth was afraid to drink it, thinking Leo had added the mixture to it. She only drank the water in her room that sat in the decanter Alex watched and took notice that the only other person who had a key, besides his father, was Clara.

One morning after his father left for work and Clara left for her weekly shopping, Alex snuck over towards Lizbeth's room. He gently knocked on the door. Lizbeth was sitting up on her bed in deep thought when she heard the knock. She was surprised to hear a knock. No one have ever done so before. She stood up from the bed and walked over to the door.

"Lizbeth? It's Alex. I know you may not want to speak to me. I do not blame you. I have been cruel to you. It was because I was misinformed. I was told you were the cruel one and, well, that you were using your youth and beauty to take advantage of my father. But several days ago you said things that made me think differently. You said you were a prisoner. I have laid in bed night after night thinking of your words. Then I realized that you never leave the house. You are...were allowed only to roam behind the white line. You hid contraceptives to not become impregnated and you will not give yourself to my father. Your anger has not been caused by ingratitude, but more like bitterness. Bitterness of being imprisoned. What I do not understand is why? Why would my father do this to you? I have so many questions and I believe only you can answer them for me. When you are ready of course".

Lizbeth placed her hands on the door as she listed to Alex's words. Then she walked away and got a piece of paper and wrote something on it. She laid onto her stomach in front of the door and slid it under. Alex noticed the paper and bent over to pick it up. Then he laid on his stomach and looked under the door to see just enough of Lizbeth's face. She smiled at him. He smiled back.

"If you are nothing like your father and now know that I am a captive here. Then call that number. Place your phone close to the door and allow me to speak to my friends. Doing so will answer some of the many questions I am sure you have".

Lizbeth lifted her head and closed her eyes. She was sure he wouldn't do it. Just then she heard cell buttons being pressed. Her eyes widened and she placed her hand on the door waiting. Then she heard the line ringing on speaker. Just then she heard him.

"Hello?"

"Philip!"

"Lizbeth!"

"Philip, say nothing and listen. Alex bring the phone as close as you can underneath the door".

"Who is Alex? Lizbeth where are you? We have been worried sick after you last message where you were yelling about being kidnapped".

"Philip, listen. I don't have much time. You have to escape. Leo has threatened to kill you and Tiara if I try to escape. He has men watching you both at all times. You have to try and escape without being noticed".

"Tiara and I have seen the men who sit outside in the car. They change shifts three times a day. We have called the police and they leave, only to return again".

"Those are Leo's men. Please, be careful. I need to know that you are both safe".

"What about you Lizbeth? How can we help you?"

"You can't Philip. Please, I just need to know you are both safe and then I will figure out what to do".

"How do we reach you again?"

"You can call this number. It's mine. My name is Alex".

"Alex, who are you? Are you helping Lizbeth? Please protect her".

"Philip, listen there is no time. Do what I ask."

Just then Alex heard the front door open. Philip tried to get another word out.

"Wait, Lizbeth...."

Alex hung up the phone.

"Someone is here. I will return again Lizbeth".

Lizbeth was so happy she placed her fingers under the door. Alex saw this and placed his fingers on hers then looked underneath the door to see Lizbeth with tears running down her cheek and onto the floor, but smiling in gratitude with Alex. They stood looking at each other this way for a moment. Then Alex heard steps coming up.

"I must go".

He rushed up off of the floor and went running down the service steps and towards the indoor pool, where he undressed himself quickly and jumped in. The person coming up the steps was Leo. When he reached the top of the steps he walked over to Lizbeth's door and placed his hand on it. He stood there for a moment silent, then removed his hand from the door and walked to his bedroom.

After the call was disconnected Philip went running to wake Tiara up. He told her everything. She jumped out of bed and they began to pack as quick as they could. Then they rushed up to the attic and took the painting Philip's mother was in and brought it downstairs. As Tiara entered the painting with everything they packed, Philip grabbed the laptop and began to schedule a portrait pickup and delivery. He purchased the shipping, printed the label and stuck it onto the portrait. Then placed it outside the side of the house. He then printed another paper that read that the portrait for pickup was on the side of the house and taped it to the front door. Then he went back to the portrait outside, opened the gate and entered it.

The next morning the delivery service truck rolled up to the house and read the note. The delivery person went to the side of the house, pickup the painting, loaded it onto the truck and drove off. Leo's men watched the whole time.

The painting went through the delivery process, until is was left a hotel. The front desk person received the delivery and placed it in room 578 as the delivery instructed requested. Especially since that room had already been reserved.

Shortly after the delivery Philip and Tiara came out of the painting.

"Just in time. Okay, as soon as we get signal we call that number".

"Who is this guy anyway, Philip?"

"That is exactly what I am going to find out. Got signal. Let me call. It's ringing. Dam, voicemail! Let me try again".

Alex was having lunch with his father at a restaurant by the water. His phone vibrated a second time with Philip's call. He declined the call. Two missed calls so far. A third call came in with Philip's number.

"Are you going to get that son?"

"It's Ben. I will let him know I am busy, so he can call me again later. When he calls this much it is either for a party or he is arguing with his parents, which leads to a party out of rebellion".

Leo chuckled. Alex answered the third call from Philip and played it cool as if he was talking to Ben.

"Ben, whatever it is, it will have to wait. I am having lunch with my father".

"What?"

"How did I know you would call about a party. You can tell me with more detail later".

Just then the waitress approached the table. Philip and Tiara heard the conversation between the waitress and Leo.

"Mr. Ferreira would you like me to refill your wine".

"No, bring the check. I have an important meeting after this lunch I must get to".

"Of course Mr. Ferreira".

"Alex, talk to your friend later. This is all the time we have together before I have to go".

"Hey Ben, later we speak my friend. I will call you right after lunch with my father".

Alex hung up the phone and Philip and Tiara looked at each other speechless.

"He's the son of Leo Ferreira? I thought his son was a kid. That did not sound like a kid. How in the world are we going to trust the son of a kidnapper".

"Tiara, you took the words right out of my mouth, but this is the first time we have heard from Lizbeth in almost three months. This is all we have to go by".

"What about your last plan. Is that still in play? What do we do about that?"

"I sent two letters in the past weeks that were made to sound like we were telling Lizbeth that she was being searched for. I was lying of course, but we already tried to get help and the police couldn't do anything to help because she is out of the country. There was no response to my letters. Either they knew I was lying or the letters have not been received yet. So now I don't know what to do. I'm the last person who would want this kind of advice, but now we do have to wait".

Tiara and Philip waited and waited. Hours had passed and the evening fell in. Philip opened the door to pay for their Chinese food delivery. As he took the order and closed the door, his phone rang. Tiara and him both ran for it and Philip picked it up first. He put it on speaker and waited.

"Hello?"

"Yes, I'm here. Now can you please explain to me what the hell is going on here and where is my friend Lizbeth".

"Please, I have just recently learned of Lizbeth situation so I do not have many answers. Questions I have, as I am sure you do as well".

"Okay, fine. Let's get through them as best we can with what we know so far. Let's start off with, who are you and how do we know we can trust you to help Lizbeth".

"I am Leo's son, Alex".

"We got as far as to figure that out, how the hell do we know we can trust you, Alex".

"Calm down, Tiara. What my friend is trying to say is..."

"I know what she is trying to say. I am not part of what is happening to Lizbeth. I just returned from abroad where I was studying at my university. When I got home I had learned that my father was married. They made me believe that Lizbeth was cruel and only interested in my fathers money, using her beauty and youth to seduce him".

"Well, I can tell you that, that is far from the truth".

"I am aware now. What I do not know, is how to help her escape. My father has way too many men surrounding the house. They check any vehicles that come in and out. It would be almost impossible to sneak her out of the house, day or night".

"Listen to me closely, Alex. There is only one way. I cannot tell you what it is. But Lizbeth will understand. Tell her the exact words I am about to tell you".

Alex raced home to give Lizbeth the message. When he got there he noticed his father was not home yet. He quietly entered the house and rushed towards the kitchen. Trying to avoid from being seen. When he looked into the kitchen he saw Clara was busy working on dinner. He then raced up the servant stairway to Lizbeth's room. There he softly knocked on the door then laid on the floor to look underneath. He saw Lizbeth come running and lay on the floor. He smiled at her. She smiled back.

"Your friends have escaped, they are safe. They told me to tell you, 578 is the way".

Lizbeth covered her face and cried from both joy and relief her friends were safe.

"There is more. I told them how heavily guarded my father's home is. The one named Philip told me to tell you these exact words. 'Request a shipment and open the gate. That is the only way out'. He said you would know what that means".

"I do. I do know what it means. But, I don't know how to open the gate".

"Maybe, I can help. What gate needs to be opened?"

"No, you can't help with this. I will be okay. I just need time. I will speak with your father and ask his forgiveness, so he will allow me out of this bedroom. Then I can try".

"What can I do then for you, Lizbeth?"

"For now, there is nothing you can do. You have done more than enough. You have saved the lives of my friends. I am forever in your debt. Now I am on my own".

"You are not on your own. Please, count with me. I want to help you".

"Thank you. May...may I ask why?"

"I feel regret to have treated so you so badly, when this whole time you were a prisoner. You must have thought the worse of me. But also, my mother was at time my fathers prisoner. I would not wish for you the same fate. The kind that makes you want to run away so quickly that you even leave your child behind".

Lizbeth took pity on Alex's response and reached out her fingers to him again. He touched her fingers and they stood this way as they stared at each from under the door.

"Thank you for being what I have not had these past months".

"What would that be?"

"A friend. Now go. I would not want you to be seen by Clara or your father".

Alex nodded in agreement and stood up and walked off. Lizbeth stood up and paced the room. She was so happy that Philip and Tiara were safe. She also understood the code 578. That was their emergency hiding place, if they ever needed one. Lizbeth now knew she had to somehow learn how to open the gate. Once she learned to do so, she would request that a painting be shipped to the states and before it did, she would hide in it. This way she would be taken right out of the house. However, she needed to get out of the room and into the hall of artwork to practice how to open the gate. It was her only hope. She saw it was 4pm and rushed to the bathroom where her last packet of birth control was hidden in a new draw. There were only two weeks left of pills.

"I know what I have to do. Let's hope it does not come to that, but just in case. I have two weeks left".

Hours later Clara walked into the room with her dinner.

"Clara, tell my husband I want to speak with him".

Clara nodded, but was suspicious of Lizbeth's request. She immediately shut the bedroom door and locked it. Then she rushed to Leo's office. She knocked twice and walked in.

"Yes, Clara. Is dinner ready?"

"Sir, your wife asked to speak to you".

"She did? Did she say about what?"

"No sir".

Leo leaned back in his chair and crossed his arms.

"Now I am intrigued. I will go to her".

Leo stood up and walked to Lizbeth's room. He unlocked her bedroom door and walked in. Lizbeth was in the balcony where she had watched the sun set. Leo walked out onto the balcony.

"You asked to speak to me?"

"I did".

He walked up to Lizbeth and stood beside her looking into her face. She lowered her head.

"I do not want to be locked in this bedroom any longer".

"I see. Yet, you cannot be trusted, can you?"

"I can. I will prove to you that I can".

Leo looked at Lizbeth wondering what was her mystery. Then he grinned.

"Kiss me".

Lizbeth suddenly looked at Leo surprised at his request.

"What?"

"Kiss me. If you want to prove that you can be trusted, do so by showing me your affection. Then if I feel you are true to your kiss. I will let you roam the house again and you will no longer be confined to your bedroom".

"Leo, your request is too much. The anger and hatred I feel towards you is stronger than any affection I could ever show you. So even if I kissed you, it would be filled with hatred".

Leo took steps closer to Lizbeth and wrapped his left arm around her stomach and waist. With his other hand he caressed her hair pushing it back. Then he softly kissed her neck.

"If you cannot show me affection yet, then I ask that you not fight me. Do not fight me any longer and I will not keep you under lock and key".

Zealously Leo kissed at Lizbeth's neck. She slightly pushed him away, but he gripped onto her even more. Then he untied the string on her dress that made it come loose.

"Leo please. I can't. Not yet".

"You can, and you will".

Leo pulled her inside of the bedroom and led her towards the bed. Then stood behind her kissing her neck as he pulled her dress down allowing to fall to the ground. Leo desperately pulled off his shirt, popping the buttons because he was too desperate to try and open them one by one. As he did Lizbeth nodded and tried to get away. He grabbed her from behind again.

"I can't Leo. Please. Give me time".

"You are my wife, Lizbeth. You do not need time to be with your husband".

He lifted her up and brought her close the bed again. Where he turned her around and began to kiss her. She tried hesitating and turning her face, but he then went down her neck. He continued pulling pieces of clothing off, almost as if he was enjoying the game. Then he began to kiss her neck gently and softly. He lifted his head and looked at Lizbeth. Her looked down to see her arms covering her breast.

"You are going to lie back and remove your arms. Reveal to me and prove that you are giving yourself to me willingly. You can hate me or despise me, but you will let me have you".

Lizbeth shut her eyes and began to breath hard from anger, while clenching her teeth. He knew she was angry and so he tried to taunt her.

"I'm sorry, is there something you want to say to me Lizbeth?"

She angrily opened and rolled her eyes to look away from him. Then sat in the bed and pushed herself back.

"Now, say the words I want to hear. Say them!"

"I give myself to you willingly, Leo".

He slowly climbed into the bed grabbing the back of Lizbeths head and chin and kissing her. She could not turn her face. He continue forward until she was on her back. Then Leo let her head and chin go and grabbed her hands interlocking his fingers with hers and putting them over her head. As she tried to turn her face away he continued kissing her neck. Leo made love zealous Lizbeth. When he was done, he laid on Lizbeth, out of breath. He smiled.

"Lizbeth. You are truly the love of my life. I will never let you go. Ask of me what you want. Anything you want I will give it to you, anything but to leave this house, and it is yours. You have truly made me a happy husband tonight".

Leo lifted himself up and climbed off of Lizbeth. Then he pulled her up and held her in his arms, placing his forehead on hers.

"You will see, my love. You will forget the life you once had and begin a new one with me. You will be happy. You will see. I will put the world at your feet. We will have children and be a family. You will love me and give yourself to me always".

Leo then pick her up from the waist and spinned her around. Then slowly let her down.

"Tonight we sleep in each others arms".

Leo let Lizbeth go and picked up his clothes. He tapped kissed her lips and went into the bathroom. Lizbeth grabbed the bedsheet and wrapped it around herself and lightly cried. Then gathered herself.

"Two weeks. I have to learn how to open the gate in two weeks or I will be trapped with his child in my belly".

Being free to walk the house allowed me to spend time in the hall of artwork again. And so there I was in front of the painting of the boat on the ocean, doing everything I could think of to open the gate.

"One would think you were looking for a passageway on that painting".

"Oh, Alex. You startled me".

"Sorry, I did not mean to. I am glad to see you are free to roam the house again".

"Yes, I am glad as well".

"I have also noticed you only come to this hall. There is so much more to do in this house".

"There is nothing I want to do here, Alex. Nothing except..."

"Leave. I know. How did you get my father to let you out of your room?"

I looked at Alex, but could not answer him. Alex walked up to me and stared at my facial expression.

"Lizbeth? Did you? Did you sleep with my father?"

"Alex, there are things that cannot be explained".

"No. Some things can be easily explained. A simple yes or no..."

"I had to! In order for him to allow me to leave the bedroom freely, I had to submit to him".

"I'm sorry Lizbeth. I didn't mean to..."

"No, it is fine. You would not understand even if I tried to explain. For woman things are different then they are for me".

"Lizbeth?"

"There are times we have to submit our bodies and allow them to taunt us and torment us for their own pleasures and sexual desires and it can be enough to want to drive any woman crazy..."

"Lizbeth?"

"But no, men do not have to deal with these kinds of things. At worse they marry a woman they are not attracted to, but at least a man needs to make no effort to do what he needs to do. And he feels nothing before, during, or after..."

"Lizbeth!"

"I'm sorry, I just....I".

Alex stepped closer to Lizbeth and embraced her. She embraced him back and began crying on his shoulder. Then she gathered herself and stepped back.

"Thank you. For not judging me and making me feel worse than I already do".

"Lizbeth, you are an amazing woman. I know my father saw that in you. But his actions on how he obsesses over you are not justifiable. They are completely wrong. You are a woman that can be easily loved. You do not care for things, instead you care for the lives of others. I am sorry you had to endure that."

"It doesn't look like it will end any time soon either. Unless I..."

"Open the gate?"

"Yes".

"I honestly don't know what gate you speak of, but I do know that you look like you need something to raise your spirits. Maybe if you feel better it can help you achieve this, this, search?"

"There is nothing I want to do more right now than to open the gate".

"One hour, that is all I ask and you can return to your work. I promise. One hour is probably all we can do before my father gets home anyway. I would not want to cause him jealousy".

"Something that would bother your father? Now you have my attention".

Alex chuckled and took me by the hand. He led me to the indoor pool. It was so big and beautiful.

"I did not know this pool was even here".

"As I have said. There is more to enjoy in this house, than just paintings. Here, I was not sure of your size, so the lady in the store helped me. She said this would fit".

Alex handed me a bathing suit in my exact size.

"How did she know my size?"

"Well, I described you. She asked for details and I told her how you were shaped here...and there...and she.."

"It's okay. It will fit perfect. I will go and change".

Lizbeth went into one of the rooms to change into the bathing suit leaving the door slightly opened. As Alex readied himself by taking off his shirt and pants he couldn't help but look in Lizbeth's direction. He paused to see her undress. He tried to turned his head, but then slowly turned back to watch her. When she walked out of the room and loosened her hair he gulped nervously. Lizbeth walked over to him and smiled.

"Wow!"

"What is it?"

"I have never seen you smile so happily before. I mean, except for underneath the door, but that was not the same as now".

"Are we going to swim or talk about my smile? I will meet you on the other side".

Lizbeth dived perfectly into the water and began to swim like a mermaid quickly and steadily to the other side. Alex stood watching in shock at how well and fast she swam. He quickly lost sight of her until she popped her head up on the other side.

"Are you coming in or what".

Alex smiled and cannonballed into the water. Lizbeth laughed and dived in again like a mermaid. Alex swam toward Lizbeth and she towards him. They met in the middle and circle around until swimming up to the surface.

"Wow, you swim so well".

"Well, when you have swum with mermaids as much as I have, you pick up a thing or two".

"Mermaids? Really? The things you say Lizbeth. Gates, paintings, mermaids? What next?"

"A race? From one end of the pool to the next".

"You're on".

Lizbeth let out a yelp as Alex tried to catch her. She quickly swam above the water to the starting point and Alex met her there.

"Ready, set, go!"

They both dived into the water and began swimming. Lizbeth was quicker and ahead of Alex. At one point she almost crossed over to his side right before reaching the end point. Alex grabbed onto her ankle. They both reached the end of the pool together.

"What was that?"

"You crossed over to my lane, mermaid".

"I did not. You grabbed my ankle and purposely slowed me down, because I was beating you".

They both had a friendly dispute as Lizbeth fought her case. Alex swam towards her showing the two sides in the water.

"See, this was my half and that was yours. You crossed over from yours, to block me from passing you".

Lizbeth laughed and kept pleading her case. Alex refused to give in. They decided to do it again. By the third time Alex continued to plead his case that Lizbeth had the habit of coming over to his side. Again he showed her the two sides. In doing so he swung his arm around Lizbeth and pulled her towards him.

"And you continue swimming over to my side like this".

Alex pulled Lizbeth close to him and they were both face to face. They both stopped talking and stared into each others faces. Alex couldn't contain himself and kissed Lizbeth. She pushed back and was shocked.

"I'm.. I'm sorry Lizbeth".

She turned around and swam over to the pool ladder and climbed out of the water.

"Lizbeth, wait!".

Alex got out of the water and chased after her. He tried to stop her by grabbing her hand.

"Lizbeth, please wait. I didn't mean to. I'm sorry. I did not want to cause you any...I just wanted you to have a swim and have fun".

"I did. Thank you".

"But, don't leave. I promise I won't do it again".

"I have work to do, Alex. Thank you for the swim, but I have to get out of this house and I only have two weeks left".

"Two weeks, why two weeks? Lizbeth!"

Lizbeth left the pool area and went towards her room. After she stepped into her bedroom she closed the door and laid her back against it. She touched her lips and felt so confused.

"No. I do not have time for any of this".

Lizbeth walked into her bathroom and began to run the water in her jacuzzi. She added bath salts and undressed herself.

Alex stood sitting at the end of the pool with his feet in the water. He kept replaying the kiss in his mind and how angry Lizbeth seemed. He grabbed his head.

"I'm such a dam fool".

He then climbed out of the pool and left the room. Lizbeth's jacuzzi was full of water and soap suds so she stepped in. She sat in the water and remembered Alex's kiss. She laid her head back and closed her eyes. When suddenly Alex walked into her bathroom still wearing nothing, but his swim shorts.

"Lizbeth! I'm sorry. I know I shouldn't had..."

"Alex! What are you doing here?"

Lizbeth grabbed a towel and quickly stood up using the towel to cover her body. She stepped out of the jacuzzi and walked towards Alex.

"You cannot be in here. If you father caught you here or Clara saw us, it would be terrible for both of us".

"Lizbeth, I know I shouldn't had kiss you. But I am not going to lie. I wanted to".

Alex approached Lizbeth and she took steps back.

"Alex, please. I do not want your father to think or believe the worse. He just allowed me to leave the bedroom. If he sees you in here he will surely lock me away again. I can't have him do that".

"Your right. I'm sorry. I don't want that for you either".

Alex turned around to walk away. Lizbeth followed behind. Alex then took a deep breath, stopped walking, turned around to face Lizbeth then grabbed her and kissed her. Lizbeth made the intent to push him back, but then suddenly gave in and allowed him to kiss her. Suddenly she realized that the kiss should not have been happening and pushed Alex back. He looked at her with regret and sighed.

"I now understand my fathers obsession with you Lizbeth. I am beginning to wonder if it is because of who he is, or the affect you have on men. You are like a drug to me. I admit I was overwhelmingly jealous when you told me you slept with him. I am fighting how I feel for you and I have never felt this before. What are you doing to me Lizbeth?"

"Alex, I have done nothing. Please, you have to leave. I am your fathers wife and this should not be happening. It is wrong and you know there would be consequences if he saw you in here. If you do feel anything for me, then protect me, by leaving this room...right now!"

Alex threw his head back knowing Lizbeth was right. He looked at her one more time, then turned and walked out of her room. Lizbeth fixed her towel and ran towards her bedroom door to lock it. Nervous and breathing hard she rushed back to the bathroom and into the jacuzzi. When she sat inside, she laid her back against it then and slide down into the water covering her face and head.

That night Leo had not been home yet and Lizbeth was laying on her stomach in her bed facing the balcony. She had left the doors open to allow the cool night breeze in. She looked at the moon and kept remembering the kiss with Alex in the pool and the passionate kiss in her bathroom.

Alex was in his bed tossing and turning. He turned facing up and pulled the cover off of his chest then placed his hand behind his head and began to think of Lizbeth. Remembering her smile, hearing her laugh, and remembering the kisses. He then climbed out of his bed and walked out to his balcony and looked at the moon.

"Lizbeth, what I would give, to have you with me tonight and hold you in my arms".

Just then, from a distance Lizbeth walked out to her balcony. When Alex saw her, he hid himself so she would not see him. He stared at her as she stood there looking at the moon. Her hair and silk nightgown blowing in the breeze. Suddenly they both heard Leo's driver pull up. Alex looked over at Lizbeth and noticed how nervous she had gotten. She took steps backwards, then turned around and ran inside. Quickly closing the balcony doors.

Alex went back into his room and with a swing of his arm knocked all the pillows off of the chaise at the foot of his bed. Then he sat on the chaise and buried his face into his hands.

He decided to go downstairs and get a drink to help him sleep, when he suddenly overheard his father talking to one of his men in the dining room area as he served a drink.

"What do you mean they disappeared?"

"The men noticed there wasn't any movement in the house for days. They checked inside. No one was in there. Their car was in the driveway and everything was still left in place".

"Did the men see anyone going or coming?"

"Nothing sir. The only movement the men saw was a painting that was picked up by a delivery service. But the men were watching. Nothing but the painting was put into the van".

"How the hell do two people escape a house unnoticed. They couldn't have left by foot. Someone would have seen them by now. Tell the men to roam the city. I want to know where they are. That is the only leverage I have on Lizbeth. She finds out they are safe and she will do everything in her power to runaway. Triple the men outside. Check every package that comes in and out. It only takes the carelessness of one man and she can escape. The man who fails to do his job, gets a bullet to the head. Tell them that, so they know they are working to stay alive".

"Yes sir".

Alex rushes back to his bedroom and closes the door. He then grabs his phone and starts to text Philip to warn them.

A: My dad knows you guys are gone. He has men roaming the town.

P: We have been hiding. We won't leave until Lizbeth is here. How is her progress.

A: She seems disappointed, so I guess it is not going well. What is it she is trying to do exactly? I want to help, but none of you are telling me what's going on.

P: The less you know, the better. Once Lizbeth learns how to open the gate and escapes, she will be free. But that man (Leo) is your father. I don't know what to tell you about that.

A: I still want to help. I do not care if he is my father. What he is doing to Lizbeth is sickening and I can't stand him for it.

P: He is still your father. You knowing too much can hinder Lizbeth's escape. Or worse. It can help him stop her or find her after she escapes. It's dangerous.

A: For who?

P: For you, your father, and worst off, for Lizbeth. If you really want to help her, just make sure she is calm and at peace. The calmer she is, the more it will help her to get the gate opened.

A: I guess I will never know what this whole gate thing is all about.

P: Maybe after Lizbeth is safe, we can share it with you.

A: After Lizbeth escapes, will I ever see her again?

P: Uh-oh....

A: Uh-oh what?

P: Are you falling in love with Lizbeth? I must warn you, you would be playing with fire. She is your fathers wife. Keep your feelings to yourself. This will cause her more confusion and panic and delay her ability to open the gate.

A: I'm sorry. I think it's too late. I kissed her today.

P:......

P:....

P: Let's try to use this to her benefit. Tell her I said to allow you to comfort her and to not fear you. Maybe your love for her can give her some kind of peace and make her feel safe enough to open the gate.

P: But I must warn you. You falling in love with her will not end well. You and your father will both be distraught after she is gone. And you CANNOT hold her back or your father WILL be the death of her.

A: I would rather die than let him hurt her.

P: Let's hope it doesn't come to that.

The next morning Clara walked into my room, rolled the cart in with my coffee and breakfast, then she left. I took my cup of coffee and sipped it as I walked onto the balcony. While in the balcony I heard my bedroom door open and close again. I found that to be odd. After Clara brings my breakfast she does not return for a couple of hours. I walked back into the room to find Alex standing there with his back against the door.

"Alex, what are you doing in here?"

He rushed over to me and pulled out his phone.

"I can help".

"What are you talking about?"

He showed me the text from Philip that read:

P: Let's try to use this to her benefit. Tell her I said to allow you to comfort her and to not fear you. Maybe your love for her can give her some kind of peace and make her feel safe enough to open the gate.

He then quickly took back the phone and would not let me see the rest of the messages.

"Why would he text that? Let me see what else he wrote".

"The other messages do not matter. What matters is what he is asking you to try. Let me help you. It is worth a try. If what I feel for you cannot help, then I will leave you alone".

I stood looking at Alex wondering if he could actually help. But if so, how would he be able to do so?

"Fine let me get dressed".

I put my coffee cup down and went to change. When I was ready, Alex opened the door and stuck his head out. When he was no one he took me by the hand and led me out of the room and down the stairs. We got up to the hall of artwork and he stopped.

"Now what Lizbeth? I have noticed that this is where you always come. Is there a secret passageway somewhere down this hall that you are trying to find?"

"Something like that".

I walked over to the painting with the boat and stood in front of it.

"You seem to be fascinated by this painting. Is this the one that carries a clue to find the gate you need to open?"

"Something like that".

"Now what then. Should I search behind them. Do you need me to take the painting down?"

"No. I need it to be silent and I need to have peace. For some reason this helps the gate reveal itself so it can be opened".

"Oh, I get it. Like the sound of the wind blowing through the hallways. That will give you a clue as to where the door or secret passageway is".

"Sure, the sound".

"In that case I will be silent, so you can listen. I will be right here if you need anything from me".

"Thank you, Alex".

Alex sat down on a bench underneath the painting next to the one with the boat I was standing in front of. I could feel him watching me, which made me feel uncomfortable.

"Alex, watching me does not help".

"I am sorry. I will stand behind you. Would that be better?"

"Yes, I think so".

After a few moments of Alex standing behind Lizbeth, he quietly took steps closer to her. He tried to be as quiet as possible as he closed his eyes and began to smell my hair. Then he carefully passed his fingers through her hair. Lizbeth turned to look at him.

"Alex, what are you doing?"

"I am not making a sound, but if this eases you and makes you fell calm, maybe it might help".

She turned back to look at the painting and reached her hands out to touch it. She placed both hands onto the painted water and closed her eyes. Alex continued passing his fingers through Lizbeth's hair. He then stepped even closer to Lizbeth, touching his body against hers. He placed his hand on her waist then laid his forehead on her head. With the same hand he used to pass through Lizbeth's hair, he then began to gently pull her hair off to the side, revealing her neck. He lifted his head and slowly came down to lay a soft kiss on Lizbeth's neck. Then another, and another. Lizbeth became very relaxed as she allowed Alex to do so. He then wrapped both his arms around Lizbeths waist and kissed her neck more intensely. Lizbeth began to feel her hands immersed in water. She could smell the ocean sea water and suddenly a gust of wind that she and Alex felt. It startled them both and Alex stopped kissing Lizbeth's neck.

"Did you fell that? Could it have come from the tunnel you are searching for?"

"I think so, Alex".

"I am sorry if I was too forward. I know something like that would relax me and I was just trying to help".

"All is forgiven. It was all in the name of help. I understand".

"Maybe, it was also something I wanted to do to you since last night that I saw you standing in your balcony. You looked so beautiful".

"You saw me last night?"

"I did. I could not sleep thinking of you and so I stepped outside and looked at the moon. Within seconds there you were".

"Alex, I think you have done all that you can for me today. Thank you".

"No, wait. You felt the breeze. Your gate is here. How do we open it?"

Lizbeth rushed off and left Alex standing there, alone in the hall of artwork.

The next day Alex was having breakfast in the dining room patio. He checked his wrist watch. Then looked inside of the house. He sat for a moment thinking, then abruptly stood up from his chair and went into the house. When he got to the hall of artwork he suddenly stopped and saw Lizbeth in front of the painting with the boat.

"I knew I would find you here".

"And I knew you would eventually come searching for me".

"Then you were waiting for me?"

"Yes, to tell you that I need to work. You distract me. So today, I want you to keep you distance from me so I can get more done".

"I see. I did not think I was now becoming a burden to you. I will leave you to your work then".

Alex felt hurt that Lizbeth wasn't as happy to see him as he was to see her. He tried to hide his feeling with frustration and instead walked off. Lizbeth felt bad treating him this way and whispered to herself.

"I am sorry, Alex. I need to do this on my own and I don't want you hurt after I am gone".

After hours Lizeth still could not figure out how to enter the painting. She couldn't even get as close as to touch the waters, smell the ocean, or feel the breeze like she did when Alex was with her. She gave off a frustrated sigh and walked out of the hall of artwork.

Alex was in his bedroom laying across his bed, deep in thought when he heard a knock on his door. Surprised that someone was knocking, he immediately got up and opened the door. Lizbeth was standing there with her bathing suit on and a towel in her arms.

"How about a swim?"

"Would this help you work better?"

"I am hoping it will".

"In that case, let us go for a swim".

Lizbeth smiled and nodded then walked off to the indoor pool. Alex ran to his bedroom draw and pulled out his swim shorts, then he ran out of his bedroom and chased after Lizbeth.

When they got to the pool, Lizbeth jumped in. Alex watched her swim underwater then rushed off into one of the rooms to change into his swim shorts. When he came out he looked into the pool and saw Lizbeth getting closer. Once she was close enough he dived into the water, interrupting her underwater swim and making her stop where she was. While still underwater he then rushed over to her and held her in his arms to where they were facing each other. He went in for a kiss and Lizbeth block him from doing so and pushed him back, quickly swimming off and back to the surface. Alex followed behind her and swam up to the surface.

Once their heads were out of the water they looked at each other. Lizbeth turned her face and Alex swam over to her. Lizbeth tried to swim off, but Alex grabbed her by the waist and pulled her towards him.

"There is something you want. Tell me what it is".

"Alex, I do not know what you want with me, but it cannot be. I am married to your father and I spend my days planning my escape from him. Once I can find a way out, I will leave and never return again. I would rather die than let him find me..."

"I know this. I know you have to find a way out. My hopes on you returning the feelings I feel for you may be in vain, but I don't care. I have allowed myself to fall in love with you. It is a choice I have made. I also know the consequences and it is a risk I am willing to take. Don't pity me, Lizbeth. Just allow me to help you, and as I do, allow me to share these moments with you before you are gone for good. Is that too much to ask?"

Lizbeth looked away sad for herself and for Alex.

"There is something else you want. Ask me, Lizbeth. I will do anything for you".

"I cannot open the gate on my own, I need to speak to my friends. Maybe they can tell me something more that might help".

"Is that all? You could have asked me to speak with them at any time. My phone is in my pants. I will go get it for you".

"No, let me".

Lizbeth pushed herself out of the water and climbed out of the pool. She rushed over to the room where Alex left his pants and pulled out the phone, then rushed over to him so he could unlock it for her. He then pulled up the number and sent the call. He passed the phone to Lizbeth and she sat down on the floor with the phone on her ear.

"Any news? How's Lizbeth?"

"Philip?"

"Lizbeth? Tiara it's Lizbeth".

"Lizbeth, is it really you?"

"Guys I have missed you both so very much".

"We have missed you so much as well".

"Are you both safe? Are you still in hiding?"

"We are. Alex has been a great help in keeping us informed on what is going on. But enough about us. How has been your progress. You need to get out of there as soon as possible".

Lizbeth lowered her head and covered her face as she silently cried. Alex pushed himself out of the water and sat by Lizbeth putting his arm around her back waist.

"Lizbeth?"

Philip knew at that moment Lizbeth was not having much progress. Tiara grabbed the phone.

"Lizbeth, answer me these questions. Have you been at peace?"

"I have, somewhat".

"Have you felt relaxed?"

"As much as I could".

"Then that leaves one more and that is taking it".

"Taking it?"

"Lizbeth, you have to understand this power is yours. How you wield it is up to you. You have to be at peace, you have to relax, but then you have to take it. You have always lived your life treating what belongs to you as if did not. Opening the gates is your legacy. It is in your bloodline. Yet, you have treated it as if though this power was something that belong to others and not you. When will you understand that you are the possessor of this power, you do not have to ask permission to use what's yours. You are not breaking any rules, you are following them".

"Tiara is right, Lizbeth. We are also aware of your newest challenge. A man who has fallen in love with you and is willing to do anything in his power to help you. Even if it means go against his father. If for anything Lizbeth, do it to protect him".

Lizbeth, looked up at Alex and he smiled at her and gently touched her cheek.

"Take all the help he is willing to offer. You are not using him, you are accepting help he is freely giving, which you so desperately need right now".

Lizbeth sighed.

"Even if this means putting his life at risk?"

Alex knew she was talking about him so he spoke up.

"Even if it means putting my life at risk".

Lizbeth nodded in disagreement and stood up from the floor and walked away.

"This is something I cannot do, Philip".

Tiara stepped close to the phone again.

"Then open that gate, Lizbeth. That is your only way out and the only way to keep him safe".

Lizbeth spoke to Philip and Tiara a little bit longer. Then said her goodbyes and disconnected the call with them. Alex then walked over to her and she handed him back his phone.

"Are you okay?"

"I will be. Thank you for allowing me to make the call".

"Lizbeth, anything you want of me, you just have to ask. I may have fallen in love with you, maybe even obsessed with you. But my love and obsession are different from my fathers. I don't want to own you or even hurt you. I would die for the opportunity that you would be mine, but I would rather be hurt, than let you hurt".

"Alex, please".

"No, don't stop me from pouring out my heart to you. Let me take all the risk. Either you find whatever gate or passageway you are looking for or I will find a way out for you. Enough swimming for today".

"Alex!"

Alex walked off and left Lizbeth standing there alone.

Days had passed and I had not seen Alex. Then one evening I heard Clara tell Leo that Alex had gone with a friend named Ben, to attend one of his many parties. I could not understand why. I had hoped I wasn't the cause of his running away. One morning as I paced my bedroom wondering what to do next. Thinking that maybe Alex's frustration was the best thing for me right now. It would make it easier for me to distance myself from him. I had to remember Tiara's words and take possession of what was mine. I possess this power, it is in my blood. I have to try again. Just then I slightly opened the door to leave my bedroom when I heard Alex say my name. I turned around and he was standing outside my balcony. His face was covered with a mask, but I knew it was him. He stepped inside and I rushed over to him.

"Alex, how? What are you doing here? How did you get up here? I heard Clara tell your father you were out partying with a friend".

Just then Alex pulled off the mask, pulled me towards him and kissed me. I admit that I did miss his absence and I did not want him to stop. So I kissed him back. After the kiss he laid his forehead against mine as we stood there with our eyes shut. Then he pulled back and looked at me intensely.

"I do not have much time. I lied about my absence to leave the house. I found a way out. I had not walked this secret path for many years. The last time I did it was with my mother. My fathers men do not even know it exist. None of them watch this path. I knew if I had time alone, I could find it again. I will come for you tonight. Be ready Lizbeth. It is a long path so we will have to run once we have climbed down. Wear dark clothing so you will not be seen in the dark of the night".

"Alex, how?"

"Lizbeth, trust me please. I will leave again and return as if I have finished my partying with friends. Then as soon as the sun comes down and it is dark, I will come to your bedroom and we will climb down and run".

Clara was coming down the hall with clean sheets in her arms. She then suddenly heard Lizbeth talking with someone. She crept over to the slightly open door and saw Lizbeth, but she could not see who Lizbeth was talking to.

"This is great news".

"It is. Finally we will be together and away from this place".

With shock to what she just heard, Clara dropped the clean sheets and quickly reached for her phone. She pulled up the camera and began to take photos as best she could. The photos she got were of Lizbeth smiling happily.

Just then Alex put his mask back on then hugged Lizbeth. Clara was able to get a photo of the masked man hugging Lizbeth. Then Alex lifted the mask from over his lips and passionately kissed Lizbeth again. Clara took photos of their kiss. She quickly put her phone away and picked up the sheets she dropped on the ground. Then she rushed off and down the service steps.

Alex climbed down the wooden trellis on the wall and ran through the bushes. Lizbeth kept watching him until he was at a distance. As he carefully ran at one point he had to hide from some men who were passing by. Lizbeth was so worried for him. Finally he passed the white line, then disappeared into the trees close by. Lizbeth sighed a breath of relief and excitedly rushed to find something to wear for the escape. She picked out dark pants and a shirt.

"Could this finally be my chance to escape?"

She then walked over to were she had hidden her last pack of birth control. When she opened it, it was empty.

"And just in time".

Not caring that Leo or Clara would find it, Lizbeth threw the empty birth control hard case into the trash can. Then walked away.

Later that evening Alex drove his convertible in through the open gate of his fathers house. He stopped to allow his fathers men to check the car as they had been told to do. Then they gave Alex the okay to drive in. When he got to the house he stepped out of the car and walked inside. He was sure to go visit Clara so she would see that he returned to the house. Clara was in the kitchen whispering on the phone with someone. When she saw Alex she laid the phone down on the counter without ending the call.

"Alex, you are home now".

"I am, Clara. Is my father home?"

"No, sweet Alex. Your father is at work today. Did you have fun?"

"I did, Clara. Much needed fun. I was getting bored being at home alone".

"But you are not alone. You have me".

"This is true, Clara. But you cannot take down a case of beer and skinny dip into the ocean like my friends and I can, with tons of beautiful woman".

"Huh, do not underestimate me Alex".

Alex laughed and grabbed a handful of cherries from the bowl on the counter, then walked out of the kitchen. As soon as he was out of the kitchen, he rushed up the stairs to his bedroom.

Clara rushed back to her phone.

"It was your son sir".

"I did not want him to return home today. He will not like what he is going to hear when I reach home and have my wife in my hands. Think woman. Did you hear anything else. A name, a voice, anything".

"No sir, they whispered. But from what I had seen, this romance Lizbeth was having has been going on for quit some time".

"And he did not enter or exit the room".

"No sir, he definitely came through the balcony".

"It has to be one of my men. One of them has to have been lusting after her and have dared to have a secret romance with MY WIFE. Prepare the room where I slept before. After tonight she will be changed from bedrooms and locked in that room. I want the windows to be locked as well. She will not see the light of day for quit some time. Whoever he is, when he comes searching for her, I will know who he is. I will have a few men I trust watch the balcony and wait in her old bedroom. When he decides to climb up again, they will be waiting, and they will bring him to me. Then I will cut his throat myself".

Clara nodded in agreement and Leo disconnected the call. Then he pulled up the pictures Clara had sent him again.

"Lizbeth. How dare you let another man touch you. Kiss you. Have what is....you will never again disobey me. And when you smile like this again, it will be for me and only me".

Leo then threw his phone and pressed the button to have the glass come down from between him and the driver.

"How much longer?"

"A few hours sir. You will be home by dinner. I assure you".

Leo then pressed the button to have the glass go back up.
He sat there furious and full of anger clenching his fist.

Lizbeth wore an off the shoulder cream colored summer
dress with a mesh overlay that covered the dress and half
her arm . She went outside to the garden to take in some
sun. As she did she slowly walked touching the tops of the
flowers that reached high up. She hadn't escaped yet, but
already felt free.

"Finally, a way out. No more of this. I am the art guardian.
I will protect this lineage. I will".

Alex had been passing by one of his bedroom windows
when he saw Lizbeth outside. He stopped to stare at her.
Then he leaned against the wall as he continued watching
her. He looked up at the sky and noticed the sun was
starting to set. He smiled and stepped away from the
window.

Lizbeth entered the house and snuck into Leo's office, but
Clara saw her go in. Lizbeth searched for a notepad to
leave Leo a note. Clara rushed off and called Leo.

"She is in your office sir".

"Perfect. We are in the driveway now".

Lizbeth searched for a notepad, when she found one inside the desk draw she laid it on top of the desk. As she did, she noticed the draw had a small latch, so she lifted it up to reveal a secret compartment. In it was her phone that she brought from the states. She quickly picked it up. Suddenly she took notice to something more frightening. There was the photo underneath it. She picked up the photo and starred at it. Then she began to have flashbacks of what Philip's mother had said, about the consequences of an evil person learning how to posses the power to open the gate and travel through paintings. The photo was a copy of the one she found in the journals, with her twin cousins and the little boy that tried to forcefully learn how to travel. Lizbeth was overwhelmed with shock. All this time she was married to that person that her family tried to hide the paintings from, the same person who stole many of her families paintings and the same person who had an evil lust to travel.

"Leo is the little boy, nicknamed Neptune. He knows about the gates".

Lizbeth rushed to put the photo and her phone back into the compartment and closed it and the draw.

"He can never know who I am. He will trap me for sure. But what if he does know. Could that be why he seduced me and asked me to marry him. No, he would have forced me by now to try and open the gate. He does not know and he cannot find out now. I have to escape tonight. I have to".

"Escape?"

Leo slowly walked up from behind Lizbeth. She turned around full a fear looking at him.

"What is it that I cannot find out? About the escape you are planning? With your lover? Come now, why so quiet, Lizbeth. You did not think I would find out that you had a lover? What I do not know, is who he is. This I want to know. SO I CAN KILL HIM WITH MY BARE HANDS!

With that he struck Lizbeth hard with the back of his hand and she fell to the floor. She touched her lip to feel the blood that came out of her mouth. He then rushed over to her and lifted her up, then slammed her against the wall. With his thumb he wiped the blood away from her lip.

"The loss of his blood will be so much more, for lusting after what belongs to me".

Alex was in the shower and was unaware that his father was home. He reached his arms out and placed them on the wall as he let the shower water hit his chest and face. He kept remembering Lizbeth in the garden earlier that day.

"Leo, please. There is no lover".

"Lies! I got these photos today. Would you like to care and explain them?"

Lizbeth looked at the photos of her and Alex kissing in her bedroom early that morning, while he wore the mask.

"Lizbeth, I just want to know his name. Tell me his name. His death will be slow and long, but then he will be dead and whatever the both of you had will be over. You will be locked away in my bedroom and no one will be able to lay eyes on you, so this doesn't happen again".

Lizbeth began to cry as she tried pushing Leo away.

"Leo, please..."

Leo began to grope on her as she tried pushing him to get away.

"You let him touch you here, and here. All of this belongs to me! You let him do so freely, willingly?

Lizbeth pushed Leo hard and tried to run. He grabbed her from behind then gripped onto face and leaned her back onto his shoulder, where he forcefully kisses her.

"You kissed him. Then you smiled. As if you enjoyed his kiss. You smiled for him. You liked it, you like him".

Lizbeth continued struggling to break free. Leo's voice cracked as if he was about to cry.

"Lizbeth, why can you not understand that you belong to me. That you are mine and no one else's. No one can have you. WHAT IS HIS NAME!"

Lizbeth stopped crying and while breathing hard looked around.

"His name. His name is....his name is Neptune".

Leo shocked to hear his childhood nickname, loosened his grip on Lizbeth enough for her to reach for the fireplace poker and swing it, hitting Leo on the leg. He yelled from the pain of the hit and Lizbeth was able to get loose. She dropped the poker and ran out of his office.

"LIZBETH!"

Lizbeth ran directly to the hall of artwork and towards the painting of the old boat on the ocean. She reached out her arms toward the painting.

"I am the Art Guardian. It is now or NEVER!"

She swung her arms open and felt a strong pull then landed hard into the old wooden boat. She quickly lifted her head and found she was inside of the painting and in the boat.

"I did it. I did it."

She looked all around and there was nothing. No island, no land, nothing.

Leo came running out of his office limping and yelling for Lizbeth. Alex heard the yelling and quickly turned the shower water off. Clara came running over to Leo.

"Clara, my men! Get the all. She has run. I want them to find her. She was planning to escape with this man tonight. FIND HER!"

Clara rushed out the front door and called the men in. After receiving Leo's orders more men ran into the house as other raised their guard outside watching to see if Lizbeth ran by.

Alex got dressed and came running downstairs and men ran pass him going upstairs.

"Father, what is going on?"

"She ran from me. I found out about her lover and she ran".

Alex took notice that his fathers sleeves were rolled up and he was hurt.

"Did you hit her?"

Leo looked at Alex not wanting to answer.

"Father, did you hit her?"

"Alex, she let another man touch her, kiss her, possibly even make love to her. I threatened to kill him, but she would not give me his name. All I wanted was his name".

"So you tried to beat it out of her!"

"She is my wife! My wife!"

"Sir, there is no sign of her anywhere upstairs".

"Keep looking. Check all the rooms. She must have hidden herself somewhere".

Leo walked off limping yelling orders to find Lizbeth as the men ran all around the house. Alex walked over to the hall of artwork and stood there wondering if Lizbeth had finally found the trap door out.

"I'm glad you were able to escape, Lizbeth. I hope to see you again. I love you Lizbeth. I love you".

Alex took a deep breath then turned and walked away.

Lizbeth was laying inside of the boat shivering in the dark. There was no sun in this painting. Just gloomy cold weather the whole time. The boat continued floating with each wave. These waves were different than regular ocean waves. They were a lot weaker in strength. Almost like a lake with waves.

"What time could it be? Or what day is it?"

The boat continued rocking and Lizbeth tried to wrap her dress closer to her body to keep warm, when a piece of it tore on the boats cracked edges. What felt like hours was actually days. Lizbeth got hungry and wanted to find something to eat, but there was no land to sail to. She tried looking into the murky dark waters, but could not see anything. When suddenly what looked like a fish swum by. Excitedly she ripped of the broken piece of her dress to use it as a net. After tying some knots on it, she dipped it into the water as deep as she could. It was not long before she caught something. She quickly pulled it up and was frightened by what she saw. It was a skeletal fish. I moved and wiggled like a regular fish out of water, but this was a fish of only bones. She lifted up by the tail as it wiggled in her hand, then she dropped it back into the water and it swam off. She tried again and again. Each time only catching skeletal fish.

"No, no, no this can't be. Who would paint such a thing. It is as if they painted death. Art is not death, it is life. Another life. A good one. What do I do?"

Lizbeth began to panic. She had no food, no water, and it was cold.

"I have to go back. I have to go back. If I was able to get into this painting, I will be able to do it again. Then this time I will stick to Philip's plan".

Lizbeth began looking for the gate to exit, but did not know where it was.

"The marker, this painting has no marker! How do I get back!"

Lizbeth let out a yell that echoed through the gloomy waters of the painting.

Leo was in the hall of artwork standing in front of the painting of the old boat. Alex was passing by and saw Leo standing there.

"Father?"

"Ah, son. I was just here admiring this painting".

"Why this painting?"

"It was Lizbeth's favorite. She would always look a this one".

Lizbeth was lying in the boat in a fetal position. Shivering in the cold, hungry, thirsty and weak.

Leo lifted his hand and touched the painting. As he did a dark cloud began to grow in the sky over Lizbeth. When Leo removed his hand from off of the painting, heavy drops or rain began to fall onto Lizbeth and all around. Lizbeth sat up quickly and opened her mouth, trying to get as much as she could of the rain water to help quench her thirst. She cupped her hands together while holding her mouth open catching rain drops. Then when her hand was full she would drink what was caught in her hands and repeat this over and over. The boat began to quickly fill up with water. She did not take notice of this and only tried to drink as much as she could.

"I don't know why she liked this one so much. It is very sad painting. The man I brought it from took his life. He was a very depressed and lonely man. Yet, he had such a great talent. Sadly he did nothing to see life for its true beauty. He painted his sadness and loneliness. Funny thing is you can look at the painting and almost feel the cold in it".

"Why do you think Lizbeth liked this painting so much?"

"She was sad. I am not truly sure what made her so sad. There wasn't anything I would have hesitated to give her".

"Maybe what you gave her was not what she wanted".

"I gave her everything, Alex. Everything".

After Lizbeth quenched her thirst, she realized the water in the boat was already reaching over her ankles. She panic and tried using her hands to dump out some of the water, but it wasn't helping. The boat continued to fill up. The more it filled up, the more the boat began to sink deeper into the water.

"No, no. Stop. This is too much. This boat won't hold".

Frantically she continued trying to throw out as much water as she could. As she did she yelled out and cried.

"Please, stop! Stop raining! Where is the gate!"

The boat filled more and more as the rain continued.

Leo walked away from the painting. Alex stepped closer to it and looked at it for a moment. Then he laid his forehead against it.

"Lizbeth, I hope you are well. I miss you. I love you".

Lizbeth heard Alex's voice loudly in the sky.

"ALEX! ALEX!"

She fell to her knees into the water on her boat and whispered and cried to herself.

"I can't find the gate, Alex. I can't find the gate".

Just then Alex took one finger and touched the painting from the top of the water and went vertically down to feel the lumps of the paint, like Lizbeth used to do. He then smiled and joined his father in the living room.

When Alex passed his finger across the painting a silver light reflected bright and Lizbeth looked up.

"The gate. The gate. THE GATE!"

She struggled to get the boat to move because it was filling up with rain water, once she was able to she used her arms to paddle it towards the light.

Leo and Alex went into the living room. Alex walked over to the bar and served himself and his father a drink. Then he walked over to his father, handed him the cup and sat in the couch across from him. Leo was deep in thought.

"One month. It has been one month now since my beautiful Lizbeth has disappeared. I had my men search for her everywhere. Everywhere".

"I'm sorry father".

"No, I am sorry. I should have never struck her. I should have kept a close eye on her, until I caught her lover. Then I could have killed him and been done with it. She would have never had the chance to run from me".

"Father, I do not think that would have been a good solution".

"What would have been a good solution then? To let him live and hump my wife whenever he wanted to? No, his death would have solved the problem. Lizbeth, would have still been with me now".

"Father? May I ask you something?"

"Go ahead, ask what you want".

"Did you hit my mother too?"

Leo looked at Alex and stared at him.

"Did you hit my mother?"

"No, I did not hit your mother. We argued a lot, but I did not need to hit her".

"Did not need to?"

"Your mother knew her place and she obeyed me".

"Then, what really happened".

"With your mother it was different. Another man loved her, but she loved me. She wanted to be with me. We married and we were happy. Then you came into the world. Your mothers joy was without limitations. We could have fought, but you, you always made her smile again. She smiled often seeing you run around the house".

"What did you two fight about?"

"Life, work, time. All the typical things couples fight about. As any husband, I ignored her rants. Doing so had it consequences. She got tired of me ignoring her and decided she wanted a divorce. I yelled back that I wanted one too. We agreed that after her charity auction she would come home and pack her things and leave, but she could not take you out of this house. That is where we argued".

"Then she did not plan on abandoning me, like I thought she did".

"No, she did not plan on abandoning you. We fought about where you would stay until the divorce. We argued there, in the hall of artwork. She was taking one of the paintings to auction off for the charity".

"Then what happened?"

"She disappeared. After that night I never saw her again".

"Did you try looking for her? Do you know if something bad happened to her?"

"I had my men search and search. But just like Lizbeth. She just vanished".

Lizbeth struggled to get as close to the light as she could. When she looked up at it, it started to fade.

"No, no. Don't. Please".

She paddled until she couldn't paddle anymore. The rain continued pouring and filling her boat to where it was almost full. When suddenly she heard a thump. When she looked up she was in front of what was left of the silver light. She quickly stood up and gripped it. Then punched at it, like trying to break it open. Then a little tear appeared. She continued hitting it until there was enough space for her to put her hand through. It was like a rubber wall. She then used the edge of the boat to stand on and push her head through the hole she put her hand through. She continue pushing through it. The same way Philip did when he was learning how to open the gate. It was as if the painting was birthing Lizbeth. With one last strong push through the hole Lizbeth's boat went under water, filled with the weight of the rain water. Lizbeth continue pushing and pulling herself through the painting.

Suddenly Leo and Alex heard a loud thump. Like the sound of a body fall. Leo jumped up and ran to see what that was. Alex placed his cup on the table and quickly followed behind. As soon as Leo was about to pass the hall of artwork, he looked down the hall and stopped in shock dropped his liquor glass, which shattered to pieces on the floor. Lizbeth was on the ground.

"Father?"

Alex rushed over as Leo ran down the hall of artwork and scooped Lizbeth in his arms. When Alex got there and saw Lizbeth he froze with shock. Leo was emotional and began to cry.

"My love your cold as ice. Alex! Have the doctor come quick!"

Leo picked Lizbeth up in his arms and rushed upstairs and towards her bedroom.

"Clara! Clara!"

Clara came running.

"Mr. Ferreira is everything okay?"

"We need the doctor. Now!"

Clara pulled out her phone and called the doctor. Leo had one of his drivers rush to pick him up.

Alex was still in shocked looking into the hall of artwork. He then went down the hall and saw all the water on the floor, that came off of Lizbeth body. He followed the trail of water across the floor, up the wall and to the painting of the boat. The painting had changed. The boat was no longer on the water. The panting was now of a boat sitting in the bottom of the ocean floor with skeletal fish

swimming by. In fear Alex took steps back and took a
tumble and fell to the ground. Still looking at the painting.

The doctor arrived and was quickly taken to see Lizbeth.
He quickly checked on her and was concerned.

"Mr. Ferreira, please. I can save her, but I need you to leave
me alone with her".

Worried Leo agreed and stepped out into the hall. Clara
took orders from the doctor to help Lizbeth. After abut
half an hour. Lizbeth was stable. The doctor left Clara
with strict orders and stepped outside the bedroom to
speak with Leo.

"Well doctor, how is she?"

"She is stable now Mr. Ferreira. But any longer and she
would not be alive right now. She was suffering from
hypothermia had severe dehydration, which is odd because
she was covered in sweet water. She has not eaten for quite
some time and is very weak. I have given Clara specific
instructions on the special diet she will need to eat and she
will need plenty of fluids. She has an IV on now. Clara will
change the bag when it is empty, to the second one I left
for her. She needs plenty of rest. She has suffered a great
ordeal. Mr. Ferreira, I do not usually ask questions bout
your line of work, but what happened?"

"Honestly doctor, I wish I new. I found her this way".

"Odd. One would think she was deserted in the middle of the ocean. Strangely enough she has no sunburns".

"Thank you doctor".

The doctor left and Leo walked in the room and stood over Lizbeth's bed, looking down at her.

Alex was in the living room shaking and with his liquor glass full. From a distance he saw the doctor leave. Then he stood up and rushed upstairs. When he got to Lizbeth's room he saw his father standing by her bedside.

"Father?"

"She's going to be okay".

"Can someone explain to me, what is going on? How did Lizbeth end up on the floor of that hall?"

"I do not know, Alex. I do not know".

Leo walked off and out of Lizbeth's room.

Several weeks later the doctor was in Lizbeth's room, giving her a last check-up.

"You have recovered well, Lizbeth. You can now return to a regular diet and activity".

"Thank you, doctor".

The doctor nodded and left Lizbeth's room. Leo sat beside Lizbeth on the bed.

"How do you feel? I mean I know what the doctor said, but I want to know how you truly feel".

"I am well. I feel better and stronger."

"Since you are able to eat well again, I will have your favorite dinner made tonight".

Leo looked up at Clara and she nodded and left the room.

"I will let you rest and tonight, I will come for you so we may have dinner together".

Lizbeth nodded and Leo left the room. As she shut the door behind him he looked to his left and to his right.

"Report to me any movement. Are the men outside as well?"

"They are sir. As you requested. There are men station outside the balcony. Anyone who comes in close will be shot on site".

"Good. Change shifts as needed and when I exit this room with her tonight, I want you gone so she does not suspect I have men guarding her door".

"Yes, sir".

Alex was listening to his fathers instruction from a distance through his bedroom door. He then quietly shut the door and paced his room.

"How can I now see you Lizbeth? I have to find a way, but how".

That evening Lizbeth stood up and took a warm shower, she then dressed herself with the dress Leo had brought to her room. She then opened her bedroom door and the men were gone. Lizbeth did not even know they were there. She went down the stairs and walked to the dining room. But there was no one there and nothing on the table. Jus then Leo walked into the dining room and stood looking at Lizbeth.

"You look beautiful, my love".

He then rushed over to her and took her by the hand.

"I told you I would come for you. Why did you not wait?"

"I was ready to leave the bedroom. I have spent plenty of time there already".

"I understand. Come, I have a surprise for you".

Leo led Lizbeth though a door she had not seen before. Behind it there were steps. He gently led her up the steps and at the top of them was a new balcony she had not seen before. It was decorated beautifully with floral vines and string lights. There was a chaise on side and an outdoor canopy bed on the other. In the middle was a table, set for two with wine and candles. He led Lizbeth to her seat and helped her sit. He then sat across from her.

"I wanted tonight to be special for you. I do not know where you went, but it must have been terrible".

"I am not ready to remember any of it yet".

"I understand. What do you think of the balcony? I had it built just for you. So we could be together tonight. I spared no expense and made sure it was completed on time. The walls are built higher to allow for privacy. I wanted it to be made like an outdoor bedroom. This way we could be alone and not seen".

"It's beautiful".

"It is indeed, but not as beautiful as you are. All the furniture is made to withstand the outdoors. Even the bed. It is made to look like any other bed, but everything on it is weatherproof. I thought of every detail. Even if it rains, we are covered. I can show you after dinner how that works".

Lizbeth forced a smile. Leo began to eat dinner and Lizbeth did as well.

After dinner Lizbeth was standing by the balcony railing looking over it with a glass of wine in her hand. Leo came from behind and held her.

"Oh how I have missed you, Lizbeth".

He rubbed is cheek against the side of her head. Then gently took the glass of wine out of her hand and placed it off to the side. Then he gently led Lizbeth towards the bed.

"I wanted to show you how this works. If we are together in bed and it happens to rains, I hit this lever and look".

A plastic covering began to roll out to cover the top of the canopy and plastic mesh side walls dropped down.

"Isn't that great. That way we can make love and not get wet. Yet still enjoy the outdoors and its breeze".

Leo hit the lever again and the plastic canopy and mesh side walls were pulled away. He then looked at Lizbeth and gently touched her face and leaned in and kissed her. Lizbeth did not kiss him back, nor did she fight back. Leo went down her neck gently. As he kissed her neck he loosened the ribbon on the back of her dress, which made the top part come loose and drop down. Lizbeth tried to catch it and hold it over her breast. Leo caressed her back as he slowly laid her on the bed. He climbed on top and continued kissing her lips and neck. Lizbeth became emotional.

"Please. Please, I cannot. Not yet. I can't".

Leo stood up and Lizbeth immediately sat up and climbed off of the bed.

"Forgive me Leo, I need more time".

Leo climbed off of the bed and leaned in and kissed her lip gently.

"And you will have all the time you need. I can wait patiently for you".

Lizbeth could not look at Leo. Only the ground. She then walked off and back downstairs. When she reached the steps to go up towards her bedroom she ran into Alex.

"Lizbeth! I have been waiting..."

"I can't. Not yet. Please".

She ran pass Alex and towards her bedroom. After she got to her room she ran inside and threw herself onto the bed and curled up as she did when she was on the boat.

A few days passed and Lizbeth chose to eat in her bedroom. So Leo called Clara into his office.

"You called for me, Mr. Ferreira?"

"I have had my wife's room and balcony guarded since her return. Any lover she had would be a fool to try and meet with her now. Yet, she will not give herself to me. More now than ever I want to have my wife and conceive a child".

"You want me to put the mixture into her juice tonight?"

"Not her juice. I want you to add it into a cup of chamomile tea, with sweet milk. Just like we drank together when we first met. I want to start anew with my wife. Things are different now".

"How so sir? Is it because of how she disappeared?"

"That is precisely why. When she has drunk her tea and is ready, I want you to let me know. This way she will give herself to me without any hesitation".

"Yes sir".

Clara left Leo's office. He sat back in his chair in deep thought.

"Things have changed immensely now, Lizbeth. It is even more crucial now that we have a child. I would be a fool not to enjoy the woman I love and to learn from her abilities. After-all, it is not everyday that one marries the only living art guardian".

Lizbeth finished drinking her tea and placed the empty cup on the tray. After a few moments Clara came into the room and took the tray away. After placing it in the kitchen she went to Leo's office.

"Sir, she should be ready shortly".

"I think I will not wait for her to be ready. I will see her now and watch her slowly desire me".

"Good idea sir".

Leo was headed upstairs and before entering into Lizbeth's room his men came barging through the front door and ran upstairs.

"Mr. Ferreira, something has come up and you are needed".

"Now? What could possibly be that important?"

The man approached Leo and whispered in his here.

"When? Who failed such a small task!"

"You know who it was sir. It looks like we will be out all night to try and fix this one".

"Let's go!"

Alex slightly opened his bedroom door and heard their conversation. He waited until his father left then came out of his room and rushed over to Lizbeth's. He pushed open the door and popped his head in to look for Lizbeth, then checked to the hall again to be sure no one saw him. Alex snuck into her bedroom, locking the door behind him.

"Lizbeth?"

He walked over to her bathroom where she suddenly walked out in her nightgown and was startled by seeing Alex in her bedroom.

"What are you doing here, Alex?"

"I do not mean to be a burden to you. And I know you have not wanted to talk, but what I have seen lately has gotten me...I have questions and I want to understand. I know you have the answers that I am seeking. Please, Lizbeth. I have been honest with you and I am asking for you to do the same with me".

Suddenly Lizbeth began to feel the reaction to the drug.

"No, no, not again".

"They are just questions that I have. It is simple, Lizbeth. Please! Do not leave me in the dark this time. I thought you were gone and safe, and now you are back in my fathers grasp again. We are right back where we started. This time it will be even harder to help you escape. He now has men watching at the bottom of your balcony and stationed at your door. I had a lot of difficulty just trying to speak with you now".

"Alex, it's happening".

"Lizbeth, what is happening?"

She tries to walk and stumbles.

"Are you okay? Do you need a doctor?"

"No. No doctor for this".

"What is it then? What are you not telling me!"

"Your father drugged me again? He gives me a mixture that make me aroused and I have no control over myself. It must have been the tea. I had wondered why I was given the tea. I thought it was to relax me".

"What can I do? I need to lay back. No, I need to...I.."

Lizbeth began to breath hard and Alex tried to help her to the bed. He laid her back and she began to gently pass the back of her hands across her face. Then touching her thighs and bitting her bottom lip as she moaned.

"Lizbeth? Lizbeth, can you hear me? Why aren't you responding? Lizbeth, what do you want me to do?"

Lizbeth began to moan and smile at Alex as she reached out to him.

"Kiss me, kiss me".

"No, Lizbeth. This isn't you speaking. This is the drug".

He leaned over to help Lizbeth sit up and she began kissing his face and cheek.

"Lizbeth, stop. This is not you. You are not like this".

"Please, kiss me. Please, kiss me".

Alex left Lizbeth sitting up and stood up. He turned around worried and not knowing what to do. As he tried to figure things out Lizbeth began pull off her nightgown. Alex turned to look at her and tried to stop her.

"Lizbeth, don't do this. Try to control it".

She continued trying to pull off the nightgown and kiss Alex. He grabbed her hands and held them at her sides. She then leaned in and kissed his neck, which weakened him.

"Lizbeth, don't do that. Please, you have to control this. Oh, that feels amazing. Lizbeth, I have wanted you for so long, but not like this. Please, I can't....."

He then abruptly stood up to get her to stop kissing him. Nervously he paced the room and as he did, Lizbeth tried to stand as best as she could and when she did she let her nightgown drop to the ground. Just then Alex turned and stood still staring at Lizbeth standing there with only a lace panty on and wobbling to hold her balance. She then fell on top of the bed and Alex came running over.

"Lizbeth, are you okay?"

She turned onto her back and lifted her waist up as she removed her lace panty. By then Alex was pleading.

"Lizbeth, please. You are so beautiful. Please try to control this, Lizbeth. I don't know if I can any longer".

"Kiss me. Kiss me".

"Lizbeth, one kiss".

"Kiss me. Kiss me".

Alex leaned in and kissed Lizbeth. She wrapped her arms around his neck making it difficult for him to back away. He tried pulling her arms off of him. When he did he back away, again he tried holding her hands down at her sides.

"Lizbeth, you are driving me crazy. I want you so badly. I wanted you for so long. This is not fair. You probably won't even remember this, or me".

"Kiss me. Kiss me".

Lizbeth moaned and groaned as she bit her lip and moved her waist. Alex let her hands go and tried to turn his face. She took his hand and placed it on her thigh. Alex took in a deep breath and gently caressed her thigh, slowly coming up from her thigh to her waist.

"I want you so badly, Lizbeth. Forgive me for this".

Alex leaned in and kissed her. Then slowly climbed on top of her. As he kissed down to her neck he suddenly stopped to get his shirt off. She placed her hands on his chest and rubbed up towards his neck where she then pulled him towards her. Before long they were making love.

After the affect of the drug put Lizbeth to sleep, Alex was also fast asleep on Lizbeth's chest. Before the morning sun crept in, Lizbeth had awoken first, to find Alex naked and asleep on top of her. She could not move without waking him up. She then had flashbacks of what happen the night before. She remember Alex coming in to talk before the the drug took affect. Then she remembered Alex begging her to stop, because he could not contain himself. Her flashbacks went even further, to the empty birth control pack, the desire for Leo to impregnate her and Philip's mother talking about carrying on the legacy. With those thoughts, Lisbeth knew what to do. She gently passed her hand over Alex's head, which woke him up. He looked up at Lizbeth and she closed her eyes and kissed him.

"Are you still under the affect, Lizbeth? I promise I don't want to take advantage of you".

She kissed him again and he kissed back. Again they made love that morning.

Later that evening Leo still had not returned home. Alex came by looking for Lizbeth in her bedroom and did not find her. He then went to the hall of artwork and nothing. There was only one last place to look. Though it was dark in the pool area, Alex swore he saw Lizbeth sitting by the edge of the pool, so he got closer to check.

"It is me, no need to wonder".

He walked over to her and found her sitting at the edge of the pool with her legs in the water. He sat beside her.

"What are you doing here? And in the dark".

"It helps try to conquer my fears of what I went through during the month I was missing".

"About that Lizbeth, I wanted....".

"Do you want to go for a swim?"

"A swim? Now?"

"It's a simple question. Yes or no".

"I have to get my swim shorts".

"Or you can just jump in naked".

"Naked? I didn't want you to feel uncomfortable".

"I would not make me feel uncomfortable, but if it does make you feel so, then I will join you".

Lizbeth stood up and took her bathing suit off and stood naked in front of Alex. Then she jumped into the water. Alex nervously began to take his clothes off and once he was naked he jumped into the water. They met under the water and Lizbeth swam over to him and kissed him. Then she swam back and up to the service. Alex followed. When they both had their heads out of the water they looked at each other for a moment. Then Lizbeth turned around and swam away. Alex when after her and met her by the ladder. Then he swam up to her and kissed her. Lizbeth kissed back and soon they were making love in the pool. Afterwards they held each other in the water for a few moments. Lizbeth was deep in thought. She looked at Alex and smiled, then got out of the water, grabbed a towel to dry herself, then put her bathing suit back on and sat by the edge with her legs in the water. Alex did the same and put his boxers on and sat beside her with his legs in the water.

"Now, what is it that you want to know?"

"Everything! I need to understand".

"Fine. I come from a lineage of Art Guardians. We have the ability to enter into any painting we please. Many have mastered the ability to enter a painting and exit a painting. I finally learned how to enter, but I still need lots of work on how to exit the painting. Philip and Tiara possess this ability to do so. Tiara is half paint and half human. Her mother was a regular person like you and I, but her father was from inside the painting. She was conceived in this world and born in this world. Philip is just a regular person who grew up with us and has been able to learn. We have been paint hopping since we were children, which is what Philip, Tiara and I have called it. All this information is just a start".

Alex sat there quietly then stood up and began to walk away.

"Where are you going?"

"This is not funny, Lizbeth".

Lizbeth stood up and went after Alex.

"And I am not laughing. The reason why I am in this dark pool room, is because I am trying to find a way to get past what I endured in that painting. The one you thought had a secret passageway in the back of it. Well, there was no passageway behind it. Just right in front of it for the person who knows how to open it. When your father was trying to beat your name out of me, I finally found a way to open what we call 'the gate' to get into the painting. I wanted to stay a day or two. The problem was, without a watch, a person cannot tell what time or what day it is. I lost track of time and the boat I was in, from within the painting kept drifting away from the gate. The painting we hop into and out of at home have a marking, so we know where the gate is and we don't get lost. Your fathers paintings have no markings. While I was stuck in the painting I heard you speak. You said you loved me and a light lit up in a vertical line. It was like you had shown me where the gate was. I did my best to get to it after a heavy rain began to sink the boat. I could not fully open the gate, I was able to get it open enough to push myself through. I was my only hope or I would have eventually drowned after the boat sunk into the bottom of the sea. Now, does that about sum it all up for you?"

Alex remembered seeing Lizbeth on the hall floor wet, and the painting changed to a sunken boat at the bottom of the sea. He sighed.

"I don't understand why you sit in here though".

Lizbeth smiled realizing that Alex believed her.

"Because where I was for a month was dark and the waters were murky. Being in here reminds me of being in there. Except I have more power here than I did there. Instead of feeling fear now whenever I am in a dark place with murky water, I will get past that fear and try to conquer it".

"A dark indoor pool does seem harmless".

"Very harmless. And there are no skeletal fish swimming around".

"Lizbeth, you do understand this is a lot to take in. What then does this have to do with my father. Is that why he brought you here. I noticed her never asked questions when he found you in the hall of artwork".

"That is a question I have asked myself for several days now. At first I thought he seduced me and asked me to marry him for that reason, but he never forced me to open any painting gates".

"Why would you think he married you for that reason?"

"Before I was born some twin cousins of mine befriended a young boy they nicknamed Neptune. This boy knew they could paint hop, but after a time he wanted to learn how to do so himself. He became greedy and forceful about learning. He ended stuck in a painting and my cousins searched for days to find which painting. Once he was rescued, instead of being grateful he demanded to learn. My cousins sent him away, and instead he stole several of my families painting then disappeared".

"What does that have to do with my father?"

"He has the same photo my cousins had. That boy they nicknamed Neptune, is your father".

"My father knows about this paint traveling stuff".

"I believe he does. What I do not know is if he knows that I am the art guardian".

"Well, after you came back from inside the painting, he now knows something for sure".

Lizbeth nodded with concern.

After Lizbeth answered as many questions as she could for Alex, they both sat by the pool together quietly.

"I know this was a lot for you, Alex. Maybe we can talk abut something else. Tell me about you".

"There is not much to tell. I have lived here all my life. My parents live here together, they fought a lot, but my mom seemed happy. Then one day she disappeared".

"When was the last time you saw her?"

"Before a charity auction. She was going to have one of the paintings in the hall auctioned off. She got all dressed up, in a red dress. And wore this enormously large diamond broach with her initial on it.

At this point Lizbeth was remembering the painting she saw of the woman on the island wearing a red dress.

"Alex, what was your mothers name?"

"I was named after her. My name is Alexandro. Her name was Alexandra".

Lizbeth abruptly stood up from the floor.

"What's wrong, Lizbeth?"

"I think. I think. Wait, I need to change".

Lizbeth ran off towards her bedroom. When she got there she grabbed a pair of pants, a t-shirt and some shoes. Alex quickly put his clothes back on and ran after her. When he got to her room she continued changing right in front of him.

"Lizbeth, are you going to explain what is going on?"

"I will, once I have an answer".

She ran back downstairs and Alex was behind her. She stopped at the hall of art work, right in front of the painting of the woman in the red dress on the island.

"Give me something sharp. Anything".

Alex looked around and found a wine opener. Lizbeth took that wine opener and touched the painting. Then gently enter the wine opener into the artwork.

"Alex, I will do my best to get back. If I don't get back in time, please don't worry".

"Lizbeth, at least tell me what you are planning".

Lizbeth stretched out her arm towards the painting and closed her eyes. She took a deep breath in and out. The golden light began to shine and the gate opened. Lizbeth took steps in and disappeared. Alex panicked at what he saw and began to hyperventilate. He stumbled over to the living room and sat down, looking back toward the hall of artwork.

I entered the painting of the island. The sun was shining bright and warm. There were coconuts on the sand, but no sign of Alexandra.

"Hello? Anybody here?"

I looked all around, even over at the waters to see if someone was swimming. She had to be in this painting, but where. Finally the woman that was trapped in the painting, in her husbands home, in the hall of artwork. This had to be it. I was sure this was the one. I walked deeper into the island in search for her.

"Hello? Alexandra?"

I must have been searching for over half an hour, when suddenly I noticed what looked like a little hut. I rushed over to it, but no one was inside.

"Alexandra! Where are you?"

I kept searching. Then I saw a woman crouched down washing a rag by hand in a pool of sweet water.

"Alexandra?"

The woman froze, then slowly stood up. She was wearing a tattered red dress that was torn in several places. She slowly turned around and looked over at me, then nodded her head.

"I must be seeing things again. Go away figment of my imagination".

"Alexandra, my name is Lizbeth. You called out to me in a dream a few years ago. I have been searching for you to help you".

"My dream. I did dream where I called out for help. She heard me for a moment. Then she didn't anymore".

"That person was me. I am here to help".

Alexandra slowly walked over to me and reached out her arm towards me.

"Are you truly real? You are not a figment of my imagination?"

"I assure you, I am real".

Alexandra touched my arm up and down and began to cry.

"You are real. You are real."

I hugged her and she almost collapsed in my arms.

"Come with me, we need to find our way back".

"I have tried. For 10 years I have tried to find a way off of this island. There is no way out".

"I may have a way. I just hope I can open the gate".

"The gate?"

"Yes, come with me".

I traced my steps back to where I had started and looked around. At a distance I could see the small end of the wine bottle opener. I continued leading Alexandra towards it.

"This is where the marker is. I will do my best to open the gate. Then we will go through it, together".

I closed my eyes and took a deep breath in and out. Then I stretched out my arms and spread them open. It worked! The gold light began to shine and the gate opened. Alexandra became afraid, but I put my arm around her shoulder and took her hand.

"It's okay, your are going home now".

We made it through and were standing in the hall of artwork. I looked over to the living room and saw Alex sitting there.

"Alex!"

"Alex. My son?"

Alex came running from the living room and stood there in shock to see his mother after 10 years.

"Mother?"

He rushed towards her and fell to his knees in front of her weeping and hugging her. She hugged him and weeped.

"My son. My son. You have grown into a man".

The doctor left the bedroom that had been Lizbeth's. It was actually Alexandra's before she disappeared.

"See mother, you will be fine. The doctor said you are in perfect health".

"I am my son, I am".

"Mother, I need you to explain to me what happened".

Alexandra was about to speak when they heard Leo downstairs.

"What has happened? My men told me the doctor was called. Where is Lizbeth?"

Clara was downstairs and did not know how to explain from the shock she felt, so she pointed upstairs. In his panic Leo ran upstairs and into Lizbeth's room. He saw Lizbeth sitting on the side of the bed closest to the balcony and Alex on the other side of the bed, with his back towards Leo. Yet, he could not see who was on the bed, until he took steps closer into the room. That is when he saw his first wife Alexandra. It was as if he saw a ghost.

"Hello, husband. It has been a very long time".

After several hours had passed I decided to take my leave and allow Alexandra to rest. Leo had been sitting on the chaise beside the fireplace drinking and still in shock.

"I will let you rest now, Mrs. Ferreira".

"Thank you sweet Lizbeth. Thank you".

She took my hand and kissed it several times. I smiled at her and she smiled back at me. I stood up and left the room. Within seconds Leo followed behind and grabbed me in the hall.

"Where do you think you are going?"

"To my new bedroom".

"What new bedroom? I never gave orders...."

"I asked Clara to move my stuff. After-all this bedroom belongs to Mrs. Ferreira. The lady of the house. Your wife. Your real wife."

"No, Lizbeth. This changes nothing..."

"Let me go, Leo. This changes everything. When I return home I will be sure to annul our marriage, which isn't valid since you now have your first wife home".

Leo grabbed me by my shoulders and pushed me up against the wall.

"I still have power over you, Lizbeth. As your husband or not, you are mine".

"No, I am not yours. Not anymore. I am free now..."

"NO! You will always be mine. You will not leave this house. I will lock you up in this bedroom. Your bedroom...."

"That is not my bedroom, I am not your wife, you have no power over me and I am no longer afraid of you".

I forcefully pushed Leo back and walked away to the bedroom across the hall from Alex's. When I stepped in I quickly locked the door behind me. Then I walked over to the nightstand draw beside my new bed and pulled out my old phone. I called Philip and Tiara.

During the morning hours Lizbeth stretched in her new bed and when she opened up her eyes she was startled by Leo, who was standing at the foot of her bed. She quickly sat up.

"What are you doing in here?"

Leo began to slowly walk towards Lizbeth's beside.

"I would have never known. I would have never thought it in a million years. What are the odds that I walked into a museum and fell madly in love with the only living, Art Guardian. I marry her and bring her to my home. I offer her the moon and stars in return for her obedience and loyalty, and instead she betrays me in the worst way possible".

When Leo stood at Lizbeth's beside, she looked up at him. Then suddenly she tried to get out of the opposite side of bed as quick as possible, but Leo jumped over the bed and grabbed her from behind.

"Let me go!"

"Now, my first wife is back. I first wondered how she returned and then remembered, I have and art guardian living in my house. She did this to me so she could break our marriage oath".

"Leo, let me go!"

"What the art guardian does not understand is that I don't need to be married to her to make her mine. If she cannot be my wife, she will be my mistress".

"I will NOT be your mistress. I don't want you to touch me ever again".

Leo picked Lizbeth up and threw her onto the bed, then climbed on top of her and held her arms down.

"You can do so willingly Lizbeth, or I will take you by force".

"I will fight you every single time. You will never again have me willingly".

"I can with a special mixture, that will have you begging for my touch".

"That will not work, Leo! I will serve my own food and drink, and the moment I feel the effect, I will travel into a painting where you cannot touch me".

Leo became furious and Lizbeth's response.

"Then by force it is!"

Leo began to kiss Lizbeth's neck as she fought to get free from him. Just then Alex barged into the room.

"Father! Get away from her!".

Leo stopped and looked up at his son. He chuckled and then slowly climbed off of Lizbeth.

"Alex, what you doing here? This has nothing to do with you. This is between my wife and I!"

"She is no longer your wife. Your wife is sleeping in the other bedroom, unaware that you are trying to force yourself onto the woman that saved the life of your wife, my mother. She brought her back to us and this is how you want to repay her".

Leo looked at Alex furious. Then he abruptly walked out of the room.

"I have to go to work".

Lizbeth climbed out of the bed and ran into Alex's arms.

"Are you okay?"

"Yes. I expected him to do this, but not so soon. I am not safe here".

"You can stay with me".

"No, Alex. If your father found out about us, it would not go well for you. I think I may have an idea".

Back in the states Philip and Tiara had already ordered for all the paintings in the museum to be packed away and shipped to the house. Then Philip and Tiara had the painting with Philips mother shipped back to the house as well. They came out of the painting and checked for Leo's men, who had left after a month of no movement in the house. This allowed Philip and Tiara to take all the steps they needed to annul Lizbeth's marriage and pack up the paintings from the home. After they packed everything in the house and loaded it on a truck, the for sale sign on the house was put up. Philip and Tiara kept watching for any signs of Leo's men. They did not want to let their guard down the whole time. After several days of driving, they reached the secret home. It was a mansion on several acres of land. This mansion was hidden in a beautiful quiet town. A safe haven that was in Lizbeth's family for years, in case they ever needed a place to keep the art safe. They hired a maid, a butler, and some security. The mansion itself was heavily guarded with great security camera systems and alarms. This was Lizbeth's wish, so they could live comfortably and protected. Once the letter of Lizbeth's annulment was delivered to the old house, they were able to retrieve and send a photo of it to Lizbeth. She was free and no longer Mrs. Ferreira, wife to Leo. Shortly after that, Lizbeth's old house was sold.

That night Lizbeth placed a painting against the foot of her bed. The painting was of a beautiful dark night sky with shining stars and a bed a grass. She then stuck a note on it that read:

Leo, this is where I will make my bed tonight and every other night, if you try to force yourself on me ever again.

Lizbeth then snuck out of her bedroom and quietly down the service steps. She rushed through the dark over to the door that led to the bedroom furnished balcony. The one that Leo had built for Lizbeth after she returned from the painting of the old boat on the ocean. She opened the door and stepped in. As she was about the lock the door, she paused.

"Wait, I have to make sure I am alone first".

She tipped toed upstairs and looked around. There was no one there. So she rushed back downstairs and reached for the doorknob when the door suddenly opened. Lizbeth startled she jumped back and Alex walked in and quickly closed the door behind him. He looked at Lizbeth waiting for an explanation.

"What is this room?"

Lizbeth nudged Alex to the side and locked the door.

"It's not a room. It's a balcony, and your father had it built to seduce me in. After I returned from the painting".

She turned around and went up the stairs. Alex followed behind. Before reaching the top he was surprised to see it was even built and how it was decorated. He continued up the steps to reach the top. Then he looked over at Lizbeth as she served herself half a glass of wine and took it down quickly. Then she took some deep breaths and sat on the chaise.

Alex then walked over to the bar himself and served himself a strong drink. Then he refilled the cup Lizbeth drank from, with more wine. He sat beside her and handed her the cup. She grabbed it and began to down it, when Alex slowed her down.

"Easy there, easy. Obviously you have a lot on your mind. Let's start with this balcony bedroom. Did you and my father....".

"We did nothing but eat dinner up here. He tried, but I could not. I ran off and he let me go".

"Then why are you up here now?"

"It will be my bedroom tonight. I didn't want to stay in mine, it case Leo returned and tried what he did this morning. If you had not stopped him, he would have…".

"But he didn't. You do not have to be afraid of him anymore. Are you afraid of him? Or are you afraid of what you feel for him?"

Lizbeth took down the wine with one breath and then stood up and walked over to the balcony edge to look out. Alex sighed then stood up and walked over to the bar. He picked up the wine bottle and walked over Lizbeth. He refilled her cup.

"You didn't answer my question".

"I'm not sure. Maybe both. I'm afraid of how he might react if he doesn't find me in my bedroom. Which is why I came up with possibly a ridiculous plan".

"Plan? And what would that plan be?"

"I placed a night painting at the foot of my bed. Then I left a note saying that I would be sleeping in the painting tonight and every night after that if he tried to do what he did earlier today".

"Yet, you are not sleeping in the painting tonight".

"No, I was worried about how he would react. So I thought if I stayed up here tonight, I could hear any commotion in the house and show my face, so he would calm down. If I were inside the painting, then I wouldn't know what was going on until I returned".

"What kind of commotion you think he would cause?"

"I don't know. But I did not want to take his unpredictable actions lightly. I was afraid he would search for me room by room if I didn't have him believe I was in the painting. I worried for your mother and for...".

"For me?"

"Well, I didn't want him to think I was with you or that you went with me. Which is why you should return to your bedroom".

"I can, but he is not home yet. So we still have time to talk. I have tons of questions anyway".

"Tons of questions? What could you possibly have questions about?"

"The times we made love...when I made love to you. Did you did you allow me to do so, because you wanted me or for some other reason?"

"Why do you ask me that?"

"The first time we were together you were drugged. I tried to contain myself, but. Well, I couldn't help myself. I wanted you so badly even before that already. I shouldn't have, but I don't regret it. I'm hoping though that you won't resent me for it."

"Alex, I do not resent you. Your father drugging me and that was wrong. Yet, I cannot defend you or criticize you".

"What about the morning after?"

"What about it?"

"Lizbeth, I am no fool. You were not under the affect of the drug anymore. Yet you woke me with a kiss. We made love, and you did so well aware that we were".

"I don't know what your talking about, I...".

"Don't play games, Lizbeth. Why did you make love me willingly that morning".

Lizbeth sighed.

"A month before, your father had taken my birth control away. He wanted desperately to get me pregnant so I would be trapped and connected him, through a child, through children. That is when you found a path for us to escape. Somehow he learned about our plan and tried to get your name out of me".

Lizbeth got emotional. Alex gently caressed her hair.

"That's when I finally opened the gate to the painting.
Little did I know I would be trapped in it for a month. I
thought I was going die in there. But then you touched the
painting, and that sliver lining showed itself through the
dark clouds".

Lizbeth took a deep breath and gather her emotions. She
then took the bootle of wine out of Alex's hand and refilled
her almost finished cup of wine. She took a big gulp.

"After I got out of the painting and was able to recover,
your father brought me here. I knew what he wanted to do.
I knew he wanted to get me pregnant. After I refused, he
drugged me, that following night. It was obvious what his
plan was. But I couldn't imagine the thought of having a
child from him, in my womb. I know a child has no blame,
but as the art guardian, my child's blood would be mixed
with his and I was afraid. Afraid if my child would turn out
evil like him. Even still, I did not want a child to bind Leo
and I together".

Alex became upset. He placed the bottle of wine on the
balcony rail. Then he drank his drink from his cup in one
shot. Alex took a deep breath and walked away toward the
bar. He served himself another bit of hard liquor. He was
about to drink it when he abruptly turned and marched
towards Lizbeth.

"So you used me! To get you pregnant? And in the...in the pool that evening? You used me again, didn't you? Here I was pouring out my heart and making love to a woman I was in love with, and here she was using me. Do you feel anything for me, Lizbeth?"

"Alex, I'm sorry. I was afraid".

Alex upset paced then drank his drink and slammed the empty cup on the table.

"You didn't answer my question. You seem to avoid my questions often, Lizbeth. Is it because you'd rather deny me a response than tell me the truth? Do you feel anything for me?"

Lizbeth rushed over to Alex and placed her hand on his arm.

"Of course I do, Alex. You are so special to me. I felt so different towards you the moment I placed my fingers under that bedroom door, and you touched them. Ever since that day, you held a special place in my heart. A friend like you...".

"A friend? You see me as a friend?"

Alex walked over to the bed and sat on it. He then buried is face into his hands. Lizbeth walked over and sat beside him.

"Alex, please. Do not ask me for anything more right now. I did not say that I would not see you differently in the near future, I am just saying that right now, you are such a dear friend to me".

Lizbeth gently pulled Alex's hands down and place her hand on his cheek turning his face to look towards hers.

"I cannot imagine losing you. I am happy when you are around and I feel safe with you. My love for you now, is that of a friend, but I am not saying that there is no hope. Where I am right now, still trapped under your fathers obsession, I cannot think of falling in love with anyone".

Alex placed his hand over Lizbeth's hand that were still on his cheeks and he closed his eyes and leaned forward toward her, touching his forehead with hers.

"I am sorry that I tried to use you. But I thought to myself, I would rather have your child in my womb a thousand times over, before having a child from Leo. You have such a good heart, I had no doubt that any child I had from you would be good and kind".

Alex passionately kissed Lizbeth.

"I'm sorry, Lizbeth. I wanted you to return the love I have for you so badly, that I forget sometimes what you have had to endure. I can't expect you to hold tightly onto a love for me when your heart has been so badly broken. I do understand that you need time to heal. It's just sometimes I get impatient and forget the reality we are living in around us".

Lizbeth smiled and caressed Alex's cheek. Just then they heard Leo's driver pull up.

"It's your father! Please, go to your bedroom. I don't want him to think we are together tonight. The goal is that he remain calm and understand my message".

Alex nodded in agreement and kissed Lizbeth again. Then he jumped up and bowed.

"As you wish my lady".

Lizbeth giggled and Alex rushed off and down the stairs. She rushed behind him and after he left she waited a moment in case he had to return. Then she locked the door.

Alex ran across the dinning room and up the service steps. When he got upstairs he ran down the hall and barged into his bedroom, closing the door behind him.

"There's hope for me yet".

Then he walked off to his bathroom and began to run a shower. When he got out of the shower he wrapped a towel around his waist and walked out of the bathroom. Just then his Leo barged into his room.

"Where is she? Is she here with you?"

"Lizbeth? Why would she be here with me? What did you do to her?"

Leo rushed over to Alex's bathroom to check for Lizbeth. He then opened the closet and looked under the bed.

"Father, what has gotten into you?"

Leo took a deep breath.

"I just wanted to make sure she wasn't hiding here with you".

"Maybe she's resting in a safe painting".

Leo turned around and got into Alex's face.

"How would you know anything about that?"

"Father, don't you dare try to force yourself onto her again".

Leo laughed nervously. Then walked off towards Lizbeth's room. Alex watched from a distance as Leo pulled the note off of the painting and wrote the words

"Fine! Now come back home and don't ever leave again!"

Leo then crumpled the paper and threw it on the floor in front of the painting and walked out of Lizbeth's bedroom slamming the door shut behind him. When Alex heard his father slam his own bedroom door shut, he rushed into

Lizbeth's room, snapped a picture of what Leo wrote and rushed back into his bedroom, shutting the door behind him.

He then texted the photo to Lizbeth. She was laying on the canopy bed looking up at the stars. She felt her phone vibrate and looked to see Alex's photo message. Then she began to respond:

L: *This is great news. Hopefully he will keep to what he wrote and not try that again.*

A: *I'm sure he will think twice before trying that.*

A: *What are you doing right now?*

L: *Looking up at the stars.*

A: *And what do you see?*

L: *Not sure, there is one that looks almost like a bird.*

A: *A bird? What kind of bird?*

L: *Good question. How many kinds are there?*

They went on texting each other for over an hour. With the last text Alex stood up and sat on his bed. The last text messages read:

A: *I wish I was there with you.*

L: I wish you were too.

With that Alex put on his sneakers and pulled out a tank-top from his draw and put it on. Then he carefully opened his bedroom door and looked out into the hall. He then snuck out and walked towards his fathers room. He put his ear to the door and listened in and heard no movement. There also was no light lit inside. Leo then quietly snuck past Leo's bedroom, then he snuck by Alexandras bedroom. Alex then rushed down the service steps. He did not want to be seen going to the door of the balcony Lizbeth was in, so he instead went through the kitchen and outside through the kitchen door. He rushed over to where the balcony was and looked up. Looking around Alex finally found a way to climb up there. He started to climb and climb. When he got to the top he jumped down.

Lizbeth was lying in the middle of the bed and she quickly sat up.

"Alex! You scared me so bad. I feel like my heart is about to pop out of my chest".

"If it did, would let me catch it?"

He pulled his shoes off and jumped into the bed and under the covers with Lizbeth. He laid on his back with one hand under his head

"What are you doing?"

"You wrote you wished I was here with you...see".

Alex showed Lizbeth the text messaging. She pushed his phone down.

"I know what I wrote. But you can't be here. Your father..."

"Should be fast asleep".

Lizbeth threw herself back down onto the pillow and looked up at the sky.

"Now, which one did you say looked like a bird".

"That one".

"Ah, yes I see it now. Definitely an eagle".

"How can you be sure".

"Trust me I am an expert star reader".

Lizbeth laughed. Later into the night they were laying on their sides facing each other. Lizbeth had her eyes closed. Alex was staring at her.

"You are so beautiful".

Lizbeth opened her eyes and looked at Alex. He then lifted himself up and got closer to Lizbeth to where above her and she turned onto on her back.

"Alex, we shouldn't".

"Let me, and this time you can place the blame on the drink".

"But, I am not drunk".

"You can blame the drink".

Alex leaned in and kissed Lizbeth. She returned the kiss. In doing so it began to grow into a passionate one. Lizbeth then quickly began to pull Alex's shirt off. Once it was off Alex rolled himself completely on top of Lizbeth and began kissing her neck while pulling down the straps of her nightgown. He then placed his hand under Lizbeth back and suddenly lifted himself and Lizbeth up together. Lizbeth's eyes opened wide from the surprise. She got onto her knees and they continued kissing as her nightgown slid down her body. Alex caressed her back and neck. Suddenly rain drops began to fall. Still holding on tight to Alex she stopped and looked into his eyes.

"It's raining. I know how to cover us".

Lizbeth tried to left go of Alex and he pressed her against his body, not allowing her to leave.

"Let it rain on us. Let it rain on us".

He passionately kissed Lizbeth as the rain came down on both of them. Lizbeth let Alex go and gently pushed at his chest. He became submissive and allowed her to lay him on his back. She then climbed onto him and Alex placed his hands on Lizbeths waist. As they stared into each others faces, Lizbeth thrusted Alex into her body and Alex to shut his eyes and bit on the bottom of his lip. Lizbeth let out groans of pleasure as she gently moved her waist, driving Alex crazy.

"Lizbeth. Lizbeth".

Alex could not contain himself and suddenly sat up grabbing Lizbeth from the back of her head and intensely kissing her lips and neck. Then he turned her over onto her back. He thrusted harder and harder as Lizbeth intensely gripped onto his back. Both their bodies wet from the rain, Alex kept thrusting and Lizbeth overwhelmed by the feeling of pleasure began to climax. Alex tried to quiet her by kissing her when he suddenly released inside of her.

Afterwards they looked into each others faces consumed and overwhelmed, then they smiled and laughed. Alex turned his face the allow the rain to fall on it and they both took in this moment and let the rain drops continue to fall on them.

 The next morning Lizbeth was in her bedroom picking up the crumpled response from Leo. Suddenly Alexandra walked in.

"Good morning dear. Go ahead and get yourself ready. I'd like us to all go down to breakfast together. I have a plan".

Lizbeth wondered what Alexandra was up to, but agreed. She then went to get ready.

Alexandra and Lizbeth came downstairs together, with Alex following behind them. They all walked over to the dining room where Leo was sitting at the head of the table. When he saw them coming he smirked. Then they all sat at the table. Alexandra sat where Lizbeth normally sat. Alex sat in his seat and Lizbeth sat beside Alex.

"I wanted us all here today to have breakfast together. I have not had much human company for over 10 years. So I am sure you all can understand when I say that I don't want to miss a moment with anyone".

"We are here with you, mother".

Leo stood staring at Lizbeth.

"Aren't we father?"

"Ah, yes, yes. We are here for you Alexandra".

Alexandra nodded at Clara and she went into the kitchen to get everyones breakfast. As she returned and began laying plates down, Alexandra extended an invite.

"Lizbeth, having been gone so long. I have not one piece of clothing in this home. Would you join me for a girls day out so I can buy me a new wardrobe? I wonder how much things have changed over these past 10 year".

"Oh Mrs. Ferreira I would love to. It would be new for us both, I have never left this house since I first step foot into it".

"Lizbeth is not going anywhere".

"Whatever do you mean, Leo? Lizbeth is not allowed to accompany me to shop?"

"You may go shopping, but Lizbeth does not leave this house".

"I do not think that is a decision you can make for her, Leo. She can decide for herself. Wouldn't you like to accompany me, Lizbeth?"

"I would love to...."

"Are we going to ignore the fact that until a few days ago, Lizbeth was my only wife. She answers to me as her husband".

"Yes father, but you are no longer her husband".

"It does not change the fact that she was...is mine".

"Not any longer, Mr. Ferreira. I have already received my confirmation that our marriage in the states has been annulled".

"That's not possible. Those things have to be done through the courts. They take months to do..."

"Not if you have friends in the system to help. Or paintings to rush things along. Making me now a free, single, unmarried woman".

Leo banged on the table angrily.

"I do not care what any papers say or does not say. Don't think that what we have built together ends, because you have a piece of paper that says so. You are still my wi... woman. And you will follow my orders, Lizbeth".

Alex became angry and the hand he had on his thigh began balled up into a fist. Lizbeth placed her hand on his fist to calm him down.

"What if I left this house altogether and returned home..."

"That will never happen. My men have strict orders to keep you in this house and within these grounds".

"I can call the police...".

Leo burst out laughing.

"The police? I own them, Lizbeth. Never forget that".

Leo abruptly stood up from the table.

"Now, if you all will excuse me, I have work to tend to".

He was about to walk off, then he stopped and turned.

"You know what, Alexandra. I think I will allow Lizbeth to join you for a shopping day. Of course you will have to grow accustomed to the eight men that will join you to keep a close eye on Lizbeth for me".

"I have no problem with extra security, Leo. If that makes you feel better. This would be a good thing for Lizbeth to get out and see the town. Maybe I can buy her some clothing as well. Wouldn't that be nice, Lizbeth?"

Lizbeth was looking at Leo angrily and then looked at Alexandra, who gave her a signal to agree.

"Yes, that would be nice, Mrs. Ferreira".

Leo continued looking at Lizbeth and walked off. They all stood quiet until the front door slammed closed.

"Forgive me, Lizbeth".

"No need to ask forgiveness. This was part of the plan, to find out if Leo still has men watching and we have learned that he does. Sadly there is still no escape for me yet".

"There will be my dear. We will all need as much protection as we can get. The man I see now, is not the man I knew 10 years ago. My return interferes with his control over you Lizbeth. We must all be watchful.

After their day out shopping Lizbeth and Alexandra came home. Alex was happy to see them both.

"Are you headed to the pool, Alex?"

"I am, mother. Did you both enjoy your day?"

"We did, besides having so many guards follow us around the whole time. Well, I will go and put my new things away".

Alexandra walked upstairs to go to her room. As Lizbeth went to follow, Alex gently grabbed her wrist.

"Would you like to join me for a swim?"

Lizbeth smiled and nodded.

"I will go change now. Your mother actually brought a new bathing suit.

"I'd love to see it".

Lizbeth walked off to change. After several minutes she walked into the indoor pool area. Alex had just began slowly brining his head out of the water. He then shook his head to get the extra water out of his hair and began coming up the pool stairs. Lizbeth tried to avoid staring at his wet body.

He then grabbed a towel and covered his chest. This broke Lizbeth's stare causing her to come back to herself. She then walked in closer to where Alex could see her.

"Lizbeth. You came".

Lizbeth smiled and Alex stared at her body in her new bikini.

"You look amazing. I mean, that bathing suit is nice... amazing".

Lizbeth chuckled and walked pass Alex and dived into the pool. He smiled and threw his towel down, then dived in after Lizbeth.

He caught up to Lizbeth on the other side of the pool. There they floated for a moment without saying a word. When they were about to speak, they spoke at the same time.

"I'm sorry. Go ahead".

"No Alex, you go ahead".

He swam closer to her.

"Lizbeth, I will speak boldly then. I'm in love with you. I know that you have been through a lot. I am willing to wait for you to heal. But I admit, while you do so, I cannot keep my distance from you. I want to be near you at all times. Even if its just sitting quietly in the same room with you. Or swimming in a pool without speaking".

Lizbeth swam a little towards the middle of the pool and Alex followed. They continued speaking and did not take notice that Leo had just arrived. He heard voices in the indoor pool room and walked over. He then saw it was Alex in the pool with Lizbeth. He hid behind the wall to listen and watch them.

"I am not asking you to do anything. I will go at your pace and wait as long as I have to. My hope would be that you would give me a chance."

"Alex, you know that it will take me time. I am truly afraid to open my heart again to anyone. What your father has done to me..".

"Was wrong. Truly wrong. I may be my fathers son, but I am not him. I do not want to hurt you for my own personal gratifications or satisfaction. Lizbeth, you are an amazing woman. You deserved to be loved and protected. To love and be loved by you doesn't need any kind of force. You give it so freely".

"Alex, your words mean everything to me right now. But still it won't be easy to just love again. And I don't want to put you in harms way".

"I understand that. And because I'm in love with you, I can be patient. I'll wait, for as long as I have to, I'll wait. Because I know that I don't have to force it. When your ready, you'll give your heart to me".

Alex swam up closer to Lizbeth and brought his body closer to hers. He then placed his hand on her cheek and came in slowly for a kiss. Alex tapped kiss her lips, then he and Lizbeth closed her eyes. Then he tapped kissed her lips again. He then came in for a passionate kiss and Lizbeth returned the kiss. Leo couldn't contain his jealousy and came forward sarcastically clapping. This startled them both and Lizbeth pushed away from Alex. Alex became upset that Lizbeth was so frightened at Leo presences.

"What a beautiful display of love".

"What are you doing here, father?"

"I heard voices and came in to see who's they were. You can imagine my surprise when I saw you Alex, and my wife kissing in my pool. How long have you been unfaithful to me with him, Lizbeth?"

"She is not your wife, father. Lizbeth is free to do as she pleases. I care for Lizbeth and I want to have a chance with her".

"That is never, going to happen!"

"Please, both of you, stop. There is no need to cause any commotion. I am going to my room".

Lizbeth swam across the pool towards the pool stairs and climbed out.

"There is no commotion, just some simple inquiries".

"Well, enough inquiries on my account".

Lizbeth wrapped a towel around herself and walked off. Leo waited a few seconds, then followed behind. Alex frustrated slapped onto the water.

Leo caught up to Lizbeth and grabbed her arm and got close to her face.

"So soon? You already seek to replace me with another man?"

"Enough, Leo".

"That is what I tell you. Enough playing this game of thinking that your are not my wife. You know very well that you are. You are mine. I was your first love and will continue to be the man you love. I am the man you will choose time and time again".

"Leo, stop it!"

"I will never stop. You know why, because you really don't want me to stop. You fight your urges for me, but it's no use. Alex cannot replace me and what I am to you. Let me go upstairs with you. Let me show you how much I love you and remind you why you became mine. Let me share your bed with you tonight".

Lizbeth snatched her arm away and frustratedly nodded at Leo and walked off.

Aggravated that Lizbeth turned him down again, he hit the wall.

It was late in the evening and Leo was sitting in his office leaned back in his chair with a drink in his hands. He sat for a bit looking at the portrait painting of Lizbeth on his wall. He began to have flashbacks of that day in the painting and how beautiful she looked. He also had flashbacks of when they first met, their picnic in the museum, and the first night they made love. Leo sipped his drink then stood up from the chair and came closer to the painting. He glimpsed over to the window and saw Alexandra and Alex sitting outside on the bench talking. He watched them for moment, then with his eyes only he looked back at the painting. Leo then set his drink down on the table and left his office and headed upstairs and towards Lizbeth's room. He came close to the door to see if he could hear anything inside. Then he snuck into Lizbeth's room and locked the door behind him. Just as he expected, Lizbeth was just finishing up her shower. He walked into the bathroom and leaned on the bathroom sink and watched her through the shower glass door. Then he began to loosen his tie and slowly pull it off. He unbuttoned his shirt keeping his eyes on Lizbeth the whole time. Leo then pulled off the button shirt and the tank top he was wearing underneath it and crossed his arms as he continued to watch Lizbeth. When she was done showering she turned off the water and opened the shower glass door, when suddenly she was startled by seeing Leo standing there. She tried covering her private parts with her hands.

"Leo? Get out or I will begin to scream!"

"There is no need for you to do so. I've come to talk".

"You are standing in my bathroom half naked, and you want to talk?"

"Actually, yes. I do".

"I am in no condition to speak to you. Give me a towel".

Leo threw her a wash cloth, she used it to cover herself below the waist.

"You think this is funny?"

"I do. It's pretty funny to me".

Lizbeth stepped out of the shower angry and tried to walk away from Leo. He gently pulled her and leaned her against the wall. Lizbeth brushed his arms off of her and he quickly lifted his arms up in the air to show he wasn't trying to be forceful.

"I just want to talk".

"Why can't you do so in a better place. Why now, why here?"

"Because this is when you are at your most vulnerable and willing to listen. Any other way, and you are a feral cat clawing at me".

"Say what you have to say and get out".

"Fine, I know I have done you so much wrong. But as crazy as it sounds, I did so because I loved you. I still love you with all of my heart and I don't think I can ever stop loving you. It is not fair how you have been stripped away from me as my wife. All in one night, because of my first wife's return? I have not seen her in over 10 years. During that time I had many lovers, but not one of those women I loved, like I love you. None of them I made my wife, like I did with you. I had to have you and I waited until you were ready. When I finally made you mine and brought you here, I don't know what came over me. I became desperately fearful of ever losing you, so I handled it the best way I knew how".

"By forcing, threatening and beating me? Are you out of your mind, Leo. That is NOT love. When you are in love with someone, you would never hurt them or cause them any pain".

"Your right. I understand that now. This was all new to me. I did not know how to handle love. The way I...the wrong way I handled it with you, is the only way I have always known how to have what I want. My intentions never were to hurt you. I just let my obsession for you get the better of me and I handled things with a constant fear in that I might lose you".

Lizbeth's eyes teared up and her voice cracked.

"You, broke, my heart. I fell madly in love with you. You were my first love".

"Yes, and I know that your love cannot dissipate overnight. I know there is still love for me in your heart".

"No Leo, that love has turned into hatred and anger towards you. You take and take, but you say that you give so much back. You only give a drop and take back by the bucket full. I am tired of your mind games. I do not know if what you felt for me in the beginning was love or just part of your game of conquest. Well, you won the game and captured your prize. But what you do not understand, is that I am not a pawn on your game board. I am a person with feelings and a heart. Feelings and a heart you broke. Instead of loving what I loved, you took from me what I loved. Even the man I fell in love with and married was taken away from me. Now what I have in front of me...I hate".

"Lizbeth, please. There is nothing I can say to remedy all the damage I have done. I regret it all, but you are a good person and I know you can forgive me".

"Forgive? Which part exactly? When you threatened the life of my friends? When you taunted and shamed me naked in a bed to force me to tell you I wanted you willingly. Or when you beat me to get a name of a lover that did not exist, but a friend willing to help".

"A friend? Who kissed my wife?"

"I am not your wife...".

"But you were! But you were, when he kissed you. And in the bedroom we shared together".

"It does not matter now, he is gone".

"I can forgive you that, and I will not try to hunt him down and gut him like a pig. But I need you to forgive me as well".

"If I forgive you, will you allow us to part ways and live our own lives".

"I can't do that, Lizbeth. You are asking me to give up my own life in doing so. Without you I have no reason to live. I cannot do that".

"Leave me alone and get out. I want to dress myself. You continue to shame me having me stand here naked like this. You enjoy seeing me this way, this is where you find pleasure".

"You think I am here to shame you or torment you? Here, a towel. No, let me wrap it around you. Is that better? Will you talk to me now".

"There is nothing else that needs to be said, Leo. I have nothing else to say to you".

"Then just listen. Say nothing and just listen. I want to make up to you everything I have done wrong. I know it will take time for you to heal from the wounds I caused, but I will wait".

"What if I never forgive you?"

"You will. You are a good person, Lizbeth. The better half of me".

"So you will take advantage of my good nature to get what you want, even if you don't deserve it".

"I, love you, Lizbeth. I don't know how else to tell you. I will divorce my wife and marry...."

"No, no, no!"

Lizbeth pushed Leo back and walked over to the other side of the bathroom.

"You must truly be out of your mind to think that I would marry you again. With Alexandra as your wife or not. I will never accept to marry you again. To be your wife, means to become your property. No thank you, I choose freedom".

"Then become my mistress. I will cater to you, to whatever you want. Alexandra will not mind. After 10 years neither of us know each other or love each other the same".

"Is it me, or do you continue to talk out of your own personal satisfaction only".

"Then tell me what you want. Tell me, I will give it to you".

"I want to go home".

"Fine, I will take you myself".

"Not with you. I want to go alone. You will never listen to reason".

Lizbeth barged out the bathroom demanding that Leo leave. He caught her arm right when she was at the foot of the bed and turned her around.

"I want to show you that I can give and not take or demand anything in return".

"I don't care about your give or take. Get out!"

"I will. If you ask me to do so...after".

"After what?"

Just then Leo forcefully pulled the bath towel off of Lizbeth and grabbed her in a bear hug pushing both of them down on top of the bed. With Leo's weight on her, Lizbeth could only use her arms to pull herself upward toward the headboard. As she did Leo followed just enough until they were both completely on the bed. Then he wrapped his arms from underneath Lizbeth's thighs, gripping them from around the top. This locked her in place from being able to move away from Leo. She could not crawl or wiggle her way out. He then went right into pleasing her with his mouth. Lizbeth fought by trying to push his head away, which he then managed to grab each of her hands one by one and interlock fingers with her.

"Leo, stop. Stop."

Leo continued orally pleasing Lizbeth. She continued trying to struggle, but it got to the point that she could not get away. The feeling became so intense that Lizbeth threw herself back onto the bed, begging for Leo to stop. After several moments of her begging him to stop Lizbeth hit her climax.

Alex eyes suddenly widened and he abruptly stood up from the bench he was sitting on. He then walked over to some flowers. He picked one and looked at it. Alexandra smiled.

"Your thinking of her again".

"I am, mother".

"Are you in love with her?"

Alex smiled and nodded in agreement.

"Well, what will you do, Alex? Your father is obsessed with her.

"I don't know. I just know that I have to try and rescue her, somehow".

"In that case, I ask you this. Does she love you in the same way you love her?"

"I believe she does, or at least she wants to. But she is afraid of my father. She is afraid that if she returns the love I feel for her, my life is put at risk".

"Do you believe she is right to think this way? The man I see today is a very different man. And his obsession with her is the kind that puts all of our lives at risk".

"I am not afraid of him, but I am afraid of what he can do to her. Before she was trapped in the painting he beat her to learn the name of the man who tried to help her. No matter what he did to her, she did not reveal my name to him. Why would she do that to protect me, unless she loved me. What's worse is that I feel like a coward for not standing up to my father to protect her. I should have been bold enough to just courageously walk her right out of this house".

"Alex, this is no fairytale story. This is different. You know very well that if you place yourself between your father and her, he will see you as a threat to getting what he wants. You and I must be patient until we can learn a way out of this. If Lizbeth leaves the house, my life is at risk. If I divorce your father and leave the house, Lizbeth's life is at risk. We must be smart about how we all escape your fathers madness. Now, I believe I have a plan".

"What would that be?"

"Eduardo, your fathers boss always had a strong love for me. I did not choose him and I chose your father instead. Eduardo was hurt, but remained a loyal friend. I will go see him tomorrow and request his protection. Your father may think he is unstoppable, but Eduardo is the only man your father knows he cannot defy. With Eduardo's protection, who knows if we can even save Lizbeth".

"I will go with you to speak to him".

"I would like that. Now, tell me about this ability that Lizbeth has with paintings".

Leo finally let Lizbeth go and she rolled over to her side pulling on the bedsheets to cover her front side. Her back was still uncovered and Leo quickly climbed over placing his body close to her back and putting his arm around her waist. She forcefully pushed his arm off.

"Don't touch me! How could you do such a thing?"

"I wanted to show you that I can give and not expect anything in return. Though I desperately wanted you and still do, I am doing my best to contain my desires to prove to you that I can".

"That is not the same thing. What you just did to me, was not control".

"Then blame me for losing control in wanting to please you and only you".

He gently stroked her arm. She tried brushing him off, but then he did it again.

"Lizbeth? Do you remember when we first met at your museum? You approached me so aggressively and strong. I knew you were angry, but I just couldn't get my eyes off of you. You looked like the most sexiest librarian that every existed".

Leo chuckled. Lizbeth's eyes began to water.

"Your hair was in a ponytail, and you had a black turtleneck top hiding all your beautiful skin. But it conformed to your curves, just like the skirt you wore. Your black framed glasses? Well, I knew early on they were not prescription. I noticed quickly the blue light reflection as you shook your head in frustration, threatening to give up the building before selling me one of your paintings. In all your anger, I could only think about how badly I wanted to kiss those angry lips of yours. I tried to gather my very bold thoughts of kissing you, and I knew that you were not going to be easy to win over. You were nothing like other woman. I invited you for coffee, but of course in your stubborn ways, we had to have tea instead. That is where you learned about the sweet milk with tea. Do you remember that?"

Lizbeth's tears began to fall down her cheek.

"Leo, please..."

"I remember wanting you to taste mine. I purposely reached out my cup so you could drink from my hand. When you did, I thought I would drop my cup from the shake I tried so hard to control in my hand".

"Leo, enough".

Lizbeth tears were uncontrollably coming down. As she sniffed from her crying, Leo leaned over and kissed the side of her head.

"My love. Forgive me. I am not trying to cause you anymore pain. I just wanted to remember what was good and pure between us. Before I became greedy and obsessed. In my defense, you are the kind of woman who would make any man lose his mind and become sick with love. I did not fight these feelings, I just gave in to them.

Lizbeth gave off a sarcastic sigh.

"You could think of me as a fool. But if I had to do it all over again, I would. The only changes I would make, is doing my best to control my obsession in keeping you away from the people you loved. All because of my jealousy in wanting you to only love me. If I had controlled my jealousy. You would still be mine today. Philip and Tiara would have visited us often roaming this house with you. And you would have smiled often, in turn making me smile to see you so happy".

Leo then curled up closer to Lizbeth and again wrapped his arms around her waist, laying his head slightly on the pillow and Lizbeth's head.

"And every night we would have slept close together, just like this. Madly in love with each other".

Leo closed his eyes and let out a deep breath. Lizbeth wiped her tears.

Before long they were both fast asleep.

The next morning Leo woke up still by Lizbeth's side. He smiled and kissed her on the head. Then he got out of the bed, got his shirt and tie from the bathroom and began to go towards Lizbeth's bedroom door. He placed his hand on the knob and looked back at Lizbeth.

"Little by little my love. It will take time, but I will win you back".

He then turned the knob and opened the door stepping out of the room wearing nothing but his pants and shoes. Alex had just come back from a run and saw his father leaving Lizbeth's room this way. Leo looked up at Alex and smirked.

"Good morning, Alex".

He walked pass Alex towards his bedroom. Alex angrily turned around to look at his father.

"What were you doing coming out of Lizbeth's room? Did you hurt her? Father if you hurt her, I swear...."

"I did nothing to Lizbeth that she did not want or enjoy. You have no place in questioning what I do or do not do with a woman that is mine and always will be".

"Lizbeth is no longer yours and if you forced yourself on her...."

"What I did with Lizbeth is no concern of yours! But if you must know, she and I had a peaceful night in each others arms".

"That is not true. Lizbeth hates you".

"Hates me? She hates me enough to allow me to spend the night with her? I think you are mistaken, Alex".

Alex became jealous and turned around and rushed to Lizbeth's room. He barged in and walked over to her. He saw her sleeping peacefully with her naked back showing.

"You let him have you!"

Lizbeth woke up startled.

"Alex?"

"Tell me, did you sleep with my father or not? I need to hear it from your mouth".

"What are you talking about?"

"He walks out of your bedroom half naked at this hour. I come in and you are completely naked and asleep. How do you think this looks to me?"

"It is not what you think?"

"Why is it everyone always says those words when they have been caught."

"It is not the same thing, Alex".

"Answer me this, just answer this. Did you or did your not spend the night with my father, here in this bedroom?"

"I guess he did?"

"You guess? Did he drug you?"

"No, I was not drugged".

"You willingly let him stay with you?"

Alex began to pace and breath hard in frustration.

"Alex, it was not like that. He snuck in while I was in the shower. He asked to talk".

"While you were in the shower?"

"Yes, but we spoke and I demanded him to leave several times".

"Until you ended up naked with him in your bed and letting him spend the night here, with you!"

"No, Alex, it wasn't like that. You have it all wrong".

Lizbeth stood up from the bed and tried to grab onto Alex's arm and he pulled away from her.

"Don't touch me. I feel like such a fool. Here I was last night sharing with my mother how madly in love I am with you, and you were in this bed rolling around with my father".

"Alex, please. It wasn't....."

Alex stormed out of Lizbeth's room and barged into his room slamming the door behind him.

Lizbeth closed her bedroom door and laid against it. She was shocked and confused at what just happened.

Alex paced his bedroom thinking of his fathers words and how he just saw Lizbeth in the bed. Then he thought of the times he and Lizbeth made love, how many times she mentioned hating Leo, and then back to remembering what he saw with his father leaving Lizbeth's bedroom. Alex could not take the anger anymore and rushed over to his fathers room. Leo had finished his shower and was almost fully dressed, except for finishing up buttoning his shirt, when Alex barged into the room. Leo came out of his bathroom and Alex punched him. Leo swung back and both men were in a full fight in Leo's bedroom. They hit furniture and began to knock things over breaking and shattering them on the floor. With all the commotion Alexandra ran out from her room to see what was wrong. She found Alex and Leo fighting.

"Stop it! Both of you stop it!"

She stood between them holding her arms out.

"What has gotten into you too? I have never seen you like this before! Is this how the both of you have handled your issues in the 10 years I was gone?"

Furious still, Alex pointed at his father.

"Stay away from Lizbeth!"

Leo furiously pointed back at Alex.

"No! You stay away from her! I have told you time and time again that she is mine".

"She is not yours!"

"No? Does she belong to you then?"

"Lizbeth belongs to no one. She is not a piece of property".

"That is where you are wrong, she may not property. But I own her heart. No matter how much she tries to hate me, I still own her heart. I was her first everything. Her first kiss, the man who first touched her body and her first....".

"Enough!"

"You really think you can take what belongs to your father. You will never have her love, like I have it. No matter how much she tries to hide it, she is still mine and always will be. Go ahead and try touching her. She will think of me when you do...".

Alex lost his temper and tried to rush his father. His mother held him back as best as he could and tried pushing him out of the bedroom. When she got him to the hall, Alex was still yelling out at his father. Lizbeth heard the commotion of yelling and ran out of her room to see Alex irate and Alexandra trying to hold him back. Lizbeth ran over to help and grabbed Alex's arm.

"Alex, stop!"

Alex snatched his arm back and looked at Lizbeth with anger. She lowered her head and he walked off to his bedroom. Alexandra followed behind him and grabbed Lizbeth's wrist.

"Come".

Lizbeth followed Alexandra to Alex's room. Alexandra went in and Lizbeth stood at the door.

"Alex, what has come over you to fight with you father in this way".

"That man is not my father! That man is a pig!

Leo walked out of his room dressed and ready to go. He looked over at Alex's room and saw Lizbeth standing in the doorway. She looked over and saw Leo. He smiled, then turned and walked away. Lizbeth took some deep breaths and lowered her head. Alex saw her.

"Did he just look at you?"

Alex went to walk up to Lizbeth and Alexandra stopped him.

"Alex, you need to calm down. You are scaring me and Lizbeth".

"I do not care mother. Let me be angry. Let me be alone".

He looked up at Lizbeth.

"Do you still love him?"

Lizbeth sigh and couldn't answer.

"It is a simple question, Lizbeth. Do you still love him?"

Still Lizbeth could not answer. Alex got even more upset and Alexandra tried calming him down.

"Do you love...".

"I do! And I do not! I hate him for all he has made me suffer and for how he still torments me. That I hate, but I loved him once. The only way to rid myself of that love is to darken my heart with hate. And never let anyone love me or love anyone ever again. I refuse to shut my heart up. But in doing so he torments with my memories of how much I loved him. He confuses me".

Lizbeth buried her face in her hands and began to cry. Alex looked at her and felt pity for her. Alexandra leaned towards Alex's ear.

"Give her time, Alex. She has not fully healed".

Alexandra turned around and walked out of the room. Alex sighed and walked over to Lizbeth and embraced her.

"I'm sorry. I'm sorry I lost my temper and let my jealousy get the best of me".

"I'm used this happening now. Men and their rages of anger and my fear and confusion. I'm tired, Alex. I'm tired. I need to get away. Please, let me leave. Tell your mother that I need to leave".

"Lizbeth, wait. Do not leave. I have better idea".

Alex left his room and went to his mother's room. Lizbeth stood there for a moment wondering what he was planning, then followed behind him. Alex walked into his mothers room and Lizbeth stood in the hall listening.

"Mother, Lizbeth and I will be taking a trip".

"A trip? Where?".

"You know where. Which one, I do not know yet, but I will join Lizbeth and I don't know when we will return. She and I both need to clear out heads. And get away from my father".

338

Alexandra walked over to him and placed her hands on his cheeks. She then leaned him forward and kissed his forehead.

"Go. Take as long as you need".

"Come with us mother, so we can ensure your safety".

"No worries, Alex. I will be safe. I have to go somewhere today to pay a visit to an old friend. I assure you that this visit will ensure my safety. Then Lizbeth will not have to carry the burden in trying to help more than she already has, by staying here in this house".

Alex nodded in agreement and hugged is mother. He then stepped out and saw Lizbeth standing there in the hall. He reached out and took her by the hand and led her downstairs to the hall of artwork. Alexandra followed behind.

"Pick one".

Lizbeth looked at Alex confused.

"You wanted to get away. Pick one. I am going with you. We can return when we are ready".

Lizbeth now understood what Alex meant. She looked at the paintings and chose the one Alexandra was in.

"Good choice Lizbeth. It was lonely there, but I admit, it was a beautiful island".

Lizbeth nodded then stretch her arms out, took a deep breath in and out, then abruptly opened her arms opening the gate at the same time. Alex reached out and took Lizbeth by the hand and they walked in together. After they disappeared into the painting Alexandra smiled, then walked away to get ready to meet with Eduardo.

Alexandra waited for Eduardo in his office. When he got word on who was waiting for him, he rushed towards his office and into the room.

"Alexandra?"

"Eduardo!"

She quickly stood up from the chair and rushed over to embrace him. After doing so he placed his hands on her shoulder and gently pushed her back.

"Let me get a good look at you. I cannot believe my eyes. I thought I would never see you again. I feared, I would never see you again. I admit there were times I thought you were....".

"Dead?"

"Every time I thought it, I wondered if it had been Leo and I wanted to kill him with my bare hands".

"Eduardo, I admit at times I felt like I would die. But I survived".

"Where were you all this time?"

"Stranded. On an island".

"Stranded, on an island?"

"I know. It sounds crazy. But it's true. I waited and waited for years. For someone. Anyone to rescue me. When I was finally rescued, I thought they were all a figment of my imagination. I had those often. When you have over 10 years with not one person to converse with, you begin to have many of those".

A tear went down Alexandra's cheek. Eduardo wiped it away.

"Well, what's important is that I did not slowly slip into madness. I remained strong and for all those years. And now, I am back".

"I don't think there is anyone in the world happier to have you back, Alexandra".

"Well of course there is. Alex is happy to have me back".

Eduardo chuckled.

"What I mean is, I don't think there is any man in the world that is still in love with you as much as I still am. Who is happier to have you back".

Alexandra placed her hand on Eduardo's cheek.

"Oh, Eduardo".

He kissed the hand she placed on his cheek and they both smiled at each other.

"Will you walk with me, in my gardens? I have had many improvements made. With the hopes you would someday return to see them".

"You had your gardens made to my liking?"

"You make it sound like I have done something wrong".

"No, it's just....".

"Anna, never liked gardens. They do not suit her either way. I was sure when I saw her walk past the flowers once, they immediately shriveled into dark gray mushrooms of some sort".

Alexandra burst out laughing and Eduardo laughed with her. He then reached out his arm and escorted her to the gardens.

Eduardo and Alexandra walked the gardens. He pointed out the changes made and Alexandra quickly leaned in to touch and smell the flowers.

"It is so beautiful, Eduardo".

"I always thought you would like it".

"Like it? I love it".

"I remembered that lavenders were always your favorite. You said the smell offers...joy?"

"Relaxation. Lavender scent allows one to feel relaxed".

"And joyous. The scent always made me think of you. And when I did, I would smile".

"I admit. While on that island, I thought a lot about you. I thought of everyone. Alex and Leo. But what felt like night when I was all alone. In front of a fire, I learned to build, I always thought of you".

"Did you say, you learned how to build a fire?"

"Is that all you heard? But, yes, I did. And how to build a hut, and dry fish, and make my very own coconut oil to fry fish in. That had a lot of trial by error, but there was plenty of coconut on the island for me to learn. With what was left from the coconut, I used as body scrubs and creams. It kept me busy, while I waited to be rescued".

"It also kept you beautiful. It is as you never even aged".

"Now you are just trying to flatter me. And I did not come for flattery. I came to ask for your help".

"Anything, Alexandra".

"I need protection. From Leo. I have been gone long and he no longer loves me the same. He is infatuated by this Lizbeth. With my return his marriage was annulled. Now he has no power over her. I feel I stand in the way between his duty with me and his obsession with her. I have finally seen my son, and I would hate for him to lose me again so quickly".

"Are you saying Leo is trying to kill you".

"I do not think he is trying to just yet, but I know it will come to that if Lizbeth grows tired of his constant pursuit for her and she leaves the house. I have asked her to stay, while I seek protection. Once Alex and I are safe, she can run and hide from Leo. Though she wanted to leave quickly after my return, I convinced her to stay and help me".

"Alexandra, you need not ask again. If so long as a hair on your head is harmed, I will put Leo to death by my hand. Even if it anything that happens to you seems like an accident, he is still dead. You can tell him that it is in his best interest that he also ensures your protection".

"Thank you, Eduardo. I feel much safer already."

"I offer you my protection for you to live in that home with him, for now".

"For now?"

"Yes, while I divorce Anna. I know she will fight me and make it a long battle, but I will have my lawyers move it along as quick as possible. Once it is done you and I will marry. Leo will give you the quick divorce you need if he is obsessed with another".

"I cannot divorce Leo just yet. If I do so now, he will surely force Lizbeth into a marriage with him and her choice to stay and help me, would become her burden".

"Then I give you until my divorce is complete. And Lizbeth is safe. Then you marry me and come to live with me. I see no better way to secure your safety. And live the rest of my life ensuring your happiness, to make up for the years we lost".

"Eduardo, I don't know how to think of you right now. Are you just crazy or in love".

"I am crazy in love with you, Alexandra. I always have been. I always will be. Even after you chose Leo over me. I let you go. You left to be with him, with my heart in your hand".

"But, you married Anna".

"Only after you married Leo. And I did so out of rebellion. I was broken-hearted and angry with you. But still madly in love with you. So much so that my relationship with Anna always remained without love".

"Eduardo. I am truly sorry. I did not mean to hurt you this way. I thought I loved Leo".

"You thought?"

"He had a way with words. After being married to him, I realized, that was all they were, words. His actions always contradicted what he said. I resented him often for that. Then he began working often and he seemed lost. When I looked into his eyes, it was as if there was nothing inside of him. There was a man standing there, but with no soul".

"Alexandra, the business I run is an agency that take out bad people. We have evaded wars, by sending in our men to take out the enemy. We also get paid really well in doing so. I hired Leo on to take care of some of the work. But he lost control and the killings became a game for him. Our agency maintains peace, from corruption. Leo took on jobs that were different from what we do. He thinks I do not know, but I have men watching him. In each report they would tell me he was more and more out of control. We are nothing like a mafia, who kill for their personal satisfaction and reputation. We are a clean agency, who kill to protect the helpless. Leo lost that concept and killed for pleasure. Then I received a report, that he has calmed himself much more since meeting Lizbeth.

"I did not know this. He always said he worked in business, but never told me what kind. Now I understand why he seemed to be losing himself in his work. Every time we fought, I thought of you and smiled thinking at least one of us was happy".

"Happy? You thought I was happy with Anna? When I made love to her, I only thought about you. The last time I made love to her she conceived our son, after that I never lied her again".

"Why?"

"She did not want me, because I called her by your name".

"Eduardo!"

"I was a young man, Alexandra. A man who was in love with a woman he could not have. My wife no longer wanted to me. So I had lovers. I am ashamed to tell you this, but I did have many lovers. I paid for their affection. And none were bothered when I called them by your name. Forgive me for sharing such a thing, I am a sick man."

"Eduardo, no. From what I am hearing, you have been sick in love".

Eduardo covered his face and silently cried. Alexandra wrapped her arms around him and held him. Eduardo cried for a moment in Alexandra's arms. Then he gently pulled away.

"We cannot have what I once wanted. But we can still have a chance to be together. We tell no one of our plans until the day arrives. After we are married it will be too late for anyone to stand in our way".

Alexandra nodded in agreement and Eduardo embraced her in a passionate kiss.

Lizbeth was standing by the shore and looking out to the waters. Alex was sitting on the beach sand, deep in thought and looking at Lizbeth.

When Lizbeth was ready she walked over and sat by Alex. He looked at her and she looked at him, then turned her face.

"I really want to understand, Lizbeth. Ever since I have met you, you have been a mystery that I am always trying to figure out and understand".

"I do not try to be. It's just that some things cannot be shared until the time is right. Like traveling through paintings. Had I told you that in the beginning, would you have believed me, unless you saw it happen?"

"I guess not. I would have thought you were a beautiful but crazy woman".

Alex chuckled and Lizbeth smiled and looked down. They stood silent for a moment. Then Lizbeth took a deep breath.

"Let me try and show you".

She stood up to find a twig and other things, then sat by Alex again. She drew a heart in the sand.

"This was my heart. It was perfect. I felt love and loved. I had Philip and Tiara and we had our paintings and travels. I understood my destiny was to protect the paintings and to keep the lineage of art guardians alive. Especially by having children of my own. Your father came and romanced me. He said all the right words and made me feel special. I fell in love with him".

Lizbeth placed beautiful shells inside of the heart shape drawn in the sand.

"As time passed, he began to lie and deceive me. Then hurt came into my heart."

She then placed small broken twigs and dried crumbled leaves into the heart shape drawn in the sand.

"To protect my heart, I built a wall. This way he could no longer fill my heart with his poisons".

Lizbeth drew a square box around the heart drawing.

"Once his words changed from cruelty to kindness the wall began to weaken. I do my best to keep it strong, but the love I felt is still in there. Underneath all the bad. I do not want it there, but I do not know how to get rid of it either. It's as if your father knows this, so he calls to the shells of love inside of my heart until he has penetrated my wall. Once in my heart again, he stirs it all together".

Lizbeth used the long twig to stir the shells, small broken twigs pieces and crumbled leaves.

"As he gets closer he fills it with more and more poison, covered with words of love and hope".

Lizbeth drops in a handful of dried crumbled leaves until it cover the shells.

"Now, what am I left with? A heavy heart and a mind full of confusion. And I do not know what to do".

Alex sighs and stands up, then he walks towards and into the ocean and jumps into the water. After a while of being under the water, he come up and walks out of the water with his hands full. Lizbeth looks over at him wondering what he has in his hands. He approaches Lizbeth and lets go a handful of seashells in all shapes and sizes. They fall inside of the heart shape drawing Lizbeth drew in the sand. There were so many shells that they covered all the small broken twigs, dried leaves, and shells she had placed in before.

"What you do is love again. Open your heart to the right person and try again. No matter how many times it takes. Until there is no room for anyone to break your heart, because instead of poison, your heart is filled with the shells of love and the desire to love and be loved!"

Lizbeth was shocked looking at all the beautiful fresh shells covering her dry shells. She looked up at Alex and he reached out his hand and grabbed Lizbeth's arm, then lifted her up.

"I want that chance to fill your heart. I want the love I have for you to consume the hurt and love you had for him. Until he is just a memory of your past. A story to tell, which ends with a beautiful love story of us and what we have".

"Alex, you say this like it is so simple and easy to do".

"No, it may not be easy, but at least you try to let me in. Let me love you. Let me help you heal. I never want to compete with him. I want to overpower his failures with my love for you. When you are ready to give me that chance, you come search for me".

Alex walked away and back towards the water. He walked in until it reached his waist and dived into the water. Lizbeth stood standing there watching Alex go in and out of the water, swimming without a care in the world. Tears began to run down her cheeks and she kept trying to aggressively wipe them away. Then she began to slowly walk towards the water. Alex turned around and saw Lizbeth coming. She then continued entering the water and walking towards him. Lizbeth stopped in front of him and placed her hand on his chest near his heart. Then she placed his hand on her chest near her heart Tears began to come down her cheeks.

"I am terrified to love again. I am terrified that you would break my heart. Or lock me away, drug me, hit me...".

"I am not him, Lizbeth. I should not pay for his mistakes. I am the man who wants to protect your heart. Are you willing to let me?"

Lizbeth looked up at Alex and bit her bottom lip trying to hold herself from crying. She then nodded in agreement. Alex smiled and sighed a sigh of relief, then leaned in and kissed Lizbeth. She wrapped her arms around his head and neck and he picked her up as they continued kissing.

Lizbeth and Alex entered the little hut that was still there. Lizbeth laid down on her back and Alex lay on top of her. He kissed her passionately as he caressed her arms, her side and her legs. Then they slowly undressed each other. Alex was sure to be gentle with Lizbeth.

"Are you okay? Are you sure?"

"I am okay. And yes, I am sure".

Alex and Lizbeth continued to kiss, when he suddenly slipped in causing Lizbeth to throw her head back and let out a pleasured groan. He then began to gently make love to her for the first time with passion. She allowed herself to feel Alex's love for her as they looked into each other eyes. She responded to his love by pulling him down and kissing him. Then slowly moving down to gently bite and kiss on his arm and neck. They continued this way until Lizbeth grabbed tightly onto Alex and hit her climax. She began loudly moaning from the pleasure. Alex released at that exact moment. Both of them allowing themselves to have no control over the feelings of pleasure and passion they shared.

Afterwards they tightly held each other close. Lizbeth softly stroked Alex's arm until they both fell asleep. As Lizbeth slept, a little silver light shaped like seed flashed inside of her traveling upward towards her womb. When it reached, it flashed brightly and then faded away.

Leo was furious throwing things around smashing them into pieces. Alexandra awoke hearing his yells and hearing things being broken.

"WHERE IS SHE! WHERE IS LIZBETH! ALEX TOOK HER, DIDN'T HE? I WANT THEM BACK NOW, SO I CAN KILL HIM AND LOCK HER UP!

Alexandra opened her bedroom door and two of Eduardo's men were standing guard.

"Both of you come inside my bedroom instead, until he cools down".

The men entered Alexandra's bedroom. One of them called to report to Eduardo what was happening and to warn the other men who they change shifts with, to watch their backs.

"Did he see you both outside my door?"

"He did Mrs. Ferreira. He asked who we were and we told him we were Eduardo's men. He laughed and was fine, but when he became this way was once he entered the bedroom down the hall. He came out of the room like a madman".

"That was Lizbeth's room".

"Then he entered the room across from that one".

"Alex's room".

"He did not find anyone and ran down the hall then down the stairs yelling the name 'Lizbeth'".

"He's desperately looking for her, but he won't find her or my son Alex".

The other guard got off of the phone with Eduardo.

"Mrs. Ferreira, Eduardo wants us to take you out of this house as soon as possible".

"Okay, yes. Let me go change".

As Alexandra went to change her clothes the guard called the other men to be ready and extract Alexandra from the home. The other men went rushing to get the car.

After Alexandra changed out her nightgown the guards pulled out their guns and opened the door and checked the hall. When the coast was clear they began to take Alexandra out of the room and down the stairs. Right before getting to the door she stopped.

"The painting. I cannot leave the painting".

"What painting, Mrs. Ferreira. Our orders are to extract you, not a painting".

"I can't let Leo find the painting".

Both guards pointed their guns and had Alexander lead the way. When she got to the hall of artwork she showed the guards the painting of the island. One guard put his gun away and took the painting off of the wall. Then they went back to the entrance of the house. Leo's yelling could be heard getting louder and closer, so they rushed Alexander to the door. Once there, the guard with the painting opened the door while the other pointed his gun and ensured that it was safe outside. Eduardo's other men pulled up in the car and they quickly put Alexander into the car and her painting in the trunk. Then they all got it and drove off.

Clara heard the commotion and saw how Alexandra was escorted out of the house. She even became afraid of Leo's rage and she rushed to her bedroom and locked herself in. Leo came out of every room searching for Lizbeth. Then he passed the hall of artwork. That is when he came to a sudden halt. He turned back toward the hall of artwork and that is when he noticed a painting on the wall was missing.

"LIZBEEEEETH!"

In the morning Clara unlocked and slowly opened her bedroom door. When she didn't hear anymore yelling and breaking, she stepped out. She began to walk the house and it was in ruins. There was not one room in the house that was not made a mess of. There was no one in the house. Everyone was gone, except for Leo who was drunk and passed out on his bed. When Clara saw him this way, she slowly closed his bedroom door.

She rolled out of the kitchen a trash can and a dustpan and broom, then she began cleaning up the mess one room at a time. As she did so, the sound of sweeping up broken glass echoed around the house in an eerie manner.

During the morning hours Eduardo handed Alexandra a cup of coffee. He then poured himself a cup and sat across of her from the table.

"Thank you, Eduardo".

"Now, Alexandra. Tell me what happened. I'm sorry I was not here when you arrived in the evening. After I rushed home my men told me you were in the bedroom. I did not want to interrupt your rest, so I waited til this morning".

"I was not really asleep, just yet. Shorty after I arrived here I was very upset. Your maid was so kind, she brought me lavender tea to calm my nerves. The tea, being here, feeling safer, it all helped tremendously. I laid myself in the bed and was calmer, but I could not sleep. I wished you had come to see me. Because last night, it was madness. What I feared came true. Alex has fallen in love with Lizbeth. But Leo is obsessed with her in a way I have never seen a man be towards a woman. It is not normal, Eduardo. He has become dangerous. I fear even for my sons life".

"Leo would never hurt his own son".

"I am not sure anymore, Eduardo. He yelled out that he wanted Lizbeth back and he knew that Alex was with her. He wanted Alex back as well so he could kill him. Your men heard his yells as he destroyed things all around the house".

"Then Leo has truly lost his mind. He has allowed his obsession to drive him into madness. It is not safe for you to return or be anywhere near that madman. You will remain here with me. I will respect you and allow you to stay in the guest bedroom. But I will have a room prepared as our matrimonial room. As soon as our divorces are finalized we wed and you will be my wife and fully under my protection".

"Eduardo, I can't. I would never purposely disrespect your wife in this way. What would she think walking these halls and seeing me here".

"Anna no longer lives here. She saw us in the gardens the last time you were here. When you came to request protection".

"Eduardo, I am so sorry. I didn't mean to cause this".

"I am not sorry. Anna and I lived in the same home for many years, but our marriage ended more than twenty years ago. She of coursed demanded a divorce after seeing our kiss. She said she would not allow me to shame her in front of our friends, so she wanted to divorce me first. As I expected, all she wanted was money and things. I agreed to her terms and she left happily, with her lover".

"Did you say, lover?"

"Anna had many lovers. Men who worked the grounds, movers, musicians, pretty much anyone she wanted. As I said. Our marriage ended a long time ago".

"In that case I will stay here with you".

Eduardo smiled and Alexandra smiled back and reached out her hand and held his.

Lizbeth was being chased by Alex on the beach. She yelled and laughed loudly doing her best to outrun him, but was not match for his speed. He caught her from behind and spinned her around as they laughed together. Then they dropped to the sand and Alex rolled on top of her giving a quick kiss. When Alex least expected it, Lizbeth smiled then pushed him and quickly stood up and ran towards the water. He jumped up from the sand and chased after her. Alex caught Lizbeth in the water and picked her up in another spin. He slowly brought her down.

"I give up. I won't run anymore, Alex".

"Good, because I am desperate to have you".

They kissed passionately and Alex lifted her in the water as she wrapped her legs around him. He then turned her back towards the waves so it pushed her closer to him each time. Then they began to make love in the ocean waters. The waves splashing gently onto Lizbeth's back as Alex pressed his cheek against her chest to avoid every wave from hitting his face. They gripped tightly onto each other, not allowing the waves or the water to stop them. Afterwards Lizbeth slide down and looked at Alex. They kissed again.

They both made love often. One the beach, in the hut, everywhere and every time they wanted to.

Alex was sitting on the beach with Lizbeth's back against his chest. He had his arms wrapped around her and was gently kissing her neck and cheeks.

"Alex?"

"Lizbeth".

"It has been almost a month now".

"It has? How do you know?"

"I keep count. While in a painting you have to, or you can lose track of time easily".

"I don't care about the time. For me it has felt like only a few days".

"While in a painting it can seem that way, because there is no day or night".

"It hasn't felt like a few days because there is no day or night. But because I am here with you. Hours seem to stop for me and I get to hold you in my arms for as long as I want to. No hiding or fearing. I can love you fully and nothing else matters".

Lizbeth looked up at Alex and placed her hand on his cheek and caressed it.

"Why couldn't we have met first. Why couldn't we have been together just like this, from the beginning".

"Because then we would not know how to appreciate all we have now. We would have taken it for granted. Sometimes adversity is needed to get a person to truly appreciate what they have. If it wasn't for my fathers cruelty, I would have never known you needed help and my protection. My heart would have been waiting for you, but we would have never even met".

Lizbeth teared up at Alex's words. She caressed his cheek again and he leaned to kiss her. Then they stopped kissing and smiled at each other.

"Lizbeth, my heart waited a long time for you. Now it's all yours. If you want it forever, depends on your answer to my question".

She sat up wondering what Alex meant. He then reached behind him and pulled out a bright shinning silver coated shell.

"Lizbeth, will you always take me to travel through paintings with you as the man you love, or how people call it in the real world, as your husband. Lizbeth, will you marry me and allow me to protect you and the paintings for the rest of our lives?"

She looked at the sliver shell and then at Alex, and was completely surprised and speechless. He then took the hand with the shell and gently rolled her hand open, dropping the shell in it.

"I know you have suffered a lot under the title of a wife. But I can promise you that it will be different with me. I may make mistakes, frustrate you, have jealous rages. Yet, I would always want to keep you safe, happy, and by my side. I want you Lizbeth. I wanted you the first moment I saw you, even though I wanted to hate you. You, weakened my walls".

Alex chuckled and lifted Lizbeth's face by the chin.

"If it's too soon and you are afraid to answer me now or you need time, I can wait as long as you want...".

"Yes!"

Lizbeth grabbed Alex's face in a passionate kiss. He wrapped his arms around her. She slowly pushed him down as she kissed him. When he was laying on the sand she sat up and pulled off her blouse then leaned back down and kissed Alex. They both continued to undress themselves and Lizbeth remained on top of Alex as she made love to him.

Alexandra was walking over to see Eduardo with a cup in her hands when two men in suits with briefcases exited the room. They nodded at Alexandra and she nodded back. As they walked off Alexandra entered the room and approached Eduardo.

"Ah, the most precious flower of my gardens. You are exactly who I wanted to speak with".

Alexandra placed the cup on Eduardo's desk and sat on his lap.

"Is that so. Well, I have brought you your cup of coffee. So if that was why you wanted to see me, then I will take my leave now".

Eduardo pulled Alexandra back down gently.

"Oh, you are not going anywhere any longer. The men that just left my office, were the lawyers I hired to handle your and my divorce. They have come early this morning to bring me the best news ever. Both Anna and Leo have signed and agreed to each of our divorce terms. With the connections I have with lawyers and judges, everything has been filed. You and I are now free and able to be married as soon as possible".

"Oh Eduardo! This is great news!"

Eduardo and Alexandra laughed with joy as they hugged and gave each other a kiss. Then he gently lifted her up, sat up from his chair and stood in front of her.

"Now, I will let you leave me for the moment to prepare for our wedding. It will be here in our gardens, where it is safer. Spare no expense my love. You will be the most beautiful bride, and I the luckiest man to ever walk the face of the earth".

"Eduardo you exaggerate. I am an old woman now, I don't know about beautiful".

"No, Alexandra. You are still as beautiful to me as the day we met".

Alexandra smiled and she leaned in and kissed Eduardo.

Later that afternoon the living room was filled with caters, florist, and dress designers helping Alexandra plan for the wedding. After they all left Eduardo watch Alexandra sigh a breath of relief. Eduardo came over to her and gave her a kiss.

"I did not realize wedding planning could be so tedious".

"After so many years alone on an island, I never thought that I would say that I am glad everyone is gone and I could have a moment to myself".

"Forgive me my love. I did not mean to overwhelm you. I just thought to call everyone to help with the planning. I was not sure how these things worked".

"Oh Eduardo. Do not mistake my mental exhaustion for anything more than happiness. I may not show it well through how tired I feel, but I am so happy. So very happy. More than I have been in years. Thank you".

They kissed again.

"Go and rest, my love. I will have Mawilda bring you a cup of lavender tea".

Alexandra agreed and left for her room. When she got to her room she went inside and sat on the bed with her back against the headboard.

"It feels like a dream come true. If only my son were here to share this special day with me".

Just then Mawilda entered the room to bring Alexandra the cup of lavender tea. Suddenly the island painting that was against Alexandra's bedroom wall lit up with the golden gate light. Mawilda yelled and dropped the cup of tea. The glass hit the floor and shattered. Eduardo heard the crash and rushed upstairs.

Alex and Lizbeth came out of the painting. Mawilda began to yell and step backwards until she bumped right into Eduardo.

"What has happened?"

"They came out of the painting!"

Eduardo looked up to see Alex and Lizbeth in Alexandra's bedroom. Surprised and afraid he stepped forward.

"What is the meaning of this? How did they get into the house and pass my men?"

"Mother? How are we in Eduardo's house?"

Alexandra jumped from the bed.

"Please, I can explain everything. Lizbeth and I can explain, Eduardo. And Mawilda, you must never speak a word of what you have just seen. If the wrong people learned of this, it could have grave consequences".

Leo was sitting in the middle of Lizbeth's bed with his back against the headboard. He was drunk and unshaven. All of her clothes scattered around the room. In one hand he had a liquor bottle he was drinking from and with his other hand he was softly touching the nightgown she wore.

"I'll find you, Lizbeth. This time when I do, we will be completely alone. No Alex, no Alexandra. No one. I have it all planned out my love. We will go to the church and you will remarry again. You will smile and be happy. Then we will run off to my secret home. No one knows of this one, or where it is. There we will be together and make love. You will desire me more than you have ever done before, and you will give yourself to me over and over and over again. You will beg me to give you children. And I will. We will have two, no three. We will be so happy. There will be no paintings...ANYWHERE! And you will not run from me ever again.

Leo picked up Lizbeth's nightgown and held it over his nose, inhaling her scent.

"I just have to find you, Lizbeth. Where are you my love? Remember, I am a free man now. Alexandra divorced me and I gladly signed. And I know why, so she could marry Eduardo. Those men here the night you disappeared, they were Eduardo's men. Eduardo was protecting Alexandra so I would not kill her, to get her out of the way so I could have you Lizbeth.

Leo chuckles and then remains still. His smile started to slowly come down and he began to gradually sit forward.

"Of course. It all makes sense now. I know where you are Lizbeth. I now know where you are".

Eduardo and Mawilda were sitting on the couch. Lizbeth and Alex were sitting on the other couch beside them. Alexandra was pacing.

"I know this is a lot to take in, Eduardo. This painting was the island I was stuck inside of for over 10 years. What I do not know is how I fell in".

"I think I do, Alexandra. When Leo was a boy he befriended a pair of twin cousins I had that learned how to travel. Leo wanted to learned and they tried to teach him. But, he became very greedy in wanting to do so and my cousins ended the friendship with Leo. He never fully learned how to open the gate, but he must have still had some ability to open it enough to where you fell in".

"Lizbeth, do you think my father still possesses this ability?"

"I do not believe so. If he did, he would have definitely tried to rescue me from the painting of the boat or your mother from the painting of the island. But he did not open the gate. I think he doesn't even know it was him that did that to your mother. As long as he does not know he has a trace of the ability, then he cannot practice to enhance it. Especially after all these years".

"This is all too much for my mind to comprehend".

"I know exactly what you mean, Eduardo. I felt the same way. Had I not seen Lizbeth and my mother come out from the paintings, I would not have believed it either".

"Maybe Lizbeth can show you, Eduardo. Can you show him, Lizbeth?"

"If and only if he promises to never share this secret. In the wrong hands, people can try to exploit it and use it for bad".

"I am not that kind of man, Lizbeth. I have no need for that kind of power. I am an old man. And I only want one thing. To retire and live the rest of my days, with the woman I love".

"Alex, get the painting".

Alex rushed to his mothers room and brought down the painting of the island.

Alexandra reached out to Eduardo and took him by the hand. Alex leaned the painting against the living room chair. Lizbeth walked in front of it and stretched out her hands towards the painting. She took a deep breath in and out, then forcefully opened her arms. The golden light showed brightly opening the gate. Alex nodded to assure

Eduardo it was safe and he walked in. Alexandra led
Eduardo in gently. Lizbeth looked over at Mawilda.

"Are you coming?"

"Oh, I don't..I..this...".

"It's beautiful in there".

"Oh, why not".

Mawilda marched over and Lizbeth stretched out her hand.
Mawilda took Lizbeth by the hand and they walked into the
painting together.

Inside of the painting Eduardo and Mawilda were amazed.
They looked around in awe.

"Come Eduardo, I will show you where I lived".

Alexandra led Eduardo to where she lived and Mawilda
followed behind them.

"I have no words to describe what I am seeing. I cannot
believe you were here all those years, Alexandra. What I
would have done to have been trapped with you in such a
place. You would have not felt so alone".

Alexandra teared up and Eduardo held her in his arms
tightly.

"I cannot dwell in the past. I now look forward to my future. Our future".

Eduardo embraced Alexandra and they shared a kiss.

They all spent some time on the beach and in the waters. Even Mawilda started to have fun trying to catch fish with her hands.

Afterwards they knew it was time to return. Lizbeth opened the gate and they all returned to Eduardo's living room. They were excited and laughed as Mawilda showed her new skills on fish catching with her bare hands.

Suddenly one of Eduardo's men came into the living room.

"Sir, there is someone here to see you. We asked him to wait outside, but he refused".

"Did he say who he was?"

"He...".

"Did not give a name. But then again do I have to? You all know who I am".

"Leo, what are you doing here?"

"It is good to see you as well, Alexandra".

Leo was clean cut and shaved and well dress again. When he saw Lizbeth he locked his eyes on her.

"I knew you'd be here".

He then smiled and slowly walked over to her. Alex gently pushed her back and stood in front.

"Whatever you want to say to her you can say it to me. Lizbeth, is my woman now".

"Is that so? She traded off the father for the son".

"Leo, what is it that you are doing here?"

"My dear friend, Eduardo. I wanted to congratulate you on your divorce with Anna. Coincidentally I have also divorced Alexandra, at the same time. Isn't that odd. That leaves Alexandra free to marry you. It also leaves me free to marry as well".

Leo looks over at Lizbeth.

"Isn't that so, Lizbeth?"

"There will be only one person Lizbeth will marry. And that person is me. I have already asked and she has agreed".

Alexandra happy to hear the news looks at Alex and Lizbeth.

"Alex? Lizbeth? Is this true?"

Lizbeth boldly stepped forward and looked at Alexandra, then she looked at Leo as she explained.

"It is true. In the time away Alex and I spent together, he has taught me how to open my heart again. Old love has been covered by new and I am happy. Happy and ready to move forward".

"No. You cannot forget your first love so easily, Lizbeth".

"Yes Leo, I can. And I did".

"May I speak you? Alone".

"No, you will go nowhere near her...".

"Alex, I will be okay".

Lizbeth places her hand on Alex's arm. He looks over at her and she whispers.

"I will be close. He can do me no harm".

Lizbeth walks off pass Leo and towards the patio. Leo stares hard at Alex. Then walks to the bar next to him, serves himself a drink and downs it. Then he take a fews steps backward, turns around and walks to the patio where Lizbeth is waiting. He shuts the door behind him and Lizbeth and he are alone in the patio. Alex, Alexandra and

Eduardo watch through the window from the living room to make sure Lizbeth is safe.

"You cannot marry him, Lizbeth".

"I can, and I will, Leo".

"Marry him and you put a target on my sons back, bringing him that much closer to his death!"

Alex heard Leo's threat and became upset, knowing he was trying to scare Lizbeth into submitting to him. Alexandra stops him. Alex then began to pace the living room. Making sure to keep his eyes on Lizbeth.

"You cannot choose for me, force me, or control me anymore. Why can't you accept that, Leo?"

"I always get what I want. Even if I have to take it".

"Like you took from my family! You tried to take their power and because you couldn't, you stole our paintings. Taking always what does not belong to you. You cause yourself this misery every time, by forcing what cannot be".

Leo walks closer to Lizbeth and looks into her face.

"Why can't this? You and I. Why can't that be?"

"It's funny how you ask a question, of that which you already know the answer to. Just because you do not like the answer, does not mean it isn't the truth. You can stay in denial all you want. You can try to justify your actions. You can use the most charming words to make another temporary escape. But the truth will always be there, and the real Leo will always come forward. Wanting people to act like they do not see the truth, is only trying to make us fall into the same denial you have when you look into the mirror".

"So, what am I supposed to do? Just sit by while you marry Alex. The boy I raised into a man. A man who is now taking away what belongs to me".

"I belong to no one. I am free and allowed to choose what I want for my own life. Alex is not taking anything away from you. Alex is choosing to love what you broke, tattered and tore. I gave, Alex my heart. He is the one I chose with the free will I have. How does it make you feel to not have what you want?"

Leo walked up to Lizbeth's face.

"It makes me feel angry".

"Then you know exactly how you make me feel each time you try to take from me what I want".

"I know what you want..."

"No. You don't. And that is why we are where we are, right now".

"I can try, Lizbeth. I can change".

"If that young boy nicknamed Neptune has not changed and his greedy ways are still there, how is Leo going to change now. What have you done to do so? Leo, do you know what I am. What my family bloodline is called to do?".

"I do. You are the Art Guardian".

"And with that responsibility I must protect the art. Protect, Leo. Not take, or destroy...protect. The person I need by my side must be willing to protect the paintings with me. How can I protect the paintings if I am locked away, like a piece of tapestry for your eyes only".

"I'm sorry Lizbeth, this is hard for me".

"And for me as well. Both of us have to let go. I have, now you must do the same"

"I am always going to love you and want you by my side".

Leo turns around and opens the patio doors. He enters the living room and looks at everyone.

"I know when I have lost. I can walk away with the last bit of dignity I have in tact. I wish you all the best on your marriage Eduardo, Alexandra.   Alex, she is a rare treasure. If you slip up. I will be sure to...".

"I won't! I know how to care for and protect the woman I love".

Leo smirks, turns to look at Lizbeth once more, then turns around and leaves the house.

Leo sat in the car and corruptly laughed. Then he told his driver to take him to the stores. When Leo got there he entered them and had the sales clerks show him all kinds of dresses and shoes, lingeries, and nightgowns. He selected all his favorite ones, paid for them and had his men come into the store to pick up all the items and place them in the trunk of one of his cars.

"Get Clara, and have her brought to the house on the cliff. Tell her to unpack all these things I have purchased and place them where they belong".

"Yes sir, Mr. Ferreira".

Leo sat in his car and told the driver to take him to the house on the cliff. When they arrived Leo stepped out of the car and walked up the very long flight of steps. His men remained downstairs. After Leo reached the top, he walked the large opened tile floor area, that included a reflective pool with a side fountain. He continued towards the railing off on the side. When he did, Leo had a full view of the beach in front of him, from atop a high cliff. He then turned around to go into the house behind him, with unbreakable windows as walls the encircled the luxurious and elegant house. He walked all around the house that made a full circled, looking to confirm that everything was in place. He then entered a code into the keypad on the glass door with no knob. This unlocked the door and he slightly pushed it open. After he walked in he pushed the door closed and it automatically locked itself. The house inside was completely furnished with contemporary style cream and turquoise colored furniture. Leather couches, glass top and marbled tables and chairs.

Leo walked through the living room and up the stairs, that led to the open floor plan bedroom. He walked passed the canopy bed with ivory sheer curtains that covered all around the bed. The bed itself had black silk sheets with a marbled ivory and black fur blanket. The bedroom had no private doors going into the bathroom. Glass window doors divided the bathroom from the bedroom and closet. The shower, bathtub and vanity sink were completely visible. Leo stood in front of the shower glass door and was pleased with the house.

"Nowhere to hide my love. I will see your every movement".

Leo exited the house by entering his code on the front door. Once outside the door locked itself and he walked down the long flight of steps. When he reached the bottom, he passed his men who immediately followed behind.

"The house is ready. Let's move to the next part of the plan".

Leo's man opened the car door and Leo sat inside. When the man shut the door the driver drove off.

After everyone was trying to get over Leo's visit, Eduardo's son Paolo walked into the living room. As he walked up closer to Eduardo he pulled his sunglasses up onto his head.

"What? No welcome?"

Eduardo recognized the voice and immediately turned around. He rushed over to embrace Paolo.

"Paolo! My son, I am so happy you came".

"I could not miss the wedding of my father with his new bride".

He then walked over to Alexandra and gave her a hug.

"Thank you, Paolo. It means the world to me that you have come".

"Of course, father".

Just then Alex and Lizbeth walked in from the patio where they had been talking about the conversation Lizbeth had with Leo. When Paolo saw Lizbeth he stared and smiled.

"I am so glad I did, father. So glad I came".

"This is a cause for celebration. I will let Mawilda have the night off and we will go to dinner. Let us go to your favorite restaurant, Paolo. Alexandra, Lizbeth and Alex will love it. The best fish you have ever tasted. After all with a day like today, fish sounds very appropriate for the occasion".

Alexandra, Alex and Lizbeth chuckled, because they understood what Eduardo meant. Alexandra walked over to Lizbeth.

"Come Lizbeth, I had some clothing purchased and delivered here just for you, and Alex. I knew you would be staying here upon your return. I don't know why, but I did have a beautiful dinner dress brought for you. I guess I was hopeful for family dinners like these".

"Alexandra, this is why I love you so. You are such a smart woman".

"Oh Eduardo, I thought you were marrying me only for my beauty".

"Aha! That too".

Alexandra smiled and walked off with Lizbeth. Alex followed behind them. Paolo couldn't get his eyes off of Lizbeth. As they walked away Paolo walked over to Eduardo.

"Lizbeth is staying here? In this house?"

"She is, Paolo".

"And Leo, her husband is okay with this? I did see him leave very angry before I came in".

"Oh no, Leo is not longer her husband. Lizbeth is free from his grasp, as is my Alexandra. But from what I can tell, Alex is very attached and protective of Lizbeth. I would not be surprised if those two are a couple".

"I see".

"Come, let us get ready for a beautiful family dinner tonight".

Eduardo walked off and Paolo stood watching as Lizbeth reached the top of the steps and turned the corner.

"I think, I will like this dinner very much. Might as well make myself comfortable in this house. There is a guest here who is extremely appetizing".

Alex, Eduardo and Paolo were downstairs having a drink together waiting for the women. Then Alexandra began to come down the stairs. Eduardo looked over and was in awe with how beautiful Alexandra looked.

"There she is. Oh my".

Alex smiled to see how much Eduardo loved his mother.

"I think you better go get her, before she gets stolen away".

"Over my dead body, Alex. I will not lose my Alexandra ever again".

Eduardo rushed over to meet Alexandra. She smiled and they walked off. Within a few moments Lizbeth turned the corner and came down the stairs. Alex and Paolo were amazed at how beautiful she looked. Alex quickly laid his drink cup down and walked over to Lizbeth. She smiled and Alex reached out his hand to help her down the last few steps. When she reached the bottom he kissed her lips.

"You look breathtaking, Lizbeth".

"As do you, Alex".

They kissed again and this bothered Paolo. He placed his drink cup on the table and walked off.

Everyone sat into the limo together. Paolo sat across of Lizbeth and Alex. He continued his drinking from the mini bar in the limo, and continued staring at Lizbeth.

"Good idea, Paolo. Open that bottle of champagne as we celebrate love, unity, and family".

Paolo popped open the bottle and Eduardo poured champagne into everyones cup.

At the restaurant the celebration continued as they ate dinner. Alexandra feeding Eduardo and he feeding her. Paolo continued to have the waiter refill his cup of liquor as he looked at Lizbeth with Alex. Alex leaned into Lizbeth and whispered in her ear.

"Is it just me, or this Paolo has not taken his eyes off of you all night?"

"I would have never taken notice of such a thing. Now I wonder, could it be true, or could it be that you are seeing these imaginary things because of jealousy".

"I am absolutely overwhelmed with jealousy, just by him looking at you".

"Is that so? Whatever should we do then? Wait, don't answer that. Because the response would be the same for the ladies at that table over there that have continuously looked over at you since we arrived".

"Do I sense jealousy coming out of the most beautiful woman in this room? Had she not told me about those ladies, I would have never taken notice of them either".

"Then we are even. They can look all they want, but you are mine and I am yours".

Alex smiled a big smile.

"Did I just hear those words come out of your mouth, or am I hallucinating from the mixture of my fish and this wine".

"When you awake tomorrow, we will know for sure".

Alex laughed and Lizbeth giggled. Paolo became jealous and took down another cup of his hard liquor.

When they got home everyone sat in the living room chatting for a moment. Then Alexandra and Eduardo said their goodnights. Paolo acted like he left the living room, but overheard Lizbeth and Alex talking.

"You don't look like you are ready for bed?"

"I'm not. I'd like to enjoy the night breeze".

"Then I will take our things upstairs, and I will meet you out in the patio".

Alex gave Lizbeth a kiss and went upstairs. Lizbeth walked out to the patio. When she reached the patio rail she placed her hands on the rail, then she closed her eyes to enjoy the breeze. Paolo waited for Alex to go upstairs. Once he turned the corner, Paolo walked over to the patio and came outside, quietly shutting the door behind him. He then walked up to Lizbeth from behind her pressing his body against hers and placing his arms around her waist.

"That was quick".

Lizbeth kept her eyes closed as she placed her cheek on Paolo's shoulder. Paolo gently touched Lizbeth's neck, then leaned in and began to kiss her neck gently. She smiled and stretched her arms back placing them on the sides of Paolo's shoulders. In his excitement Paolo began to move his hand up from Lizbeth's waist until he reached her breast. When he did he began to kiss Lizbeth's neck more aggressively, then with one hand he grabbed onto one of her breast and with his other hand he went down and through slit of her dress and grabbed her between the legs.

"Alex, not here. Alex, slow down".

Paolo became more aggressive and grabbed onto Lizbeth tighter and tried to pull up her dress. She struggled to pull it back down.

"Alex! Alex! What has gotten into you?"

Just then Alex was coming down the stairs and saw Lizbeth struggling with Paolo. He became furious and rushed downstairs. When he opened the patio door he heard Lizbeth.

"Alex! Stop! What's wrong with you!"

"He is not me!"

Paolo let Lizbeth go and when she turned around and saw it was Paolo and not Alex. In her shock she covered her mouth to stop herself from yelling out. Alex rushed him and hit Paolo in the face knocking him over. When Paolo was on the ground Alex rushed him and grabbed him by the shirt. Alex was about to hit Paolo again when Lizbeth grabbed his arm.

"If you ever touch her again I promise I will...."

"Alex stop! Please stop!"

Alex let Paolo go and stood up. Lizbeth pulled him inside and they went upstairs. Paolo scoffed with frustration and stumbled as he got himself up. Then angrily walked off to his bedroom.

The next morning everyone was up early preparing for Alexandra and Eduardo's wedding. Paolo came down to have breakfast with Eduardo. When he did Eduardo saw Paolo's face from Alex's punch.

"Paolo, your face. What happened?"

"Ah father, last night as I walked into my bedroom I accidentally walked into the door".

"I am not surprised, with all the drink you had last night. Try not to drink so much today, that way you do go walking into anymore doors".

Paolo scoffed and rolled his eyes.

Eduardo and Alexandra had their wedding as planned. The ceremony was held in the garden. The reception was underneath a large white tent and everything was decorated beautifully.

During the reception Alexandra and Eduardo approached Alex and Lizbeth.

"Alex my love, you know I am saving a dance for you this evening".

"Only one, mother. I hope I can get that one dance tonight, seems like Eduardo has not let you go all evening".

"I admit, I have been a little selfish tonight. I want Alexandra all for myself. I do believe it is time to share her, but just for a little bit".

"I think I should take this dance chance quickly, before Eduardo waltz you away again, mother".

They all laughed together. Then Lizbeth gagged and covered her mouth.

"I'm sorry. Excuse me".

Lizbeth rushed off.

"Is she okay?"

"I think so, mother. This is the second time today. It must be something she ate?"

"Now wait a minute, I have served the finest tonight. Only the best for your mother, Alex".

Eduardo and Alex chuckled, but Alexandra was concerned.

"Gentlemen, I think I will go check up on my future daughter-in-law. Then we will have that dance, Alex".

Alexandra walked towards the house where she found Lizbeth in the bathroom throwing up.

"Are you okay, Lizbeth".

"Oh goodness, I think so. Must have been something I ate".

Lizbeth came out of the bathroom.

"I'm fine now".

"Lizbeth? When was your last...you know?"

"My last....oh oh. It was last month".

"Aha, and this month?"

"It...should have been...I think I'm late".

Alexandra looked at Lizbeth waiting for her to catch what she was trying to say.

"No. It can't be. Alexandra, it must have been something I ate".

Jut then Mawilda walked into the house.

"Mawilda! Can you have one of the servers rush out to the store to pick something up for me".

"Of course mam, what would you like".

Alexandra leaned into Mawilda's ear and asked for a pregnancy test.

Mawilda looked at Alexandra belly surprised.

"Not for me. For Lizbeth".

"Ah, yes. Okay".

"And quickly, please".

"Alexandra, please I don't want to be a burden. We can do this another time. It is your wedding day".

"All the more I want to know. This would be the greatest wedding gift".

She grabbed Lizbeth by the hand and they returned to the party.

Once Mawilda gave them the sign that the pregnancy test was delivered. Alexandra snuck out with Lizbeth and went to Lizbeth and Alex's room.

Alexandra paced the bedroom in her wedding gown waiting. Lizbeth came out the bathroom.

"Okay, it says we should know within 15-20 minutes".

"Good, then we wait".

Eduardo began looking for Alexandra wondering where she was. He walked over to Alex.

"Have you seen your mother?"

"I have not. I myself am looking for Lizbeth".

"Ah, there is your mother now".

Alexandra approached calmly and took Alex by the hand.

"Come Alex, I owe you a dance".

She led him to the dance floor and signaled the musicians to play. When they did she and Alex began to dance.

"Were you with Lizbeth?"

"I was".

"I she okay?"

"She is".

"I was getting a little worried. You two were gone for a while".

"Alex, you know that I and Eduardo are too old to have children. But grandchildren. That would my greatest joy".

"It would?"

"It...would".

Alex looked at Alexandra confused as she stared at him. Then she nodded her head towards the house. Alex was still somewhat confused and then he caught it.

"Lizbeth?"

"I think you should check on her".

"Mother! Is she....".

Alexandra smiled a great big smile. Alex's surprised looked turned into excitement. Then Alex kissed his mother on the cheek and went running towards the house. Eduardo walked over to Alexandra.

"Is everything okay?"

"Eduardo, we are to be grandparents".

Eduardo surprised burst out laughing. He picked up two glasses of Champagne.

"Everyone! A toast! Today is truly a special day. Not only did I marry the woman I love. But we together shall have our first grandchild. It has been confirmed".

Everyone cheered and clapped for them. Paolo smirked then sipped his drink. Eduardo kissed Alexandra and he took the champagne glass out of her hand, laid it down on the table and took her for a whirl on the dance floor as they both laughed and kissed.

Alex barged into the bedroom where Lizbeth was sitting in a chair. She quickly stood up.

"Is it true?"

"It must have been the painting. I was taking care of myself. I promise I was. But I guess the birth control had no effect in the painting. It must have been then".

Alex rushed over to Lizbeth and grabbed her in a tight hug.

"Oh my love! You have made me the happiest man today".

He lifted her up as she yelled out and laughed. He then spinned her around with joy.

"I love you! I love you! I love you, Lizbeth!"

After Alexandra and Eduardo's wedding. Planning for another wedding began. This time it was for Alex and Lizbeth's wedding. It was not going to be a big party. The only invited guest were Philip and Tiara, who were desperately awaiting to finally see Lizbeth.

When they got to Eduardo's house they ran out of the car and all three embraced each other as they yelled out from joy and laughter.

"I have missed you both so much!"

"And we have missed you!"

Philip picked up the painting his mother was in to show Lizbeth.

"I brought mom too, we can visit her later".

Alex, Eduardo and Alexandra looked at each other confused with what Philip said about his mother. Alex shrugged his shoulders then came down the outdoor steps and approached them. Philip looked up and saw Alex for the first time.

"Okay, so did my sunglasses just fog up or did I just see the most handsomest man that fell onto planet earth".

Tiara also shocked to see how handsome Alex was elbowed Philip on the arm.

"Sorry, did he hear me? Sorry, your just...your gorgeous".

Lizbeth burst out laughing.

"You must be Philip".

Alex reached out his hand to shake Philips.

"You must be right. Wow that is a strong hand too".

Alex then stepped over and gave Tiara a hug.

"And you must be Tiara".

"That's me".

"Come, meet the rest of my family".

Alex led the way and Lizbeth jumped in between Philip and Tiara and locked arms with them.

"Tiara got a hug, I didn't get a hug. Is that customary here?"

"I wouldn't hug you either if you were undressing me with your eyes. Did you have to be so obvious".

"Tiara, I was just being honest".

Lizbeth just laughed with joy.

That evening Lizbeth, Philip and Tiara had been sitting out in the terrace, each with a cup of wine in their hands talking for hours.

"Well, I will be the first to admit it then. Alex is a hunk".

"More than that Philip, he has an amazing heart".

"Okay, so what's wrong with him, because you cannot be that gorgeous and have a good heart too".

"I beg to differ. If a good looking man is raised properly and with a good mother like I was, then he can be handsome and have a good heart".

Alexandra walked up from behind them.

"I meant no offense".

"Oh none taken. You are actually right. It is very difficult to find a man with both these qualities together. Like my Alex and my Eduardo".

"I do admit, for his age, Eduardo is top of the list too".

Alexandra laughed at Philip's comment.

"I think I like you already".

"See, Lizbeth, Tiara, I won the mother-in-law over already".

They all four laughed together.

"Seriously, guys. Is everything really as peaceful as it should be?"

"Good question, Tiara. Did Leo really accept your marriage with Alex?"

"I hope so. I spoke with him, but he is so unpredictable, I just don't know".

"Lizbeth is right. The Leo I saw after coming out of the painting is a complete stranger to me. He made me very fearful. A fear I never felt towards him before. His obsession with Lizbeth has changed him".

"I just don't understand. All he had to do was love her. Lizbeth loved him. Instead he tried to cut her world out of her life and keep her for himself".

"I agree, Tiara. And lets not forget he even threatened to cut his son out of Lizbeth's life to keep her. What kind of man threatens his own sons life?"

"A man who is losing his mind. My Alex tells me he does not know the man his father has become".

"You guys! Do you think the travels have anything to do with his mind slipping into madness. I am the art guardian. In my blood is the lineage of travels. Could it be something about what's in me that causes this in him".

"Lizbeth's your right! There is only one person who would know for sure".

"Your mother, Philip!"

"Let's go!"

Alex walked up from behind and overhead them speaking.

"Where are we going?"

"Oh, Alex this is for educational purposes. Just Philip, Tiara and I will travel into the painting Philip's mother is in. Hopefully she can help us understand".

"Lizbeth, if I am going to be the husband of the art guardian, I think I would need to learn something too".

"And I the mother-in-law".

"Where is everyone planning on going?"

"Eduardo! We are going to ask Philip's mother some questions".

"I see and where is she?"

Philip smiled, lifted up the painting in his hand and pointed at it.

"Ah, now I see. Well, let me let Mawilda know we will be gone for a bit".

"Wait a minute, everyone can't go!"

Alex looked at Tiara.

"And why is that, Tiara?"

Tiara thought for a moment.

"Good question. I guess we can".

Tiara walked off towards the house, Philip followed behind.

"Don't forget your sunglasses people".

Eduardo leaned over to Alexandra's ear.

"Sunglasses? Whatever for, it's nighttime now?"

Alexandra shrugged her shoulders not understanding why either.

Before long Lizbeth opened the gate for the painting Philip's mother was in. They all entered in. Once the gate closed, Mawilda quickly placed the painting in her bedroom and laid it against the wall for safe keeping. Then she went about her chores.

Once in the painting, Lizbeth saw Philip's mother at a distance and waved.

"Lizbeth!"

She came quickly over and Lizbeth ran to her. They embraced each other tightly.

"Oh my dear girl, it has been so long. I am so glad to see you safe".

Once everyone reached Philip's mother they stood there waiting. Philip's mother looked over at everyone.

"And who are all these people?"

"Mother, this is Lizbeth's fiancé Alex, his mother Alexandra, and her new husband Eduardo".

"Oh, we have the whole family here, don't we".

"Yes mother, but we have come because we need information. Where did you put the journals?"

"Dear me, it's the journals we seek. Every time we need those, something is in the works. Come, follow me. I stored them here".

They all gathered outside a wooden hut Philip's mother had built for herself. Inside was a wooden chest. Tiara and Philip carried it out.

"All of the journals are here?"

"Yes, Lizbeth. After your desperate call for help many things were hidden in here for safe keeping. My dear girl. What you must have endured, must have been terrifying. I am truly glad you are safe now".

"Yes mother, and look at the hunk she's going to marry now".

They all chuckled except for Alexandra.

"Forgive me for prying, but you live in this painting? By choice?"

"I do. This is my home and I can never leave".

"But I was trapped in a painting for over 10 years. I would have escaped with the first opportunity given to me. Why do you stay by choice? I don't understand".

"Alexandra, we should have explained earlier. Philip's mother had terminal cancer in the real world. She was given less than a month to live. Tiara came up with the idea to try and bring her into the painting before...before".

"What Lizbeth is saying is that I was going to die. Coming into the painting saved my life. Here in this painting there is no cancer. I age like I normally would in the real world, but there is no disease here. We all know disease is manmade anyway. Here you find what the artist paints. Artist do not paint disease, illnesses, suffering, or pain".

"Actually mother, some do paint suffering and pain, but in those painting we do not enter".

"Just like the one I was stuck inside of, in Leo's home. The one with the old wooden boat on the ocean".

"I see. So if you returned now to the real world..."

"I would be dead".

"So you are not trapped, you are surviving. You are a brave woman indeed".

Alexandra became emotional and Philip's mother rushed over to her and embraced her. After she cried it out she took a deep breath.

"Well, I didn't mean to cause any delay. Let us find out what we have come to learn. Hopefully this will allow us all to survive safely and in peace".

They all began to talk and search in the journals until Alex stood up.

"I think I may have found something. This is talking about the obsession of a man".

Philips mother rushed over to Alex. He handed her the journal.

"Yes, here it is. It says the man fell in love with an art guardian and all was well. They traveled through paintings together, but when he could not learn to travel it made him very angry".

"Just like Leo when he was a boy".

"Yes, Lizbeth. Now it also says here when she would travel alone for short periods he became very angry that she was gone, even if it was for a few moments. Something that never bothered him before, began to drive him to sudden rages and outburst".

"How did she get away from him, mother?"

"It says here, that the art guardian hid in a painting with her children for several years. She raised them and educated them from inside the painting. When a traveler entered the painting, he told her that her husband had died after slowly slipping into madness with her disappearance. It goes on to say that this happened because of his greed. When they lied together like husband and wife, there was a connection that took place between their bodies. He became hungrier and more possessive of his wife. The power to travel can amplify greed in a man".

"So if a man already has a lot of greed from within, making love to an art guardian will make his greed for her and for what's within her, amplify to a level of driving him crazy?"

"That sounds exactly right, Philip. Now more than ever we have learned that the man an art guardian chooses must be of a kind nature and not filled with a senseless amount greed.

Tiara, Lizbeth, Phillip and Philip's mother looked over at Alex.

"Oh no, I am not full of greed. I have had Lizbeth and been apart from her and I do not feel obsessed. What I feel for Lizbeth is love. I have felt jealousy, but never to the point to want to lock away".

"He's right. Alex has been the same man with me before and after making love to me".

"I think this answers our question then. Lizbeth really isn't safe. She will never be safe. Leo will obsess over her always".

"Tiara is right. This also puts Alex at risk. His father is no longer in his right mind".

"Then what do they do? Hide away in a painting for the rest of their lives?"

"Good question, Alexandra".

"Unless. Unless, he is locked away in a painting".

"That's a great idea, Eduardo. Can't we have Leo locked away in a painting? Like I was for all those years".

"That is a possibility, Alexandra. But which one".

"The island, where I was".

"That would seem like a good idea, but if he was able to open the gate to where you fell in last time, Alexandra. How do we know he won't spend years trying to get out.

And if he does, he will have learned how to open the gate to come out and go into a painting. Whatever painting he is trapped into, it has to be a painting where he wants to stay and won't try to get out".

"Lizbeth is right. It has to be somewhere he is willing to stay and will not care to escape from".

Everyone sits there, thinking. Then Alex's face lights up.

"The portrait. The portrait of Lizbeth. It's resemblance of Lizbeth it out of this world. If he is obsessed with Lizbeth, what better place to trap him, then with Lizbeth. In the portrait of her".

"Wait, your saying he had a portrait made of Lizbeth?"

"He did, Philip. And after the portrait was painted he had me dressed in the exact same manner when he revealed it at Eduardo's party".

"Yes, I do remember that night. He revealed the portrait in my home".

"This sounds amazing. But we still have one problem".

"What's that mother?"

"Well, Philip. The Lizbeth in the portrait would need to have two things. Love for Leo and she must never bare him a child. Especially from within the portrait. Children conceived and born in a painting, with one human parent have the ability to travel easily at a very young age without having to learn or make effort. It just comes easily to them, like second nature.

"Just like me".

"Exactly like you, Tiara".

"How then can we ensure that the Lizbeth in the portrait will love Leo and not bare him any children?"

"There is only one who can help. They call him, The Painter. His name seems very common, but his powers are not. He has the ability to use his paintbrush to create what we are hoping for, by simply stroking the brush onto the painting, with these special requests in his mind".

"Are you saying that with a stroke of his paintbrush, the Lizbeth in the painting will love Leo. And not bare him any children?"

"That is correct, Philip".

"Well, where do we find, The Painter".

"That is what I do not know, Alexandra. We have not needed any help from The Painter in years".

"Maybe the journals?"

"We could check, but The Painter travels often. To find him would be through word of mouth. The last time we saw him, he was at your grandmothers funeral, Lizbeth".

"The odd looking man with the brushstroke on his cheek".

"Yes, that was him. After that day no one has heard of his whereabouts".

"Sounds like we are going to have to do a lot of paint hopping to ask around."

"Alright, when do we start?"

"As soon as Lizbeth and Alex have been married. This will at least offer the protection of Lizbeth having a husband, so Leo can never force her to marry him".

"Great idea. She will be married and with her pregnancy, he can't impregnate her".

"What? What pregnancy?"

"Oh my, Lizbeth. I am so sorry, I thought they knew".

"It's okay, Alexandra. I had hoped for better circumstances to share the news, but what better place than here next to the woman who was like a mother to me".

"Oh my dear girl! You are going to be a mother. This is great news. The lineage of Art Guardians shall indeed continue".

Philip, his mother and Tiara stood up excited and hugged Lizbeth.

"Where was she conceived? In the real world or in a painting?"

"It was in a painting. I was taking my birth control, but some how in the painting the birth control had no affect".

"Indeed this girl will be the strongest of all. Two human parents, yet conceived in a painting. That has never been heard of".

"How do we even know she will be a girl?"

"Oh my dearest, Alex. All art guardians born are girls. For some reason it is automatic. After the firstborn there are other children and the mothers have sons, but the first is always a girl. Well, this will be a wonderful wedding indeed. You must tell me all about it".

"Actually, Alex and I we were hoping to have the wedding ceremony here. Of course we will have all the legal actions done in the real world, but the ceremony would be here. I couldn't think of getting married again, without you by my side. I should have never married Leo, without ensuring I could trust him with the truth. That would have been the right way. Alex knows my truth and he is and will be part of who I am".

"Is it just me or is this the most exciting day ever. We learned how to defeat the bad guy, with the exception of having to locate The Painter, there is a wedding and I'm going to be an uncle. I'm just ecstatic right now"

"Philip, I couldn't agree with you more".

"Piña colada's on me people, let's go".

Everyone began walking over to the tiki bar. Alex approached Philip.

"They sell piña colada's in a painting?"

"Of course they don't sell piña colada's in a painting. They give them away. Money is never needed in a painting, everything is free".

Eduardo and Alexandra overheard Alex and Philip. Surprised Eduardo looked at Alexandra.

"Who would have thought I needed to work so much for retirement. We should have just retired into a painting".

Alexandra chuckled.

Leo was leaned back in his office chair deep in thought and with a drink in hand. Suddenly he got a call on his phone and place the call on speaker.

"Speak".

"Mr. Ferreira, we have an update on the prize".

"Go ahead".

"She and Alex have obtained a marriage certificate. They are now legally bound together".

Leo clenched his fist in anger.

"Go on".

"We have heard there is a wedding ceremony within a few days. No one knows where. They have not reserved any venues or churches. But there has been word about a honeymoon location".

"Where?"

"It will be on the beach of Lagos, the Mei Praia. We have confirmed date and time of their trip".

"Good".

Leo disconnected the call.

"There will be no wedding night with Alex, my love. Because for the rest of our lives, we will be together in our own, forever wedding night. You will see, my love.

Tonight, I celebrate my own bachelor party. These will be my last nights alone without you, Lizbeth".

Leo put the drink cup on the table, stood up from his desk and walked out of the office. Then he called his driver from his phone.

"We leave now".

Once he stepped outside the house his driver was waiting. The driver then drove Leo to a fancy bar. Leo got out of the car and stepped in. He looked around and saw beautiful women. He tried to make a selection, when he noticed Paolo sitting at the bar tipsy. Surprised to see him, Leo walked over and sat by him.

"Paolo, nice to see you".

"Ah, Leo. I have not seen you in quite some time".

"This is true. What brings you here tonight?"

"I am going home tomorrow. I came to visit for my fathers wedding. He is wed, so now I go home. Besides, the next wedding is one I am not invited to".

"Wedding? There is another?"

"You haven't heard? Lizbeth is set to marry your son, Alex".

"Ah, yes. I have heard".

"And this does not make your blood boil?"

"Alex has been disowned as my son. And as for Lizbeth, she is missed, but there are many more woman to appease me. Just look around".

"This is true. But Leo, you know how we men are. We always want what we can't have. It is the thrill of the game. You wanted Lizbeth and lost her. I wanted Lizbeth and had her in hands, until Alex took her from me".

"You had her in your hands?"

"I did. Of course she thought it was Alex, but for just a few moments I was able to have her close in my arms. I admit, I still want more".

Leo became jealous hearing Paolo talk like that about Lizbeth, but refrained himself from showing it. Instead he called the bartender to refill Paolo's cup to keep him talking.

"Forgive me if I offend. I just assume since she is no longer your wife and now bound to your son Alex, that you would hate her for doing such a thing".

"Yes, I could hate her. But I much rather forget her. Which I already have done".

"You have? I don't think I would do so well forgetting a beautiful woman like her. She is a hard to catch, but an extremely rare treasure".

Leo continues getting furious hearing Paolo talk about Lizbeth like that.

"So, tell me. What do you know about their wedding? Will it be held in your father Eduardo's house".

"Oh you didn't know?"

"No, tell me".

"They will have the wedding privately done in some secret place. I of course am not invited. Their honeymoon is a lie. They have made reservations at a resort on a beach in Lagos, but they are not going".

"How do you know all of this?"

"I overheard them speaking. They did not know I was listening. The fake plans were to throw you off their trail in case you were following them. Their honeymoon night will be in one of my fathers Villa's. Their honeymoon and the rest of their lives. They are moving to this villa. It was supposed to be my villa, but my father gifted it to them. Had I meet Lizbeth first, that would be my and Lizbeth's villa".

"Where is that villa?"

"You know where it is? It is the first villa my father brought. You went to one of his parties there".

"Ah yes, the one on the beach".

"That one".

"I know it well".

"They installed all this new security to stay safe inside from the dangerous Leonardo Ferreira".

"Are they that afraid of me?"

Paolo shrugged his shoulders.

"Well, Paolo. It was good to see you. I will leave you alone to your drinking".

Paolo nodded and Leo walked away. After doing so Paolo looked in Leo's direction and saw Leo leave the bar.

"I'd love to see your face, Alex. When your father crashes your honeymoon night. Serves you right for stopping me and ruining my chances with Lizbeth. Ah, Lizbeth".

He scoffed and took down his drink, slammed the cup on the bar and demanded more alcohol from the bartender.

The wedding day was here and Philip and Tiara were helping Lizbeth get ready. Philip added the finishing touch by placing the crystal hair comb into Lizbeth hair. Philip and Tiara leaned in and looked at Lizbeth's reflection in the mirror.

"You look so beautiful, Lizbeth".

"Philip's right, you look amazing Lizbeth".

Lizbeth looked at them both and reach out her hands placing them on Philip and Tiara's cheek.

"I don't know what I would do without you both. If there is any beauty in me, its because of the love I feel radiating out of me right now. It almost feels like a dream. Like I'm going to wake up and still be locked in that room. Pinch me and tell me this isn't a dream".

Lizbeth began to tear up.

"Oh no, Lizbeth, don't cry. Get her a tissue, Philip".

Philip rushed to get a tissue and Tiara sat on the bench next to Lizbeth.

"Listen to me. You have been through so much. But what you endured made you stronger. Had it not been for that, you would not have learned how to open the gate. You did that, all alone. This is not a dream. This is real, and you made it this far by remaining strong and not quitting. Now go and live your forever happy".

"Tiara is right. You deserve it Lizbeth. And as soon as you guys leave for your honeymoon villa, Tiara and I are going on our search for The Painter".

"I want to go with you guys, I can't leave this up to you only, it is my fight and all my fault for choosing Leo the first time.

"But if you had not chosen Leo, you would have never met Alex. So maybe it was worth the mistake. And you do not need to worry. Philip and I will be glad to go on this search".

"Yes, and I need some adventure in my life right now. I love my mom, but I can only have so many mango coconut drinks on the beach. She is safe and healthy, that's all that matters to me, and I will come visit her as soon as I get back. And Tiara, well, you know she always needs an adventure. Let's face it they should have named her Quest or Risk Taker. I mean why Tiara? That's something you put on your head. Lizbeth should be wearing a Tiara".

Tiara and Lizbeth rolled their eyes and laughed as they stood up to leave.

"I do like the name Quest".

"See, I always come up with the best ideas".

Philip and Tiara walked Lizbeth down the hall of Eduardos house and stopped at the bedroom Philip was staying in.

"Are you ready?"

"I am".

"We will see you in there".

Philip kissed Lizbeth's cheek and walked in the room. Tiara hugged Lizbeth tight and went into the room. They then closed the door and Lizbeth waited in the hall, alone. In the room was Eduardo, Alexandra and Alex waiting for Philip and Tiara. Philip opened the gate to the painting his mother was in, and everyone entered in. After the gate light went out, Lizbeth reached for the doorknob and heard a door at a distance slam loudly. No one was supposed to be in the house.

"Hello?"

There was no answer. Lizbeth took a few steps to see if she could see anyone, but there was no one. Again she heard a loud noise. Lizbeth became afraid.

"No, no, no".

As she rushed back to the bedroom door, before opening it she heard a call to her.

"Wait for me! Wait, wait!"

Mawilda came running down the hall. Lizbeth sighed a breath of relief.

"Oh, Mawilda, it's just you".

Mawilda rushed over, opened the bedroom door and led Lizbeth in. They walked in front of the painting and Lizbeth opened the gate. Mawilda rushed into the painting. Lizbeth took a deep breath then entered the painting. From a distance everyone saw Lizbeth walking towards them. Alex was overwhelmed.

"Wow, she looks so beautiful".

"Yes, she does, Alex".

"You all are going to like this one".

"What did you do, Tiara".

"Watch, Philip".

Lizbeth passed a place on the sand that moved and attached itself to her dress like a train. As she got closer and closer to Alex, just a few feet away the train began to seem like it was breaking apart as each piece flew up in the air revealing it was a butterfly. Each white butterfly that came apart from the train took on its original colors of blues, oranges, purples and yellows. Everyone was in awe at the sight.

"Now that is genius. Why didn't I think of that. From a cocooned trapped caterpillar to free as a butterfly. I love it, Tiara".

When Lizbeth reached Alex the ceremony began. They looked into each others eyes and said their vows, exchanged rings, and for the sand ceremony they used two large shells to scoop the sand from beneath them and placed it into a glass shell shaped vase.

Tiara and Philip were emotional trying to hide that they were tearing up.

The wedding reception lasted three days. Yet no one took notice that it did. Philips mother had huts built for everyone who needed rest. She had layers of leaves placed on them to darken them inside, since there was no night in the painting.

Lizbeth and Alex had a special one made for them further away.

Lizbeth woke up and caressed Alex's face. He opened up his eyes and smiled at Lizbeth.

"Good morning, husband".

"How do we know it's morning. It could be the middle of the night in the real world".

"That's true. But since we make our own time here, then it is morning for us".

"I like that. I like that very much. I could get used to be the husband of a paint hopper".

Alex leaned in and began kissing Lizbeth. Then slowly rolled on top to make love to her.

Philips mother was standing by the shore looking into the water. Alexandra came out of her hut and joined her.

"Do you think heaven would be like this for all of us?"

"I don't know about everyone else's heaven, but for me, this is for now. After-all in the real world, I am no longer alive. I guess you could say this is my temporary heaven".

"Well, it is a beautiful temporary home. What makes it all the more precious is being surrounded by your loved ones. For 10 years, I was alone. No one to speak a word to, laugh with, hold in my arms. Why is it we take for granted so many things in life. Simple things, like a funny joke or a conversation".

"That is something I have wondered myself since being here. Life has so much to offer. Yet it is those little things that build it into a life. Mistakes, hurts, loss, all of these make us feel like life is lost, but it's not. As long as we have breath in our bodies, we rebuild. Like you with Eduardo. Lizbeth with Alex, me still surviving. Some things are fair and some aren't, but it's up to us to choose to be happy or not, with what we are dealt".

"You are a very wise woman. Thank you. Though you may not have known this, I struggled and hid my anger. I seem okay to everyone, but I was furious. Alone on that island I let out so many screams and frustrations as the years went on, and no one came. At one point I lost hope and thought I would never be rescued. I have dreams that I am still on that island. Then I wake up in a warm bed and I can't help but cry. Then I realize that I have gained so much back. Not the way I would have wanted, but I have been given a second chance. Why waist it, right".

"You are absolutely right, Alexandra. We have both been given a second chance. Let us not waist it".

They smiled at each other and embraced as they looked out into the ocean.

After we all returned back from my wedding inside the painting, we were all exhausted, but everyone was in good spirits. After some much needed rest Philip and Tiara said their goodbyes to me, to start their search in the states for The Painter. Alex and I packed our things to move into the villa. My job was to do as much research as possible to find where The Painter could be and give Philip and Tiara clues on where to search. Alex would work on locating any and all places that paintings were stored near us, to allow us to do some painting hopping for clues. Everyone wanted us to remain inside the villa as much as possible, to stay safe and protected from Leo. I did not like the idea of being trapped again, but at least this time I was with Alex.

We worked on our search during the days. And at night we made love over and over again. I admit some days I would watch him as he bathed, prepared us a meal, or when taking a swim in the ocean and I wondered, maybe even feared, if he would change and become like Leo. But Alex was different. He smiled often and lived in the moment. He wasn't obsessive or selfish. He did not tell me I was his queen, he made me feel like his queen.

"Lizbeth, are you coming for a swim or what".

"Of course I am".

I walked out of the house to meet Alex at the beach. Suddenly someone grabbed me from behind and covered my mouth and nose. I struggled to get loose, but then felt dizzy. Things got blurry, then everything went dark.

Leo's man pick Lizbeth up and rushed over to Leo's car. He gently placed her in the back seat and shut the door.

"Good job men. How long will she be this way?"

"She will sleep for several hours, Mr. Ferreira".

"Well done. Here is your payment. And remember. Not a word of this to anyone".

Leo rolled up his window and the driver drove off. The men got into their car and drove off in the opposite direction.

While on the beach Alex started wondering where Lizbeth was. So he decided to come get her. When he came up the stairs and walked towards the door he saw her towel and sunblock bottle on the floor. Alex rushed into the house.

"Lizbeth! Lizbeth!"

He looked everywhere and could not find her.

"Noooo! Lizbeth!"

Furious Alex threw a chair across the room. Then he dropped to his knees.

"I will find you Lizbeth. I'm so sorry, I should have protected you".

Then he let out a yell of rage.

Alex returned to Eduardo's house and fell into his mothers arms.

"I have to find her, mother. I have to rescue her".

"You will, Alex. You will".

Philip and Tiara were told and they began to speed up their search. Alexandra and Alex did all they could on their end to provide as much information as they could to Philip and Tiara. Eduardo used his connections to help search for Leo and Lizbeth on his end.

When Lizbeth awoke she was lying in a bed with black silk sheets and an ivory sheer curtain all around her. When she sat up, she looked down to see she was wearing her old nightgown. The one she wore in Leo's house. That is when she began to panic. She moved the sheer curtains and stood up from the bed and found herself in a bedroom with glass walls and doors. She took some steps forward and saw the view. That is when she realized that she was up on top a cliff. As she stepped closer to the glass wall, she heard Leo's voice.

"Do you like it? I selected this design with you in mind. It's high up, with no place to go, but down. And in this house, everywhere you go, I can see you, my love".

"Leo! What have you done? Where is Alex? Did you do something to Alex?"

"Alex is fine. He must have spent several hours looking for you. But as time passes he will stop his search. And you and I will continue our lives here, together, happy. Just you and I. And the best part is...look...not one single painting. Anywhere. The beach and the sky are our artwork".

"Leo, you are losing your mind. This cannot be. You cannot kidnap me. I am Alex's wife!"

Leo rushed over to Lizbeth and she tried to turn around to get away from him, but he grabbed her arm and turned her to face him.

"You are no one's but mine. Your my wife. No paper changes that. I was your first, I made you mine".

"No! Let me go! It doesn't matter if you were my first or not. What we had is over.."

"Never! You are always going to be mine".

"I, am, not, your, property! I am a human being not an animal!"

Lizbeth pushed Leo back and he loosened his grip enough for her to come loose.

"Stop this, Leo. Please. This has to end".

"Your right. You are absolutely right, my love. If I end Alex's life. Then everything changes, doesn't it".

"No! Leo, no. Don't do this to me. Don't threaten me this way. Not again, please".

Leo walked up and grabbed Lizbeth's face.

"Then lets make this simple. You obey me and accept the fact that you belong to me. Then we will go on to live our lives here as a happy couple. You will love me and give yourself to me. Everyone will forget you ever existed and we will continue on. Just me and you. Do you understand? Do you understand!"

"Yes, Leo. I understand".

"Good. Now tell me that you love me. I want to hear you say it".

Lizbeth began to cry. Leo leaned in and whispered into her ear.

"Tell me you love me. I need to hear you say it, my love".

"I love you, Leo. I love you".

Leo kissed Lizbeth's lips then slowly let her face go. He then took her by the hand and walked her to the closet. When they walked in the lights lit up.

"This is your side my love. I was sure to purchase all your favorite product and things. But this here. All the clothing,

I chose. Here, this is what you will wear for our dinner tonight".

Leo then led and sat her on the vanity bench. He leaned in to kiss her shoulder.

"Now, do what you do. Where you dress up just for me. I even got you that lipgloss you always wore for me".

Looking up at Lizbeth's reflection through the mirror, Leo gently passed his thumb across Lizbeth's lips.

"The one that made your lips looks so tempting. All I wanted to do was kiss them".

Leo turned Lizbeth's face to his and he sat on the vanity bench. He then caressed her face and touched her lips with his thumb again. He kissed her lips gently. Then laid his forehead against hers to fight the urge to do more.

"I have to be patient. We will have plenty of time together. I want to take my time with you, Lizbeth".

Leo stood up and walked out of the room. After a few moments, Lizbeth silently yelled pushing away all the makeup on the vanity. Then she began to desperately cry.

In the evening, after Lizbeth was ready she looked into the mirror and stared at herself. She took a deep breath and started to make her way through the bedroom. As she did she noticed there was no door, just railing and steps going downstairs. She began to do down the stairs until she ended up in the living room where Leo was waiting.

"There she is. The most beautiful wife any man could ever hope for".

Lizbeth slightly smiled. Trying to fake it in front of Leo.

Leo slowly approached her, then placed his hand on her waist, gently pulling her towards him. He then leaned into her neck to take in her scent. Leo continued breathing her in all the way up to her ear, where he kissed her neck, right below her ear. Then continued with more gentle kisses down her neck until reaching her shoulder.

"Ah, Lizbeth. I have missed so much. I'm so happy to have you back".

Leo then purposely dropped his drink on the floor and grabbed Lizbeth tightly with both his hands. Then started to lustfully kiss her neck and caress her back.

"Leo, wait. I need time. Please. I need time".

Leo came to sudden stop and let out a breath, laying his forehead on Lizbeth's shoulder.

"I know you want to be with me, Leo. And I will not fight you. I only ask that you give me time. It is too soon for me. We haven't seen each other in a long time".

"Forgive me, my love. You are right. I can be patient. I can wait for you to give yourself to me".

Leo tapped kissed her lips and smiled.

"In that case. Come, Clara has prepared a great dinner for us".

As Leo spoke and led Lizbeth to the table she began looking all around. She noticed the doors had no knob or lock on them. Nothing but a keypad. He sat her down at the table, then sat himself down.

"Where are we?"

"You have already seen for yourself. We are up top a high cliff. Where no one can find us. I had this house built to my specifications. I knew that you were hard to tame, so the doors are locked by codes. I am the only one who knows the codes. Below this cliff, I have a swarm of men guarding the house day and night. No one can get in, and no one can get out. You do understand this. Don't you, my love?".

Lizbeth nodded. As she remained at the table with Leo, he spoke about many things. But Lizbeth did not pay any attention to him. Instead she kept trying to search for a way out.

"Lizbeth?"

"Yes?"

"You haven't eaten much at all".

"Yes, this is true. I am not hungry, Leo. Being forcefully taken away from my home....".

"That was not your home. Your home is wherever I am".

"Yes, right. I'm sorry. I just need rest".

"Here, I have something for you that might calm your nerves".

Leo stood up and prepared a cup of tea with sweet milk in it for Lizbeth and placed it in front of her. She froze in fear to see the cup.

"Leo, I...".

"It's not drugged. I promise".

"Please, Leo. Please don't do so. I will give myself to you willingly, just please don't drug me".

Leo reached out and touched Lizbeth's cheek taking notice that she was afraid. What Leo did not know was that Lizbeth was afraid to be drugged, because she did not know what effect it would have on her unborn child.

"Easy my love. Let us forget the tea. I can see I have much work to do in order to regain your trust again".

Leo pulled the tea cup back. Then stood up and reached out his hand to Lizbeth.

"Now then, let's go for a soak. I have been desperately waiting the day to be together in our pool with you".

Lizbeth took Leo's hand and he escorted her outside where the pool was. Again Lizbeth looked around everywhere trying to find a way out. Leo stopped in front of the reflective pool. It was dark outside and only the moonlight lit the pool. Leo turned to look at Lizbeth and leaned in to whisper in her ear.

"Take off your clothes".

"Maybe I should do so inside, so I could change into a bathing suit".

Leo chuckled.

"You don't need a bathing suit for this pool. No one will see us. There is no one here, but you and I and the open sky".

Leo then began to remove his jacket. He then dropped it onto the floor, while keeping his eyes on Lizbeth he then slowly untied and pulled off his tie, then his shirt, pants and shoes. He stood in front of her naked.

"Now, your turn".

He approached her and placed his arms around her back to unzip her dress. Then he gently pulled the dress down until is passed her shoulders and dropped to the ground. Leo then rubbed on her back and kissed her shoulder and neck as he removed her bra. All that she had on left were her lace panties.

"I will let you keep those on. To prove to you that I can be patient".

Leo then walked in backwards down the pool steps leading Lizbeth into the water by her hand. Once they were in the water deep enough to where it almost reached their chest, Leo grabbed the back of Lizbeth head, gently gripping onto her hair and he began to forcefully kiss her. Lizbeth tried pulling back her head but couldn't. She then turned her face to stop Leo from kissing her.

"Leo, please. I can't".

She pushed Leo back and turned around to leave the pool, but Leo grabbed her and pulled her back, pressing her back against his chest.

"I told you that I would be patient and wait to make love to you. But I did not say that I would not kiss you and caress you. I can gently touch what is mine".

Leo groped on Lizbeth's breast and lustfully kissed her neck. She struggled to push his hands off of her and as the water moved in a wave form, she suddenly caught a flashback memory of Alex in the ocean waters. She saw him standing in the water all wet and waves splashing onto his back. Lizbeth smiled imagining Alex and saw him walk over to her and gently hold her from behind.

"Please, slow down".

Leo surprised at her request, then slowed himself down.

"I can slow down for you, my love".

Though Leo said these words, Lizbeth heard Alex's voice saying them. That is when she stopped fighting Leo and instead she felt Alex touching her. Leo spinned Lizbeth around and kissed her lips. She kept her eyes closed and continued envisioning Alex. Leo then began kissing her neck, caressing the back of her neck and back. Lizbeth submitted herself.

"Alex".

Leo abruptly stopped. Angry he grabbed Lizbeth's face. She opened her eyes afraid. Leo was furious.

"I am not, Alex!"

He pushed her face back and walked out of the pool. Lizbeth was surprised with herself that she called Leo by Alex's name.

That night she laid in the bed very still as Leo had his arms wrapped around her. She waited for him to be asleep. Once she was sure he was, she slowly lifted his arm and slide out from underneath. Slowly she stood up from the bed, looking back often to ensure he was still asleep. She rushed down the stirs as quickly as possible. When she reached the living room she rushed to the doors touching and checking everything. Desperately looking for a way out or anything she could use to call for help.

"Lizbeth?"

Suddenly she heard Leo call to her. Lizbeth opened the kitchen cupboard and grabbed a cup. Leo lifted his head from off the pillow and looked around. Then he immediately stood up from the bed and looked down over the railing from the second floor. He saw Lizbeth in the refrigerator.

"Lizbeth?"

She acted as if though Leo startled her. Leo came rushing down the steps and into the kitchen towards her.

"Leo! I wasn't doing anything wrong. I just wanted a drink. I was sure I could do that myself without having to wake you up".

Lizbeth placed the juice decanter back into the fridge.

"If it bothers you, I won't do it again".

"Oh, Lizbeth. You make me sound like such a cruel monster".

He rushed over to her and pulled the juice decanter back out from the fridge and filled her cup halfway.

"Of course it doesn't bother me. This is your home, our home. I just got worried when I did not see you in the bed. It's not like you can escape, but I still do not want wake up in the bed without you there by my side".

Lizbeth gave a fake smiled and drank some of the juice. Then Leo took her hand and led her back upstairs to the bedroom, where they laid in the bed and he tightened his grip around her and went back to sleep.

Alex was on the dining room table at Eduardos house. It was full of papers and maps. He was having a video chat together with Philip and Tiara.

"There is a possibility that we are getting close. Tiara and I are on our way to the airport now. From our last paint hopping were heard rumors that The Painter could be in Paris. Where did you say the name of the museum was again?"

"From what I am seeing here it says there is one called The Louvre. It's the only one that has had recent deliveries of paintings".

"How did you find that out?"

"Eduardo has connections in places I never thought he would. When you get to the museum tell them you are representing Eduardo. They will give you a pass to explore beyond the normal tourist area".

"You got it! Hey, Alex. We will find her. And we will find The Painter to get this done and keep her safe".

"I won't stop until I do, Philip".

"We are here at the airport now. Over and out".

Alex smiled at Philip's call out.

"Over and out, Philip".

Alex disconnected the call. Alexandra walked up from behind him and placed a cup of lavender tea on the table for him. He looked at the cup and thought of Lizbeth, sipping from a tea cup and smiling.

"We will find her, Alex. This is lavender tea. It will help calm the nerves".

He smiled and picked up the cup and sipped the tea. Just then Eduardo walked in.

"I just got word that Leo hired a contractor to build him a home on a cliff".

"This is great information, Eduardo. Where? What cliff?"

"That is what we do not know yet. I have my men trying to tract down the contractor. Leo hired someone from out of the country. We have called the contractor, but he is not answering because he is doing work for another client. His secretary tells us he won't be back for another week".

"Another week? That's too far away, Eduardo. Surely we can find another way. Maybe permits that were requested in order to build. They could have some address or location".

"Good idea, Alexandra. Let me make some calls".

Lizbeth woke up and Leo was not in the bed or in the room with her. She stood up out of the bed and carefully peeked her head out to look downstairs. From a distance she could see Clara working on breakfast. Lizbeth then looked everywhere for Leo, but did not see him. Then she moved up a little more, still hiding from Clara's view. That is when she noticed Clara always carried her phone in her apron.

Lizbeth went to get herself ready. When she was done she walked down the steps and was headed to the kitchen to get closer to Clara. Then she heard the glass door unlock.

"Ah, my love. Your awake".

Leo looked over to Clara and saw she was still making breakfast.

"Shouldn't be much longer. Come with me. I want to show you what I do for work".

Lizbeth looked over at Clara disappointed and followed behind Leo. He brought her outside of the house and down the stairs. She looked everywhere for a place to run or hide. Any form of escape. But she and Leo were surrounded by men.

After they got downstairs from the cliff, she followed Leo to a secluded area on the beach, near the cliff wall. There were some men waiting with their guns pointed at another man on his knees. When the man on his knees saw Leo he began pleading.

"Mr. Ferreira, I beg of you please".

"See this man, my love. He was caught trying to steal a large briefcase full of a lot of money. Too much money".

Leo reach out his hand and one of his men handed him a gun. Leo took the gun and as the man began to plead again, Leo took one shot to the head. The man dropped to the ground. Lizbeth began to yell and tried to turn and run. Leo grabbed her from behind as she struggled to get loose.

"He was punished for trying to steal what is mine. No one, takes what is mine".

Lizbeth continued yelling and struggling to get away from Leo. He let her go and she ran off.

"Watch her".

The men nodded at Leo and followed behind her. When she tried to rush towards a car, one of Leo's men grabbed her by the wrist.

"You don't want to do that, Mrs. Ferreira".

Terrified Lizbeth ran up the stairs towards the house on the cliff. The men followed behind until she was halfway up to the top. Then they stopped and allowed her to continue alone. When Clara saw and heard Lizbeth coming she rushed to enter the code, which unlocked the door. Lizbeth ran inside and up to the bedroom. She then sat on the floor with her back against the bed and desperately cried.

When breakfast was ready Leo ordered Lizbeth to sit with him at the table. It was quiet, as Leo ate his breakfast. Lizbeth just stared at the table.

"Your still not hungry, my love?"

Without moving her head Lizbeth looked at Leo. He looked at her and scoffed then smirked.

"I wanted to you learn about the kind of work I do. It is important to me that you do so, since I will have to do much of it here. It's quiet and secluded. The perfect place to shoot a man in the head. Yet, I also wanted you to see what I was capable of. If I am defied".

Lizbeth did not say a word and just stared at Leo.

"How else do you think I pay for all the luxuries I give you? Did you think I sat in an office all day?"

Lizbeth then turned her eyes away from Leo and back onto the table again. Suddenly she gagged and jumped out of the chair and towards the bathroom. Leo smirked and continued eating his breakfast.

"The first one is always the worst".

Then next day Lizbeth was up when Leo was dressing and getting ready to go. She acted like she was still asleep. After Leo was ready, he stopped by her beside and caressed her hair. Then he turned and walked down the steps. She opened her eyes and watched as he entered his code and unlocked the door. He covered the keypad each time, making it hard to see the numbers being entered in. He then left the house and went down the stairs. Lizbeth jumped out of bed and got herself ready.

As soon as she was dressed in some white palazzo pant with white crop top, she went down the stairs with a beige sunhat in her hands and looked around to see if she could see Leo anywhere. After not seeing him anywhere, she rushed to the kitchen.

"I want to go out, open the kitchen door Clara".

Clara paused what she was doing and looked at Lizbeth suspiciously. Then she looked around for Leo.

"I know you have the code. You let me in yesterday. I want to enjoy the sun and breeze. I will be standing here. I cannot go anywhere, Leo's men surround the bottom of the cliff. It's not like I'm going to throw myself over".

Clara hesitantly pulled out her phone from her apron and searched for the code. When she found it she looked at Lizbeth, who turned her head away. Then Clara entered the numbers. As soon as she did so the door unlocked and Clara slid her phone back into her apron. Lizbeth then used her sunhat and brushed it in Clara's face as a distraction so she could slip her hand into Clara's apron and take the phone. Lizbeth then went outside and to the farthest part of the cliff railing. Though she could still be seen by Clara, she could only see Lizbeth by constantly stretching over to do so.

Lizbeth covered the phone with her sunhat and lifted her chin, only using her eyes to look down. She quickly dialed Alex's for a video chat. Alex was at the dinning room table with his mother going over maps of the areas where cliff homes were built, when he suddenly heard his phone. He looked oddly at the incoming call. He answered the call and begun to see Lizbeth.

"Lizbeth!"

"Alex!"

Lizbeth in her emotion started to cry while still looking upward.

"My love were are you? We are searching for you".

"I'm being watched in a house with windowed walls on a cliff near a beach. I don't know where. Leo has codes on the doors so I cannot escape".

"Where is he now? How were you able to call me?"

"He is out. But he will be back soon. I stole Clara's phone. You will not be able to call me again. I will be throwing this phone over the cliff so Leo never finds out that I called you".

442

"Lizbeth, Philip and Tiara are in Paris they believe they are close to finding The Painter. We are also checking on recent building permits to find where you are. We will find you and rescue you".

"Alex, you cannot come here to rescue me. Your father killed a man before my eyes. I fear what he or his men will do to you. Listen closely. I have a plan. This is what you must do".

Lizbeth shared her plan with Alex and he agreed.

"Three days, Alex. Try to find The Painter please and after three day watch the painting for any movement".

Just then Lizbeth heard Clara bang on the glass door. She knew Clara had just realized her phone was gone. At that moment Leo has just reached the top of the stairs and Clara rushed over to the living room door. When Leo saw Clara running he quickly entered the code and came into the house, pushing the door closed behind him.

"My phone is missing. My phone is missing".

"Where is Lizbeth!"

"She is there".

Clara pointed to where Lizbeth was and Leo rushed over to the kitchen door.

"He's here. I have to go. I love you, Alex".

"Lizbeth!"

Lizbeth disconnected the call. And immediately shutdown the phone. As Leo entered his code to open the kitchen door, he entered the wrong numbers and frustratedly had to do it again. Lizbeth then place the phone in her hat and swung the hat to act like she was going to put it on. In doing so the phone was catapulted over the cliff hitting rocks along the way and breaking into pieces. Leo got the door open and rushed over to Lizbeth who was playing calm and cool, while leaning on the rails. When Leo reached her, he aggressively grabbed her arm and began searching her body, throwing the sunhat over the cliff.

"Where is it!"

"Where is what!"

"Don't play stupid with me Lizbeth! Where is the phone!"

Lizbeth became dramatic and emotional.

"I don't have any phone. Let me go! Your hurting me!"

Lizbeth broke away from Leo's grip and looked at him as if he were crazy. He calmed himself.

"Lizbeth, forgive me. I thought you....".

Lizbeth walked off and left Leo with his words in his mouth. He nodded and let out a breath. Then he angrily turned around to look at Clara who was behind him.

"Find that phone!"

Clara nodded and rushed off. Leo stood looking out at the beach for a moment, then frustratedly walked off.

Alex banged on the table in frustration.

"Dam you father! Dam you to hell!"

Alex aggressively pushed all the things from on top of the table to the ground.

"Alex!"

"If it wasn't for his greed and selfish ways, my wife and unborn child's life would not be at risk right now".

"Calm yourself, Alex. Stick to Lizbeth's plan. It is our only chance. Trust that she will be okay".

"I should have protected her".

"Lizbeth is a strong woman. She has endured your fathers aggression, hunger, thirst, cold temperatures and still she survived all alone. Do not think, that because she is a woman, she is vulnerable. Lizbeth knows what she is doing".

Alex sat in the chair and placed his elbows on his thighs and grabbed onto his head. Then his phone rang again. He rushed out of the chair to answer. It was Philip and Tiara.

"Alex! We found him! We found The Painter! What's the plan!"

Alex and Alexandra let out their excitement. Alex began to explain the plan to them.

Philip and Tiara returned with The Painter to Portugal. They met with Alex at the airport, who came to pick them up.

"Where is The Painter?"

"He's here. With my mother".

Philip lifted the painting his mother was in.

"Why did he not come in the plane, with the both of you?"

"Have you ever seen The Painter?"

"No, Tiara. I have not".

"When you do, you will see why it was best to bring him in the painting".

They all got into Alex's car and drove to Leo's house. When they got there they saw that his father still had men watching the home.

"How do we get in?"

"I know a way, but we will have to wait till dark".

When night fell, Alex took them through the path only he and his mother knew about. Alex then snuck in through an unlocked patio door.

Philip and Tiara followed behind.

"Breaking and entry. Is this enough adventure for you Tiara Quest. It's nothing like entering into a painting. This is sneaking into the real deal".

"It sure is 007".

"Funny, that was...no, that was not funny".

"Both of you hurry up, it's this way".

As they snuck into the house, Philip got a look around.

"Tiara, is it just me or is it too dark, but are these walls painted a horrible dark turquoise blue?"

"It's an ugly turquoise blue".

"I thought so".

Alex led them to his fathers office. The only light on was the one over Lizbeth's portrait.

"Oh my goodness. When you said he had a portrait made, I thought it was just a really nice painting. This looks like a printed photo. This is surely a talented artist".

"Philip is right. It has almost no flaws".

"Is that a bad thing".

"No Alex, that's actually a good thing. Some people in the paintings have flaws that cause them to show they are artworks and not human. The more real she looks the easier it will be to deceive Leo that this look-a-like is Lizbeth".

"Okay, let's get to work then.

As Alex climbed to reach for the portrait painting, Tiara opened the gate and entered the painting Philip's mother was in, to let The Painter know it was time. The Painter followed behind Tiara and walked out of the painting. He was tall, thin, odd looking. He wore a black suit and had a brush stroke on his cheek. When Alex turned around with the portrait of Lizbeth and saw The Painter standing there he was startled.

"And that is why we brought him through the painting".

The Painter spoke with a slow deep speech and tone.

"You must be Alex".

"I am he".

The Painter looked at Alex oddly.

"You are different. Very, very, different".

"Different, how?"

The Painter passed his hand over Alex like it was a paintbrush. And a silver light streaked.

"Yes, I thought so. You have a child coming. When your child is born. Seek me, and I will explain".

"Yes, sir. But unless we work on this plan, I don't know what will happen to my child".

"Bring the portrait to me".

Alex came closer to The Painter with the portrait painting of Lizbeth. The Painter looked at it for a moment. Then he reached his hand into his jacket pocket, without taking his eyes off of the painting. He pulled out of his jacket pocket a paintbrush, with it he stroked the womb of the painted Lizbeth. Then he stroked the location of her heart. Both spots The Painter stroked sparkled in silver. Then faded.

"It is done. She is now barren and will love the first man she lays eyes on".

"Oh thank you, thank you sir".

"Remember, all adjustments come with a cost".

"How much do you want? I will pay anything".

"He does not mean money, Alex. It means switching the painting can have a cost to it. Sort of like a give and take".

"What Philip is saying is that, we took the ability for her to have a child. For that she gains something. And for giving love, she loses something".

The Painter nods once in agreement.

"How do we know what was lost or taken?"

"We don't, unless we enter the painting and wait to find out".

"But we don't have time, Tiara".

"I know. It's just a chance were going to have to take. The most important thing is taken care of with the fake Lizbeth, which was the ability to love and not bare any children. Now, we need to find the real Lizbeth, before Leo finds out she is pregnant with your child".

Alex nodded and turned around to hang the painting back up on the wall where it was.

"Philip, I will take The Painter back. You guys can sneak us out. That's one less person to have to sneak out".

The Painter lifted his hand.

"I will stay here. There is much art calling to me from that direction".

"That is where the hall of artwork is".

"Then that is where I shall go".

The Painter turned around and walked out of the office. Alex, Philip and Tiara followed him from a distance. When he reached the hall he stopped. Then before walking into the hall a silver light flashed and The Painter was gone.

Alex, Philip and Tiara looked at each other.

"Guys, we got to go".

"Philip's right. Let's get out of here".

They all three snuck out safely and climbed into Alex's car. They then got to Eduardo's house and waited for Lizbeth's call to let her know it was done".

After three days had passed Leo came upstairs for dinner. He saw only one place setting that Clara was preparing for him.

"Is Lizbeth still eating upstairs?"

"Yes sir, she says she still feels ill".

"I will give her one more day, then I want her at the table with me".

"Maybe you should give her more days, Mr. Ferreira. Maybe a month?"

"Why would I do that?"

"For the baby".

"The baby?"

"I know Lizbeth's time. I have checked her trash and nothing. It must be she is...".

Clara signaled Leo by tapping her belly.

Leo caught what Clara was trying to say. He sat there, thinking as Clara walked off.

Later that evening Leo went up the stairs slowly. He looked over at Lizbeth and stared at her. She looked over at him then quickly turned her face.

"Are you still angry with me?"

Lizbeth did not say a word.

Leo walked over to the shower and turned it on. Then he came back over to Lizbeth's bedside and began to undress himself while. When he was completely naked he leaned in and scooped Lizbeth up by the waist.

"Let's have a shower together".

He began to undress Lizbeth who looked directly at him angrily as he did so. After she was naked he led her to the shower and walked into it, pulling her gently inside with him. He closed the shower door then grabbed Lizbeth and began kissing her as the shower water wet them.

"Leo. Leo, please".

Leo chuckled.

"See, I knew I'd get you to speak to me again".

Lizbeth scoffed and backed away from him bumping into the shower wall. He moved up on her and pressed his body against hers. Then he looked at her face.

"When you were planning on telling me?"

"Telling you what?"

Leo rubbed his hand down Lizbeths side and onto her stomach.

"About the baby".

Lizbeth eyes widened.

"See, Clara knows these woman things. She tells me your pregnant. What I can't understand is how I could have done that, if we still have not made love. So if you are pregnant. Who's is it?"

Lizbeth gathered herself.

"If Clara knows so much, then ask her what happens to woman who endure high levels of stress. It's call being late or missing a month altogether. Obviously being kidnapped, seeing a man shot before my eyes, and being yelled at for no reason can take its toll on a woman's stress level. Ask her that".

Lizbeth pushed Leo hands away.

"Calm down my love. This means, if you are not pregnant, than I can get you there. You will carry my child inside of you, Lizbeth".

Leo kissed Lizbeth and she tried turning her face.

"No. No more waiting. I'm going to have you right now, in this shower".

"Leo, I wanted to ask for something and now Clara's assumptions have ruined my chances".

"Ask me for whatever you want...after".

Leo lustfully kissed Lizbeth and began groping her body. This time Lizbeth could not fight him off, he was determined. Lizbeth closed her eyes tightly and grabbed onto Leo's arms as he picked her up and pressed her against the shower wall. There, Leo began to make love to Lizbeth intensely.

After the shower Lizbeth was drying up then she sat on the vanity seat. Leo walked over and laid in front of her a lingerie.

"This one, my love".

"Leo, I wanted to ask..".

He kissed her neck and walked away. Lizbeth angrily picked up and slammed the lingerie onto the counter.

Knowing she did not have a choice Lizbeth slowly put the lingerie on, Leo watched her through the glass walls as he waited for her in the bed. When she was ready she walked out of the bathroom.

"Come here".

She slowly walked over to him, then suddenly stopped.

"Leo. You said after".

"Of course my love. After I have you, over and over again".

"No, my request is a small one. Depending on your response, would depend on how happy I may feel right now, this night".

Leo quickly slid out of the bed and pulled Lizbeth close to him. He began kissing her waist and thighs.

"Tell me my love. What is your request".

"I want a painting".

Leo abruptly stopped. He stood up and wrapped the bed sheet around his waist.

"A what?"

"A painting. Just one".

"You think me to be a fool? You want a painting so you could go into it and hide from me?"

"No. That is not true. Besides, how can I hide if the painting will be in your possession. You would know where I was. I do not want to travel into it anyway. I actually don't even think I can".

"Which painting is this?"

"The portrait you made of me".

"Why would you want that one?"

"I want to gaze upon myself in a time that I was happy with you. Before you changed and broke my heart".

Leo paced a little.

"It's only one painting, Leo".

"I know it is!"

"And with it, I want everything I wore that day. The dress, the jewelry, everything".

Leo was surprised at that request.

"Were you really happy that day".

"I was".

Leo caressed Lizbeth's cheek.

"It's yours. The painting, the dress, the jewelry".

Lizbeth smiled a real smile this time.

"Ah, there it is. That smile. My Lizbeth's beautiful smile".

He gently grabbed the back of Lizbeth's head and kissed her. Then turned and laid her on the bed, where he climbed onto her and made love again.

Everyone was at Eduardo's house having a silent dinner. Alex, Alexandra, Eduardo, Phillip and Tiara were deep in thought as Mawilda came around the table serving. Suddenly a ring tone broke the silence. Eduardo pulled his phone out of his pocket and placed the call on speaker.

"Sir! The painting is moving".

Everyone stood up in shock.

"Did you hear me sir? The painting is moving".

"I heard you! Follow the painting! Do not be seen. And be very careful".

"Yes sir. We will provide with location details. Turning on GPS now. Can you see our location, sir?"

He waved at Alex who rushed off and opened the laptop. He then gave Eduardo a thumbs up.

"Yes, we have your location".

"We will keep you updated sir".

"Thank you".

Eduardo disconnected the call. Philip in his excitement jumped out of his seat.

"Oh my, oh my. She did it! Lizbeth! You did it!".

Philip then got emotional. Tiara tried comforting him.

"It's gonna be okay, Philip. And your right, she did it".

"That's our girl, Tiara. That's our girl".

Alex did not say a word. He intensely kept his eyes on the laptop screen the whole time. Alexandra came from behind and placed her hands on his shoulders. This startled Alex.

"It's just me".

"I'm sorry mother, it's just....".

"I know, I know. Keep your eyes on that screen".

They all came together and stood encircled around Alex as they all watched the laptop screen.

Almost an hour into the drive and finally the GPS marker came to a stop. Alex kept his eyes on the screen. Philip, Tiara, and Alexandra looked at each other. Then they looked at Eduardo and waited. When suddenly Eduardo's phone rang again. He immediately answered the call.

"Sir".

"Yes?"

"We found it".

Everyone started to cheer.

"I don't think anyone should celebrate yet, sir".

They all began to calm themselves.

"Sending images now, sir".

The images began to come in. Alex slowly sat back in the chair from what he was seeing.

"Are you getting the images sir?"

"We are".

"The house is high up on that cliff. Unreachable and unclimbable without being seen. Leo had dozens of men guarding. It would be almost impossible to get it".

"You have done well. Now, get out of there before you are seen".

"Yes, sir".

Everyones excitement turned into concern again. Alex stared at the picture of the portrait being brought up to the the stairs of the house.

Phillip placed his hand on Alex's shoulder.

"Our Lizbeth has come this far, let's not lose hope yet, Alex. We know she has a plan. Let her see it completely through".

Alex nodded.

In the morning when Lizbeth woke. She stretched a little and was startled by Leo's touch on her arm. He was lying in bed behind her.

"It's just me, my love".

He kissed her shoulder a few times. Then he gently turned her around to face him. He then leaned in and kissed her lips.

"Good morning, my beautiful wife. You have made me a happy man. You let me make love to you and make you mine again. I missed so much making love to you. Tonight, I want to be in your arms again, but first. I have a surprise for you".

Lizbeth's face lit up. Leo lifted himself and pointed to the foot of the bed. Lizbeth sat up and there in front of her was the portrait painting. She pulled the blanket off of herself and rushed over to it. Then gently touched it.

"I had it brought in last night, while you slept peacefully".

"Oh Leo, thank you".

As Lizbeth passed her hand on the painting and over the heart it sparkled lightly. This surprised Lizbeth.

"It's been done".

"The what? What's been done?"

"Oh, I meant the painting. It's been done. It's been brought to me".

Leo stood up from the bed and walked over to Lizbeth. He lifted her up gently.

"You can get anything out of me. Just ask as nicely as you did last night and I will give you your hearts desire".

Leo kissed Lizbeth's lips. She smiled happily.

"There is my wife's beautiful smile".

"Tonight I want to wear everything in this portrait. Just like that day".

Leo was happy to see Lizbeth's new found joy, but he also became a little suspicious of it.

That evening Lizbeth dressed herself up in the red dress. She followed the portrait to ensure her hair and makeup were identical. Then she put all the jewelry on. She stood up and walked towards the painting, taking and earring from her jewelry box. She stabbed the earring into the painting to mark the gate. Just then Leo came upstairs and saw Lizbeth.

"I am at a loss for words. You look so beautiful, Lizbeth".

Lizbeth smiled. Leo approached her and gently passed his hands down her back.

"Come, dinner is ready for us".

Lizbeth went to follow and suddenly stopped.

"Wait. Can we bring the painting downstairs?"

"What for?"

"I have already been able to see it well enough to dress myself tonight. But its home location can be downstairs".

Alex again found Lizbeth's request odd, but he walked over to the painting and picked it up. Lizbeth went down the stairs and Leo followed behind.

Leo laid the painting against the living room table and led Lizbeth to the dining table where they sat down to have dinner together.

Alex, Tiara, and Philip were sitting outside. Alex had a drink in his hands. No one was speaking. Just when Philip was about to say something, Alex abruptly stood up.

"I can't wait anymore. I'm not just going to sit here. It is an hour drive from here. If Lizbeth gets out of this, I am not going to have her drive an hour to get to me. That is too much of a risk. I want to know she is safe, with me, in my arms".

Alex walked off to his car. As soon as he opened the car door and sat inside, Philip sat in the passenger side and Tiara in the back seat. They both startled Alex, who thought he was alone.

"How did you...".

"You didn't think you were going alone did you. You took the words right out of my mouth".

"Philip's right. Took you long enough though. Let's get out of here".

Alex nodded and quickly drove off.
After their hour drive they park at a distance from the house and turned off the car lights.

"Now. We wait".

Alex stared at the house intently.

After dinner Leo stood up to serve himself a drink from the bar. Clara walked off with their finished dinner plates and to get desert. Lizbeth knew this was the time. She stood up from the chair and walked in front of the painting. Leo saw from as distance as Lizbeth stretched her arms out to the painting.

465

"Noooo!"

Leo came running over, but before he could grab Lizbeth's wrist the gate was opened.

"Lizbeth, you lied! You said you could not travel into this painting!"

"I did not lie, Leo. I told you could not travel into this painting, because I knew you would not want me to go alone. Come with me".

Lizbeth stretched out her hand to Leo. He hesitated.

"It would only be for a stroll. I am the Art Guardian, Leo. I need to travel through paintings in order to stay alive".

"What do you mean".

"Leo, if I do not travel I waist away and die early. So, come with me. There is no where I can hide, this painting is locked in this house".

Lizbeth smiled and reached out her hand again. Leo was still hesitant, but slowly stepped toward Lizbeth. When he was close enough Lizbeth, she grabbed onto his hand and pulled him in. Clara saw him enter through the gate and disappear and she dropped the tray with all the deserts and began to yell. No one could hear her through the glass doors. She tried getting out of the house, but could not do so because she did not have her phone with the codes.

Lizbeth came through the painting and Leo was behind her. The gate closed as they look around a room with grayish blue painted walls. There was a chair in the middle of the room where the painted Lizbeth sat. Lizbeth began to look around the room. She walks toward a window in the far right hand corner of the room. When she looked out she saw the painted Lizbeth picking flowers outside.

"Leo. Let's look around the house. We can split up to do so. Then we can meet down in the gardens".

Lizbeth went to walk off and Leo grabbed her arm.

"No you don't. We are not splitting up. Don't think you can take me for a fool, Lizbeth".

"I'm sorry, Leo. I thought you would have enjoyed coming here. I see you do not. Maybe we should go back".

Leo continued looking around the room.

"It looks so real. It's been so long since I have entered a painting. I did not remember how amazing it all looked".

"I does indeed. Let's look around to see what is outside of this room".

Before leaving the room, Lizbeth took another glimpse and saw the painted Lizbeth was still outside.

Leo began walking down the hall and Lizbeth followed behind. She counted the rooms as they passed them, to ensure she would remember her way back. They then made it downstairs to the kitchen. On the table was a bowl with fruit. Leo picked up a fruit and bit into it.

"So sweet. It tastes so real".

"And satisfies just like the real thing".

"What is outside?"

"Let's find out. I want to pick some flowers anyway".

Lizbeth let Leo lead the way. As he stepped outside she followed behind. He then took steps forward and looked at the sky.

"It's night at home, yet here it is almost as if the sun just went down. What time could it be here?"

There was a silence. Leo turned around and did not see Lizbeth.

"Lizbeth? Lizbeth?"

He began to search for her outside. As soon as he walked off, Lizbeth came out from behind the door holding her shoes in her hands and rushed back upstairs. As soon as she reached the top of the second floor she began counting rooms to help find the right one.

Leo continued searching for Lizbeth and found her picking flowers.

"There you are my love. I was looking everywhere for you. Let us not split up again. I would not want to get stuck in here".

The painted Lizbeth looked at Leo and smiled happily. Being the first man she had seen, she immediately fell in love with him. She then shyly smiled at him.

"Let's go. How do we get out of here?"

The painted Lizbeth mumbled. Leo looked back her.

"Did you hear me? How do we get back?"

Again the painted Lizbeth mumbled. She could not speak a word. Because the painted Lizbeth was given the ability to love Leo, she lost the ability to speak.

Leo became frightened and knew this was not the real Lizbeth. He turned frantically looking up towards the house to see if he could see Lizbeth in any of the windows, when suddenly he saw a bright golden light in the room upstairs. The light shined brightly then dim out.

"LIZBEEEETH!"

Lizbeth walked through the open gate still shining bright in the real world.

Just then from a distance Alex was dozing off inside the car. Philip and Tiara were asleep. He shook off his sleep and lifted his head. Just then he saw the light.

"There it is!"

Philip and Tiara woke with a startle.

"Look, the light".

Then the light went out.

"Is this the first or second time, Alex?"

"I don't know, it's my first time seeing it".

"We have to find out if she just left or just returned".

"I'm going to get closer".

"Alex, we can't be seen by any of Leo's men".

"I'll be careful, Tiara. You guys stay here".

Alex climbed out of the car and carefully started sneaking his way closer to the house.

When Clara saw Lizbeth she began yelling out of fear again.

"Don't take me, please. Don't make me disappear".

"Open the door then!"

"I don't know the codes. Leo had them on his phone".

"Don't tell me didn't write them down somewhere".

Clara thought for a moment. Then nervously remembered where they were written. She rushed to the kitchen and completely pulled out one of the draws, dropping everything from inside onto the floor. Then she reached her hand in touching the top and pulling out an envelope that was taped there. Lizbeth snatched the envelope from Clara's had and opened it. When she saw the numbers she was surprised.

"These codes are the dates Leo and I met and when we got married".

She rushed to the door and entered the code. Clara was standing a few feet away from Lizbeth, afraid of her. Lizbeth rushed over to her and grabbed her by the neck. Clara afraid yelped out. Lizbeth brought her outside the house and they went down the steps together.

"You will tell the men that Leo fell off the cliff and that he is dead. If you tell them he is in the painting, I will throw you in there".

Nervously Clara agreed. When they got downstairs the men called to Lizbeth to stay where she was.

"Your boss is dead. Go, send men up there to find him. You won't find him because he is dead".

The guard in charge sent two of his men who rushed upstairs.

There was no sign of Leo anywhere. They rushed back downstairs.

"Mr. Ferreira is not anywhere in the house sir".

"I told you your boss is gone. When you have the time you can search for his body over the cliff".

Lizbeth pushed Clara forward.

"Mr. Ferreira is gone. Over the cliff. He's gone".

"You all no longer answer to Leo. I am your new boss now. If you want to be payed for all your hours spent guarding this house, then leave quietly, now".

The men looked around at each other. The guard in charged looked at Lizbeth.

"Full payment for our services, Mrs. Ferreira".

"Agreed".

The guard signaled his men to leave. Lizbeth pushed Clara towards the guard.

"Take her with you".

"What do you want me to do with her?"

"Take her wherever she wants to go, but I no longer want to see her again".

Terrified, Clara rushed over to one of the cars and sat inside. The guard wondered why Clara was so afraid of Lizbeth.

"Do you need me to leave any men to protect you here, Mrs. Ferreira?"

"No, I will be fine. But I do need a phone".

The guard handed Lizbeth his phone and she dialed Alex's number. The phone rang inside the car and started Philip and Tiara. The rushed for it and picked up.

"Alex?"

"Lizbeth? Alex is trying to find you"

"You are here?"

"We are. Alex couldn't wait any longer".

"Come to the house. Leo is gone".

"We will be right there!"

Philip jumped over to the driver side and began driving the car. Tiara had her head out the window searching for Alex. When she saw him she yelled out to him.

"Alex! He's gone. Lizbeth did it!"

Philip stopped the car and Alex rushed to the car and jumped into the passenger side.

Lizbeth handed the head guard his phone and he turned and climbed into the car. Cars began to leave one by one. By the time Philip, Alex and Tiara rolled up in the car, there were no guards left. Alex rushed out of the car and ran towards Lizbeth.

"Alex!"

Lizbeth ran towards Alex and they excitedly embraced each other.

"Lizbeth, are you okay? Is the baby okay?".

"Alex, we are okay. We are okay".

Alex and Lizbeth held each other again. Philip stood standing by the car trying to hold his tears back. Tiara came over and threw her arm around him.

"It's gonna be okay. It turned out to be a happy ending".

"It did. It did".

Eight months later Philip and Tiara returned to Portugal, to be there for Lizbeth and her firstborn. They excitedly ran over to her, but gently embraced her and jumped around her.

When the time came for Lizbeth's baby to be born, everyone was rushing and trying to remember everything that was needed to bring to the hospital. Two cars left Eduardo's house. One with Alex, Lizbeth, Tiara, and Philip. And the other with Alexandra and Eduardo. When they got to the hospital, Lizbeth was rushed into the labor room. Philip, Tiara, Alexandra, and Eduardo waited in the lobby.

After a few hours, they were all allowed to go back and see Lizbeth. When they walked into the room, they saw Lizbeth and Alex smiling but slightly worried. Philip was the first to express concern.

ı oh, what's going on?"

"Yes, is my granddaughter okay?"

Alex was holding the baby. He slowly approached them and uncovered the babies face.

"Yes mother, your grand-son is fine".

When they looked at the baby boy, they noticed he had a paintbrush stroke on his cheek that sparkled with a silver light. Philip and Tiara's eyes widened.

"She's a he. And he is not an art guardian. He's a painter. Known as, The Painter".

With Tiara's words Philip passed out and Eduardo caught him in the air.

Leo's house on the cliff was dark and untouched for eight months. It had an eerie feel to it. The painting still laid in the same place it was left.

Suddenly the painting moved. Then a little more. A hand then began to push through. Then a head, followed by a body, which landed on the floor. It was the body of an unshaven long haired man. When he lifted his head up. It was Leo.

Made in the USA
Middletown, DE
01 May 2022

65012409R00265